RIVERDOWN

By

Scardthomas

This book is a work of fiction. All persons are the product of the author's imagination.

Any resemblance to actual persons, living or dead is purely coincidental.

Fictional names have been used in the immediate topography, although some geographical scenes and buildings, within The Lake District, were used as models.

The actual location of Lastwater is fictional.

This edited edition was published in .

To my lovely wife, Helen.

Some of the tales depicted in this novel's concern with an animal rescue centre were based on real life traumatic occurrences involving various wildlife and domestic animals, in which, Helen played the lead role in their eventual recovery. This, so beautifully gives evidence to her caring passion for all those less advantaged than herself.

CONTENTS

PART TWO. 1983.

THE WINTER OF SIXTY-THREE.

The ice lay on lake Windermere in the winter of sixty-three.
A young man loved a quiet girl; fair, soft-skinned and pretty.
They tramped the snow laden fells aside the drystone wall;
With rope, boots and ice-axe they climbed the peaks of tall.

The black dog followed them as they wandered free to roam.
Vistas of beauty blessed their eyes often seen by them alone.
The period of the nubile pair: a sweet spell of time occurring,
At the springtime of love with a summer harvest recurring.

At the thaw, clouds of mist hung about in every place,
The lovers drew closer still, they had the future to face.
The time had come to part and head homeward separately.
Thus, a chapter closed, and the young man went to sea.

PROLOGUE

In the late afternoon of Tuesday 25th September 1956, two twelve-year old boy scouts clambered onto Cloud Point, which formed a substantial promontory by the lake known as Lastwater, in the county of Cumbria, northwest England.

It had been and still was a hot day despite the lowering early evening sun and the lengthening shadows from the fells across the water. The anticipation of their swim filled the boys' minds with a seductive feeling of excitement. They were under strict instructions from the scoutmaster not to enter the water until his arrival. Already clad in swimming trunks, they sat down near the end of the point looking across to Shimdorie Island and beyond to the distant shoreline on the other side of the lake.

The late summer camp had been fortunate to enjoy fine weather in a place notorious for heavy rainfall. Not only had they experienced dry conditions every day, but, also, for the time of year, unusually, the temperatures had remained warm until the evening set in. Today was their last, before packing up camp in the early morning ready to return to their hometown of Rochdale in Lancashire.

One of the boys, Alex, did not have the slightest intention of waiting for the arrival of his leader and the other scouts attending the camp site. He could not see or hear any sign of them approaching. Their imminent arrival would probably be heralded by shouts coming up through the wooded area that separated the campsite from the lakeshore. Alex's parents knew only too well this trait in their son. He might be told, strictly, not to touch, perhaps, a newly arrived tasty morsel in the refrigerator. Later, he would blatantly disobey. "Oh sorry, I forgot," was the usual excuse backed by a well-practised facial expression of fake surprise. Sometimes, he would be punished – but not usually. This was a percentage of risk he had obviously worked out from an early age. On this occasion, he would simply remark on emerging from the water to an irate scoutmaster, "I'm really sorry Sir – I slipped!" It was not, however, the spoken word that often or not decided his fate. This depended on his ability to refrain from allowing a fateful smirk to appear on his countenance.

Lastwater was becalmed. It had been so for the last two weeks.

The boys sat near the edge oblivious to the discomfort of the harsh volcanic rocks on their posteriors. The water had a considerable depth right here; steep shelving taking place immediately below them. The gentle lapping of the water heightened their expectation of the sudden rush of relief to their hot bodies when they dived in. It had been so every afternoon of their camping trip so far: the highlight of the day. This was why they had asked permission to go on ahead of the others having finished the rope bridge task allotted to them.

Alex rose to his feet and without waiting for his companion to utter a syllable – dived. The execution was perfect. Vertical – but not quite: legs and feet totally aligned. There was no splash.

The other boy, Ben, jumped to his feet shouting the disappearing swimmer's name. At the same time the scout leader made his entrance at the beginning of the promontory. He had gone on ahead of the rest of his charges feeling edgy about Alex's untrustworthy nature. Ben, standing right at the water's edge where Alex had last been seen, looked towards the approaching man in alarm as the lithe fellow leapt athletically from rock to rock. At any moment, Alex would surface near at hand with an explosion of disturbed water.

By the time the leader had drawn close, Alex had been underwater for nearly three quarters of a minute.

"Where's Alex?" he asked in a casual manner, not in the least out of breath. Quite naturally, he thought he must be somewhere on the other side of the point exploring or some such. Ben said nothing. He stared at the deep water beneath his feet and slowly, very slowly, he half raised his right hand and pointed. The scoutmaster looked at the lake waters and then at the now visibly frightened boy before him. "Has he ...?" the man's facial expression abruptly changed. "Has Alex entered the water!?" An almost panicky tone inhabited those last words.

" Yes Sir. He's just vanished – here."

The broad shouldered, anxious man's entrance into the water was not in the same class as Alex's had been. It was more of a clumsy duck-dive, but the purpose was effective: to get down under as fast as possible. Ben received a liberal quantity of lake water over his head in the process. His hair lay lankly over his forehead, dark and glistening in the failing sunshine.

The seconds ticked silently by – and gradually the disturbed surface of the lake returned to its former calm. Thirty seconds ... forty-five ... fifty.

Nothing.

The boy spread his vision wider hoping and expecting his scout leader to at least come up for air. He ran outstretched fingers of his right hand over his face in extreme anxiety.

A minute and a half ...

Ben, who had no wristwatch to refer to, knew this passing of time only as an age.

Gradually ... he raised his head and looked without knowing why towards the island in the centre of the lake. The expression on his face was so desperately moving – a mixture of stark fear and apprehension muddled by questions – Where? Why?

As though in answer a strange deep noted unearthly sound reached him from across the lake. He could make out an area of disturbance near the shoreline of the island standing out starkly alongside the mill pond calmness elsewhere. The strong, low cast sun's rays created transparent bright gold highlights on the surface of the broken water.

The sound of the other boy scouts approaching through the woods reached his ears. Leaving his towel behind, he started to scrabble wildly over the rocks towards them, but really – anywhere – just to escape – from *the nightmare*.

PART ONE

1982

CHAPTER ONE

LASTWATER, CUNBRIA MARCH 1982.

Four-year old Emma Hunter stared at the young red squirrel, wide-eyed at the sheer cuteness of the creature. It looked at her with round, high-lit black eyes, while standing on its hind legs, bushy tail arched behind, nose twitching and ears flicking. One of the shorter front legs was held against a white belly splinted and bandaged; the other seemed to hang under the injured leg in support.

This was the latest admission to Bray Castle's bird and animal recuperation centre run by Suzanne, wife of Dalmar Hunter, the National Trust curator for Bray Castle. The centre had become an important part of the fund raising attributed to the trust attraction as a whole. It was frequently visited by mothers with young children throughout most of the year, it being a wet weather favourite. There was plenty of the latter here; the castle being situated adjacent to the inland waterway known as Lastwater, in the mountainous region of the Lake District in Northwest England.

The animal sanctuary had been incorporated into three substantial outbuildings whose drystone construction was still totally sound. The interior required extensive work in order to bring it up to the standards necessary for animal and bird husbandry, however, in the end, it all worked extremely well for the occupants and public viewing. Conveniently, there was an old undercover passage between the castle and the outbuildings. Suzanne Hunter realised, from the beginning, the importance of allowing public access. The entire viewing area separated the recovering birds and animals from unwanted human interference by means of a substantial glass screen, which blotted out alarming scents and noise. This appeared to work very well. Although many of the patients, being from the wild, were wary of people in general, having only sight of them greatly reduced their apprehension. They tended to accept the grinning faces after a while and treated them with disdain.

Suzanne was careful never to place any animal in the viewing area she considered too unwell or at risk through shyness. The red squirrel, for the time being, was housed in a cage sympathetic to her natural woodland surroundings, in an area not visited by the public. Occasionally, small groups of school children, sworn to a silent routine were allowed in under strict supervision.

Despite the encumbrance of Michael, Suzanne's two-year old son who had wrapped himself around his mother's left leg; Emma received a dig in the ribs. "What's its name?" the playful daughter asked.

Suzanne shrugged and pursed her lips in thought. "Haven't got that far yet. Any ideas?"

"Well – it's a girl – isn't it?"

"Yes. How did you know that?"

"Bea told me," Emma said in a casual manner. Bea short for Beatrice was Suzanne's main helper at the centre. "Then – it must be, Suzanne." The girl ducked and stepped nimbly to one side before her mother could give her a quick cuff.

Bray Castle lay a quarter of a mile from the western shore of Lastwater. It was separated from the lake by deciduous woodland on one side and pastureland with rocky outcrops on the other. This latter was formerly used for sheep grazing. In the centre a path ran down by the edge of the trees and shrubs to a jetty and boathouse by the lakeside. Many visitors came here just to visit the grounds and enjoy the panoramic viewpoints across the water.

The estate was reached by road from a single

carriageway off a major road some four to five miles northwest of Grasmere. Quite an impressive gate structure announced the beginning of a long driveway. To one side was a small lodge house, nowadays uninhabited. It was used by the ground staff for storage and utility purposes. The drive was bordered all the way on the right-hand side by woods, while the pasture wound its way to join that by the castle on the left.

A dower-house lay to one side of the castle with its own garden area. For many years it had been run as a private guest house for visitors but was now used as the Hunter's private accommodation.

The castle looked like a pocket-sized version of a much bigger medieval construction; about the size of a reasonably large manor house as far as accommodation went. It was the battlements, towers and magnificent entrance that transformed it. However, a visitor would not find here a Norman keep or Saxon moat. This construction was built in the early part of the nineteenth century by one of Manchester's wealthy industrialists of the time. Despite its youth, as castles go, it did have charm. Most of the stone used to construct the walls came from excavation near the slate quarries at Coniston, where layers of granite had to be removed to acquire the right volcanic stone. The battlements were shaped in a lighter tone alternative and this paler stone was used for aesthetic reasons, plus the extra effect achieved with some apertures carved in the shape of the crusader's cross. The whole gave off a pleasing ambience: not too aggressive. The entrance arch and massive oak doors looked authentic enough.

Around 1955, the then owners handed over the entire estate to the National Trust organisation. For many years, it was used as an outward-bound style college for students wishing to indulge in the various mountain and lake outdoor sporting activities. It was during this period that a jetty was added alongside the boat house. The kitchen was enlarged behind the castle subtly hidden from public view. The cavernous first floor bedrooms used by the original family were easily converted to dormitories.

Due to an unfortunate boating accident the school lost its funding and closed in 1979.

Eighteen months later Dalmar and Suzanne took over the running of the estate as a tourist attraction. Originally, in the early summer of 1975, the couple met and entered into a dramatic courtship, during which Dalmar became, for a while, something of a reluctant national celebrity due to his bravery in despatching the most dangerous freak reptile ever known. The couple married and moved to Cumbria in 1977. Dalmar gave up his job as a personnel manager for a Southampton firm, taking a reduction in salary to work for the National Trust on various projects throughout their vast areas of responsibility in the Lake District National Park. Two years later, this paid off when he accepted the challenge of curator at Bray Castle. As the position came with accommodation for him and his family, they were able to rent out their family home in Grasmere, which provided enough funds to cover mortgage payments and general maintenance.

The only disappointment, particularly for Suzanne, was that her uncle Reginald who used to live with her mother's eldest sister Maggie in Grasmere, died soon after she and Dalmar had moved there. Suzanne, particularly in her teen years, usually spent part of her summer school holidays with them. But Maggie, after her husband's death sold their home and moved down to Somerset to be near her sister.

When Suzanne had finally summoned her daughter back to her presence, she mentioned to Bea that she was going to try and put Michael down for his mid-morning nap.

After they left, Emma followed Bea through to the public viewing area in order to start various chores among the inhabitants. There were already several visitors on the other side of the glass, and they were obviously curious as to what might transpire. However, the jobs were fairly mundane and feeding time would not be until much later in the day.

In the very first pen, kept secure from the other residents, lived a magnificent red dog fox that had been caught in an illegal trap. The veterinary practice who first received the animal when it was brought in by the Royal Society for the Prevention of Cruelty to Animals were unable to save the injured front leg, and it had been amputated. That was four weeks ago and already the fox seemed competent on three legs. It was expected that he would be released shortly. Whether he could adapt to catch prey considerably less fleet of foot than he used to be, would have to be monitored, but others with similar disabilities had survived before. When Bea and Emma entered the pen, he slunk off to the far corner – looking at them with head hung low. The two girls set about cleaning and providing new straw, changing the drinking water and making sure his bed area was dry.

Next along the line was a stoat in transitional winter to summer coat of tan over white: a rather grubby white. It was nowhere to be seen. In fact, visitors rarely saw this animal, its natural activity being nocturnal. If someone managed to spot the resting little fellow, they might notice that there appeared to be nothing wrong with it. The stoat had been found, apparently lifeless, by an estate volunteer worker. When it was placed on a little bench, in the centre, it suddenly woke up and had to be promptly caught with a net before it could wreak havoc. Suzanne had decided that if it continued to act in a normal manner, they would soon let it go.

Enjoying its recuperation was a fully grown, female Fallow deer coloured a striking light reddish brown dotted with white spots. She had been discovered with a nasty parasitic skin infection. Vets at Keswick had held out little hope for her survival, but, thankfully, they found a cure, of homeopathic origin, and she was sent here to be sure that all trace of the infection had been eradicated before letting her go back into the wild.

The last two pens in this section were currently unoccupied.

Suzanne and her staff had created two large further pens for hedgehogs and rabbits – frequent visitors to the centre with various injuries – usually the result of road accidents.

The red squirrel, now known as Sue, was the only resident of the private area at present.

Also, under the auspice of the rehabilitation centre were two sheep grazing on pastureland by the lakeside, the result of a stomach disorder caused by eating remnants of plastic bags cast aside by careless walkers on the fells. Both had to be operated on to remove the binding plastic in their intestines. It was quite usual for Suzanne to take on farm animals as well as those from the wild. This could be of great assistance to farmers, and they were more than willing to make a contribution for their keep.

After having successfully put her son down for his midday nap, Suzanne came back to help Bea and her daughter with mucking out work. Despite having given birth to two children, she had managed to revert back to the slightly fuller figure she possessed before becoming pregnant with Emma six years ago: curvy, some people would call her. Suzanne's major enchanting feature was the brightness of her eyes; deep nut-brown on sparkling white. When she smiled, it was very engaging. Cumbrian county television companies had been using her to talk about the patients at the centre. Her knowledge had not come easily. She attended a zoological course at an agriculture college before obtaining a degree in animal husbandry at Lancaster University. She achieved this qualification as an adult student, before becoming pregnant with Michael. This had meant that the care of Emma, during her toddler years, had often been delegated to a part time nanny.

John Dalmar Hunter was thankful the rain had stopped although it would not have made much difference to his immediate plans. The Land Rover he was driving reached the top of a steep incline among the lower fells above Lastwater. Dalmar immediately turned off the narrow road onto a rough pull-in. He opened the driver's door, jumped out, and before doing anything else went to the rear and opened one of the doors. Out clambered a snuffling adult Tri-Colour Rough collie, with his glorious thick coat coloured mostly black with white markings under neck, chest and belly. Sable areas occupied the upper legs. He gave his owner a grateful lick on his right hand, before wandering over onto a grassy, rocky area just above an almost sheer drop to shrub-land some seventy feet below. The dog had been here many times before. It was a favourite stopping place for Dalmar when he returned from supply shopping at a near-by town, or the village post office. The reason being that from this vantage point the whole of Lastwater and the surrounding fells were set out before him.

Today was not the best of days. The sky was overcast with grey cloud casting a dull hue everywhere. There was little wind and the waters of the lake wore an opaque gun-metal calm. The hilly terrain rose up on the north and southern slopes still bearing a cover of winter bludgeoned, rust coloured bracken from last year's growth. With the advancing spring season this would soon be transformed. In the east and west valley areas showed off variegated greenness and everywhere there where outcrops of volcanic rocks – some of which, in the strange light, appeared almost black. Away in the far distance to the west lay the higher mountains near Derwentwater, and in the east, on the other side of the valley the lower slopes of the mountain known as Helvelyn rose gloriously majestic.

Even in this light Dalmar loved this place. He never stopped considering how lucky he was to have met and married Suzanne, who introduced him to this part of the world properly. He had once taken a holiday here at the age of twenty and had vowed, one day, to return. Now, it was truly magical to share all this with his family.

Their vantage point was some way up the slopes of White Crag looking down on Diamond Gill that tumbled over numerous smooth contoured boulders in a steep descent towards the lake. Where the mountain stream met the main body of water, there rose out of some trees the roof of Lastwater Rowing Club. It had an illustrious history, racing river rowing boats of all classes, mostly in the north of England, but, sometimes, when they had an exceptional crew in any of the categories, Henley regatta on the Thames was on the annual schedule. Their own regatta, not a large affair, was always popular because of the different conditions provided by open water. This year they were missing out on a big regatta at Cheshire due to failing to get their entrance documents done in time. Otherwise, they would be making the long journey tomorrow. As it turned out – this was considerably more than just a shame.

Shimdorie Island covered in shrubs and Rowan trees lay near the centre of the lake opposite Bray Castle, whose tower turrets appeared over a substantial woodland area. In the near distance at the western extremity, about a mile and a half away, a farmhouse connected by several drystone walls could be discerned. This and Bray Castle were the only inhabited buildings. It left the northern shores of the lake an excellent area for wildlife. Even the path for walkers showed little use because it did not lead to a major mountain trail.

'Time to go. Work awaits,' Dalmar thought to himself. "Fly – come," he called to the dog who ambled over somewhat sluggishly. This dog had been his faithful companion for the last eight years. They had shared some sad and dramatic times. Mostly though, it had all been joyful. When his master and mistress had moved to the Lake District, Fly had revelled in it; the landscape of his birth right. At nine years old, he might be expected to be slowing down, but not Fly – there was plenty of spring left in him. However, now – he used it only when *he* wanted to.

Before driving off Dalmar cast one more glance over the

lake. Suddenly, his attention was caught by a strange change in the water just this side of Shimdorie Island. It was a colour change – or – appeared to be. Then, just as quickly as it had appeared – it began to disperse spreading tentacles out over the water. Dalmar stared at the spot for a while. Then he blinked and started the Land Rover engine.

Visitors to Bray Castle had to use a double independent doorway to pass through from the animal area to the bird sanctuary. This area had become by far the largest section in the centre. From all over Lakeland and beyond, veterinary clinics, not to mention the general public brought birds of most varieties here for treatment. By far the greatest contingents were wing injuries: most but not all survived; the main ingredient for recovery being security and care. This is what they got here in abundance. It was always a great moment when they were released back into the wild after the injured wing showed obvious signs of being complete once again. Sometimes, it would be necessary to return a bird to a specialist habitat, but most were set free from the castle itself, to begin a new chapter in their lives.

This morning a wood pigeon was to be given back its freedom. Emma had named the bird Sammy. He had been found by some tourists on the road approach to Bray and it was presumed that he had been hit by a vehicle. In this case Suzanne used her own knowledge without consulting a vet. Quietness, sustenance and shelter were all that was required to allow the wing to mend naturally. It had taken – just three weeks.

They took Sammy out to the lower courtyard on the wooded side of the castle. From here he would be able to fly off a rampart, and if he should get into difficulties, the fall would be cushioned by a thick growth of rhododendron bushes. Emma brought the pigeon with her in a pet basket and placed it on the ground. "Go on then – undo the straps," said her mother. The four-year old had trouble loosening the buckles with her little fingers; Suzanne had to give her a hand before Sammy waddled out.

When he first came to them his right wing trailed on the ground fully open. Now, it was neatly folded back onto his body. Sammy turned a seemingly questioning eye on the two of them before immediately hopping and fluttering about exercising the stiff wing. Then, apparently satisfied, he went to the edge of a raised rampart. Without hesitating, he took off. There was no downward passage in the flight. He flew almost straight up to land on top of one of the lower side towers. Then he turned his head, and, once again, appeared to be looking at them with one eye. Making an announcing call, he stretched his wings and in a long beautiful glide – went away into the treetops.

"Bye Sammy," shouted Emma. Both mother and daughter waved after him. It was an emotional moment. Frequently, after events like this they might see a similar bird in future weeks or months and wonder if it was the one, they had cured. Emma would always call after them by name, and, sometimes, because the behaviour of a particular bird suggested it, she was probably right.

CHAPTER TWO

"WHERE HAVE THE ROWERS GONE?"

The next day, Sunday 21st March, dawned to a similar overcast sky as the day before.

It was to be a black, black day.

By tomorrow the tranquillity of Lastwater would be shattered. The area would be the subject of shocking headline news throughout the country.

At ten-thirty in the morning, Dalmar could be seen striding down the path heading towards the boathouse at the water's edge. This path was bounded on one side by meadow and the other, deciduous woodland. He was a tall man, in excess of six feet with wide, square shoulders: an athlete's physique suggesting a middle-distance runner rather than a sprinter. He walked with a fluid movement – long striding. His dark hair glistened in the still air, and, as usual, the slight curl throughout his locks caused several strands to fall over his left eye. Those eyes usually took on a pacific blue hue – deep and purposeful. He was carrying a metal toolbox in one hand and a carpenter's saw in the other. Despite his position of responsibility his all denim attire was something he could usually get away with, although, during the week he often wore a blue sports shirt with the National Trust logo on the breast pocket depicted in gold. He hardly ever wore a suit, and no one seemed to mind.

Trotting purposefully on in front, tail swinging from side to side, head held high, the magnificent collie heralded their passage.

The one disadvantage to most curator positions within the National Trust was that it demanded attention seven days a week. The only day when Bray was closed to the public was Christmas day. At least they had that over farmers.

Adding to this responsibility, Dalmar had managed to persuade the Trust to build an observatory on the extensive roof structure at the castle. There was very little light pollution in the area. Nevertheless, his superiors had taken some persuading, not just for the capital layout, but, also, a mountainous region with its extra rainfall was hardly ideal due to a high risk of cloud cover at night. In extreme cases a residential visitor staying for a week with the intention of using the observatory might not be able to do so. Such visitors were warned of this possibility. However, most were happy to switch to more general tourism and day- time pursuits applicable to the Lake District. The observatory was treated more as a bonus night-time activity. Although, despite this; it was proving popular among students of the science for all ages.

A canteen housed in the old kitchen area at the back of the castle was used to give residents their evening meal. A total of five guests could be accommodated in the converted dormitory areas at any one time. Also, on hand was a residential qualified astronomer who could guide those observers that required tuition. He was a retired widower in his late sixties and the task suited him admirably. The arrangement, so far, had worked out very well because the fellow became highly thought of by his students, so developing a beneficial reputation for the centre. This also relieved Dalmar of having to attend at night when he really needed to get some sleep.

The curator's purpose for the visit to the boathouse was to make some minor repairs to the wooden sluice gate, which prevented other craft from entering the enclosure. It was a very impressive boat shelter being constructed from volcanic rock in the same manner as many of the cottages here about, although, the architect had been tempted with some flamboyant extras to compliment the castle.

During the years of occupation by the original family, some rather special small craft had been used for recreation purposes; whereas, the outdoor activities school had possessed two sailing dinghies and one small rowing boat. All that occupied the boathouse now was a similar rowing boat, maybe even the original; no one seemed sure. This meant that the boathouse was considerably under used. It had been this fact that prompted Suzanne to suggest there might be some way a sanctuary could be created for the sole use of injured water birds: something that was much needed. Dalmar promised to look into the practicality of a conversion and change of use, although, secretly, he was beginning to wonder if the wildlife cause was beginning to take over. But, perhaps, that might be a good thing.

Meanwhile, further along the southern shore of the lake towards the east, the rowing eight were getting ready to cast off from the boathouse belonging to Lastwater Rowing Club. (L.R.C.) They were considered a highly competitive team and held out great promise for this year's competitions with young men ranging from the ages of eighteen to their late twenties. The eldest was the coxswain who had accumulated several years' experience with eights including a spell at university.

There had been some doubt the evening before, as to whether this morning's practice session would go ahead due to the suspect weather. However, having heard a forecast predicting much the same conditions all day, where it might well rain, but without a strong wind; the all-important factor, they decided to carry on as arranged. L.R.C had the disadvantage of open water, which in strong winds could quite definitely result in the sinking of an eight-man crew sized boat. Racing boats were designed with shallow draughts. While the same disadvantage applied on a river there was far less shelter out on a lake. The stroke oar, John Singleton, known as Johno, had contacted everyone involved to let them know today's practice would go ahead.

All the team had arrived in good time. Quite a few of them had some way to travel. Two lived in the neighbouring county of Lancashire. By ten-forty-five all was ready for the off, and the boat had already been taken off its hanging rods on the boathouse wall and set in the water.

As they pulled away from the jetty the cox, Ben Homer, set a course to pass to the south of Shimdorie Island. He knew Johno wanted the main speed trial to be later after they had gone way past the island down to the western end of the lake. The return journey along the northern shore would provide the necessary unhindered fast run and strong effort.

Two women, both retired primary school teachers, were resting having found comfortable positions to sit on the promontory known as Cloud Point, almost opposite Shimdorie Island. One of them was enthusiastically studying the scenery. She adored all aspects of this particular part of Cumbria. There was an atmosphere about this valley and its lake that thrilled her. Probably, it was due to a strange ambience of friendly wildness. There was nothing bleak about it and even on a day where the natural colours were all dull, it still held a magical enchantment. Her companion was engrossed in a book. They had put their car in the hidden parking area below and to the side of the castle, and, by design, taken a stroll down to the lake shore. Cloud Point was their viewpoint and resting place before returning to have a cup of coffee in the canteen. Due to the lack of March's usual biting north-easterly winds they were warm enough for the time being.

Janet, the woman looking at the scenery, caught sight of the approaching oarsmen out of the corner of her eye. To start with, they were coming almost straight towards her.

With his back to the lake, Dalmar, at the boathouse, was puzzled about something. He stood there scratching the top of his head in confusion. On a post halfway along the jetty, the usual lake water mark level was indicated by a small painted white line. Oddly, and without satisfactory explanation, the water was gently lapping some three inches above it.

On the racing eight, Johno, the lead oarsman was satisfied with the rate of strike he had set all the other seven rowers for the time being. There was a good rhythm with this crew, and he was quietly confident of achieving something in May at the Tees Rowing club regatta, despite missing this weekend's racing at Chester, although he had not got over the club secretary's blunder, just yet.

He chanced a quick glance over his left shoulder, not because he did not have complete confidence in Ben's steerage: he was reckoned by many to be the finest cox in the north of England – just out of curiosity. He noted they were coming up to the island. The crew pulling away behind him were made up of the two bow men, both six feet two inches tall with strong, muscular bodies: Michael and Michael, referred to as the two Mikes in rowing circles, simply because they always seemed to compete in the same team and in the same positions. Then came the engine room consisting of Sam at number 3, a wiry red-headed terrier sort of guy, Philip at position 4, dark and handsome, Charles (Charlie) number 5, the heaviest fellow – all muscle: number 6, awesome Anthony they called him, swarthy and dour. And at number 7, the youngest member of the team, at just eighteen years old, Daniel, a blond head turner for the girls with a shy streak.

All of them had one thing in common. They were aware of the smooth rhythm and power behind their rowing. They were confident. They were proud. And there was no doubt about it, they did seem to be moving exceptionally fast over the calm water. Unfortunately, this was not due to their skill alone. They did not know it, but something else was assisting their passage.

Janet, from her vantage point on the end of Cloud Point was fascinated by the rowing team. The dark blue carbon fibre hull, so low in the water, moved swiftly over the surface of the becalmed lake – almost noiselessly – such was the skill of its oarsmen. Each rower seemed to feather their blades in unison before squaring them to enter the water at the beginning of each pull on the oars. Neat puddles formed by the blades at the completion of each stroke.

The combination of the double rows of long oars, supported by the riggers, gave an impression of some giant water creature scudding over the surface. All the crew, except for the coxswain who sat hunched at the stern moving backwards and forwards with the on-off power of the rowers, were a complete machine winding up to release their full power. They were kitted out in dark blue shorts and white with blue striped vests. The crew was now almost up to the eastern end of the island and the extra shadow made the spectacle stand out even more.

The lady was disturbed from her observation by a comment made by her companion, Brenda. "You really must read this novel after me – it is quite riveting." Janet turned her head to acknowledge the remark.

At this exact moment, Johno glanced to his left. They were moving past the eastern end of Shimdorie Island, and the stroke noticed that Ben was steering his usual course close into the bank so as to give the boat a virtual straight line heading towards the northern end of the lake. Noticing their speed over the water, he wondered if the cox might easy up on the stroke rate to avoid the catching of a crab by one of the oarsmen. He felt a surge of pride at their apparent skill. He was not to know that their progress was being assisted by an all-powerful force. Suddenly, he was distracted by a strange and alarming expression enveloping Ben Homer's face. Abruptly, without saying a word the expression further changed to one of extreme consternation. There was no doubting it. At the same time Ben pulled sharply and urgently on the steerage rope to bring the boat hard to port. Johno swung round. He cried out in alarm and disbelief. The boat ... was about to plunge down an enormous hole in the lake to the accompaniment of a dreadful noise that blanked out everything.

Johno was the only one of them to utter a sound. The rest – dreadfully – did not have time.

As the cry travelled over the water, Janet urgently turned her attention back to the lake – a part hidden from her companion's view. She stood up. 'What was happening and what was that frighteningly eerie sound?' Her mind was confused. "Where have the rowers gone?" she said in a raised voice.

Also attracted by Johno's shout and the strange sound which seemed to envelope it was Dalmar. He was in the castle rowing boat tethered to a ring on the stone wall part of the jetty. He had just managed to get the sluice gate open. For the first time that he could recollect the base of the slatted wooden construction was down to the level of the water – enough to cause rot worries. He was further distracted as Fly, having roused himself from his prone position at the end of the wooden jetty, started to bark. Dalmar had not heard him bark like that in years. He jumped out of the little boat making it clunk against the stone wall and took the two steps up to the pier deck in a single stride. Seeing nothing immediately to be concerned about he yelled to his dog, "Fly – quiet!" The collie immediately obeyed, but he did not look happy. He kept thrusting his elongated jaw lake-wards, as though trying to solve a problem by scent.

Then Dalmar noticed the lady standing on the end of Cloud Point further along the shore. She was pointing towards the island with an outstretched arm. Unable to locate the direction from which the cry emanated, he could only be sure of one thing, it had been masculine in nature. He decided to go and see the lady on the promontory. She had not moved, he noticed, and was still standing at the water's edge looking out over the lake. Another woman had joined her.

Due to Fly's uncharacteristic barking display, Dalmar sensed something untoward. He set off at a fast jogging run. Fly followed. After negotiating the twisting trail along the lake shore under beech and ash trees they approached the point. Dalmar slowed to a walk so as not to alarm the women. He clambered over the rocks towards them. They ceased their conversation and looked at him suspiciously.

"Hello," said Dalmar. "Sorry to intrude. My name is John Hunter, the curator of Bray Castle." He paused to give them a reassuring smile. It was Fly who accomplished that reassurance. When they saw the handsome animal, both ladies were instantly at ease. He did tend to have that effect on people. As a younger dog, he would have gone up to them expecting some attention, but not nowadays. Dalmar addressed his next remark to the lady he had first seen. "I was working over there," he pointed along the shore to the left, when I heard a man's cry: sounded urgent. My dog started barking and I saw you pointing at something on the lake. Is anything the matter?"

Brenda was the first to speak. Both ladies possessed clarity of speech and could not be accused of mumbling at any time. "I don't think so. My friend is concerned about a rowing boat." She turned her attention to her companion. "Janet, it must surely have gone on the other side of the island?"

"I think I'm going bats," replied Janet, she was obviously still flustered. "I could have sworn they were rowing between *us* and the island ... although they were certainly some distance from here." She shook her head – "Must be as you say Brenda. That shout – it sounded so urgent – also, something else, another noise – and then the dog barking and I thought I saw a disturbance in the water right over by the island ... Must have imagined it."

"When you say they...?" Dalmar was about to ask.

Janet pre-empted his question. "Oh, quite a lot – like one of those university boat-race what's its."

"A rowing eight?"

"Yes - had to be. At least that number."

Dalmar took this as confirmation. Adding a cox made nine anyway and he knew the eight-team boat often went out practicing on a Sunday morning.

"I'm afraid I didn't see it," Brenda joined in. "I was sitting back there reading. "Think it must have been obscured from my view – mind you I wasn't paying much attention."

Dalmar nodded. It was possible that the boat was moving, blind to them, on the other side of the island, perhaps cutting over to the eastern shore. If they intended to row down to the western end of the lake – it would have long since passed the island and returned to their view – although somewhat distant.

"Are you visiting the grounds?" asked the curator. This might have seemed an obvious question, although, some people like to have a look around the castle as well, a pleasure they had to pay for.

"Yes," replied Brenda. "We love it here. To be followed by a cup of your excellent coffee."

Dalmar grinned. Their canteen had a reputation for its coffee, which, honestly, surprised him. "Thank you," he acknowledged. "Anyway, don't let me disturb you further." Immediately, Fly walked on knowing they were leaving.

"It was nice to meet you," said Brenda graciously. She gave a low wave with her right hand. "Your dog is beautiful," she commented as an afterthought.

Janet still appeared to be pre-occupied with the lake. This did not escape Dalmar's attention. Even so, he returned to the boat house – dog and man adopting a loping run. As soon as he arrived at the jetty, he again looked out to the west ... nothing. There were no boats in that quarter of the lake that he could see.

Quickly, Dalmar climbed down into the Bray's boat and, using the side of the drystone wall, pulled himself and the rowing dingy back into the shelter closing the sluice gate as he did so. At first, he could not believe it. There was no doubt though. The bottom of the gate was now clear of the water level by six inches – where it should be. More puzzlement.

The curator decided to abandon his repairs for today and collecting his tools he made his way out of the boathouse by the side door, which was located at the rear of the building and clear of the jetty. He called to Fly and set off up the path towards the castle. On the way he noticed the two women some way behind. Out of politeness he turned to acknowledge them. They waved back.

He suspected Suzanne might be at the animal centre. She was – with his daughter and son attending to the little red squirrel. A little breathless he said, "Darling – I need to pop down to the rowing club urgently. A visitor to the grounds has seen something odd out on the lake. It needs clarification."

If he expected his wife to accept that – he was mistaken. "Pardon," she said. "Something odd?" She looked at him with her sparkling eyes; those endearing few tiny dark freckles just above her cheek bones obvious in the shelter's crisp lighting. Dalmar thought she looked cute in a white roll-neck jumper with her virtually black hair falling over the edges on each side of her head. These two were confidants as well as lovers. In that, they were lucky.

"A lady was concerned that the eight-crew and their boat, which she had been watching opposite Cloud Point, appeared to have vanished. I know it is hardly likely, but I must check it out," then he added, "in person," indicating a telephone call would not do. There were reasons here. Dalmar had his own water area's security to consider.

At this Suzanne did not question him further. She knew, as did most people who lived hereabouts, that Lastwater had a history going back for centuries of mysterious unexplained drowning accidents where the bodies of the missing were never found. This did not apply exclusively to people either. "If you are not back in time for lunch – I'll keep a plate-full in the oven."

"Thanks."

"Can I come?" asked a little girl's voice.

Her father looked down at the serious face of his daughter. He smiled. "Not this time sweetheart. He hesitated before adding, "Anyway, this little chap needs your attention – and yours," he quickly chucked Michael under his chin before he felt left out, then he proffered a finger in the squirrel's direction, who was studying him warily. "Just going to cadge a quick coffee from the kitchen, then I'll be off with Fly. Bye you three." He blew kisses at them and went around to the back of the canteen.

The Sunday crew were working and seemed pretty busy for the month of March. "Hello Trishia, can I grab a coffee from the thingy?" Dalmar pointed at a percolator bubbling away in the corner.

A harassed looking portly lady, obviously in charge here, waved an arm. "Alright for some," she muttered. Dalmar smiled.

After his refreshment – he managed to steal a chocolate biscuit before joining Fly outside in the courtyard. He threw a plain digestive at the grateful animal.

When they reached the favoured viewing place below White Crag, Dalmar pulled in. On this occasion he did not let Fly out; his intention being to be on his way again soon.

Studying the scenery, while enjoying light refreshment, a gentleman who was sitting on one of the exposed boulders courteously said, "Good morning – or is it afternoon?" Seeing the National Trust logo of oak leaves and acorns painted in white on the Land Rover's dark green body had aroused his curiosity.

Dalmar glanced at his watch, "Just gone noon," he said, "I don't suppose you have seen a rowing eight out on the lake?"

The man replied, "Yes." Funny you should ask that. It must have landed somewhere – possibly Bray Castle. I noticed it earlier when I was on my way up from the car park by the A591. "They were moving so smoothly – a good crew by the look of it."

This confirmed the fact that there had been an eight out there. He took the opportunity to look all over Lastwater. There was no sign of any boat. He gave the man a, "Thank you," and departed as politely as possible. It was obvious the fellow was in for a chat.

On arrival at the club, Dalmar parked the Land Rover in the member's car parking area. Actually, he was not a member, but he knew his presence would be tolerated.

Leaving Fly in charge of the vehicle, he knocked on the club house entrance door. There was no reply, so he pushed it open and entered.

He found a club official behind the neat little bar at the corner of the member's lounge. They knew each other. "Dalmar – what brings you here?"

"A fool's errand, I hope Jim. Has your eight-crew returned yet?"

"About ten minutes before they get back – I should guess," replied Jim, looking at the clock on the wall. "Why?"

"Mind if I wait?" Dalmar then went on to relate the morning's events at Cloud Point.

Jim was not concerned, but he did understand the other man's desire to have the matter explained. Non-members were not allowed to purchase drinks; however, Jim tempted the intruder to a glass of light lager beer. They both went outside to await the arrival of crew.

Out on the jetty area were two oarsmen getting their individual sculling crafts ready to go for their practice session. It would be the coxless fours turn later in the afternoon.

Jim, last name Derby, introduced the curator and explained the reason for his visit. For the first ten minutes the men talked in good humour. After that Dalmar noticed some serious looking glances being made, particularly towards the northern shore, right across the lake opposite them. Johno's crew should be much nearer home than that by now. After all, the idea had been to make a fast run on the homeward leg. They should be back – and fatigued. Unusually for him – in this situation, Jim lit a cigarette. He normally refrained from the habit at the club.

By and by, the overdue time reached half an hour. Jim suggested that the two scullers go out, one to take a course this side of Shimdorie Island and the other on the starboard side. He went into the club house and returned with two bright yellow radio handsets, which he proceeded to test. Satisfied – he handed one to each oarsman.

When the skull boats had departed, Dalmar, his task over, although unresolved, thanked Jim for his hospitality and left. Fly was very pleased to see him, nuzzling the back of his head enthusiastically, as he climbed into the vehicle.

CHAPTER THREE

"YOU WILL BE ALRIGHT OUT THERE?"

Dalmar had in mind a visit to Bray's observatory. Perhaps the powerful telescope could be brought to bear on the lake instead of the sky. He hoped Brian Cussen, the astronomer, was available.

As it happened, Brian was about. There had been no night duties for the last four days due to completely overcast skies. Dalmar found him having his lunch in the canteen after he deposited Fly on the front lawn of the Dower House. When there the dog knew that is where he must stay until told otherwise. This suited Fly very well. He was guarding the family in his master's absence. At least that is what people thought. Possibly, it was an accurate assumption, anyway, Fly always looked proud and there was shelter available under the front porch if he needed it. Emma frequently made sure his water bowl was topped up, unless the rain did it for her.

Brian Cussen was a slim man with a full head of greying hair. One physical attribute he possessed was a blessing in disguise for his profession. He had brilliant eyesight, even for his age. His hearing was not so good, but he accepted that and knew that it would not be long before he would have to wear an aid to compensate. Dressed in his usual blazer, white shirt and Fellow of the Royal Astronomical Society's tie; grey trousers with polished, deep tan leather lace-less shoes, he greeted the curator. "Hello Dalmar," he said. "What ails you?" Brian thought he detected worry lines on his face.

When he heard the news, he pushed his almost empty plate to one side and escorted the curator through to the central hall of the castle interior, via the back entrance. There were only two visitors looking around. An attempt was being made to bring the ground floor reception rooms and a library back to the style and content of the occupation by the original family. At least, necessary repairs to walls and particularly the ceiling plaster's ornate decoration were complete, but the rest had some way to go. A lot of it depended on donations to the National Trust in the kind of period furniture and fittings required. They tended to be added as they became available. The desired effect was getting there.

The two men made their way up the central wooden staircase. This was a beauty – good strong solid oak with banisters to match. Avoiding the bedrooms and wandering tourists they went through a corridor to a rear door. Brian produced a substantial iron key and unlocked it. From here they had to negotiate a narrow stone spiral staircase to the roof area. A sturdy doorway gave them access. A much more modest key was used to open the observatory itself.

Brian had to unlock the telescope from its position on the motorised revolving drive unit. Once free, both men lifted the telescope off its supporting arms and mounting. It was very heavy being a solid brass construction, which gave wonderful stability when viewing the heavens. With difficulty they took it out onto the roof and carried it over to the edge of the front parapet. This should give the best panoramic view of Lastwater. While Dalmar supported the scope, Brian attached a heavy metal tripod to its mountings, a tricky operation during which the curator had to take the full weight of the great telescope. There then followed a quick focusing operation before Brian vacated the eyepiece for the curator.

First of all – the curator decided to get used to what he was looking at. Limited experience with high magnification telescopes had taught him that it usually took a while for the brain to register the enormous change in focal length. What he saw – made him gasp. He took his head away from the scope and shook it – in disbelief. Brian had lined up on Shimdorie Island. For a telescope used to looking at distant stars, the result was staggering. Dalmar could make out individual rocks, plants, trees and pebbles being gently lapped at the water's edge. It was as though he had been magically plunged right into the island itself from half a mile away.

Having satisfied himself that all was well on the island, he moved the telescope right over to its right-hand periphery to try and get a look at the goings on at L.R.C. The actual boat house, apart from its roof, was not visible, due to woodland in the foreground, but he could clearly see Jim and another man, dressed in a dark suit, looking out over the lake on the small pier, presumably in radio contact with the scull boat oarsmen. Dalmar then turned his attention to carrying out a thorough scan of the northern shore. It took a good ten minutes during which Brian was courteously silent. Finally, Dalmar brought his head up. He had, of course, seen through the scope for its intended purpose, to view the night sky, but this was the first time he had used it in this situation. "Quite remarkable," he said.

Brian gave a curt nod. "I take it you saw nothing comforting?"

"Unfortunately, not." The tall man pushed the lock of hair away from his left eye. "Perhaps I had better go and let my wife know the latest. She will be anxious."

"Why don't I continue to look?" The astronomer suggested. "Have you had your lunch?"

"I'll grab something while I'm at it. Be back in about half an hour ... okay.?

"Absolutely," affirmed Brian, at the same time giving out a knowing smile.

Dalmar found his family in the kitchen at the Dower-house. There was an appetising aroma of roast lamb. Emma was attempting to feed baby Michael in his highchair. It looked to be a task that Suzanne was somewhat nervous about. She wore a wistful expression. Her husband found it endearing. She turned her attention to him with a questioning look. He shook his head. The colour started to drain from his wife's face. Quickly Dalmar added, "I expect some explanation will come to light. They've got two skull boats out on the water looking right now; both are in radio communication with the club."

Suzanne still looked shocked. Her attention was distracted as Michael pushed the spoon, full of baby food, away from his sister, annoyed at her persistence. Any minute now and it would be spilt over goodness knows what. "Emma – be patient darling. Remember what I told you."

Dalmar carried on. "After leaving the rowing club, Brian and I got the big telescope out of the observatory. We've mounted it on a tripod, on the roof, over-looking the lake. Amazing what you can see."

Suzanne was about to suggest that the children might like to have a look, and then she realised that the roof of the castle was one of the last places she wanted them to be. "Just about to serve up – you timed it well." She added, "It's a worry isn't it – you know – Lastwater's history?"

"Yes," her husband confirmed. "But – eight rowers – they can't just have disappeared!"

Suzanne saw the point. The colour was gradually returning to her cheeks, although she was not smiling.

During the week, Dalmar usually fended for himself during the day leaving Suzanne free to attend to the children. They had their family meal together in the early evening. On Sunday's though, they often had a traditional roast lunch together. Today, Dalmar ate quickly and asked Suzanne if he could have his pudding later. He was anxious to return to the roof of the castle.

Before going there, he put through a telephone call to the rowing club. "Hi Dalmar," said Jim when he heard the identity of the caller. "It seems your questioning was justified – not a sign of them."

"Nothing. The scullers drawn a blank?" asked Dalmar.

"For now – yes – they are still out there looking for any sign. Got the club president with me and the coxless-four crew have just turned up. They will be going out to search as well. I have notified Ambleside Mountain Rescue. They've got an inflatable with an outboard motor. The chief constable of Cumbrian police has given us permission to use it." Motorised craft of any description were banned on Lastwater for wildlife conservation reasons. This was obviously considered an exception.

Dalmar felt his brain chill and there was a funny feeling in his stomach. He wished he had not eaten quite so much roast lamb. 'An eight-man crew and their cox were missing on Lastwater – how?' His mind raced.

"Look Jim, I must get off the phone and free up your line, but if there is anything, we can do this end. You are welcome to use our jetty for whatever. We have taken the big telescope out of the observatory and mounted it on the castle roof. Had a thorough search in all the inlets and bays that we can see, including this side of Shimdorie Island. That is where the lady saw your crew from Cloud Point this morning. We have spotted nothing unusual yet; will keep on looking."

"Thanks, Dalmar – will let you know if there any developments."

"Bye Jim – good luck."

Suzanne had been listening to the one-sided conversation, which told her that there was no news. She went up to her husband who was standing still by the telephone in their hall. She put an arm through his and looked up at him. "My god," he said. "This is crackers!"

"What's happening?" she asked.

"They have called in Ambleside Mountain Rescue with their boat. Had to be done of course, the crew are more than two hours overdue now." He looked down at her with a partially open mouth. The top row of teeth were not quite straight. She loved this in him. "I have told them they can use any of our lakeside facilities." Suzanne gave a gentle nod. "What bugs me," he carried on, "is the nothingness – no sightings of anything." It was obvious what he meant by that, oars, personal kit, plastic bottles: most of the crew took a drink with them. Nothing."

He told his wife that he would be back soon and went off to see Brian on the roof after letting Fly into the Dower House kitchen for his mid-day treat.

The astronomer was now wearing a lined jacket, which he kept permanently in the observatory, and was in the process of opening a heavy-duty plastic sheet with eye holes in each corner. He had felt the presence of rain likely and decided to be prepared. He considered that it might be a good idea to leave the telescope in its current position for a while. In which case, it was not just rain now that the instrument must be protected from. Clear skies were forecast tonight so there would probably be a layer of dew in the morning.

Dalmar told Brian about the latest news at L.R.C. "Well I have seen the one-man boats out there. You don't need a telescope for that," Brian commented. "Although – I have been busy. Think I have been all over the lake visible from our viewpoint, including the inlets where the streams come down. It is amazing how many of them there are. I didn't realise."

"Yes, I know. Must be a huge volume of water in total," agreed the curator.

"Now then – this may not seem important at this moment, but I think your wife would soundly disagree. Over there," Brain pointed along the shore to the west, "where that large patch of reeds is. Do you see?"

Dalmar followed Brian's pointing finger. "Got you," he affirmed.

"Can't be sure of course – but I think there is an injured otter lying there. It is definitely an otter and it seems very still. Wouldn't have thought it would be sleeping there. They usually go into a den, don't they?"

"Think so. We will have to consult our resident expert." Despite the serious occurrences, Dalmar managed a small smile. "Can I see?"

"Yes, I have the scope focused on the animal." Brian

pointed to the telescope.

When Dalmar looked through the eyepiece he was astounded. It appeared that right in front of him lay an adult otter visible through a multitude of reeds. It appeared to be lying on its side with the head turned away from them – and very still. Dalmar raised his head sharply. This could be bad news. A pair of otters had been released into the lake area last summer. They had been reported as doing well. Fish stocks were currently good, and the Wildlife Trust had come to an agreement with the officers of the Lake District national park, who administered the whole of this area. Consequently, a ban on angling was put in force for the next five years. Otters had been steadily declining in the United Kingdom during the nineteen-fifties and reached crises point in the early sixties, due to pesticides getting into their food chain. They were now recovering gradually.

Dalmar said out loud, "This must be the breeding season. That could be a female." Brian showed his concern in the expression on his face. "Can I leave you in charge up here? Drag a chair out of the observatory. I'll ask someone to bring you a cup of something, shall I?"

"Why don't I go and get it. They are a bit busy in the canteen." Apart from anything else, the astronomer needed to pay a visit to the toilet.

"Okay. Let's go. We'll see what Suzanne thinks." After negotiating the spiral staircase, they went off in different directions.

Dalmar went through the ample hall to the front door. Doris Appleby was on duty taking entrance fees off visitors and handing out leaflets with historical information. The castle, being rather young, did not have a lot of that. She said that they had been quite busy, although not overly so. Doris was a middle-aged lady with a joyous but efficient side to her personality and rather enjoyed this part time job – meeting all kinds of people. She had just been chatting to some old boys from the outward-bound school days. They were very impressed, remembering its rather tatty interior when they were there. Doris told the curator this thinking it would be bound to please him. He mentioned to her about the missing boat crew, keeping it low-key, purely for management reasons. A panicky receptionist would not help matters at all. Doris, however, did not seem bothered. "Probably gone ashore with a crate of beer," and she laughed.

As expected, Suzanne was very distraught about the otter. She obviously could not leave her children and accompany Dalmar in the boat. Being Sunday there were no groundsmen on duty; this would mean her husband must go alone. Suzanne was a little concerned. "You will be alright out there?" She knew he was a strong swimmer but the morning's events ...

"Don't worry," he said. "I'll wear my waders." These were special rubber boots that came right up over his thighs. Suzanne was not comforted with this. It was not what she meant. She let it go with a frown. The otter's possible distress won. "Tell you what – give me half an hour's start and then come down to the jetty to give the children some fresh air. I'll meet you there, hopefully with the otter." He thought for a second or two. "Should I take anything – blanket?"

"Might be useful. If you can get hold of the otter, handle it carefully. And bring it back safely. That's all." She narrowed her eyes at him. Dalmar knew what that meant. It was a kind of instruction rather than a plead and just said soundlessly, 'Be careful.'

"Okay, I'll do my best. Might be nothing wrong with it ... hope so." He managed to get away before Emma found out what was going on. She would have delayed matters with a bombardment of questions. Fly was decidedly put-out at not being called to join him; especially when he saw his master in his waders. He loved going out in the boat. The dog grunt-barked his disapproval and went into a sulk, slinking off to hide in the shrubbery in the back garden.

It took Dalmar no longer than fifteen minutes to get out

onto the water in the rowing dinghy. He had noted that the sluice gate at the boat house was still clear of the water. Things seemed back to normal in that direction. The sound of an outboard motor could clearly be heard in the eastern part of the lake. Ambleside Mountain Rescue had, presumably, launched the inflatable at the beach there. Actually, the sound was more than clear: it was downright intrusive but would have to be put up with in the circumstances. Already, birds of many species were taking to the air; the noise would be totally alien to them.

Dalmar pulled on the oars in a practised rhythm. He felt ill at ease. The usual enjoyment he experienced when out on the lake was badly tainted with a forbidding leaden atmosphere. The lack of light due to the overcast sky and low cloud level did not help. The peaks of the mountains to the west were draped in a hanging mist, and the slopes of Helvelyn to the east were dispersed into a blanket of grey cloud.

It did not take long to row across Tadpole Bay, so called because during the spring, on certain days, the shoreline could be encrusted with them. If a passer-by were to cup their hands and submerse them, at the water edge, and then lift them clear allowing the water to cascade out – the palms of those hands would be full of a wriggling brown mass of life: hundreds of tadpoles.

As he approached the line of sandy coloured reeds, Dalmar turned his head around to get a close look. The dark shape of an animal could be seen lying amongst them. He shipped his starboard oar and gently steered the bow end round with the other, so as to come alongside as close as possible. The boat bumped up across the shallow mud bank about six feet away from the prone animal. Taking hold of the rope, secured at the bow end, Dalmar tried stepping out with one leg. The wader clad foot only sank in about three to four inches. This was not uncommon here – there would be a bed of hard rock immediately beneath the mud.

Dalmar secured the other oar and inched forward

through the tall reeds. This was an action that should be bound to disturb the animal if it were merely sleeping, something that was quite possible for an otter during the daytime; except that they usually rested in a small cavern, perhaps below a lakeside tree, which they entered under water. Soon Dalmar was able to confirm that he was looking at an adult otter. At first sight it looked to be lifeless. Then he noticed that it was breathing and the one eye he could see was fully open. It made no attempt to turn its head to look at him, indicating, conclusively, that all was not well. What momentarily confused him was why this otter, injured or not, chose to make the difficult passage through the reeds? Their land movement was awkward, the body being designed for momentum in the water. He found out when he got really close. On the other side of the animal was open water.

Dalmar returned to the side of the boat and, using the rope, pulled it along to the extreme end of the mud bank. He was then able to come back along the other side until he was almost up with the animal. He partially fell once, on the ultra-slippery surface, even the deep tread on his waders could not prevent it, but, thankfully, the thick rubber covering on his legs prevented a nasty skinning, as his left shin cracked against naked rock. He winced and cursed at the same time, before recovering his balance and a two-footed stance.

Now that the otter was more visible to him, he was sure it was a female. It did not seem long enough or wide enough in its body to be otherwise. Secretly, Dalmar was grateful, for if it came to have to lift her, matters would be a lot easier. With a slow unhurried movement, he got as close as possible to the otter dimly aware that, never in his life, had he been so close to one before. He felt awed.

Dalmar could see that the animal was greatly distressed. Her breathing was spasmodic and sounded laboured. Wet oily fur on her flat head hooded two dark eyes and a damp black nose jutted out from under, surrounded by long thick whiskers. On each side of her head protruded small rounded ears.

Dalmar knew the claws on her short forelegs were sharp and powerful, so his first task was to try and get the blanket under the body, in order to wrap her before trying to lift her into the boat. He brought the bow of the boat closer still, until he was able to reach in and grab the blanket. Carefully he placed it over the otter. Then he proceeded to try and turn her over. Amazingly, she let him, from which he came to the unsettling conclusion that she must be very weak. She made not a sound.

When Dalmar was satisfied that his patient was fully wrapped in the blanket with its head and tail protruding from each end, he took her weight and carefully lifted. Her heaviness, initially, surprised him, feeling the pressure on his spine. With caution he placed her in the stern of the boat. Then, quickly, he embarked and pushed off.

As he started to row back into the main body of the lake, his attention was caught by something in the water twenty to thirty yards away. It was another otter. 'Of course, he thought to himself, 'the other half of the pair – the male.' As he took in the size of this animal, he now knew he had been right, this one was not only longer but heavier as well. It was lying on its back and appeared not the slightest concerned at his presence. From his side on view, Dalmar could see that the animal was holding onto something. Its short front legs where clasped to it and, although hidden from sight, presumably so were the hind legs. Whatever it was - looked to be long and thin. Judging by the protruding end beyond the animal's tail, it could be a branch that had broken off a tree.

Slowly, the otter drifted around to an end on view with the head farthest away from the watching man. Dalmar realised the otter was fast asleep, lying on its back, listlessly. What he now saw caused his body to stiffen and the expression on his face to harden to one of deadly seriousness. Lying across the animal's chest held in its claws, as though giving extra buoyancy was the blade of an oar. At the other end, trailing in the open water, what Dalmar had originally thought was a broken branch, now could be clearly made out to be the fractured end of that oar. But it was not this alone that caused alarm – it was the dark blue on the blade with a narrow, white horizontal stripe just before the curl at the end of the blade: the style and colours of Lastwater Rowing Club.

CHAPTER FOUR

"OTTERS DON'T DROWN..."

As our man studied the sleeping male otter he was in somewhat of a quandary. The priority should be to get his patient, the female, back to Bray as soon as possible. The poor thing looked to be in a highly critical state. But ... Dalmar had to have that oar, currently cradled like a float, along her mate's belly.

His dilemma was solved just then. With a loud mew the male awoke. It looked at the man in the boat in what can only be taken as astonishment. Not for long: releasing the broken oar, he rolled over to sink beneath the surface. Dalmar could just make out the streamlined body diving down and away.

Quickly, with a couple of strokes, the waiting man was on the drifting oar. He caught hold of the end where it had been broken and brought it aboard. It was longer than his dingy, giving evidence that the break must have occurred, near the gate, where oar meets hull in a racing boat. Disappointingly, there could be no doubt that the item was not the result of forgotten lost property. Judging by the overall condition and the stark, splintered area at the fracture itself, it was relatively new.

This event was witnessed by Brian Cussen on the roof

of the castle through the telescope. He could quite clearly see the long object that Dalmar had just brought on board with the broken end sticking over the stern of the rowing dinghy. It did not take much to realise its significance. He had also witnessed the successful transfer of otter to boat. It now occurred to him that he would almost certainly be more useful down at the jetty. He could see, with the naked eye, Suzanne trundling along with Michael in his pushchair, and little Emma running on ahead as they made their way down to the lakeside. He set about securing the plastic sheet over the scope and tying it down securely. If the wind grew strong, the sheeting could be lost; the roof area being rather exposed. He knew it would take some untying, but better that than the other.

Over his shoulder Dalmar noticed the arrival of his family on the jetty. Emma was standing on the end waving at him. He returned it cheerily. Suzanne, holding tightly to the pushchair with the toddler well strapped in, was looking at him enquiringly. He gave her a thumb up sign, before getting on with the job in hand.

Our lone rower let his eyes fall into Tadpole bay's depths as he progressed. He said to himself, 'What is your secret?'

Apart from checking his direction twice, Dalmar came on across the bay as quickly as he could. When he drew in the oars to let the boat drift up to the jetty, he was breathing hard with the exertion.

A shout of surprise from Emma greeted him at the sight of the otter, with two audible gasps from his wife: one, on noticing the state of the animal, and the other at the significance of the broken oar. "Oh," was all she could say.

Michael made a reasonable comment, "Big fish," he said pointing at the otter.

'First things first,' thought Dalmar. "I'll lift her out and place her on the ground up there," he suggested and without waiting for an answer proceeded to do so.

"What's wrong with it?" asked an immensely curious

four-year old. "Mummy – is that an otter? Really! – an otter?" Her eyes were wide with wonder.

"Yes, now stand out of the way so daddy can bring her up." She had noticed life in the animal. Dalmar was very careful. As he climbed the steps with her cradled in his arms, she mewed at him with eyes wide open. He laid her down and opened up the blanket. Suzanne was at the otter's side in a flash. She was not a vet, but she had enough knowledge to know that there was a major breathing problem here. Quickly she opened the otter's mouth and peered in looking for a blockage. She was greeted by gurgling noises and a load of bubbles. Suzanne said, "What!" out loud. "I don't believe it. Darling - this animal's half drowned." As the otter was lying conveniently on its side, Suzanne immediately started applying pressure in upward strokes with the palms of her hands along the otter's back. If anything, the otter's breathing became worse and more traumatised, when suddenly it gave an enormous cough, and out of its mouth shot a good quantity of water forming a serious puddle next to her.

"Urgh," gasped Emma, jumping back out of the way. Michael giggled.

Dalmar was amazed, while full of admiration for his wife's action. "Well done love!" he said with emphasis.

The improvement in the otter's well-being following a severe coughing fit during which more water was expelled from its lungs – proved dramatic. After looking around her for a while, she started to flounder along the jetty in an ungainly fashion. Dalmar made to go after her, but his wife placed an arm on his to dissuade him. When, the previously all but dead animal reached the end of the jetty, to Emma's delight, it dived off and swam away as though nothing had happened. They all watched it glide beautifully through the lake's calm waters, back across the bay so as to re-join its mate.

"Never did find out if she was pregnant," said Suzanne.

Dalmar could not believe his ears. 'That's my wife,' he

thought.

Just at this moment Brian Cussen arrived. He looked in the boat and around the group on the jetty. "Where is the otter?" he asked.

After he had been greeted by Suzanne and her daughter, they brought him up to date. Suzanne was feeling very satisfied.

Brian looked puzzled. "Half drowned you say. Otters don't drown – not even half-way." This gave them all something to think about. Dalmar had already made up his mind, but for the time being he kept his thoughts to himself.

Very soon the party were on their back up to the castle, Dalmar carrying the dreadful oar. Suzanne, with rather damp jeans from her attention to the otter, had merely confirmed with her husband that those were the rowing club's colours on the blade. As he did so – she went silent. 'Did this mean that nine young men had actually drowned out there within hearing distance of their own voices?' Her mind, of course, did not want to believe that.

Brian, making himself useful with Michael's pushchair, told his boss that he had seen him retrieve it through the telescope, and informed him that from his vantage point on the roof there appeared to have been no sightings of the missing crew.

Apart from a curious inspection Emma did not ask any questions about the oar. She was used to her father bringing discarded items out of the water.

As soon as he decently could with consideration for his children, Dalmar placed the oar in the back of the Land Rover and summoning a grateful Fly – departed. He had thought about phoning the club first but decided that sight of the salvaged item was probably more important.

On the way, he pulled in at the White Crag observation point. This time he let Fly out for a sniff around. A single, winter worn, shaggy sheep moved off from browsing on the verge. It need not have worried; the dog never disturbed these animals having been trained not to, long ago.

All the rowing boats were still out on the lake, clearly visible, even though the light was starting to darken with the approaching end of the day. Ominously, it seemed to the distant watching man, an inflatable with outboard motor hushed, lurked in the waters immediately adjacent to the southern shore of Shimdorie Island.

Seven minutes later Dalmar pulled into the rowing club's car park. Although Ambleside Mountain rescue's vehicle must be still down at the car park by the main road, there were now two marked police cars here. And, generally, considerably more vehicles than had been here this morning were in evidence. It occurred to Dalmar that, presumably, most of those that had been parked for the greater part of the day belonged to the missing crew of the racing-eight.

Leaving the oar and the dog in the back of the Land Rover, Dalmar entered the club's neat wood construction building with its cleverly designed single section sloping roof. He found Jim talking to a senior uniformed policeman out on the jetty.

Jim, looking almost desperately morose, introduced them. "Chief Constable of Cumbrian police, George Lipoce. Dalmar Hunter, curator of Bray Castle for the National Trust."

After very brief pleasantries the curator of Bray Castle addressed them both in a hushed tone. There were several men around in hearing distance. "Think you had better come and look at this – found it in the lake." If both men could look even more serious, they did so now. "It's in the back of my vehicle."

Following a quiet exit from the club – there were only a handful of members directly in their way – Dalmar approached the back of the Land Rover and opened its rear doors. Immediately he told Fly to sit before the animal could move. The oar stood out like a message from hell lying there, with blade towards them; the stem going all the way to the front windscreen between the seats. The broken end was lying, starkly, hard up against the glass.

Jim Derby's pallor blanched. He looked about to stumble. Dalmar half put out an arm in support. "Oh – Christ!" he exclaimed. Putting a hand to his forehead, he said, "I'll get Douglas ... the chairman," and rushed back into the clubhouse.

While he was gone, Dalmar had time to tell the chief constable where, and in what circumstances the salvaged item was found. Jim Derby came bustling back, virtually pulling a very reluctant portly gentleman with a full grey-white beard along with him. It must be said; Jim kept himself in a very good state of fitness. The many rowing years he had spent at the club had given him strong leg and upper torso muscles. He had not allowed them to run to fat, unlike the chairman Doug Saunders who constantly appeared to be out of breath.

It was in this state, all red in the face, that Douglas surveyed the oar in the National Trust's Land Rover. He made similar enquiries about where and when off Dalmar, whom he had not met before, but somehow introductions, at this time, seemed pointless. Then he just stared at the oar for perhaps half a minute before turning to the Chief Constable. "I am officially notifying you that the nine members of our first eight crew are missing – presumed drowned – on Lastwater."

There then followed a dreadful silence. It was broken by George Lipoce. "I shall need names, next of kin, addresses – phone numbers." Jim glanced at Douglas, received a nod, and went off to get the information required.

The policeman and the club chairman briefly discussed the matter of informing the press. It was decided that this should be done after all next of kin had been told.

There was an awkward moment before Dalmar broached the subject of what to do with the oar. Douglas thought they could find a niche in the club's administrative office for the time being. With a grunt or two he reached into the rear of the vehicle to retrieve it. First, though, he had the presence of mind to give Fly's long nose a quick pat and tried hard to smile. The dog had already picked up the strong negative atmosphere. He duly whined.

Before leaving, Dalmar again made it clear that Bray Castle's waterside facilities would be fully available for whatever purpose. He knew that an underwater search would be necessary.

On the return journey, Dalmar switched the car's headlights on in the dip position for the gathering gloom of twilight.

The first matter to attend to on arrival back at the Dower House was to notify his immediate superior in the National Trust organization, the regional director for the Lake District national park, Jack Twentyman. He got through to him at his home near Keswick. Dalmar received the reaction he had been expecting followed by instructions: a complete ban on public access to the lake, as far as possible. However, National Trust employees must not interfere with the authorities carrying out searches. In fact, quite the opposite, they should assist in any way possible. Dalmar's responsibility only extended to the water frontage on the Bray estate.

The entire Lake District of north-west England was designated a national park, and in this case, it would be park wardens who would be primarily responsible for patrolling the majority of Lastwater's shores.

Thankfully, a four-year old girl and a two-year old boy were not yet aware of the tragedy that had befallen the locality in which they lived. It would not be possible to keep the whole matter from them, particularly Emma, but Suzanne was hopeful that she would not suffer the horror that all the adults undoubtedly would. The parents were able to get both children off to sleep in good time that evening, even Michael seemed tired and went down earlier than usual.

After Suzanne had completed her check on the patients in the bird and animal centre around nine o'clock, topping up water containers where necessary and removing uneaten food, she went to have a long talk with her husband over the day's awful events and how it would affect their Monday's duties at the castle. For example, that day was usually put aside for most of the administrative duties. Dalmar did not have a secretary. They coped with all the correspondence between them.

What her husband had to say interested her greatly. He opened by asking if she knew what her brother and his family's plans were for the imminent Easter school holidays? They had two children aged six and four, Charles and Holly.

"Actually – I don't know. Haven't spoken to Chris (short for Christine) for a while – why?

"Don't say anything until I have had a chance to speak to Jack. Look – I think we need a geologist in on this little lot." He stopped to put his mug, half full of hot coffee, on the small table next to his chair. They were sitting next to each other on an ample settee in the Dower House lounge. A log fire, in hot ember mood, provided sufficient heat. The room's two radiators were turned off. "I have noticed some very strange things about our lake recently, and, it occurred to me that if I can get permission to consult your brother – then why not?"

"Great – it will be good to see them. Nice for Emma too. She and Holly usually get on." Suzanne grimaced as she said this, remembering a couple of dodgy times, but they were a year older now. "What strange things?" she asked, recalling the earlier conversation.

"Well – it's because of the coincidence with the tragedy. This morning when I first went to the boathouse, I noticed that the lake water level was very high: higher than I have ever seen it before. Okay, we have had a lot of rainfall recently – but why should that freak level suddenly disappear just after the eight-crew disappeared?"

Suzanne took a while to take this in. Her reply was sensible. "You obviously think there is a geological reason.

Apparently, my brother, surprisingly, is considered a good geologist."

Dalmar made no comment on this. Whenever Suzanne and Tim, her brother, got together it would not be long before the sibling rivalry of old reappeared. He moved the subject, in general, on. "And then there is the otter. As Brian said, who ever heard of an otter drowning – partial or whatever?" Dalmar leant forward and stared at the soft peach coloured carpet. "Unless ... it got caught in some ... in a very powerful current?"

The main ten o'clock news on the television already had the event as their main item. A distinguished, senior politician's resignation was downgraded to second place. The announcement was made by Cumbria's Chief Constable to a group from the media outside Lastwater Rowing Club. Numerous, powerful lights seemed to have magically arrived for the purpose. All next of kin had apparently been informed and a list of the missing was sombrely read out by George Lipoce.

Dalmar and Suzanne went to bed soon after the news fearing a hectic day tomorrow. Suzanne needed a cuddle. Her security had received a nasty knock. One thing led to another and they made love. That is how it was with these two: it happened – naturally. Titillating foreplay was not part of their repertoire: a choice preferred by both. The staged dinner for two in an expensive restaurant was not for them. When they went out, they both preferred it to be with the children.

An hour later when they were sound asleep, the telephone next to the bed rang. Dalmar groped for the handset. "Yes?"

"Mr Hunter?" came a crisp male voice. Then he announced who he was and what newspaper he represented. "Could we have your opinion on this awful drowning accident?"

"Appalling," said Dalmar and put down the receiver. He immediately followed this up by pulling the plug out of the socket fixed to the skirting board. He was just about to climb back into bed when Michael, from the cot room next door, started crying. Mumbling something about, "Staying put," to his wife, Dalmar went to attend to him.

Suzanne was grateful, but now lying in bed in a new twilight sleep she wished her husband's body was close at hand. The apparent disaster that had overtaken their idyllic neighbourhood created within her a desperate need for comfort. She thought to herself that she needed it more than Michael at this time, before motherhood kicked in and she waited patiently.

When they had first come to live at Bray Castle, she knew about the sad history of unexplained drowning accidents on the lake. No bodies were ever found. There were recorded events going back centuries, although none could be verified as being accurate, apart from the two that had taken place in the nineteen hundred's where competent witnesses had given their evidence. As time had gone by, Suzanne had come to believe that there was no longer any threat. In view of the tranquillity and beauty surrounding them, it was not surprising. That feeling of serene security had now been shattered.

Soon, Dalmar returned. She grasped him in a necessary embrace. He responded - somehow understanding. His wife ... trembled involuntarily.

CHAPTER FIVE

"I MAY HAVE YOUR MAN."

The Hunter's alarm clock had been set for six a.m.; a full hour earlier than usual. By a miracle it did not wake Michael.

Dalmar grabbed his black wool dressing gown from the bathroom and went downstairs to make Suzanne a cup of tea.

It was not until he opened the curtains in the lounge that he realised dawn was about to break, and, for the first time for quite a while, sunshine was waiting in the wings. It looked to be a cloudless sky.

The phone rang.

And so, it started, telephone call after telephone call. The police were getting a team of divers together. The favoured point for their operation was to be the jetty and boathouse at Bray Castle. Dalmar was told to expect them any time that morning. Jack Twentyman called to tell them he was on his way. And then there was the press: only a few enquiries fortunately; most of the questions would be directed at the rowing club. Also, there were numerous calls from friends and relatives recognising the location on the news broadcasts and in the papers.

Dalmar had a suspicion that there would be many more visitors than they would normally get on an insignificant March Monday. And he was right.

When he went over to the castle at eight, the view over the lake to the northern fells, in normal times, would have pleased him greatly. With the arrival of full sunshine – the magnificent colours of the vista were put on display. On the lower mountain slopes, the soft pinks of the heather with deep blue where shadows darkened the ravines and hollows, together with the woodlands by the lake still showing their winter dressing of nothingness – looking from this distance like stippling artist's brushes in silhouette. The short grazed lower slopes were now a pleasant pale green interspersed with the odd solitary oak or clump of rowan. The lake itself, the dull grey now erased, held a vibrant compliment to the cerulean sky, with a virtual royal blue hue and the trees and shrubs at its edge were reflected in unison.

Emma attended play school three mornings a week at Grasmere village. This was one of them. Bea started things going at the animal centre before Suzanne joined her at 9.30. She was a stout girl in her early twenties; rather plain, with, usually, untidy light brown hair. However, she had a tender heart. Somehow, her general appearance did not seem to matter in her N.T. sports shirt. This job suited her and she – it. Naturally, Bea only had one topic of conversation that morning: the rowing disaster. The first patient Suzanne wanted to see was Sue, the red squirrel. Here, at least, there were encouraging signs. The little chap was sitting up on his hind legs, all tawny and sandy, munching away on a nut kernel Bea had just given him. The good news was the fact that she was using both of her little front paws to grip with, the splint was now no more than a support. Suzanne reckoned she would be able to remove it within a week or two, subject to confirmation from Ursula, the centre's usual vet. All the other animals and birds seemed to be doing fine, and, as yet, there were no new admissions. She went outside to check on the sheep and after that – there was no avoiding it – the paperwork.

On her way back she found two of their volunteer staff on duty at the castle entrance. Edna and Mabel, two senior citizens, frequently did a stint here. They lived at Grasmere village and were grateful for something to do. This morning, obviously due to the tragedy, they were talking in whispers, almost as though they were in church. Suzanne spent a little time with them.

The most distressing thing about the disaster, as it was

to the whole nation, was the sight of eighteen grieving parents, wives, girlfriends and, tragically, four young, now fatherless, children frequently shown on television. This was a severe young manhood loss. Admittedly, not on the scale of wartime casualties but nine young men gone – vanished – disappeared – how – why? What made it worse was the lack of any real evidence. The atmosphere this created, especially locally, was horrible.

Poor Janet, as the last person to see the rowing boat and its crew, was interviewed so many times; it was starting to have an effect on her nerves. She even imagined in her dreams the matter to be, in some cruel way, her fault for not spotting a vital clue. "What *do* you mean? – an entire nine men in a rowing boat just disappeared before your eyes?" was how one uncaring reporter put it. It was time for Brenda to be that special friend in need – and she was.

The police diving operation went on for ten days. The canteen staff at Bray Castle were kept constantly busy, The National Trust insisting on providing refreshments for the divers and their crew free of charge.

They did not find anything.

The broken oar now became an almost hallowed object, there being no doubt that it was from the lost boat. A thorough search of all the shore areas, particularly the mud banks and endless reed beds went on for a few days more. It was important, where possible, to prod beneath the surface; a ghoulish job. There were two residents of Lastwater that took great exception to all this as the breeding season was upon them. These were a pair of Mute swans who repeatedly hissed and flapped enormous wings, especially at surfacing divers.

Lastwater Rowing Club broke the current ban on access for craft, other than those used in the search operation, on the lake. They came out with all their remaining boats, including the old eight wooden hulled racing boat, on the second Sunday after the tragedy.

The weather had not reciprocated the conditions of the

past lost Sunday morning. It was dull and overcast – yes – but a steady rain fell, not the all soaking type – just rain. However, it thankfully took out the overall pale gun-metal grey tone in the water breaking it up into countless crystal droplets constantly on the move.

Every rower was dressed in their best regatta kit. A service of remembrance was to be held for their lost comrades. The Bishop of Lancaster, in full ceremonial robe, embarked on a small craft especially sent up from the river Thames in London. It was a very smart wooden boat used at river funerals. The important thing was that it was powered by oarsmen. All motor craft were banned for the occasion. The vessel was launched from its transporter at a small shingle beach at the eastern end of the lake. Two large inflatables transported the relatives, one to the north-eastern and one to the south-eastern end of Shimdorie Island. At exactly eleven o'clock, the nearest hour to the heart-breaking disappearance of the rowing crew and their craft, the bishop rose to his feet in the bow of the small barge. He raised his mitre as high as his arm would allow. Seeing the signal, all the oarsmen in every boat raised their oars and pointed them skywards, an act that took some doing when there were two oars to handle, both of which were very heavy. They had practiced this. First, the bow man was assisted by the number two oarsmen, and then each in turn going down the boat with the cox able to help the stroke man. The single scullers settled for one oar. At the same time, the relatives on the inflatables jettisoned literally thousands of white tulip petals especially obtained from Amsterdam. The whole created an emotive scene which brought tears to the eyes of not just the next of kin.

Following this the bishop gave a short address, which included naming all nine club members lost presumed drowned. As he read out each name, he cast a handful of tulip petals onto the lake. Only this time they were not white, they were yellow signifying sunshine for eternal life. Nobody seemed to notice when, but the rain had stopped.

The Hunter family watched from the castle roof with all staff members and any visitors who wished to. It had become a favourite vantage point for the media as well. There were three television cameras set-up there. Brian and Dalmar had dismantled the telescope from its tripod and put it back in the observatory a few days after the unexplained tragedy.

In normal times, Lastwater would have been extensively visited by researchers from media organizations for quite a while, because of the colossal mystery surrounding this and other tragedies on the lake in the past. On the 2nd April, Argentina invaded the Falkland Islands, a British protectorate in the South Atlantic Ocean, and for the next two and a half months the United Kingdom was involved in a military confrontation. Effectively, the Lakeland disaster was forgotten. This certainly did not apply to local residents or the relatives of the missing loved ones who still wanted answers. But, blessedly, Lastwater returned in a relatively short space of time to its usual peace.

The day before Good Friday, on the 8th April, a few days after the ceremony on the water, Suzanne's brother, his wife and two children arrived late in the afternoon. Timothy, a sandy haired young man with a perpetual grin was popular because he was easy to get on with and reasonably intelligent. Christine had classical good looks and even after giving birth to two children, together with advancing years, it had made no difference. Male eyes were frequently turned upon her: blonde and beautiful with green eyes and high cheek bones. Her figure was simply, alluring.

On the same day a new arrival arrived at the recuperation centre, a beautiful tawny owl. How this wonderful looking creature had come to be treated by a veterinary clinic was a matter of complete luck. From what could be ascertained it had been hit by a falling branch during a fierce squall, the type that sometimes occurs without warning amongst the mountains – even in the valleys. Completely unconscious, the owl landed in a flat-bed truck carrying turf, which had been travelling along the A66 main arterial road. It was discovered while the gardeners, at a hotel in Bowness-on-Windermere, were unloading the turf for the laying of a new lawn. If the bird had landed hard on the tarmac road, which lay directly under its perch where it was roosting, it would have been killed; if not from the fall, then certainly as a result of being hit by fast moving traffic. After being allowed to recover quietly at the clinic, the owl appeared to have suffered no serious effects. However, it was thought prudent that under the watchful eyes at Bray it could be monitored for a few days just to make sure.

And so, it was that Charles, Emma, Holly and young Michael were treated to the wonderful sight of being able to see a magnificent adult Tawny owl close to. They were mesmerised by the bird's big dark eyes and the, apparently, revolving head. It was placed in a glass fronted housing with a good perch, not forgetting the need for a plentiful supply of food and water. Due to its spell at the clinic it seemed already to have lost its shyness in front of human beings. No doubt that would return once released back into the wild. Suzanne used to find birds of prey the hardest to feed. Where do you get supplies of dead rodents and large insects? She found a source as a result of her television appearances by appealing on air. Someone who made a living by showing flight demonstrations by fast moving birds of prey and taking them to perform at shows and schools contacted her. She never had the problem again.

Tim Westward and Dalmar Hunter were finally able to find somewhere quiet on Easter Sunday evening after the children had all gone to bed. Tim loved it in this part of England, although he would have preferred to visit out of a holiday season. It tended to get too busy for his tastes, so he was very grateful to be able to come to Bray and Lastwater's recreational environs, which was not as busy as some parts of the National Park.

Dalmar had already given Tim an indication as to why he wanted to speak to him about Lastwater's dark side, on the telephone, before he brought his family up for the visit. He had also obtained clearance for a consultancy fee from his employers, if required. The National Trust had come to an arrangement with the trustees of the Lake District National Park.

However, Tim's opening remarks were, initially, a surprise to the curator. "I have given the matter a great deal of thought," he said. "The thing is, I really don't think I am qualified."

"Are you sure?" Dalmar queried with one eyebrow raised.

"To put it in a nutshell – I'm a rock, mineral and strata man – what you need is, probably, a marine geologist who has specialist knowledge in freshwater geology."

"Help," said Dalmar, "and where do I find one of those," then he added because he felt it necessary, "who won't cost a fortune?"

"I don't know about fees – but, it just so happens, I may have your man: name of David Fresher. He studied with me at university. According to reports, he has been getting some amazing facts together on lakes in Kenya and other African countries. Apparently, it is helping with irrigation plans considerably." Tim paused to glance at his brother-in-law. "I know that he is out of the country working on a contract and is not expected to return to the U.K. until September. Some way off – but – if I were the National Trust, I'd wait. He is your man – without a doubt."

"Considering his reputation – won't he be expensive?"

"Sorry – can't answer that one. Why don't I make some enquiries? Won't do any harm."

It was left like that. The problem had been going on since human occupation around here. An answer might be urgent but not in the time scale of things. Obliquely, Dalmar wondered how it might affect fish stocks. 'If, whatever, had sucked down a large racing rowing boat and its crew, nearly drowned an otter; what about fish?'

Dalmar and Suzanne managed to get time away from the castle to go on a family walk up Loughrigg Fell with Tim, Christine and their children. Being only a thousand feet in height it was manageable for small children. Dalmar would take Michael on his back. They were very lucky, choosing a day when, although not completely sunny, it remained dry, and stayed like that for them to thrill at the seductive views over Grasmere. Fly utterly revelled in these outings.

The two four-year old girls were surprisingly capable of making it to the top. It was the adults who lagged behind. Six-year old George was the first to the cairn on the summit. They found a comfy place to sit and indulge in a light picnic lunch. From this vantage point they could see over to the west and the bulk of the highest mountain in England, Scafell Pike. It still had a tiny cap of snow on its top, like icing on a cone shaped tea cake. To the south, Windermere, England's largest inland waterway stretched away ahead of them.

Being in a seated position, they began to feel the chill from the increased wind strength due to the height, so it was not long before they all started the descent, Dalmar taking extra care with his burden.

The next evening, Dalmar and Suzanne took advantage of a baby-sitting offer from their guests, and they went to see the big movie of the time, E.T. It made a change for them. They had not been to see a film for more than two years.

Ten days after Tim, Christine and the children had returned to Hampshire, Tim Westward wrote a letter to Dalmar. He had managed to contact his old student friend. It was good news. If the National Trust provided him with food and lodging, the fee for his services would be modest and he could make himself available in late September, as expected. Dalmar wasted no time in providing confirmation after checking with Jack Twentyman.

One of the challenges facing Suzanne in the near future was to put her animal husbandry learning into practice in the proper manner. It had been decided that the Bray Castle estate's extensive meadow areas, either side of the woodland running up from Cloud Point, could be used to graze sheep in small numbers – instead of, as now, the odd one or two who were recuperating from accident or illness.

To this end, to start off with, five ewes and their lambs would be arriving for one pasture and the same amount for the other. The date allocated was Tuesday 27th April.

As can be imagined there was great excitement when the morning of this day arrived. It was not one of Emma's nursery school days so she would be able to enjoy the arrival. The breed of sheep, concerned, was Herdwick, a strain exclusive to the Lake District. They were hardy and tended to be territorial so avoiding the necessity of thorough fencing. The dry-stone walls and boundary fences already in place would suffice. They would be able to stay in these pastures right through the winter.

At last, a cattle truck pulled up at the car park near the castle. Tom Sherigold, a shepherd who worked for the National Trust climbed out. He would be helping Suzanne and a couple of groundsmen to settle the new arrivals in. The National Trust leased several small farms with Herdwick sheep herds. Most of these farm holdings were bequeathed to the N. T. by the children's writer and illustrator, Beatrix Potter, after her death in 1943. The ten ewes and lambs had come directly from them by arrangement. When they had successfully shepherded the first five ewes and their lambs into the pasture by the Dower House, they then had to drive out and back along the road to the access point on the other side of the woods to reach the pasture for the remaining sheep. Herdwick ewes have an angelic feminine face and their lambs are all black in their first year. Emma was smitten, especially with the lambs high pitched bleating as they demanded to stay close by their mothers through the operation. It all went very well, and, from now on, Bray Castle had its own small sheep farm.

CHAPTER SIX

"SOMETHING ABOUT THE TASTE."

Well into the month of May, Dalmar and Fly were out at the western end of Lastwater. They had walked the two and a half miles from Bray. It had been something Dalmar had been planning to do for some time, but an opportunity had never come about until now. In his opinion, the extensive reed beds all along the western side of the southern shore of the lake is where salvage relating to the disappearance of the rowing eight could end up. And the best way to spot something would be to do it thoroughly and slowly, in other words, on foot. Being a day in the middle of the week when everything seemed to be covered at the castle, he broached the subject with his wife. It was a fine morning and Suzanne backed him. It would be good for Fly and give her husband a chance to get rid of some cobwebs.

On their route they repeatedly left the narrow road to get nearer to the shore along Tadpole Bay and study every nook and cranny. Now that the growing season was well on new greenery was sprouting up all over the place. All the while, the background sound of new-born lambs bleating kept them company.

About mid-morning they moved higher up along the course of Sonnet Gill. At one point, Fly climbed out onto a rocky outcrop supporting a large cantilevered slab. Dalmar, for obvious reasons, had taken along a camera. He could not resist this pose and felt for the instrument in his light back-pack. Crouching down below the outcrop, he was able to get a shot with the dog standing out against a lone blue sky. Fly's head was stretched towards the lake, his nose intent on something in the air, the abundant dark coat on his back combed straight from a recent grooming glistened in the sunlight. The soft, white under-fur looked invitingly cuddlesome and his legs stood strong and steady. It ought to be a good photograph, although some people would not have a great deal of faith in the photographer. He once shot an entire film in central Wales, while on a weekend break with Suzanne, using the incorrect ASA setting. All the photographs were so dark, it made the sunlight resemble that cast by the moon in the middle of the night. One of the prints had been framed. It hung in a Dower House corridor. Everyone thought it to be an atmospheric picture of a full moon's light over a reservoir. Dalmar rarely let on.

The cantilever stone, on which Fly now lay stretched out, turned out to be an excellent observation point. The lake, resplendent in its fine weather colouring with all the beauty surrounding it at the height of the growing season, lay out before them. The reed beds now looked like giant green grasses having lost their tan winter colouring, and the western valley was lush with vivid hues in the shrubs and meadows. In the distance, the faint domed summit of Great Gable could be seen poking above the crags, situated this side of the large inland waterway called Derwentwater. Lastwater, itself, known as the lake with the bluest water showed of this attribute today. The colour, under a cloudless sky, at this time of year, could best be described as a lighter shade of royal blue. Gliding over the water, just this side of Shimdorie Island, were the pair of white Mute swans with five light-brown cygnets following in line.

Dalmar got out his binoculars and, focussing on the reed beds, began a thorough scrutiny. He was looking for anything foreign to the flora, mud, rock and water. And he found something. From this distance the subdued greenish-ochre colouring partially matched the surroundings. It looked to be either a piece of tarpaulin or canvas and not very big. Dalmar took, as a marker, a scots pine, one of a group just off a large reed growth, whose lofty structures dwarfed anything else in the tree department, anywhere around Lastwater.

It took the two of them about twenty minutes to descend Sonnet Gill. Dalmar, without waders, still managed to get out among the reeds some fifty yards from the pine in his walking boots.

He was in for a disappointment. What he had seen from the crag was not a piece of canvas, it was nothing more than a matted mass of last season's water lily leaves.

Making his way back towards the tall tree, he was surprised to see Fly snorting and trying to extricate something from a hollow in the bank made by exposed tree roots. He kept prodding and hooking at whatever it was with a front paw. When Dalmar came up to him he spotted the cause. Tucked around a bend in the hollow, out of sight and floating in a shallow miniature pool was a light blue, plastic bottle, complete with screw top. Dalmar extracted it. He shook the water off. This was likely to be discarded litter, but, just in case, he put it in his backpack.

After this he had a good look around the area for fear, he might have missed anything. His attention was interrupted by a gruff low bark from Fly. Looking up, he saw a man approaching along the path coming from the west.

A voice with the soft vowel tones of the Cumbrian dialect hailed him. "You's t'curator man at the castle?"

"Guilty," replied Dalmar. The man looked friendly. Dalmar had seen him driving farm vehicles about on several occasions, often when one of them had to pull in off the road to allow the other to pass.

T'is my farm yonder," he said giving Fly a welcoming pat.

Ah. Then I'm very pleased to meet you," Dalmar had often thought it was high time he got to know this man and his family. The opportunity had not arisen because; unless the farmer and his wife were directly involved, they kept themselves very much apart from anything to do with tourism. Or so it seemed.

"Ae – how'do, name of Legg, call me Chris."

"Dalmar Hunter."

"Owz'that – Dal..?

Dalmar spelt it out for him. "Unusual.Still – there-you-go."

Dalmar entered into a dialogue with the farmer, particularly about current farming economics in the area. Chris tended to be non-committal almost as though he were talking to someone from the Inland Revenue. He got much more lucid when they got on to the subject of the boat disaster after Dalmar had explained what he was doing just now. It occurred to him that Chris might have found something himself, but although he said they had not, at the same time, he had not been looking, so anything unusual might not have registered.

"If you lives here – you's don't go on t' water. Simple," said Chris. "We're always taught to keep clear – right from t'cradle."

"You probably know more about the lake's dark history than anyone?" Dalmar was suddenly very interested in what Chris had to say. However, typical of his clan he was far too busy to talk now. But he did suggest that he bring his good lady over one day so that she could meet his wife. They could have a good yarn then. Therefore, it was partially arranged. Chris would get his wife to telephone.

Dalmar and Fly enjoyed a light luncheon of sandwiches except that the dog's was more biscuit and ham than bread. After carrying out further exploration along the southern bank of the lake, Dalmar decided to leave it at that for today. The rest of the lake, and by far the least important in relation to where the rowing eight had supposedly disappeared could be explored later. They arrived back at the Dower-house in the middle of the afternoon. Leaving Fly on the lawn, Dalmar went to his office. There were no immediate problems to do with the administration of the estate, so he put through a call to the L.R.C. There was no answer and he left a message on the answerphone installed there, just mentioning that he had found a light blue plastic bottle. There was no label to signify a drink's brand.

When Suzanne asked him if he had found anything, he mentioned the item. She also thought it was probably an uncaring person's rubbish: the object, for the time being, remained on Dalmar's desk. Suzanne was delighted at the possibility of meeting Chris Legg's wife. She had been concerned that after two years they still had not got to know these important neighbours.

Later that day, Suzanne was enjoying a long cuddle with her husband on their sitting room couch. Dalmar had put on a record he was very much into at the time, the soundtrack from the film Chariots of Fire, a film about past British athletic achievement, which had been a big success last year. It was not Suzanne's favourite, but she was grateful for a chance to keep her man in one place and hold his attention.

At the recuperation centre, the only animal not released since March was the fallow deer. She had had such a serious infection and it was taking time to bring about a final cure with the homeopathic treatment. When they thought it had completely cleared up, on two occasions, the skin irritation returned.

The three-legged fox had been successfully repatriated to Grizedale Forest, and the red squirrel was now somewhere in the woodland at the castle estate. Other animals were coming and going. The centre was busier than ever and even more popular with visitors.

The ten ewes and their lambs were all doing well. Suzanne was really pleased. Michael loved to watch them from the back garden at the Dower-house. There was another very interested observer as well – a certain tri-colour collie. However, Suzanne had no need to worry about him. He had long ago been trained to leave sheep well alone.

On Friday evening, Dalmar took a phone-call from Jim Derby calling from his home in Keswick. After a chat about how matters were going on, Jim asked, "This bottle you found. Was it in the water?" The curator explained, telling him about Fly's curiosity and the fact that it was hidden from view. The next question took Dalmar by surprise. "What was in it?"

After a pause he replied, "Air – empty."

"I see," Jim's tone was serious. "Johno had been using a blue bottle for a couple of months before he went missing. Whereas the other rowers always took along a beverage in theirs', usually water, Johno didn't. Apparently, he liked the lake water – something about the taste – tangy mineral touch – always used to bring back a full bottle. You see - they hadn't long been out, so when they went down that bottle might have withstood sinking – being full of air. Well – it would have done." Dalmar remained quiet – shocked at what was sitting innocently on his desk in the castle. "Thing is – if it is what I think it is – it's the property of his next of kin – a young widow." There followed an audible sigh. "I shall have to take it to her. Are you around tomorrow evening?"

Dalmar said, "Of course," and a convenient time was arranged for Jim to pick it up. The revelation had a similar effect on Suzanne. She went quiet. Nobody else was told about it.

Dalmar was acutely aware that, for the first time, as far as he knew, the rowing club now referred to the trauma as a boat going down, instead of – missing.

The running of Bray Castle had resumed its former equilibrium, the senior management of The National Trust organisation being satisfied, as were the officials of the lake district National Park, together with their tenants, Lastwater Rowing Club, that nothing more could be done, apart from a sense of wariness concerning swimming activities on the lake, until David Fresher the freshwater geology expert commenced his research in September. Certainly the L.R.C. carried on with its training exercises on the lake, not as though nothing had happened, quite the contrary, but they carried on. Anyone who lived within a five-mile radius, and there were not many of those, had always treated Lastwater with the greatest respect due to the historical tragedies associated with it. The March event was, although emotionally dismal, just another one.

Jim Derby arrived promptly at 9 o'clock the next day. Dalmar had already transferred the bottle to the Dower House and, after introductions; Suzanne left the two men alone in the lounge while she went upstairs.

Jim confirmed that the article was Johno's at once. "I'm not looking forward to delivering that," he said emphatically.

"No – don't suppose you are," Dalmar sympathised. "Can't you ring first?" He shrugged his shoulders. "Be a shame to have to go twice if she wasn't at home."

"Yes," agreed Jim. "I might just do that." He reached for the glass of Irish whisky Dalmar had poured him. After a drink he brought out a packet of Senior Service cigarettes. Dalmar had to search for an ash tray. Considering his smoking habit, it was surprising Jim was such a fit man.

"Tell me," broached the curator. "What is the opinion at the club? Okay, there have been drowning incidents before on this lake – to my knowledge no bodies have ever been recovered. A boy scout and adult scout leader were lost off Cloud Point in 1956. The boy got into trouble. They say the leader dived in and in his desperation to find the lad under water – after all, the boy was his direct responsibility – stayed down too long and got into trouble himself. That sort of thing is quite common, especially when a parent is trying to carry out the rescue."

"Yes – and those lads – attending the outward-bound

school right here in'79," said Jim, "took a boat without permission, in the dark. I know for a fact that they were heard singing on Shimdorie Island. Heard tell that they had a crate of beer with them."

"So – both these could be explained – but an eight and its entire crew. All we have is part of an oar and a plastic bottle?" Dalmar studied Jim's face as he put this to him.

"Do you know – and I have this from a reliable source," replied Jim. "Some of the police investigating actually think the whole thing was faked, and all nine of them now live abroad somewhere? Some sort of life insurance swindle."

"What!?"

"Search me – daft isn't it. Anyhow – to answer your original question. Nobody seems to want to know as to how and why. Some of the members, because they are still in contact with grieving relatives don't wish to discuss the actual incident or the underlying reason. Meantime we carry on doing what we do – row. It's given our competitive urge an extra edge. We have no eight – well we could get one together, but it was decided, out of respect, to cancel all competition entries for that category this year. An anonymous donor is letting us have a brand-new carbon fibre boat. The scullers and the coxless four are doing really well."

"Congratulations. In the circumstances – it is remarkable,"

"Thanks. Anyway, everyone seems content to wait for your man's opinion. Maybe we will have to take some action then." Jim hesitated. "Actually – I have a feeling some members, bizarrely, don't want to know."

"Surely someone must have a theory?" Dalmar's facial expression was quizzical.

"You see," began Jim, "up 'till now there hasn't been any need for one. As you just pointed out, other events could be explained. I can tell you – Lastwater isn't alone in this. Windermere has a dreadful reputation."

"Really – I didn't know that," Dalmar looked surprised.

"Worse really. But then it's a huge lake compared to Lastwater; must be three times the size. They blame the marshy shallow areas – like quicksand apparently."

The two men talked about other things for a while, the Falkland Islands conflict in particular, until Jim left cradling the blue bottle. Given Jim's comments, Dalmar did not broach the subject of his forthcoming meeting with the Legg family. He intended to find out as much about Lastwater's sinister past from that source himself.

During the next week Suzanne was invited by Daisy Legg, Chris's other half to go over with the children for tea on Saturday afternoon.

Suzanne made it a rule never to get involved with domestic animals at the recuperation centre. However, something occurred which caused her to make an exception. She got to hear of a family who lived at Patterdale, a small village at the southern end of Ullswater, the second largest lake in the national park. There eight-year old son had a rare form of terminal cancer. He was not expected to live for more than a year or two. Apparently, the boy was devoted to the family pet cat, a five-year old tortoiseshell female who was suffering from an epileptic condition, which brought on violent fits. When they occurred, it was very distressing for the boy. This did not help his condition.

The cat had been treated with traditional medicine for some time, but it had had no effect. A vet who used both traditional and homeopathic medicine thought she could help. However, a place separated from the boy was needed so that both the cat and the boy could be away from any trauma while the treatment was progressing. It was reckoned it would take about four weeks, and then the cat ought to be able to return to the family home without suffering any more fits. Suzanne was approached to see if she would be willing to provide that temporary home. She readily agreed, although she had no intention of putting the patient in the centre. She considered this was a case for

Fly, who was very tolerant of cats, to play a part. So, on Thursday afternoon, the mother and the sick boy came over to the Dower-house at Bray. If all went well, they would be leaving the domestic animal with them for treatment and rest.

Shortly after Rosalind, the mother, and Jacob the boy, plus little Petula, the cat, had arrived another car drew up outside. It was Helena Shorford, the vet who had contacted Suzanne about the matter. She was a slight woman, in her early thirties, with auburn hair and an elfish face that hid an amazing intelligence. Before ringing the doorbell, she said hello to a curious Fly who was being kept outside, in the meantime, so as not to alarm the cat.

Over tea and cake Helena explained to Jacob and Emma, who was intently interested, plus a curious Michael exactly what was going to happen. Petula would be given medication of homeopathic origin. This would start right now. She persuaded the cat to take the first pill wrapped in a piece of chicken breast right there and then. Also, she would be undergoing a change of diet to mainly dried food with lots of fresh water. Jacob, a naturally quiet boy, seemed to accept this and the need for a temporary separation from his pet.

During their visit, Dalmar finished his work and went to say hello. He felt full of sympathy for Jacob, who because of a fair complexion was very pale due to the effect on his blood cells caused by the cancer. He suggested that when he came for one of his periodic visits to see how Petula was getting on, he might like a quick tour of the castle, especially the battlements. Jacob brightened at this.

Dalmar also got into conversation with Roz, who must be suffering beyond comprehension. She was an incredibly striking looking woman. Loosely she would be described as a platinum blonde. Certainly, in the light that Dalmar was seeing her, the hair was the palest hue of blonde, almost calico. Add to that the lightest of blue eyes – well – she could certainly command a presence. She told him that it was a good job they lived in the Lake District, England's wettest area because Jacob loved the rain. Dalmar was aware that this was quite common with terminally ill cancer sufferers. Roz had a part time job with an equestrian organisation near the southern end of Windermere, which she was trying to hang onto, although, it was proving difficult due to the attention Jacob needed.

At the parting, there were some tears, and, bless her, when little Emma put her arm around Jacob, she even got a watery smile in return. Before they left Jacob was introduced to Fly, whom he quite obviously adored and kept ruffling his glorious neck of soft white hair.

CHAPTER SEVEN

"SOMETHING TO DO WITH A BOX."

At three o'clock on Sunday afternoon, Dalmar parked the National trust Land Rover outside Lastwater Farm, by the look of it, traditionally built from local volcanic rock materials. Daisy Clegg and her two daughters, Justine, eight, and, Lucy, six, came out to meet them. The girl's initial attention was taken up with Fly, whom they instantly adored and could not wait to introduce him to the two farm sheep dogs, who were currently snoozing in-doors having been out with Chris Legg, most of the morning, on the fells.

In no time, it seemed, following introductions, the two older girls took Emma and little Michael off on a tour of the farm outbuildings to show them the lambing sheds in particular. Suzanne and Daisy followed behind, while Dalmar was invited inside to join Chris in the farm kitchen.

Daisy possessed virtually the same physique as Suzanne being slightly full in figure, but not overly so. She had a tint of red in her blonde hair, several freckles on her cheeks; now brought on in the late springtime sunshine, which they had all been enjoying for quite a while recently. Her disposition was constantly cheerful, balancing the rather dour attitude of her husband; a very tall man of six foot three. He was strong, slim and fit with the same fair complexion as his wife. It follows that both daughters were of similar appearance.

Suzanne had last spent time on a Lakeland sheep farm in 1976 when she had been invited to see around a larger concern in the Langdale Valley. Because this one was more compact, she found it easier to grasp the whole enterprise, and found it intensely interesting because of her own little venture at Bray.

Justine and Lucy were very patient with Michael as he toddled around obediently obeying everything the older girls told him to do. He particularly enjoyed getting in close with the lambs and it took some time before they were able to entice him away. However, next on the list was the free-range chicken enclosure. Here, he was introduced to a great gathering of young chicks. Many are the people who have pondered this question, 'how could anything as adorable as a tiny golden chick turn into something as gawky as a chicken?'

At length they all returned to the farmhouse to find their men in earnest conversation about Lastwater's latest sad event. This was put in abeyance, in front of the children, and Daisy started to lay up for their tea, ably helped by her daughters. Suzanne suddenly realised what was coming. This was not going to be tea and cake, it would be a full-blown high tea: probably two boiled eggs followed by sandwiches, and then cake and going by her past experience it would be an extremely filling fruit variety. Thankfully, due to this outing they had put off their usual Sunday roast lunch. As it turned out, all her family, even Michael, showed no lack of appetite. The eggs being new-laid were perfect having a taste, with the compliment of hot buttered toast, second to none.

Fly was introduced to the two border collie sheep dogs. After much sniffing they seemed to be at ease with each other and settled down.

Not until after the meal when the children had gone off to the front room with the dogs did the subject of Lastwater return. Chris Legg did not usually expound on the subject especially when it involved the telling as regards his own family's history. He was a direct descendant of the Legg's, who had run Lastwater Farm since the original owners left to emigrate to North America in the late seventeen hundreds. The type of farming had never changed: sheep and poultry. He married Daisy, a farmer's daughter from Coniston in the south-west of Lakeland, when they were both in their late teens. Unfortunately, his mother and father both died before he reached the age of twenty-five, leaving their children without grandparents on his side, although Daisy's mother and father were both still active in farming and they often met up.

Dalmar thought it prudent to tell Chris why he wished to know about Lastwater's history in general. He explained about David Fresher's commission.

Naturally, Chris was interested. He explained, at some length, why it was that he encouraged his children to stay well clear of the water, and why his parents had done the same to him. In the year of 1851, the family had lost an entire generation. Only due to a re-marriage and having a child late in life did the family line continue.

In that year they had been enjoying a late summer during the last weeks in September when instead of the usual heavy rainfall, periodically, there was none.

This prompted the farmer's wife to take her two young children on a mid-day excursion by rowing boat for a picnic to Shimdorie Island.

They never returned.

Apparently, it is known that they landed on the island due to evidence provided by picnic remains found later, also excited children's voices were heard by a shepherd on White Crag coming from across the water. Neither the occupants nor any trace of the boat were ever found.

During Chris Legg's recitation, Daisy remained silent. When he had finished Suzanne made a low-voiced comment, "After that, it is amazing that your ancestor, the farmer at the time, managed to carry on."

"You are right there an'all," Chris confirmed. "The old fella be something of a hero to us."

More happenings going back in time, some of which might be hearsay, were divulged. These tragedies did not all exclusively involve human beings; there was an event where one of the farm's sheep dogs became lost in the early nineteen-hundreds.

After confirmation from Chris, Dalmar was able to ascertain that no trauma occurred after the dog's disappearance until the tragic loss of the scout and his scout master in 1956, off Cloud Point. This established that there was nothing regular about the phenomenon.

Before Dalmar had a chance to climb into the driver's seat of the Land Rover when they were about to leave and goodbyes had been said, with a promise of a return visit from Suzanne, Chris Legg caught hold of his arm. "There is something you should know. We don't usually mention it to off comers, but this 'ere geology man might be interested. 'Tis rumoured that the original family that emigrated to America have the secret to the Lastwater mystery – something to do with a box. That's all I know mind." Chris used the broadest ancient Westmorland dialect for the first part of that sentence ("Saumethin' tau djur wit' ae baux") as though mimicking from a distant time.

"Oh – right. Might have to get back to you on that Chris. What part of the United States?" asked a very curious curator.

"Virginia. Got a very big spread by al' accounts."

After they left, Suzanne asked her husband what had been said. When he told her, she was even more curious.

During the following week Pet, the cat, responded well to her medication. She had stopped having fits and seemed at ease with life. Fly was particularly good to her. He seemed to take on the role of guardian in the same way that he did with the children. Jacob and his dad came for a visit on Wednesday, late in the afternoon.

Dalmar was glad of this; he wanted to put an idea to the father. The plan, for which senior management approval was not sought, was to invite Jacob and a few of his primary school friends to come over and play in the grounds for a couple of hours. They would be supervised all the time in order that none of them strayed too near the lake's shores. Afterwards, they would be given drinks and cake or biscuits in the canteen. Jacob's dad, Frank, was delighted. Nothing was mentioned about the need for urgent arrangement in view of Jacob's serious condition. Both men understood this, and it was why Dalmar had muted the idea early in their association. Suzanne had already given it her utmost approval and said she would arrange things with the boy's mother and the school. It was to be a school outing for a chosen few. Brian Cussen was going to be involved. It would be daylight, but he could give them a short talk up on the castle roof.

Government Health and Safety inspectors called unexpectedly on the next day. Dalmar held a very low opinion of this profession. On one occasion, a few years ago, he had been enjoying a lunch with two old friends in a large pub style restaurant in north Hampshire. During their meal a man of lowly height entered the pub by a side door, just near where Dalmar and his friends were seated. He was carrying a clip board and looked self-important. His attention was caught by a chandelier lighting arrangement where small clay flowerpots had been used as lampshades. The man tut-tutted in an obvious manner. A little while later he could be seen behind the bar holding up samples of beer in a glass. He seemed to be haranguing the staff. Shortly after that the landlady brought out a large free-standing ladder and placed it under the chandelier. She then climbed up to the very top and set about removing the flowerpots. The ladder wobbled. Dalmar immediately got to his feet and went to support the contraption. "Thank you," she said, looking down with a smile. Fortunately, the woman was wearing trousers, so he was able to look up and ask the reason for her actions? The lady mouthed down in a hushed voice. "Health and safety. We've got an inspector here. Apparently, these might fall on someone." She made no attempt to hide her sarcasm.

Dalmar's reaction to this not only surprised the landlady but his companions as well. The reason being because he did not respond in a low tone of voice, in fact, quite the opposite, making sure anyone within a thirty foot radius, inspector included, who was seated at a table further into the restaurant hiding behind a newspaper while having his lunch, heard every word. "The only inspectors a business such as this requires – are its customers!" 'Nobody had given any thought to the landlady's safety,' he registered to himself.

It was Dalmar's misfortune to have an overbearing self-important inspector, on this occasion, at Bray Castle. Fortunately, his colleague a thorough but practical lady was the opposite. The two of them spent a great deal of time arguing about matters of hygiene, particularly in the canteen, plus safety regulations for staff and the general public elsewhere.

Dalmar managed to keep a reign on his temper, only giving vent to veiled sarcasm now and then. On one occasion Mr Hemp, the man disgracefully given such a job by people who should be ashamed of themselves, suggested to the curator that a person could fall on the polished wooden stairs even though anti-slip treads had been put in place. "If they were that drunk, they should bounce," said Dalmar, turning his back on the idiot.

Mr Hemp was not going to take that. It was time to exert his authority. "And supposing it happened to a child?" he said petulantly.

Dalmar came straight back. "That could only happen if the child was playing on the staircase. Parents are asked to prevent this by way of a notice clearly displayed at the entrance. My staff cannot be held responsible for undisciplined children. Are you saying these anti-slip treads are not satisfactory?"

"I would suggest – the centre of the staircase should be roped thus providing hand holds for people who are not using the banisters."

"You have not answered my question?" replied Dalmar.

Mr Hemp was beaten. He did not usually come across anyone this forceful. "Well – it is up to you of course." He made to make a note on his pad.

It was a good thing that this inspector had not come

alone for he might well have, temporarily, closed the estate to the public. However, his colleague managed to persuade him to give a report demanding various improvements within a time scale. There was only one matter that, initially, presented a real problem. The current fire alternative escape route from the upper floor was ruled as unsatisfactory. It wound its way off down a back staircase gaining an exit thorough the kitchens. It was suggested that a route be opened up through one of the entrance porch construction towers that did a dual job of support for the large overhead structure, and, also, gave an alternative access to the roof area. To make an opening from the first floor into the one tower possessing a stone spiral staircase running up its, virtually, full height, might present structural problems. This would mean expensive specialist architectural consultancy. Naturally, Jack Twentyman was horrified when the matter was reported to him. Secretly, while he congratulated Dalmar and his staff for having passed the inspection overall, he had been a little worried that his man might not have been able to contain his natural abhorrence of all government inspectors, whatever they were checking on, and foul things up. He very nearly did.

Brian Cussen knocked on Dalmar's office door one morning sometime after eleven o'clock. After an invitation, he came in, or rather, was pushed in by an extraordinary young woman. What she was wearing did not really matter because it was all covered in a tightly buttoned grey raincoat. Her ample blown-about auburn hair set-off a serious well-structured face, completely devoid of make-up or lipstick, with clear, piercing blue eyes and a strong but well-proportioned nose. She was smiling or was it sneering? It was hard to tell which. Her bulk looked strong rather than plump and judging by her sturdy legs was well supported. "As I haven't received an invitation *since* you arrived – I decided to come anyway," she announced in a, probably, fake high society dialect. "I would have expected that you would have had the courtesy to have extended your compliments at the very least."

Brian shuffled up to gain Dalmar's ear at close quarters. "Found her wandering around – insisted on seeing you," he whispered. "Think she's as pissed as a newt. Sorry." Then he quickly made his exit indicating with a hand motion that he would wait outside in case he was required.

"I think you will have to explain? – madam. I am not aware that we have offended anyone," Dalmar said as he studied the creature before him. In the circumstances, he stayed seated.

"Name of Adred," the woman said expecting immediate recognition.

"Right," said the curator still none the wiser. "How can I help?"

"I do not require any help." She looked at him in an affronted way. "Do you not know who I am?" As it happened the lady was well in control of her senses and not inebriated as Brian had thought. She appeared to be fighting a strong emotion.

"I am sorry…" Dalmar began.

"I represent the oldest surviving family from these very parts. In fact – it was my family who used to live here before this monstrosity was built." As she declared this, she opened her eyes wide and tucked in a surprisingly comely chin.

"Oh – I see." Our curator suddenly got interested, but he was to be disappointed if he thought he might glean further information about Lastwater.

Raising her shoulders as high as they would go the woman went to the door, opened it wide to reveal a furtive astronomer and stated loudly. "So – I shall expect to hear from you." And she left with loud, thudding, exaggerated footsteps on the wooden flooring – just like that.

Brian was very contrite, feeling he might have done more to prevent the lady from getting her way. Dalmar alleviated his worry by saying, "Actually, it might turn out to be interesting." He told him about the family connection.

The Hunter's had arranged for Jacob and his father to come over together with seven school friends. After Jacob had said, "Hello," and given Pet a cuddle, all the boys were taken off to the woodland area. Fortunately, although not a particularly fine day, it was not raining. All of them received a pleasant surprise. They were each given a handsome toy western rifle and a supply of cap strips. They were then divided into two teams of four by the National Trust groundsman, Trevor and Nigel, his student helper. One team advanced from the south and the other from the castle itself. Simply, they had a wonderful time shooting at each other as they met, darting from tree trunk to tree trunk, clambering over rocks and diving into bushes. The bonus was that they were able to keep the rifles – minus caps; Suzanne thought it a good idea to leave that to parent's approval.

After this Brian Cussen gave them an entertaining chat on the castle roof. There were some students present, who usually helped out in the canteen, whose job was to keep them from climbing on the battlements, which one lad would have done given the chance. He seemed to have no fear of heights at all. It was with some relief that Brian was able to herd them all down to the canteen to finish off the afternoon.

During all this Jacob often looked very tired, but he kept rallying at the sheer joy and excitement – a special boy's own experience.

The weekend after this Dalmar finally persuaded Suanne to let him take his children out on the lake in the castle's rowing boat, but not until he had explained why he was sure the lake was safe at the present time. He told her about the water level rise he had noticed before the rowing club tragedy, and its subsequent return to normal afterwards. He assured her that there was no way he would take his children out on the lake if he had any doubt. She knew she would have to one day, so reluctantly, she gave in. He chose the Saturday morning when everything was organised at the castle; the sun was shining and there was very little wind. He was under a strict promise not to be gone for more than an hour. Prudently, in order to concentrate on the safety of his children he left Fly at home – too much whimpering.

Emma was given the task of making sure that Michael did not stray from his seat alongside her in the boat. Just as a precaution, Dalmar attached the boy's toddler reigns to his right wrist while he rowed. He decided to avoid going near Shimdorie Island and instead headed out over Tadpole bay, intending to cross to the eastern shore of the lake before heading home. Michael loved it and kept trailing his hand in the water uttering pleasing little boy talk.

When they got in close to the shore near a bank of grassy covered rock they were treated to a wonderful sight: a very rare sight. Emma spotted them first. She let out a gasp, "What are those?"

Her father had eased up on the oars due to the proximity of the bank. He turned to look in the direction of Emma's outstretched hand. Swimming in the shadows cast by an oak tree's branches were two wet furry heads, with two other little heads between them and the bank. The pair of otters with pups.

Dalmar put a finger to his lips indicating to the children to keep quiet. They did and enjoyed some minutes watching the family. This must be one of the first occasions when the pups would be old enough to swim. The mesmerizing sight was further enhanced by a collection of yellow flag iris growing in the shallow water adjacent to the bank. The substantial blooms were reflected in the water and two of the pups were swimming amongst them breaking the images into little ripples of bright yellow.

The wildlife adventure continued as they made their way back across the lake. Out of nowhere, they were surrounded by several Mallard ducks with their young. The distinctive glossy green head of the drake and white collar made the brown female ducks look rather ordinary, but they all possessed a glorious purple patch on their wings. In truth, Michael was more delighted by these than the otters.

When they got home, they both took great delight in making their mother envious, although she was pleased they had had the experience. The sighting of the pups was very good news. They would have to inform the wildlife society concerned of the successful breeding.

Monday 14th June, the Falkland Islands conflict ends with a satisfactory outcome for the United Kingdom.

Late on Tuesday afternoon, Dalmar entered the front door of the Dower-house after having been in lengthy discussions with an architect concerning the proposed new fire escape route from the first floor of the castle.

He was greeted by both Fly and his wife who explained that Mary and Jacob were here to take Pet home. The treatment had been successful so far, the cat had suffered no further fits, although further medication would be necessary for a month. Naturally, Jacob was pleased and excited at the prospect of having her home again.

Suzanne explained to her husband that because Roz liked poetry, she had shown her some of his. Dalmar did not publicise the matter but one of his hobbies was the writing of verse. He had written very little in recent years. "Oh, poor you," he said aside to the lady.

"No ... I loved what I have managed to read just now," she said with sincerity written all over her face.

"She likes the one called 'Rain'. Apparently, Jacob likes rain," said Suzanne.

"Any chance of a copy – just that one," she hurriedly added thinking that it might have been interpreted as a copy of the lot.

Dalmar tried not to show it. He was enormously flattered. "Yes, of course," he simply said.

After they had all enjoyed tea and cake, Roz gathered her things together in order to leave. Emma was unashamed to give a tearful goodbye. Suzanne made a promise to see Jacob and Pet soon although no one was quite sure when. But it was a sincere wish from all of them and not just for emotional reasons.

CHAPTER EIGHT

'I HAVE NEVER LOVED SO MUCH IN THE RAIN.'

Two new arrivals at the animal recuperation centre were causing much excitement in the Hunter household. They were a couple of five-month-old Roe deer who had both been injured in the same road accident. Fawns always follow their mother's closely whenever they cross over a thoroughfare. On a busy main road in southern Cumbria, the mother had miscalculated, and both her young had been hit by a van. It had not been travelling excessively fast, fortunately, and a veterinary clinic had been able to splint broken bones on each deer. Initially, it was thought the animals had suffered no further serious injury.

Suzanne had agreed to be a guest speaker at The British Veterinary Association dinner to be held this year in the City of York. She was terrified at the very thought of it but had been persuaded to carry it out. They were very keen due to the Bray Castle, Animal Resuscitation Centre's success. Normally, it would not make economic sense for vet practices to attend to wild animal injuries. Now in this area they could due to the fact that the costs would be recovered by Bray from a proportion of visitor admission charges. Suzanne had to keep a record of the account on the bird or animal's arrival, and then, when they had enough in the kitty, she would request an invoice from the veterinary practice concerned. The scheme worked well. This and other matters she would be explaining at the dinner in a week's time. Suzanne planned to stay the night with a cousin who lived just outside the county town of York.

Dalmar would be looking after the children while she was away.

Jacob was off to hospital for the final chemotherapy session. Suzanne had arranged to visit him and his mother two weeks later. This was to give him time to get over the treatment, which, usually, left him feeling lousy.

Just before this, Dalmar received a letter from a schoolteacher at a secondary school in Carlisle. It requested an interview where the interviewees would be three twelve-year-old schoolgirls chaperoned by the teacher. They were carrying out a project on localised events and had chosen the recent rowing club disaster on Lastwater for their subject. It had puzzled Dalmar that they should want to see him and not an official at the rowing club, but he decided to go along with it. Ever since the end of the conflict in the South Atlantic he had been expecting an approach from the wider press. It did not actually occur to him that this might not happen, especially from the most likely source – the region's newspapers or television broadcasters – for fear of damaging the tourist trade to the area. Tourism was the number one industry for the Lake District.

The interview occurred two days later following a quick response to Dalmar's telephone call agreeing to the project. While two of the girls showed their age with their rather immature questions, the other girl, whose name was Elizabeth was very much the opposite. It was quite obvious what her career intentions were going to be. The teacher, Mike Parsons, after the initial introductions, left the running of the interview to his pupils. They started by asking him about his responsibilities as curator of Bray Castle and quickly moved on to the recent tragedy, followed by as much history of other traumas as they could get. Following the Hunter's visit to the Legg's farm he was able to give them virtually everything. There was one matter he left out. Chris Legg had told him about the family connection to a Virginian farm in the United States in confidence, and so it remained.

One of the fawns at the recuperation centre showed signs of recovering earlier than the other. He was on his feet with a front leg splinted and bandaged and seemed to be managing quite well. The other, a female, remained very quiet. Bea was concerned. Suzanne, when she saw the deer immediately asked the vet to call. He said he would be there in the morning of the following day. Unfortunately, the small deer further declined and died during the night. This was very much the downside of what they were doing here. It sometimes happened. In this case the fawn had obviously been more severely damaged by the accident; almost certainly an undetected internal injury. Suzanne always had great difficulty with these occurrences. Either she kept her daughter away from the centre as much as possible, so that the grief caused by such an instance could be avoided, or she involved her. She chose the latter on the basis that such events were far rarer than the eventual repatriation to the wild of the majority.

During the springtime and early summer, Dalmar frequently spent much of his time out with the ground staff helping with woodland management and fence or wall maintenance. Actual coppicing in the wood areas was carried out in the autumn months. This had been neglected for many years and they were still trying to catch up in order to get the natural ecology back on track. During these activities Fly was always in evidence. The dog always enjoyed them.

Such things as the lawn and general appearance work, Dalmar could leave to the garden expertise of Trevor. First impressions when anyone drove up to the castle were important. The extensive sloping lawn to the left of the main building always appeared well trimmed and all the drive areas looked free of weeds. Particularly attractive were the dry-stone walling incorporating miniature towers set back from the castle entrance. Cleverly, rowan trees had been allowed to grow amidst the structures.

When the time came, Brian Cussen drove Suzanne to the rail station at Windermere town where she would start her journey to York. Her relative would meet her at the other end. This was the first time she had left either of her children. They made a joke of it, but it was quite an emotional parting. Dalmar had his work cut out to make things cheerful again. He resorted to a children's video of Thomas the Tank Engine that had just been released. It did the trick, particularly with Michael, his obvious enjoyment rebounded onto Emma.

The next evening Suzanne found herself being introduced as the guest speaker at the dinner for practicing veterinary surgeons, mostly from the north of England. Some had travelled down from Scotland and others from the Midlands.

As each food course was consumed, Suzanne who had been sitting at her place on the top table among highly estimable company felt utterly apprehensive. When she stood up to speak, the palms of her hands were clammy and she was quite sure she would not be able to utter a word, let alone project her voice so that everyone could hear her. Normally, she was a person known for her sense of humour, and she was aware that this had been lacking in her personality in recent months, as it had for most people living or working near Lastwater.

The men and women before her, she had always had a great deal of respect for, not just because of their qualifications, but, also, for what they did. She had decided to start with an amusing story that concerned an acquaintance who liked to adopt elderly cats in need of a home. When this lady took her new charge for an initial and introductory visit to her vet, the gentleman took one look at the black and white feline face and said, "Well – you landed on your feet – didn't you?"

Whereupon the cat looked the man full on, turned around, presented her backside and proceeded to spray the unfortunate vet full in the face with her urine. He hardly had time to close his eyes. Nearly everyone in the room laughed. They all knew that although cats were usually very clean animals, sometimes they showed their strong disapproval by such actions. It was as though the cat was thinking, 'This is what I think of you.'

Suzanne started her address by telling them of the situation when her husband became curator of Bray Castle two and half years ago. It, very soon, became obvious that the venture would not be commercially successful by relying on receipts from visitors to the castle alone. It did not have any significant history and there was simply not enough attraction to rely exclusively on tourism. It was therefore agreed that she would use her knowledge to create the bird and animal resuscitation centre. She told them how it had gradually taken shape with the arrival of the first patients through to the established centre it was today. After that she went on to explain how veterinary practices could make financial sense out of the arrangement. She was not aware of it, but the diction in her voice was passable and no one was in the least bored. When she had finished – she smiled – probably from intense relief: if nothing else enchanted them – that did. The applause was very loud and sustained.

The next day, Dalmar sneaked some time off to take his children to meet the train carrying his wife home. He had trouble containing a very excited boy and girl on the platform before the train's arrival; all they wanted to do was run around.

Prompted by the schoolgirl's interview, Dalmar asked his wife if a return visit for the Legg family could be arranged in order to glean further information about the lake. They came on Sunday afternoon, 4th July, complete with the two Border collies. Suzanne reciprocated the high tea – replacing the boiled eggs with a cold meat salad: a seasonal choice. Her cake was lighter too – a lemon sponge with succulent clear icing. Chris Legg seemed to like it – devouring two large slices.

Dalmar showed them all around the castle and took

them for a stroll in part of the grounds.

When they were down at the boat house looking across to the island, the scene of the Legg family tragedy all those years in the past, Dalmar broached the subject of the farm's original owners moving to the United States.

Chris Legg, with one foot resting on a raised ledge at the edge of the small pier squinted across the lake in the late afternoon sunshine; his golden hair glistening in the lowering warming rays. To Dalmar and his wife's amazement he proceeded to do something he had not done before in their presence. He took a smoker's pipe out of his jacket pocket followed by a tobacco pouch and filled the bowl of the pipe in a one-handed action. All the while he said not a word, and it was not until he had applied a lighted match and got the tobacco properly smouldering, exhaling large quantities of smoke that he deigned to reply to Dalmar's, apparently, ignored question, although he was actually contemplating his reply. Dalmar realised this and waited patiently. Cumbrian men were known for their often carefully considered responses to questions.

Little Michael and Fly could not take their eyes of him during the whole operation. They were completely mesmerised by the puffs of intoxicating tobacco smoke evaporating in the lakeside air. Young Emma, although she had witnessed a man smoking a pipe before was fascinated at the way Chris carried out the habit.

Chris's voice broke the atmosphere. "Lastwater Farm, to al' accounts were started by the Posselthwaite family in the fourteenth century. Some say they were one o' the first with the Herdwicks. O'course, over the centuries there were many hardships usually to do with illness, either to the stock or to the folk. There is talk of a flood in 1512 when all the lower fell grazing land was underwater."

"What caused them to sell up and leave the country was a combination of things. First – the fire that destroyed most of the interior of the farmhouse. A lot of the stonework survived. However, a youngster were in charge and he was tempted by the new world. So, they upped and left for good an'all. Anyhow, 'tis said there is something else. All we know is that it where to do with a witche's curse from the deep past. This was known as THE DREAD CURSE. The family blamed their various misfortunes on this and were convinced that by leaving the area it would be no more. As to the curse's origins – well – we don't know. 'Tis a mystery. This was in the late seventeen hundreds." Here Chris paused to take a few puffs on his pipe. He appeared to be thinking hard at the same time.

At the end of the jetty, Daisy Legg was busy keeping an eye on the girls and all three dogs. Michael remained with his mother, on reigns, still staring at the vision of the pipe smoker. Both Suzanne and Dalmar were listening to Chris avidly.

"It is said that they took with them the secret of Laswater contained in a wooden box." Again – the pause. "That is all we know – 'cept an address for a ranch, spread – whatever they calls it over there in the state of Virginia. As far as I know – no one from here has ever been in contact with anyone – o'er there. 'Cept for this address – that is. Came – out of the blue a few year back."

"Any chance of having that address?" Dalmar did not hesitate to ask this.

"By al' means," replied Chis. "Daisy will see to it."

"Do you know anything about the family that used to live on this land before the castle was built?" asked Dalmar.

"Very appropriate," said Chris with a grin. "It was one o'their ancestor's, apparently, who was the witch I referred to. She was burnt alive."

The finality of this statement made Suzanne gasp in horror. "I know," said Chris – but they were pretty barbaric then, especially o'er superstitious matters like that."

"We had a woman call and see us; said her family used to live here before the castle was built. Went by the name of Adred?"

"Ah – Adred Dread. Haven't seen her in years. She is

the only Dread left an'all. When she departs this world –
that'll be that." Chris said with finality.

"So – the *Dread Curse* - yes?" asked Suzanne.

"Aye. Although I'm not privy to the reason for it. It was
the Dread's who named some parts around the lake,
including Shimdorie Island. T'was always known as The
Island afore."

"Don't suppose you know where Adred lives now,"
asked Dalmar. He was becoming more and more convinced
that he should try and contact her.

"No – I don't. Sorry," answered the farmer.

"Ask Doris Appleby, the lady you's have working for
you. She might know." It was Daisy who spoke picking up
on the conversation. Chris looked at her enquiringly. Dalmar
nodded and thanked her.

Shortly after this the Legg family returned to their farm.

Due to the L.R.C. tragedy Dalmar had done nothing
about coming up with plans for the water bird sanctuary at,
or adjacent to, the boathouse. In discussion with Suzanne
they had decided to shelve the task for twelve months.

At length, the time came for Suzanne to go and see
Rosalind and Jacob at Patterdale. Jacob had recovered
from the effects of the chemo treatment, but Suzanne was
shocked to see that his outward appearance, particularly
relative to the colour of his skin, had deteriorated. However,
the young boy seemed to enjoy playing with her children.
He took a particular pleasure in fussing about after Michael
– hardly letting him out of his sight.

Before settling down to afternoon tea, they all went for a
stroll around the village as far as Goldrill Beck. Suzanne
was delighted when Pet, the cat she had nursed, chose to
sit on her lap while they were having tea. Roz and Suzanne
had developed a friendship since their first meeting when
Pet was brought to them. They held similar values in life.

As they were leaving, Suzanne handed Roz an
envelope which contained a copy of Dalmar's redrafted

poem entitled 'Rain.' Roz thanked her and placed it on the mantelpiece against a clock.

A few days later, the specialist at the Royal Lancaster Infirmary took a blood test from Jacob in order to ascertain how he was doing after the final chemotherapy in the program. He also carried out further tests together with a full body scan. When the conclusions were communicated to his mother and father a week later, the news was awful. The chemotherapy session had had no effect. The cancer was spreading to other vital organs in his body. Shortly, Jacob would have to go and stay at a children's hospice in order that twenty-four-hour care could be administered.

When they returned from the hospital with this information. they immediately went to collect their son from a neighbour who had been looking after him.

Late that afternoon, after her husband had gone to put in a couple of hours work in an insurance office at Ambleside, his regular employment, Roz sat watching her child playing with Pet in their front room. He had a piece of string with several knots tied at the end, which he trailed around and around while Pet kept darting after it. When she caught the knotted area with her claws, Jacob would quickly pull it way, where-upon Pet would pounce after it, tail twitching furiously.

It was raining outside: a constant full-bodied downpour. Jacob kept glancing out of the window, occasionally exclaiming and pointing excitedly. The sky had darkened, and his mother switched on a standard lamp to provide a warm ambient light. She took the envelope, left by Suzanne, off the mantelpiece; opened it and read.

RAIN

I have never loved so much in the rain.
And felt so warm and dry and calm.
The wet curtain parted
To reveal a pillow soft face.
The feel of the rose petal
My fingertips entrance.
And when my lips brush gently,
It is the same.
How I dream and dream that feel,
Until the dream is dreaming me.
Dream on dream.

I have never been so at peace in trust.
When his unseen hand reaches out
Mine will so do,
For the sky carries a mesmeric message,
Cloud evading, sure to a searching mind.

I awake early in the morning
To try and cool his fevered brow
And let him know
That I lie
Not far away – waiting ...
Hoping.

CHAPTER NINE

"THIS IS THE KIND OF THING YOU WANT TO KNOW."

The next time Doris Appleby was on duty at the castle, Dalmar wasted no time in asking her as to Adred Dread's whereabouts, and he made it clear why.

"A lot of people misjudge that lady and no mistake," was her opening remark. "She might be forthright with her views and I would say a bit loud, but she never did anyone any harm. Considering the way, she lives, she is always clean and although her dress sense is bizarre, nobody could accuse her of wearing dirty clothes."

"How do you mean?" asked Dalmar.

Doris was in full flood liking nothing more than to expound on a gossipy topic. "It works like this. During the summer months she lives rough, usually sheltering in a cave on Sty Head Pass." Doris furrowed her forehead at this point as though she was not sure of something. "At least, so I'm led to believe. 'Course that could be exaggerated. Anyway, during the season she keeps the self-catering properties at Seatoller and Seathwaite in good order in between lets. Now – her expenses are minimal – so she saves up enough money to rent a room during the winter, usually at Ambleside."

"She came to see us here in May this year. Is that out of the ordinary? I mean we are some way from Borrowdale," asked Dalmar confused. The two villages Doris had mentioned were at the southern end of Derwentwater. Although Adred could have come across country, it was not an easy trek involving seven or eight miles of mountainous terrain.

"Naow – if she has a week to kill between jobs, she has been known to wander far. That is one very fit lady!" emphasised Doris.

"She has asked me to invite her over;" Dalmar held both of his hands open in an as it happens gesture, "in order that I can pick her brains about Lastwater's history. It would be useful if that could be arranged. How does one go about it – if she is of no fixed abode?"

"Easy – just pass the word. I could start the ball rolling if you like? However, if I were you, I would think about doing this the other way around. I reckon she will think a lot more of it if you do." Doris looked at the curator over the top of her spectacles in a knowing sort of way. "She might cooperate more."

"Really," acknowledged Dalmar. "I might just do that. Leave it with me before saying anything. Sounds like a good idea." Actually, what Dalmar liked about it was that there would be less risk of an unprepared, embarrassing encounter on the premises.

"What people don't know about Adred is that she comes from a very intelligent family going back to the year dot. One of her ancestor's was a professor in the sciences or some such. All of the children from each generation did well at schooling. She, herself, speaks with quite a posh accent."

The curator thanked Doris and said he would let her know what he planned to do soon.

The following day, Dalmar met Suzanne, Emma, Michael, Roz and Jacob as they were leaving the bird sanctuary during the afternoon. He was on his way down from the office to get himself a cup of tea from the canteen. When he saw Jacob, he found it very difficult not to show his dismay. The poor little boy was pale beyond belief and his eyes were sunken and dull. He walked with a stoop to his shoulders. Roz saw it in Dalmar's eyes. She placed an arm on his by way of saying hello, although she could not hide the distress within her, it showed under her smile.

"Great to see you both," Dalmar forced his speech into a joyful tone. "Been sorting out our feathered friends?"

"We have been here for quite a while," ventured his wife. "Jacob is a very keen animal lover like our Emma." What she did not mention was so was Roz – very much so. At her part time occupation helping to run a riding school, she was a very good horsewoman and her understanding of this animal, in general, was well known. "Just taking them over for tea at the Dower-house – don't suppose you can join us?" asked Suzanne.

Dalmar raised a grin. "That would be nice – but no. Got to get hold of Jack. He wants some figures."

"Try and get over before we go," suggested Roz. "Would be nice to catch up."

"Okay," he replied, and then thinking on – there was a pallor on Jacob's face that he did not like at all. "No – that's a promise." He smiled broadly at all of them. Michael wanted to stay with his daddy, until Suzanne informed him about a certain chocolate cake waiting for them. Magically, his temporary preference for his father's company disappeared.

When Dalmar made a promise, he would keep it. If there were ever any doubt, no promise would be forthcoming. Accordingly, he arrived at the Dower-house a good ten minutes before Jacob and his mother were due to leave.

Without sounding like favouritism due to Jacob's illness,

Dalmar made it clear, before they left, that any friend of his wife was more than welcome to visit whenever they chose. One of the things he had learnt from Suzanne since being married to her resulted in his question to Jacob as they were getting into their car. "How's Pet doing?"

Jacob gave him a full smile. "Oh – she's great thanks." He chatted on further eager to give a full account of her well-being.

Roz never mentioned anything during this visit. The grim fact was that her son would be going to a hospice on Saturday. He was not expected to return. While Suzanne would probably visit him there, it was unlikely Dalmar would. This might be the last time they would see each other.

It was now the busy period at Bray Castle being the peak holiday time while all the summer school holidays were in full flow. However, Dalmar knew this would be a good opportunity to get to see Adred Dread over in Borrowdale. She would be kept at it on the changeover days at the holiday rental cottages, and an audience should be possible late in the day, before she disappeared to her cave shelter in the evening, the exact whereabouts of which was something known only to her, apparently.

Dalmar informed Doris Appleby of his intentions and asked her not to mention it to anyone. He figured that he would have more chance of a meeting if he used the element of surprise. Suzanne understood why her husband wanted to do this, it was in order to gather as much information about Lastwater's history before the arrival of David Fresher late in September, but she was not too happy about it. He was really needed on site during this time. To make amends, Dalmar made sure all the paperwork was up together before he went and ensured all the recent takings were banked on the morning of his departure. He only intended to be away until late in the evening of the same day.

On Friday afternoon, the sixth of August, Dalmar parked the Land Rover in the public car park at Seatoller, a village at the southern end of Borrowdale. Here he started to make enquiries about contacting Adred. At a small village stores they directed him to try a couple of holiday lets near the bridge. "She might be working in one of them," he was told.

He drew a blank at both, but, luckily, while he was knocking on the door of one of the cottages, he met a man who asked if he could help? "I'm trying to contact a lady by the name of Adred Dread – rather urgently. I was told she works here on Friday's."

"Been and gone," the man said. His face was not unfriendly. He explained that the preparation for the next holiday visitors would have been concluded that morning. "She also does three cottages at Seathwaite." This was the village further along towards Derwentwater. "But I think they have a different change-over day. I could pass on a message – if that's any help," the man offered. Dalmar thought that he looked to be a person of some importance locally. As a result of this character judgement, he told the man who he was, and informed him that he wished to see Adred in order to gain information concerning her family's history before the arrival of a geology expert in September.

The man introduced himself. He was on the parish council and lived in the village. "At a guess I would say she has purchased some supplies and gone back to her – perhaps one should call it a *lair,* up Combe Gill. No one knows exactly where she hangs out. But I can tell you that it is not up Sty Head Pass which is popularly believed. She dwells, in the summer months, somewhere beyond the cave area at Bessyboot. They tell me, although I am not privy to this knowledge myself, that the only way to contact her is to go up to Tarn at Leaves and call out." At this the gentleman grinned doubting that Dalmar would undertake such an adventure.

He was wrong.

Returning to his car, Dalmar collected a light backpack

which contained two items, a waterproof jacket and an Ordnance Survey map of the area. He took from the glove compartment a bottle of Californian red wine, two small, clear plastic tumblers and a corkscrew.

From the village store he purchased a crusty loaf of white bread, a solid wedge of Red Leicester cheese, a bunch of watercress and several florets of white grapes. With the whole lot in his backpack and after studying the map, he set off.

The wettest area in England was not living up to its reputation today, thankfully. It was quite the opposite, hot and sunny. Dalmar was clad in light denim jeans, a light blue short-sleeve shirt and on his feet, he wore a pair of north American Indian moccasins. Normally, on the fells, he wore good strong boots with ankle support. Today, he had been caught out thinking that he would not have to trek very far. He was not concerned.

Dalmar moved differently when he wore his moccasins. He seemed to claw at the ground on each step and the muscles at the back of his legs rippled with the movement. Making his way back down the road he had motored along earlier, he passed over Strands Bridge and then located a path going off to the right so as to follow the route along a gentle escarpment above Combe Gill. The way was easy, and he enjoyed himself finding a cooling breeze that caressed the sides of his face preventing perspiration forming on his hairline.

He had to continue along this path for at least two miles, so it became a little monotonous, but as he came up to a miniature ravine housing another stream know as Rottenstone Gill, the path became intermittent and more interesting. Because he was wearing moccasins and the ground underfoot was probably the driest it ever got during the course of a year, he found himself using poise and balance, with the occasional raised arm, leaping from boulder to boulder and grassy knoll to grassy knoll. Nearing the top, he was flanked on one side by Bessyboot at 500 metres, and Rosthwaite Fell on the other at 650 metres above sea level. As the grade lessened, he came to one of Lakeland's prettiest, in terms of situation, small lakes known as Tarn at Leaves.

It was now early evening, but the sunlight would be around for another three hours before he need to make the return journey. Wasting no time, he cupped his hands over his mouth and shouted, "Adred!" several times. There was no echo, but it did sound loud and intrusive on the gentle seen. The only other noise he had heard since leaving the sound of running water behind him was the occasional bleating from sheep.

He sat down to wait.

After about five to six, Dalmar was about to give vent to his lungs once again when he suddenly noticed a figure silhouetted against the northern sky that had crested on the summit of Bessyboot. He was sure it was a youngish looking woman wearing a dark coat. Dalmar felt as though he were being intrusive. He gave a salute style wave with his right hand. The woman started down towards him. Dalmar stayed where he was taking his backpack off his shoulders and laying it on the ground. He was standing right on the shore of the tarn next to a couple of sizeable boulders. As she approached, she undid her coat buttons revealing a pair of blue jeans and what looked like a navy-blue smock on her upper body. He was surprised to see that her hair, looking full in body and much sleeker than the last time he had seen her at Bray was coloured a deep auburn. It glinted in the evening sunlight and set off her tanned complexion to great effect. As she drew close, those grey-blue eyes did not waver from their straight trajectory towards his.

"Well – if it isn't Mr Curator. What brings you out here? Surely not to see the likes of me?" There was an air of sarcasm in her tone.

"Actually Adred, I need to talk to you urgently. Oh – and I've brought us some supper." He indicated his backpack on the ground up against one of the boulders.

Adred flicked her hair back over her shoulder. Dalmar was surprised. She seemed considerably more attractive than the apparition that had appeared in his office several weeks ago, red faced and wild looking.

"Urgent?" she asked suddenly curious.

Dalmar quickly explained about the forthcoming geologist's visit, and how it was necessary to gather as much historical information concerning Lastwater before his arrival. He suggested to her that after the awful tragedy earlier on this year, something needed to be done in order to prevent such a happening again.

"So – you want to know about the Dread family history?"

Dalmar thought - that said it in a nutshell considering the actual meaning of the name. "Yes," he affirmed.

She pointed a finger at the pack. "What have you got in there then? No wine I suppose?"

Dalmar smiled. "A bottle of red."

"Ah. You have just bought yourself a willing participant." Adred returned the smile. Dalmar was amazed to witness a mouth full of healthy-looking white teeth in goodly number.

They seated themselves on the boulders and Dalmar pulled the cork on the wine bottle; poured them both a tumbler and handed one to Adred. She took it in a hand that was not exactly manicured but clean even to the nails. She smiled again.

"Cheers," said Dalmar and the young woman put the little tumbler to her lips. Expecting a course gulp, Dalmar was again surprised. She did it elegantly and her expression showed enjoyment at the taste and effect.

"Okay," she said, "what do you want to know?"

"Simple." He gave her a knowing grin. "Just go back as far as the history of your family at Bray allows."

Adred opened her eyes wide. "Well!" She thought for a while. "Actually, it won't take that long." She took another sip of her wine. Dalmar began to wonder if this was the same woman who had called on him at the castle. There was no loudness of voice, no aggression; even her facial muscles seemed – softer. Unknown to him, there was a reason. She was not putting it on - she had a purpose.

Dalmar interjected quickly. "I mean was it a farming family. Were you in competition with the Posselthwaites at the other end of the lake?"

"No. We were not farmers except in a smallholding kind of way. Self-sufficiency – mediaeval wise if you like, although a normal practice if you had the land: a few sheep, poultry, vegetable garden – that kind of thing. No – we were teachers. My great, great, great – whatever – grandfather was the first teacher at Grasmere school. The position stayed in our family for a hundred years or more."

Adred glanced at Dalmar. "However – That's as maybe. This is the kind of thing you want to know. Can't tell you exactly when but around the date 1500 there was an appalling tragedy. A young man from Lastwater Farm enticed a girl – a fourteen-year-old girl – from Bray House to spend a night with him on Shimdorie Island. To be honest that is our side of the story. The Posselthwaite's may have a different reckoning. But they're not here – so we can't ask them," she added with a kind of finality. "Anyhow, they both disappeared presumed drowned. They found a small boat in the marshes which belonged to the farm. That's how they came to this conclusion, plus stuff found on Shimdorie, I believe."

"Is that where the curse originates from?" Dalmar was recalling the conversation he had with Chris Legg.

"Yup – probably said in anger. The girl's mother, a Dread of course, was blamed for all kinds of misfortunes the Posselwaites suffered in future years. She was burnt alive at Cockermouth. They accused her of being a witch. Horrible!" Adred shuddered.

Quickly, Dalmar moved on. "I know about the flood of 1512 – what else?" he asked, opening his hands and holding them in an expansive manner.

"Other farming misfortunes, but most of all in 1505 a

relative of the Posselthwaites, a teenage boy, fell to his death from Striding Edge on Helvelyn. In those days they didn't normally climb the mountains. Left them well alone, not having the kind of kit we have today. It was in winter too – good cover of snow apparently."

"I didn't know that," remarked Dalmar. "Strange. Was it suicide?" Striding Edge, an infamous ridge near the summit of Helvelyn mountain, had been the site of several tragic accidents over the years where climbers had fallen to their death.

"I really don't know. It was so long ago. Can't really rely on the gossip of ages," she grinned shyly at him.

"Anything else?"

"Oh yes – the most important bit." It'll cost you another drink and you mentioned supper. For now – I need more than liquid."

CHAPTER TEN

"WELCOME TO MY BATHROOM," ...

It might have been where they were, or what he expected, but while eating their supper without talking much, except for Adred's murmurs of appreciation at the simple repast, Dalmar realised the person before him was not wearing any cosmetic application to her face, and yet it did not seem to mar her appearance as a woman. Most people would agree that she was not beautiful in the true feminine sense, but she had something.

Dalmar had made up his mind before this evening's encounter that he would not ask questions about her night shelter. It was believed she slept in a cave. So be it, but, from her appearance, it did not look as if she did. Unlike the first time he had laid eyes on her at Bray, her clothes were in good order; her hair was combed, and she exuded a pleasant womanly aura.

Dalmar decided to put a question in a subtlety different direction. "Forgive my curiosity, but don't you get lonely out here?"

Her answer surprised him. It was the kind of reply he might have made. "Yes," she said. Dalmar looked at her and waited. She gazed back at him, searching his eyes. Finally, she shrugged her shoulders. "Just – the best solution – that's all." 'Solution to what?' would be the obvious follow up, but Dalmar left it at that. He did not want to pry.

When they were left with just the grapes and the wine, her visitor invited Adred to continue from where she had left off. "You mentioned that there were still important facts concerning your family to tell?"

Adred wrinkled her nose, whether to clear an itch or due to thought discomfort only she knew. "Professor James Dread," she said.

"Sorry – I'm not familiar..."

"Never met anyone who is," she interrupted. "Fact is though – he discovered the secret of Lastwater."

"Which is?" Dalmar had a feeling he knew the answer to this question.

"Wish I knew. It died with him."

"How come?"

Adred shifted her position on the boulder stone being careful not to spill her little vessel of wine she was cradling in her right hand. "Well – the evidence, apparently, disappeared in two directions. There was a lot of stuff written down that got burnt – maliciously – I am led to understand. And there was a small box he made that was supposed to contain the secret. Rumour has it that it went to the United States when the Posselthwaite family sold up and emigrated. My father told me someone in their family stole it claiming it was part of the curse against them, so it may well have been destroyed."

"Anything else?" encouraged Dalmar.

"Sorry to disappoint – but it might be worth trying to find out if there are any surviving descendants of the Posselthwaites in the States." She paused before draining her drink. "It was James Dread; he was a professor in the sciences by the way, who put names to various geographical parts of Lastwater – like Shimdorie Island for example. Apparently, after the malicious damage to his work he became very secretive with his studies; never told anybody about anything and kept all the information to himself – which is a great shame. Did you know that it was Professor Dread who gave the lake its name?"

"What – Lastwater?"

"Yes. Even the Legg's took it up and used it for the farm in due course. The only original topographical name left is your place – Bray."

"Any significance to Shimdorie? ... I mean it is unusual."

"Not that I know off." She pursed her mouth in a kind of so what attitude.

"What about your parents? Where do they live?"

Adred looked at Dalmar with astonishment. "Don't you know I am an orphan?"

"Oh, I'm sorry – I really had no idea..."

"Come to think of it – why should you," Adred realised, but she was taken aback that this information had not been passed on to him. "My mother died when she gave birth to me. My father, the last male Dread, didn't make it to my first birthday."

Dalmar felt sorry for her. But he made no comment. It would not help.

"It had to be a man who gave me my first name," she carried on. Think it was the schoolteacher in him. Dread is an awful surname, but I am told, he named me Adred to prove that letters were only letters, Adred is an anagram of Dread.

Dalmar, being a poet, did not agree with the philosophy, however, he remained silent. Privately, he thought both names unattractive. It appeared she rather liked her first name. 'Just as well,' he thought to himself. "That was rotten luck – about your parents. No other relatives? Not even a distant cousin?"

"Nu-oh," she replied with a slight laugh. "Well – who knows? Not to my knowledge anyway. At least the inheritance provided the executors of the family estate with sufficient to pay for my education. The family home in Kendal was sold up."

"Where did you live though – in an orphanage?"

"Yes. And from the age of four I went to a Roman Cathlolic convent and stayed there until I was sixteen. When the other girls went home during the school holidays – I stayed on."

Her visitor made no comment. It was hardly his business to enquire further. Adred made a small smile. "Guess that's about it."

"Okay," said Dalmar. "Thanks – you have been very helpful." He looked about him; the sun seemed to be going down. Shadows were lengthening. He picked up the two tumblers and put them in his backpack.

"Fancy a swim before you go?" Adred asked the question in an enticing kind of way.

"What – here?" Dalmar pointed at the waters of the tarn.

"No. I know somewhere *much* better." She jumped to her sandaled feet. "Follow me."

Her guest did not have much choice really. He picked up his pack and the still half full bottle of wine, the remainder of the grapes, and went after her as she walked ahead of him with a remarkable undulating hip movement. Adred was not an overly tall woman. This did not tally with descriptions that had been passed on. Dalmar found it all strange. He concluded that it must be to do with the overall conception of the Dread family from Bray as tall, austere, secretive and intelligent people.

Adred led Dalmar amongst tough short grass and heather up through a rocky mini ravine to crest a small mound in the hilly terrain. She pointed down a steep slope to a large rock outcrop. "Go down there and around to the left. I'll be with you very soon." Then she moved away from him to disappear from view over a large jumble of scree and boulders.

Her guest did as he had been bidden. She had not been lying. He found himself alongside a beautiful, good sized pond completely hidden from any of the pathways hereabouts. It was virtually surrounded by miniature cliffs. The only sensible access being the slope he had just come down. The late day sun streamed in from the west casting a deep shadow on the side where he was standing. It was like looking at a liquid surface of dark blue tinted gold. Dalmar had never seen anything like it, either in actuality or photographically. Hearing a sound behind him he turned to feel Adred next to him. She was carrying a white towel. Dalmar raised his eyebrows. He wanted to say he did not have any swimming trunks but desisted.

Adred touched him on his left shoulder and then climbed up the back of the large slab of rock that formed an overhang over the water. When she reached the top, she quickly released the waist button on her jeans and let them drop. She pulled the smock over her shoulders revealing breasts that needed no support whatever. She pushed down a pair of pale blue knickers and executed a dive of beautiful style entering the water without a splash and hardly a ripple.

The visual experience left Dalmar partially stunned. He followed her up to the summit of the rock and started to disrobe. The sight of her body as it was revealed to him etched against the deep blue of the evening sky had caused a stirring in his loins. By the time he dived into the water he was already starting to fly the flag for England. The ice temperature that hit his body as the water closed over his head soon put an end to that. When he surfaced gasping, not for air, but at the shock, he heard a gurgling giggle behind him. As he spun about, a shining wet dark-haired head of appealing charm grinned at him. "Welcome to my bathroom," she said.

Dalmar laughed amid further gasps. "Sorry for invading your privacy, but – thank you," he said light heartedly.

The two of them swam about for a few minutes. Dalmar could not recall anything as invigorating as this happening to him before, and he had not exactly led a sheltered existence during his youth. Adred swam very well. Her freestyle was far superior to Dalmar's, his preference being the breaststroke. He asked her where she had learned to swim so well. "Boarding school," she replied. He knew what she meant. Some such establishments were extremely well equipped in the sports department.

Without announcement, Adred walked out of the pond at the base of the slope. She picked up the towel and draped it around her body while languidly looking at the floating man who was lying on his back enjoying the moment.

Eventually, Dalmar came out of his reverie. The cold was starting to get to him. He turned his head to see the girl looking in his direction. He smiled at her and made for the bank.

As he clambered out, she moved up behind him and passed the towel, which he reached for and immediately gave the hair on his head a vigorous rub. Suddenly, he felt the girl's fingers caress the lower part of the cleft in his buttocks. They moved tantalisingly slowly up, to come to rest below his coxes. Dalmar turned and seeing her in a squat position went down to sit alongside. Before he could take her face in his hands, she pushed his shoulders to guide him to lie on his back against the long-stranded grasses by the water's edge; then she moved onto him in a straddle position. When they had connected Dalmar looked into her face. Her eyes were shut tight, but the rest of her features showed intense desire. 'She must be at the most potent time of her cycle,' Dalmar dimly registered. This heightened his sexual want for her; something that had come about unexpectedly in the last quarter of an hour. She started to move on him with slow small strokes, partially opening her mouth to facilitate her breathing which became more intense, and, after a while, her movement, sublimely erotic, built up to a faster momentum before she let out a single – moaning cry. She slowed to almost a stop while keeping her motion going at a gentle rhythm. Her perfume was that of the heather and the grass; sweet and musty. Gradually, her hips brought on a vibrant thrusting movement, although still controlled. She kept this up, uttering minute gasps every now and then for a minute or two, until the blood rush to her nipples signalled an urgent pulsating thigh tremor to herald climatic moans of ecstasy. Her fantastic excitement brought the man under her to a shuddering ejaculation. As her harsh breaths began to subside, she laid her head on his chest letting a peaceful calm descend. The bare skin along his back was uncomfortable against the hard ground. He bore it without complaint.

After about fifteen minutes during which Dalmar let the girl rest on him, she suddenly raised her head under a mass of tousled hair. Adred blinked, shaking off her drowsiness. "The night is closing in. You must go." Her voice was husky. She put the tip of her finger to his lips and climbed to her feet. "I don't make a habit of this sort of thing. In fact, you are the only person who has ever visited my private bathing area." She looked at him appealingly. "I trust you to be discreet. Somehow, I think you will be," and she finished with a glorious smile. It took away all the sombre atmosphere surrounding her.

Having already retrieved their clothes from the rock they used as a diving platform she dressed and, without waiting for him, picked up the towel and started up the slope. At the top she turned to him so that her form was silhouetted against a deep blue sundown sky. To choose a last image of someone – this was perfect. The now, almost black auburn hair glinted like phosphorescence in the last rays of sunlight. Her strong facial muscles, cast into shadow, gave her a dusky diffused profile. "Oh – just in case you might worry. There will be no babies," she said in a partially raised voice. And then she was gone.

When he was ready, Dalmar put the backpack on one shoulder now containing very little and climbed the slope. At the top, there was no sign of Adred. He picked up the half full bottle of wine, made sure the cork was secure, and left it in a prominent place for her to see along with the grapes. Whether the birds would leave any of them for her was debateable.

After this, he started off at a jogging run being careful to land securely at each step. With only moccasins on his feet he could easily turn an ankle on the rocky paths, so he was especially careful going down the steep descent by Rossthwaite Gill, and, at times, slowed to a hesitant lope. By the time he got to the escarpment overlooking Combe Gill it was dark. Moonlight from a cloudless sky gave him a grey landscape of ghostly forms to negotiate. The sound of a waterfall in the tumbling stream could clearly be heard.

It took him three quarters of an hour to get back to the car park and the Land Rover. There was a red telephone box there and he used it to call Suzanne.

"I was getting worried," she said.

"I am sorry. Got stuck on the fells talking to Adred. Got the information we want. I'll tell all when I get home. Too late to say goodnight to the children I guess?"

"Yes," replied his wife. "They are both soundoze."

"Okay – see you in around three-quarters of an hour an hour."

On the way, he was sure of one thing, he would not be telling quite all! He felt no guilt about what had just happened, but he was aware that his love for Suzanne had received some kind of absolute confirmation.

When he got home, he mumbled to his wife that he needed a quick shower, explaining that he had had to run down from the fells in order to beat the night closing in.

Afterwards, clean and robed he told her of his strange

encounter; well, most of it. Suzanne sat with her mouth partially open throughout. She had, like others, heard the rumours that Adred lived in a cave during the summer months, but had never really believed it. They still had no actual proof that she did, but – unless she had a tent concealed somewhere up there among the crags. It was likely.

Dalmar astonished Suzanne by announcing that he wished to visit Virginia, U.S.A. before David Fresher arrived late in September. This reminded them that Chris Legg had not, as yet, given them the address they needed to contact the ancestors of the original Posselthwaite family. Dalmar resolved to go and visit them tomorrow. Then, pleading tiredness, he went to bed.

While lingering in the twilight of sleep a thought occurred to him. During the lovemaking with Adred, she had not given any suggestion that she wanted to be kissed, neither had she proffered her lips to him. According to his experience with women in the past, this was unusual. He wondered if it had anything to do with the total abstinence from her childhood of parental love. Sexual gratification appeared to have been her only need.

In the morning, it was his turn to get a surprise. "Why don't we both go?" asked Suzanne after breakfast and in between attending to children's requirements.

"What – to the Legg's?" her husband asked.

"No – silly – the States."

"But who is going to look after the estate? It's the high season."

"How long were you intending to go for?"

"Actually – just a few days."

"Look – we haven't had a break from here since we arrived. I'll see if mum and dad would like to come up. Tim and Christine might like to visit with the children. Bea can run the animal centre. She's got two student assistants over the summer. They should be able to cope with the sheep as well. Trishia and Sue will be alright in the canteen providing all the supply ordering has been done. The others all know what they have to do."

"Okay, but what about the overall bit? Jack won't have time to arrange a stand in. I want to get it over with within the next couple of weeks because of the annual N.T. conference looming."

"Why not suggest Brian. He could manage for three days – surely?"

Dalmar's brain ticked over. It *was* a good idea and he was beginning to warm to the thought of some moral support on the trip. "Hmmm – sounds good actually."

"There you go then." She came up and kissed him all minty breathed having just cleaned her teeth.

As it happened, when Dalmar put the idea to Jack Twentyman, he was immediately all for it, realising the importance of giving the geologist as much useful information as possible. The minimising of bad publicity for Lastwater, was paramount, not to mention the safety aspect to visitors and staff. He even volunteered to be on site, most of the time, himself.

CHAPTER ELEVEN

"SOMEONE A BIT WORRIED?"

It was now the first week in August and Bray Castle had never been so busy. The staff reckoned a lot of it was due to a morbid curiosity. The public could not visit Lastwater Rowing Club, and this was the next best thing. The real reason being that they wanted to see the lake itself close up, as well as Bray Castle, together with its other attractions. Some tourists were aware that the last sighting of the lost rowing team was from Cloud Point located in the castle grounds.

Despite this and the preponderance of questions from visitors to staff on the subject, the atmosphere was starting to get back its old cheerfulness and there was rather more banter about generally. Even Suzanne seemed more like her old self. This was about to come to an abrupt end. On Tuesday afternoon she returned from a visit to see Jacob and his mother at a hospice near Kendal. She was, firstly, horrified to see Jacob as a pale imitation of the boy who had played in the woods here not that long ago, and, secondly, Roz informed her that he was not expected to live for more than another four weeks. The poor mother's distress affected Suzanne deeply.

At the end of the week, Dalmar heard back from the United States following his letter of introduction to a ranch in Virginia. The current lady of the house, although a descendant of the original family, was not a Posselthwaite by name. She had married and taken her husband's name, Madison. The letter contained some very good news. They still possessed documents relating to her ancestors in England, and he and Suzanne were welcome to pay them a visit as soon as they liked.

Emma Hunter had become very taken with some goings on in the bird department of the rescue centre. This was not to say that there was not much of interest in the animal sector; it was just that something rather special was taking place. No less than four Nuthatch fledglings from a late breeding had been found by the side of the road near Keswick. They needed frequent feeding and constant attention so that they might be brought to adulthood. Emma seemed to have taken the task on as her individual responsibility. Nobody minded, despite her tender years. Both Bea and Suzanne kept a watchful eye on the proceedings. They need not have worried. She was achieving wonders. The breed had not been known to exist in Lakeland before, being far more common further south.

Really, just the size of a normal garden bird when adult, Emma, nevertheless, seemed to appreciate their rarity even though as fledglings they had yet to show the glorious blue-grey backs with chestnut coloured bellies when fully grown. As a tree-dweller the baby birds needed a diet of seeds and nuts.   Bea helped Emma prepare a mash of these ingredients with a little milk on a daily basis.

The major problem they had at the centre, currently, was the large population of hedgehogs brought in as a result of road accidents. Usually, the animals did not survive what was frequently a night-time collision, but there seemed to be a preponderance of near misses lately with damaged legs and feet. Anyway, they were coping.

Dalmar and Suzanne decided to make the trip to the States soon after the August bank holiday weekend. Her brother and his wife would come to stay from Thursday 21st, covering the Hunter's absence from the next Tuesday through to the following Sunday, giving them three whole days in Virginia. Suzanne's parents would not be able to come to Bray, but that did not really matter.

Despite his time in the Merchant Navy, Virginia was somewhere Dalmar had never been, and Suzanne had not even visited the U.S.A. before. Fortunately, both their passports were valid. Naturally, she was extremely excited, although she tempered it in front of the children. She knew she would miss them almost at once after leaving home. They decided to travel to Manchester on Monday afternoon and stay overnight somewhere near the airport. They would be flying out around mid-morning arriving at J.F.K. airport, New York, in the early evening. Then they had another flight to undergo down to Richmond, Virginia and would not arrive there until nearly midnight. The plan was to make a leisurely drive by hired car on the following day in order to reach their destination; a horse farm owned by the Posselthwaite descendants situated a short distance from the Blue Ridge Parkway.

However, something happened before then. It did not affect their departure date, but it *was* highly emotional. Roz phoned Suzanne on Tuesday, 10th August. Jacob had died the day before. Suzanne felt desperately sorry for her. It was bad enough for the father, but for the mother to lose her only child... Suzanne had no idea how she would cope if it happened to one of hers. When alone, she was reduced to copious tears herself.

It was not possible for both Dalmar and Suzanne to attend the funeral. One of them had to stay behind and look after the children and keep an eye on things at the castle. Suzanne went. It was a dry and sunny morning at the little Patterdale churchyard where they buried him and, unsurprisingly, there was a huge turnout. The church knave could not accommodate all the mourners. Many had to stay outside and listen, as best they could, through the open doors. Suzanne was one of these. After the service she promised Roz, while giving her friend a long hug, that she would be in touch when they returned from the States. She did not want to get in the way while family and long term friends were mourning the passing of the poor boy. Suzanne had only become a friend to Roz recently because of the situation with her son, but something told her – it would continue.

Christine Westward climbed out of the car and stretched her body after the long car journey. An excited Charles, followed by Holly were the next to appear and their immediate attention was drawn to Fly who came, tail wagging, at a furious rate. Tim Westward took his time. The door to the Dower-house was flung open and Emma rushed out. Suzanne appeared cradling a glass of red wine in one hand while trying to stop a rampant two-year-old boy. Tim grinned at the scene. Looking at his sister he said, "Things much the same then?" while making up and down movements of hand to lips with a make-believe glass.

"Oh – behave Tim!" was her greeting to her brother.

That much had not changed anyway.

Christine raised her eyebrows. "Oh come on you two. Tim, you are ruining my chances of getting one of those drinks – so – yes – behave." After that they all got down to being polite with their greetings. Although, by the devilish look in Tim's eyes – it would not be for long. He obviously needed to make up for lost time.

What a contrast this light-hearted arrival turned out to be compared to the last visit so soon after the rowing club tragedy.

The Monday of Dalmar and Suzanne's departure arrived with a rush; it seemed, to both of them. Jack Twentyman had been at the castle with Dalmar all morning attending to last minute matters and making certain that his boss was thoroughly briefed of any pending events. Brian Cussen had been allowed to stay in his bed having been up most of the night with a full contingent of sky watcher students. Both Dalmar and Suzanne had made sure that all day to day administration was up to date for their respective responsibilities.

Emma and Michael were occupied with Tim and Christine's two children, so the departure was, fortunately, not tearful and Fly did not appear to notice, although, he earlier made anxious dog whines at the sight of two familiar suitcases in the hall, but it was soon forgotten. Considering this was the first time either of their children had been separated from their parents, it was remarkable what a little subterfuge could achieve.

On the way down to Manchester in their hired car, Suzanne, however, was sad. It tempered the excitement that she naturally felt for the adventure that lay ahead. After an uneventful overnight stay in a hotel near the airport she had recovered sufficiently to enjoy the flight to the United States. They landed at J.F.K. airport in the early evening and were soon on their way to Richmond without experiencing any delays in the transfer. But, by the time they arrived at their hotel, apart from taking in the relaxed attitude of the taxi driver, they were too tired to take any notice of culture or architecture.

The next morning, after a light breakfast, they set off in a rented Chevrolet Impala along route 64. Suzanne referred to the car as an ugly, lollipy tank. But once on the highway she appreciated its ride comfort and given the outside high temperatures, the air conditioning. She was glad she had packed cotton summer attire. Dalmar was comfortable too, in his lightweight sky-blue denim.

Suzanne had enjoyed looking at the colonial architecture while riding through Richmond and its suburbs, but now out on the open countryside, she was beginning to grasp the feel of this vast country compared to her own's somewhat smaller scale environment.

They made good time on the freeway, allowing for frequent stops at interesting places.

Thwaite Horse Farm lay under the peaks of the Blue Ridge Mountains. The sixteen-acre horse breeding centre was the third venture successfully established by the descendants of James and Harriet Posselthwaite, the original immigrants from England two hundred years ago. They started farming arable products initially, in a situation nearer to the Atlantic coast where, in those days, such a locality was more secure. They switched to a mixture in the nineteenth century, adding tobacco and finally selling that farm to commence horse breeding in the early twentieth century under James Posselthwaite the third. They struggled to survive for almost an entire generation before the farm eventually prospered: the man responsible being Cyril, James's eldest son ably helped by sister Cherry.

Cyril married a girl brought up on a spread situated further south. They had the one child, a daughter, who was now grown up and married with two young girls. Her name was Emily Madison and they were continuing were Cyril had left off. He and his wife, Hester, had retired and moved nearer to Charlotesville.

Dalmar drove through the entrance, a wooden archway construction, to Thwaite Farm just after six p.m. local time. Considering they were five hours behind the time in Cumbria, U.K., they were both a little weary. It was their bedtime.

They were greeted warmly by Emily, a cheerful but strong faced looking woman. Her features were fairly dark, like Suzanne's, suggesting a Celtic origin.

Suzanne was fascinated to know about the workings of the farm, but Emily respectfully suggested that that could wait until tomorrow. She considered it would be more appropriate to feed them and let them get some sleep. A barbecue was in the process of being prepared to satisfy the immediate requirement. They were now joined by two extremely curious little girls whose names were Trudy and Tracy. After prolonged introductions during which both girls wanted to know if they had ever had tea with the Queen and would not believe that they had not, they were finally escorted to their room in the ranch-house style building. They were given twenty minutes to freshen up, and the daughters reappeared to take them both to the large patio area around the back, where they were greeted by the strong aroma of steak and poultry being cooked on two large grills suspended over burning charcoal set in hand built brick housings.

Justin Madison, Emily's husband, held out an enormous hand of welcome to Dalmar and greeted Suzanne with a smacking kiss on her right cheek. He was a huge man, like a giant, tall and wide, without, it seemed an ounce of excess fat. Sweat poured from his brow as he tackled with the heat from the burning coals and the still high temperature of the evening sun. It did not seem to bother him, as though it was an everyday occurrence. The liquid loss was amply replenished from an eleven-gallon keg of Budweisser. Dalmar accepted the offer of a glass of the same. It became obvious after a few polite queries as regards to their flight and travels that Justin's favourite topic of conversation was horse farming and being the layman, Dalmar was more than happy to listen. However, he was soon joined by Suzanne, who had initially made friends with the two girls explaining that she had children of the same ages. She prolonged Justin's prevailing with constant prompting queries. Suzanne looked stunning in her simple navy-blue dress and Justin became quite taken with her, thankfully, in a polite kind of way: the gentle giant. He had a glorious smile showing two rows of healthy teeth. Dalmar reckoned it was due to a diet of steak. Those laid out smouldering on the barbecue grills looked huge. Dalmar was very hungry and he could feel his mouth salivating. Emily eventually came out from the kitchen area carrying numerous salad bowls on a large natural wood tray with every conceivable variety of summer vegetable, not to mention some enticing looking crusty rolls of bread. The sauces stacked out on a side table with the cutlery and plates numbered among them brands and ingredients neither Dalmar nor Suzanne had ever heard of.

Over this feast, Emily explained to their quests that they had gathered together quite a lot of documents. Some, her father had let her have from his possessions and together with the collection here it amounted to a sizable file. The vast majority were to do with sheep farming records of the time in north-west England. "Anyhow – we will not say any more on that until tomorrow – O.K.?" She spoke in a soft Virginian drawl. Suzanne, because she sensed she should, nodded her agreement and Dalmar was far more interested in enjoying his meal.

Emily did express her concern about the rowing boat accident. She said they had heard all about it over here. "Did you folks know any of the missing guys?" she asked. Suzanne explained that none of them lived locally. The rowers would have visited the club at the lakeside on a regular basis, but, although, they often saw them out practicing nobody at the castle had known any of them personally.

"Well, that's some..." Justin left the sentence unfinished. He had a deep voice to go with his frame. Dalmar thought he sounded like a character out of a western movie.

After eating some fruit, Trudy and Tracy went off to bed. They both possessed bubbly characters sporting long bouncy chestnut hair with healthy complexions.

The four adults chatted quietly by the dying charcoal embers as the sun went down. The Hunters were in for a treat. The sunset over the Blue Ridge Mountains was breath-taking. It caused long periods of silence as the four of them gazed and took it all in. Justin said that they often had what he called, "Blue-time sun-downs, but this one was one of the best he had seen."

Following a giant milky coffee, Dalmar and Suzanne went to their room with very full stomachs.

The next morning the two of them shared a waffle with syrup for breakfast. Suzanne could have done with just a cup of coffee, but she did not want to disappoint Emily after all her trouble. While the two women were clearing up, Dalmar was invited to start perusing some documents laid out in two boxes on a table set in an alcove by a giant window in their front room. He was told he could look at what he liked, however, Emily suggested that it might be wise not to muddle the two boxes contents. "One belongs to my father and this little lot I have gathered together from some cousins and our loft," she indicated the appropriate container with her right hand.

The breakfast remains cleared away, Emily and Suzanne found Dalmar with a few papers he was studying in front of him. Emily asked, "Anything interestin'?"

"He glanced up. "Well – nothing to do with the Lastwater anomaly – but did you know that your family, certainly in the earlier epidemic of 1350, completely escaped the Black Death?"

"Actually – yes. My dad told me about this. Because my ancestors were livestock farmers there were not a lot of rats about. It was arable farming that attracted most rodents –

which, I guess, every schoolgirl or boy knows spread the disease in Europe in the first place."

Dalmar smiled at her. "According to this entry in some kind of weekly diary – the lady seems rather proud of the fact." He thought for a while. "When you consider that they had no idea what caused the foul disease in those days, it is not surprising: probably thought they were purer than other people – or something like that." The other two could see the point.

"Don't you find a lot of those documents difficult to read?" asked Emily. "Impossible with some of them – I reckon."

"Yes – they used quite a lot of different characters to us. And these varied from region to region as well. Also, the sentence structure is strange in places – as though it were written in a kind of dialect. Tell you what though, although some of the ink – and we are presumably talking quills here – has faded, it is still legible."

"That is probably because my family kept it away from sunlight. In recent times my mother placed acid free protective sleeves in the other box," Emily told them. "Anyhow you guys. I have to tell you we would like you to take all of that back to England with you, so you don't have to worry yourselves right now."

"Are you sure?" Suzanne was agog.

"Yup," Emily replied emphatically. "One day, when our daughters are older, we should like to come over and visit the old place. It would be a real thrill to know some of the stuff was on display in a museum?"

"I'll arrange that for you with pleasure," said Suzanne. And she meant it. She had the contacts and knew exactly where to go and who to see.

"I'm very grateful," commented Dalmar, it did seem a bit daunting to sift through them all now. "May I suggest that after the freshwater geologist has been through them – we let the Legg family at your family's old farm site have a look, and then my wife can do her stuff. I assure you there is no one better to arrange it."

"Yea – that's a fact. Look – tell you what if the Leggs need to keep anything – then go ahead. Hell – there is plenty there," she finished with a flourish. "Now – come on, Justin is going to give you a tour of the farm and then you are both going for a ride." She beamed at them. "O.K?"

Suzanne was delighted and it showed. She had hoped this might happen. Dalmar was a little nervous and tried his best to hide it. He had not ridden a horse since he was a teenager. "Great," he said with a fake grin.

Emily was not fooled; she saw through it. "Someone a bit worried?" She took his arm as he stood up. "It's alright – we will look after you." There was a teasing grin on her face.

CHAPTER TWELVE

"IT'S EMPTY," SHE SAID.

Justin thought they might like to see something of the farm husbandry before they went out for a ride. Suzanne was very taken with the brooding mares and their foals. She could have spent all day with them.

For some reason, Dalmar had forgotten that they used a different style saddle, the western saddle, which made the riding a lot easier for him. Not so his wife who was used to the discipline of the European type. However, she soon adjusted her posture and really enjoyed their long trek over the pasture lands of the farm and beyond through unimaginatively beautiful Virginian countryside.

When they returned to the ranch-house, Emily had a surprise for them. "How would you folks like to hear a real good gospel choir?"

As it was the last thing he expected, Dalmar stood with his mouth slightly ajar. Suzanne, on the other hand, came straight back, "Would we?" was all she said, her face covered in smiles while showing off her dimples.

"My folks are travelling over to Charlottesville to watch a concert taking place tonight. They suggested we join them, truth is – they have already reserved tickets."

"Emily – this is something I have always wanted to see." Suzanne was really enthusiastic. A little unsure, Dalmar just nodded in agreement, but, then he thought he might enjoy the experience.

After a shower and a light meal, the three of them left in the farm's big station wagon for Charlottesville. The two girls were left in the care of their father who made it clear that he was not a gospel man; in fact, he gave Dalmar a sympathetic glance just before they departed.

Emily's mother and father were thrilled to meet the Hunters and asked masses of questions about the U.K. Her father, being a Posselthwaite, was very intrigued to hear, firsthand, about his family's original sheep farm, which they had occupied for some four centuries: a truly remarkable dynasty.

As things turned out, it was Dalmar who enjoyed the concert more than his wife, simply because so much of it was melancholy. It was obviously this choir's preference. However, they did perform some upbeat, cheerful numbers which Suzanne enjoyed. That was the sort of thing she associated with gospel singing: lots of ecstatic smiling faces throughout the performance.

It was during a particularly brilliant rendering of the river shanty, 'Oh Shenandoah' that an amazing thought occurred to Suzanne. Dalmar, so entranced by the performance, failed to notice her sudden start of surprise and disbelief when the extraordinary realisation occurred. At least, it was extraordinary to her because she was amazed that no one had ever mentioned it before. What triggered the revelation was the constant reference to the noun *river* in the lyrics of the song.

Quite out of nowhere, it dawned on her that Lastwater had no outflow. There were plenty of streams, becks and gills feeding it off the fells; abundant in volume when considering the sum total of them with their constant tumbling water courses nearly always in full flow. But there was no river taking the water off, either to join another river, or with a course straight to the coast. Apparently – nothing at all. 'How could this be?' As her mind registered the fact, firstly she put a hand to her mouth to stifle a gasp, and then she kept glancing sideways at her husband wanting to share her thoughts, but he was so obviously sent by the emotive song, judging by the rapt expression on his face – she gave up. During the haunting melody, some would claim the greatest of them all; it was amazing that she was able to think about other matters. Perhaps it was the melancholic feel to the music that conjured up the sadness of recent events on Lastwater, or perhaps she just transposed one waterway to another.

Dalmar became convinced that he had never heard anything so beautiful. The choristers were resplendent in their powder blue and white gowns and they swayed in perfect unison to the music's rhythm. The folk song was performed so well that it had an effect on the audience of entrapping them in the ambience. The choir had a way, through the arrangement, of causing an effect by clever choral harmony on the repetitive river phrases using tenor, treble and then bass rolling over and over just like the river Shenandoah itself. When the performance came to an end the applause was ecstatic.

Cyril Posselthwaite, although well on into old age, seemed remarkably spry. He was most interested in chatting to Dalmar during the interval of the concert – wanted to know all about Bray Castle and its meagre history. The man's countenance reminded Dalmar of several other similar facial appearances he had seen in Cumbria – both young and old. 'Must be a tribal trait,' he thought.

On the way back, Suzanne sitting in the rear of the station wagon seemed strangely preoccupied and rather subdued; so much so that Emily, from the driving position, asked her if she had enjoyed the performance. "Well – was it what you expected honey?"

Suzanne put her host at ease at once. "It was fantastic! – lovcd it – thank you so much for taking us." Suddenly, through impatience, she decided to talk about her startling discovery concerning Lastwater. She had planned to wait until she and Dalmar were alone, but when she thought about it, Emily's thoughts on the subject might be useful. She would have the geography of her own vast country to refer to. "May I explain what is bugging me though?" She carried straight on without waiting for anyone's invitation. "During the rendition of 'Shenandoah,' an extraordinary thingy – thought – occurred to me."

"Oh dear," joked her husband.

"No – listen you. This could be important." The tone of her voice made Dalmar half turn in his seat to study her face.

"It was the repetition of the word, 'river.'" She paused to give Dalmar a direct look. "You see – there isn't one."

Emily said, "Sorry – not with ya honey." She was not quite sure what Suzanne meant by *bugging* either.

"Emily, I'm sorry, this must seem strange to you. But the fact is the lake where we live – well it does not have a river connected to it." She glanced again at her husband whose facial expression changed from passive curiosity to a slow dawning amazement. "Does it?" Suzanne added.

"But it must have," said the man.

Suzanne could see the expression on Emily's face in the rear-view mirror. It said, 'how could such an obvious fact have gone unknown?' – or something like that.

"Without an outflow of some description the lake would burst its banks all the time," Dalmar was still thinking as he said this. "A river course must be formed over time."

"It must be seeping away then. What about the end near the rowing club? Isn't that marshy?" suggested his wife.

"Not sufficiently," said Dalmar confidently. "This is something that is going to need explanation. I mean does anyone know of any inland waterway that does not have an out-flowing river to start with? A pond – yes: they dry up and sometimes flood, but a lake ... no. Not possible."

Emily started running through lakes in the U.S. in her mind, but she could not think of one that did not have a river associated with it. She did not necessarily know their names, but she did know they existed. At length she could not contain herself, "Get real you guys – you mean no one knew about this?"

"Does seem ridiculous, I agree," remarked Dalmar. "Must be an explanation, but I cannot think of one for the moment. What is amazing is that it takes a brilliant rendering of 'Oh Shenandoah,' to awake my wife to the realisation. Why?"

"Well – there you go," said Emily with a chuckle. "There's no accountin' for the brilliance of us girls." Suzanne laughed with her.

When they arrived back at the farm, Justin joined them for some coffee curious to know if his guests had enjoyed the evening, to which they both nodded enthusiastically. Their daughters had long gone off to bed and were sleeping soundly.

While they were sitting in comfy chairs in their front room looking at the deep blue night with its myriad of tiny shining stars through the big window, Emily brought in a plain brown carrier bag and placed it amidst the coffee mugs on a low table. "Dad gave me this after the concert – says if it is alright with me, and it is, you can take this along with you as well as the documents. Same deal – perhaps a museum might like to show it. Don't know its exact age but – well – I guess possibly three hundred years old."

Suzanne gasped.

"This," added Emily, "apparently contains the secret of Lastwater. I was told that as a kid and all those a'fore me, I guess."

Dalmar raised the obvious question, "Which is?"

Justin immediately roared with laughter and Emily had to shout above it as she held both hands out, "Sorry – haven't a clue!" She proffered a hand towards the bag, inviting one of them to take a look.

Justin, controlling himself, said, "Don't get too excited." His wife gave him a reproving glance.

Suzanne stood up, bent over and peered inside the bag, almost as though she were afraid to touch whatever lay inside. "Go on – take it out," Emily encouraged her, "it won't bite yer."

Gingerly, Suzanne placed her left hand on the top of the carrier bag to hold it steady and put her right hand inside. She brought out a wooden box about eight inches long, four inches wide and two and a half deep. Dalmar thought that although the carpentry was not expert it must have taken some doing, because, if he was right, it was made from English hardwood oak. The most obvious attraction about it was the painted lid showing a coloured map of Lastwater and its shores. Not only was it painted well, but it appeared to be scaled accurately. Someone had gone to a lot of trouble to get it right. "Lastwater," he said pointing to the picture. "No doubt about that."

The most likely question came from Suzanne. "Did it come over when your family emigrated?"

"Yes," Emily confirmed, "always used to be on display, like an ornament, going way back. My mum hated it. When it was her turn, she made sure it was hidden away and dad didn't mind."

"I don't know whether you know this? But this ties in with a rumour we heard. That the secret of Lastwater went away with your family," said Dalmar.

"Well – is that a fact." Emily looked amazed.

Justin gave that chuckle of his. "I hope you folks haven't come all this way for that?"

Dalmar and Suzanne laughed this off, but they were secretly thinking in the affirmative.

"Have a look inside," invited Emily. She was a little surprised that Suzanne had not yet tried to lift the lid.

There was no locking mechanism or catch. She just pushed the lid up. It could easily close on the hinges under its own weight. "It's empty," she said.

"Yup, that's about the size of it," Justin chuckled all the more.

"May I?" indicated Dalmar with outstretched hand. Suzanne passed it over and sat back down. Looking at the lid again, close to this time, her husband realised that this small but detailed work of cartography had been executed with oil paints of, presumably, high quality, because the illustration was, almost, as new – not even a scratch in all that time. He looked thoroughly, trying to decipher if there had been any past family alterations, by a child for instance, but there was no sign of any over-painting using a foreign medium. All looked original. What struck Dalmar was the authenticity, because the artist had used a pallet for the water, uniquely attributable to Lastwater, which was evident under the right weather conditions – a lighter shade of royal blue. He opened the lid again. The empty box told him nothing. "Do you think it might have contained something once?" he asked.

Emily shook her head, "Not that anyone can remember – and you'd think they would if there had."

Dalmar nodded in agreement, closed the lid and turned the box over. It was on the underside that the only damage revealed itself: a pea sized hole, obviously the result of some minor accident. He put the box back on the table. 'No secrets,' he thought to himself.

Despite Justin's obvious amusement, Suzanne thanked Emily profusely for her and her father's generosity in letting this strong family artefact go back to Cumbria. Again, she promised to do the necessary and hoped they would see it someday on display. "We will certainly show it around and see if anyone has any ideas," she finished.

The next day the Hunters were free to do some sight-seeing on their own.

They chose to take a look at the world-famous Blue Ridge Parkway and drive down as far as Roanoke, taking their time, ensuring that they view as much of the scenery as possible. High on their list of priorities was to acquire some presents to take home not just for Emma and Michael, but Tim and Christine's children as well. They enjoyed the experience and wished they could have explored more of the non-commercial route, but time ran out and they had to head back to Charlottesville before too much of the afternoon had passed.

On Saturday morning, Dalmar and Suzanne said goodbye to Justin, Emily, Trudie and Tracy, thanking them for all their hospitality and generosity. They had never expected to be given so much attention and could not hide their appreciation. Suzanne promised to stay in touch and keep them informed as to museum displays and so on.

They made good time to Richmond, on this occasion choosing to make only a couple of rest-breaks; this gave them time to take a walk around some of the old town after a meal at their hotel.

The next day, the return flights went without a hitch and, on arrival, they drove straight off from Manchester Airport in a hired car to make their way up the M6 towards the Lake District.

On the way, Dalmar thought Suzanne might doze off; it had been a very early start for them in order to catch up the five hours local time difference, but she was too excited with the anticipation of seeing Emma and Michael, although they would be tucked up in their beds when they arrived. Seeing that she was fully conscious, he said, "I've had a thought."

"What's that darling," she acknowledged expecting something fairly mundane before turning to look at him. What she saw was a mischievous glint in his eyes.

Dalmar had been aware that something was hatching in his wife's brain; she had been thoughtful virtually all the way home, especially on the long flight across the Atlantic Ocean. He had known her for long enough to know when to spot the signs. Also, this time, he had a strong conviction as to what it was all about, and that it almost certainly involved Rosalind Maidment. "You know the old stable block behind the kitchen area at the Castle?"

Suzanne suddenly looked a little peeved. "Ye-es," she said in an uncertain manner.

"Well – the castle and its surroundings would make an excellent equestrian centre." Then he added, "Would it not?"

Suzanne turned fully sideways on and glared at her husband.

Dalmar continued. "And, of course, we know just the person to run it – don't we?" One glance at Suzanne, and he could not hold the ruse any longer. He burst into one of his loud belly laughs.

Suzanne yelled at him, "You sod – you knew I was thinking along those lines –didn't you? And – just for the record it was *my* idea!" Then she pouted.

After Dalmar had calmed down and acquiesced, there was only one topic of conversation all the way back until the turning off the M6 motorway to the Lakes. The whole thing had been as a result of Justin Madison's excellent informative attention while showing them around Thwaite Horse Farm. Although Suzanne had no aspiration to be a horse breeder, she could see the restoration of the old stable block, now only used for storage, giving huge potential for a thriving equestrian centre and a further attraction for holiday makers.

When they drove up to the Dower-house at one o'clock in the morning, the children may have been in bed asleep, but when Tim opened the door to them, a certain very excited collie came bounding out to greet them and Suzanne made sure she gave him plenty of attention. Christine came down the stairs in her robe to say 'hello,' and hear all about their trip.

The next morning, all the children were delighted with their presents from the Blue Ridge Mountains. Fortunately, none of them had woken when they arrived. Although Dalmar and Suzanne's siblings had missed their parents, especially at bedtime, the fact that their cousins were staying had helped enormously. Christine said hardly a cross word had been said between them. There had only been minor bickering between the two youngest.

Dalmar had to cope with messages from Jack Twentyman and Brian Cussen. The latter would not be surfacing until later and Jack was not due until mid-morning. However, he was pleased to find only normal Monday morning administration requirements pending; everything had run smoothly in his absence – more or less. Anyway, there was nothing urgent to fret about just then.

CHAPTER THIRTEEN

"A MERCILESS, PERILOUS INLAND WATERWAY."

As soon as she could, Suzanne went over to the animal centre to see how Beatrice and her holiday students had got on in her absence.

Sadly, one of the ewes in the meadow had passed away due to a sudden illness and her lamb still required some mother's nourishment to supplement her grazing diet. This was being done at the centre by bottle feeding. They brought the lamb in at night to give it protection from foxes and other predators: so far, it was surviving without too much distress. There were some new residents, yet another hedgehog, a pigeon with a broken wing, which was not expected to survive and two other smaller birds with leg injuries. These latter two, hopefully, when healed, would learn to adapt to life with one leg.

When Jack Twentyman arrived, he had nothing untoward to relay to his curator, but he was full of curiosity to learn all the details about the trip and its main purpose. Dalmar brought him up to date and with only four weeks to go before David Fresher arrived, they decided to leave all the available material, including the box, for his attention before passing them on to other interested parties.

When Dalmar broached the subject concerning Suzanne's equestrian suggestion, much to his amazement, considering how his superiors had been so cautious at the animal centre inception, Jack was enthusiastic and promised to look into a budget proposal. He also agreed that Roz Maidment should be sounded out, because without somebody able to run the operation professionally, it would never get off the ground. Too much specialist knowledge was required: horse acquisition and husbandry, teaching, equipment – just to identify a few.

Tim and Christine Westward stayed on until the end of the week. This meant that they could take Emma and Michael with them on holiday sightseeing trips, thus helping out their mum and dad, and, in turn, Suzanne kept them comfortable at the Dower-house: a very amicable arrangement considering they all got on so well.

Suzanne sent a long letter of appreciation to Justin and Emily in the States. She inserted it in a package containing information about Bray Castle, together with an invitation to come and stay sometime in the future. If, at that time, they were no longer the resident curators, she was sure accommodation could be made available. She also sent some candy for the girls and a large bar of Kendal mint cake for the adults. She hoped that it would clear U.S. customs inspection.

Roz received a message from Suzanne, the next day, on her answer phone, while she was at work, informing her that they had returned from the States. When Roz called back it was later in the day. "How are you managing?" Suzanne came straight to the point.

"To be honest – crap;" there was a sigh. "To be expected I suppose." The poor lady sounded as though she meant it. They talked about the situation, in general, after Jacob's death. Then Suzanne asked her if she had thought about getting involved in a project. "Yea – actually, Frank and I have launched a new charity. We have called it the J.M. Fund for seriously ill children – not exclusively terminal cases. We are trying to think up ways of fund raising to get it off the ground."

This took Suzanne by surprise. Her intention was to announce the plans for the equestrian centre in order to provide a distraction from her grief. The charity would be doing just that; also, at the same time, fulfilling a need to assist others in a similar plight to their own recent experience. Suzanne decided to leave mentioning the equestrian project for the moment and invited Roz over after her stint at work on Friday afternoon.

Tim and Christine, Dalmar and Suzanne were enjoying a glass of wine before their evening meal on Thursday. They were seated outside in the late day August sunshine looking over Lastwater and the distant fells. It was a scene none of them ever tired of. Fly lay stretched out on the grass, apparently asleep. "So," broached Tim Westward, "you reckon you are pretty well armed with information to help David when he arrives in just – what – about a month's time – isn't it?"

Dalmar hesitated before replying. "Actually – I think we have done our bit, if you know what I mean. Whether he can use any of it remains to be seen."

Christine interjected. "You have interviewed the farm people at the end of the lake, you have seen this Dread girl; you have been to the United States! For God's sake – done enough! I should say so. Mind – I find it infinitely amusing that you fly across the Atlantic ocean in order to discover the secret of Lastwater, and come back with an empty box and some dog eared papers no one can understand – plus – as a direct result of this trip, Suz here comes up with the brilliant idea for horsey stuff right here."

Tim coughed on his wine. "Only because she got the vibes at the horse farm – it would probably have happened sooner or later in my opinion. She didn't have to go half across the world."

"It was the sheer exhilaration I felt at the horse farm that got me going Timothy!" This was followed by an exasperated sigh. "Oh – you wouldn't understand." She looked at her sister-in-law for sympathy and got it. Anyway, after the ribaldry, everyone agreed that it was a good suggestion and they all drank a toast to its birth.

In the morning, the Westwards prepared to leave on the long journey to return to Southern England. Everyone felt sad. It was as though they were subconsciously aware, particularly the grown-ups, of impending trials on the horizon. Christine made a point of taking Dalmar's hands in her own; looking him in the eyes and imploring him to be careful. Once on their way, Tim asked her about it. "Don't know," she said. "Felt a wobble in the family security – particularly where he is concerned." She shrugged her shoulders not being able to add anything further.

That afternoon, Roz knocked on the door of the Dower-house door, fittingly, still wearing jodhpurs from her morning session at work. Her long pale hair whispered about in the strong breeze, strands of it had stuck to her lips which she brushed aside deftly. She was smiling bravely, and it helped illuminate her wan face a little.

Over the next hour, Suzanne finally got around to telling Roz about Bray Castle's proposed equestrian project. "Fancy the job of running it?" asked Suzanne straight out.

Roz was dumbfounded. At first, she could only think that this might interfere with the running of Jacob's charity, then as time passed and the two of them thoroughly discussed the implications, in that she would not be expected to work seven days a week. Help would be at hand and that help would be trained and managed by her in the shape of qualified students seeking part time occupation, and by existing staff at Bray, including Suzanne herself. Gradually, the sheer excitement of bringing the venture to fruition got the better of Roz. She still had the presence of mind to want to discuss it with her husband before committing herself, but, in reality, it was just what she needed. There was no doubt that she was ably qualified to carry it out. Despite the offers of assistance from Suzanne, to start with, until business had built up, she was quite sure she could manage it on her own, by limiting the days when the service would be available, provided the animal's welfare was looked after seven days a week. The priority was to get the old stable housing up to modern day standards, most importantly as regards the comfort and safety of its new occupants. Until the National Trust had given a definite go ahead, Suzanne suggested she kept the matter secret apart from her impending talk with Frank.

Dalmar arrived in time to see Roz before she left. He greeted her warmly. "Roz – really wanted to see you. Got an idea." He seated himself down and then said, looking at her expectant facial expression, "You need to raise funds for your son's charity. I have a suggestion that should bring in quite a bit."

"Oh, and what is that?" asked Suzanne puzzled. He had not mentioned anything to her. Poor Roz was beginning to wonder if she could take any more *great ideas* just now.

"A sponsored swim. I intend to swim from the eastern end of this lake to Shimdorie Island and back."

"What!" Suzanne almost shouted in her disbelief.

Rather stupidly her husband said, "Good one – yes?"

"No," immediately said Roz. "Sorry – I won't hear of it."

"For heaven's sake Dalmar; you must be joking. You have responsibilities. You cannot go diving – Into what has been labelled a merciless, perilous inland waterway. Don't be an idiot!"

"Actually, you didn't know but ...." Dalmar said this in an off-hand manner, "Last summer I swam from Cloud Point to Shimdorie Island and back – twice." And then, as an afterthought, while the two ladies were staring at him, he added, "On different occasions – of course."

Due to the lake's dubious history nobody went swimming in it. Nobody – ever!

"Oh – give me strength!" exclaimed his wife.

Undaunted, Dalmar carried on. "Look – I would arrange for rescue boats to be on stand-by – at no cost – and it would raise a lot of dough – you must admit, provided we spread the word.

"The nine young men who were lost earlier this year – *actually* – were in a boat," commented his wife succinctly, while apparently, studying the fingernails of her right hand.

Roz's initial dismay began to subside as it dawned on her the potential for acquiring a large sum in a short space of time, so that the fund could really start working. Her original alarm over safety had been checked when Dalmar mentioned the stand-by boats in the plural. She kept quiet, waiting to see if Suzanne would acquiesce.

"Darling," Dalmar appealed to his wife, "I would not put myself foolishly at risk, I assure you. I have given it a great deal of thought. It is the superstition people have about Lastwater I am playing on. There should be no risk if things are properly handled simply because I am a good distance swimmer. Also, I have no intention of venturing along the southern shore of the island. Plus, I have a contact in Carlisle who may be able to help with the press, and your connections with the television company should be invaluable."

Suzanne gradually started to see the logic; her initial panic subsiding. Her facial muscles went from high tension to awareness. However, her eyes sparkled dangerously like a female tiger at bay.

Dalmar let her think for a little while before asking tentatively, "Do you see?"

"Yes – damn you," she replied in a very soft tone, giving Roz a whimsical grin. And then she thought she would shock him by asking a simple question ... "When?"

His reply astounded her. "Ah – given that a lot of thought as well. To avoid unnecessary crowds causing hindrance it would be better carried out on a weekday, and preferably before David Fresher arrives, so that his studies are not disturbed."

Suzanne wanted to suggest it be done some time after the freshwater geologist's visit, but she immediately realised that winter might arrive by then. Also – 'the sooner the better for the charity's sake, which was the whole object of the exercise,' she further considered.

Roz lent across in her chair and spoke almost in

confidence to Suzanne, "Are you sure?" Then thinking on, "Tell you what, chew it over for a couple of days. Won't hurt."

"Nope – he'll be okay." She laid a hand on Roz's arm. "I just panicked – being over cautious I guess."

Roz looked intently at her. "No, you weren't," she said. "You can never be that."

In the early evening, Dalmar spent more time with his children than he normally did trying to make up for lost time. Michael was given a treat trying to catch a table-tennis ball his father kept lobbing him from a pile of plenty, although, his father kept a watchful eye making sure the little boy did not attempt to put one in his mouth. Additionally, Emma enjoyed an extra-long bed-time story.

Afterwards, he asked his wife if she had had a moment to broach the subject of Lastwater's lack of a river outflow to his brother. Being a geologist, he might have the answer. "You must be joking," was her reply. "I wasn't going to give Tim the chance to tease me. There is probably a very simple explanation. Thought I would leave it until David Fresher gets here." Dalmar nodded, but he felt disappointed. Tim would have been sure to have known and he had deliberately left the matter alone, given that it was Suzanne who had originally come up with the quandary.

The next day, in the afternoon, he asked Brian Cussen if he had any knowledge about it. Brian looked baffled to start with. However, this was not due to ignorance; it was purely because, as concerns Lastwater, he had never noticed the geographical oddity. Eventually he said, "Actually I do have knowledge of something similar. While spending some time in Canada many years ago, I learnt that there are one or two lakes in British Columbia with no obvious outflow. It is believed that water runs away underground to join tributaries of other rivers."

Dalmar nodded. "I rather thought that might be the case. Otherwise Lastwater would be an oversized pond," he added with a smile.

The four surviving nuthatch fledglings now looked like young adult birds. Their plumage showed off the contrast between the orange undercarriage and the slate grey backs associated with the breed. It was time to entice them to learn to fly. There was no going back on this. After shepherding and encouraging them to fly by gentle handheld launches, they would have to fend for themselves in the estate's wooded areas. Emma, who, proudly, had patiently carried out thrice daily feedings for some time, invited little Michael along with his mother to share in the occasion, although he was a little too young to fully understand. All went remarkably well. Two of the nuthatches took to flight at once. They did not go too far, but they were competent. The other two took rather longer with lots of flapping about inexpertly on the ground, but after about the sixth attempt all four of the birds had disappeared from view amongst the shrubbery. It was time to leave them to it, although Emma was naturally very reluctant.

There was no need to inform the children, but the reality was that not all of them would survive. They would have to run the gauntlet of birds of prey and land-based predators until they were more competent at looking after themselves. With the natural shortage of their species in the area, it might be difficult to find a mate, even if they survived the winter. But matters had to start somewhere, and somehow.

Dalmar, Frank, Roz and Suzanne wasted no time in getting things together to organise the sponsored swim. Before proceeding, Dalmar checked with Jack Twentyman that the national Trust would have no objection, and, also, with the Lake District park authorities. There seemed to be no problems providing that a safety boats were arranged. In fact, both organisations were positive in their outlook. Jack volunteered to stand in for Dalmar at Bray Castle on the day and the National Park offered to provide personnel to man the safety boat. They had an inflatable of their own with an outboard motor.

The two couples held a meeting at the Dower-house on

the following Monday evening after the children had been put to bed. The date agreed upon to hold the event was Friday 24th September; the day before David Fresher was due to arrive.

Dalmar and Suzanne would handle publicity with the media, while Frank and Roz would concentrate on local fundraising in the area. Collection boxes had already been put in place in various public buildings and a few amenity shops had them on display in Grasmere and Ambleside. An attempt would be made to add Bowness, Windermere and Keswick before the event.

Dalmar had to ensure that the course was clearly understood by all. He would enter the water at the little shingle beech by the eastern car park and swim toward Shimdorie Island. Someone would be on the island to check landing and provide some king of refreshment, probably just a drink.

Needless to say, it being a school holiday time, Emma overheard talk at the castle about her dad's forthcoming swim. She was not in the least worried and jumped up and down with excitement when her mother confirmed it.

Dalmar's one and only call to canvas the media was to the teacher at the Carlisle secondary school, Mike Parsons, and particularly requested if he had any contacts with the press. Mike said he was busy just at that time but would get back to him. Considering that the teacher was not working due to the summer school holidays, or so Dalmar thought, he was a little disappointed at the immediate lack of enthusiasm. The next morning, he received a gratifying surprise. Not only had Mike contacted a local newspaper group who were willing to inform, not just Carlisle, but all the towns in the north-west of England as well. Also, much to Dalmar's amazement, Mike said he would like to participate as a swimmer.

Why Dalmar should have thought he would be the only sponsored swimmer was something of a mystery, because as soon as Lastwater Rowing Club got to know about it, two of their young men, both extremely strong and competent swimmers, volunteered as well. And then one of Frank Maidment's work colleagues asked if his seventy-two-year-old father could have a go. It would not be just his age that would be the draw; as a much younger man he had once swum the English Channel!

Dalmar began to panic. As a breaststroke swimmer he might well come in last. The two rowing club members would be bound to be first. Although he knew nothing about Mike Parsons' capabilities, it would not surprise him if he would easily out-perform him in terms of speed. 'Why would he have volunteered if he was not an accomplished swimmer? Oh well, grin and bear,' Dalmar thought to himself.

Suzanne's efforts with local television and radio organisations were proving enormously fruitful. Everyone pledged their help by informing the general public in appropriate programs from now until the date of the swim.

The Maidment's activities with point of sale marketing were progressing well. Keswick was now well represented. This left only the more local towns at the southern end of Lake Windermere. It was still a big task; however, they were both confident of finishing in time.

CHAPTER FOURTEEN

JUST THEN – IT STARTED TO RAIN.

A couple of weeks before Emma started school, Suzanne and Bea were discussing matters in the office she shared with her husband. It was mostly to do with feed supplies. Little Michael was playing happily on the floor with a new toy. He had just celebrated his fourth birthday and would be attending play school for the first time later in the week.

There was a tap on the door and a beaming Jack Twentyman entered. "Good morning," he said acknowledging both women saying at the same time. "I have some good news."

Dalmar was not present. He was out working with the ground staff on woodland management. "How are you Jack?" asked Suzanne in greeting, adding, "and the family?"

"All well, thank you. This little chap alright?" he said bending down to give Michael a gentle prod in the ribs. The boy was used to Jack by now and enjoyed his cheerfulness. The Regional Director received a cheeky giggle in response. "Look – can't stop – on my way to Keswick. Just thought you would like to know we have received clearance, in principle, for the equestrian program."

Suzanne and Bea both gasped and showed faces full of smiles. "Wow!" exclaimed Suzanne.

"So – we need to arrange a meeting to get things started. Get that husband of yours to give me a call," said Jack.

"Okay," Suzanne replied showing exultance in her manner. Jack stayed on for five minutes chatting to the excited girls. He declined an offer of coffee pleading lateness for an appointment. Nevertheless, he still found time to stop his car and give Fly, who was doing his guard duty at the Dower-house, a short pet. He loved that dog. Fly

146

responded with a gentle "gruff" and stuck his nose in his face. Ever since they had first met, over two years ago, the dog had taken to the older man.

The only difficulty encountered by Roz during the organisational endeavour for the sponsored swim was bureaucratic. Local government expressed their concern over safety measures. It took many anxious telephone calls before they got the go ahead to hold the charity event. All kinds of other difficulties evaporated whenever the reason behind the sponsored swim was mentioned. Cost free assistance with poster advertising. Broadcasting details regularly on local radio and television and announcements in newspapers – all this bumped up the pledges of support made by the general public and local businesses for all five of the swimming participants. Of great assistance was the offer of a Cumbrian radio station to take payments by credit card on the day of the event thus creating a live broadcast, on and off, throughout. This news made Dalmar even more anxious. However, he kept it to himself. *And still bringing up the rear the curator of ...* He could hear it loud and clear in his brain.

With only a week and a half to go before the swim, Jack, Dalmar and Suzanne sat down to come up with a program to launch the equestrian activity at Bray Castle.

It was agreed that the accommodation in the stable block could sensibly house six ponies. This would suffice to start with. Pastureland was available on the grassland below the front of the castle stretching down to the lake shore. The sheep currently grazing there would be moved to join the others on the eastern side of the woodland. Initially, the object would be to create a riding school and, when ready, pony trekking could take place on the lower fells in the area. Roz Maidment had agreed to become the stables manager, but it had yet to be decided when she would start.

Dalmar suggested that the stable house renovation should take place immediately and he volunteered to get builder's estimates. Suzanne was qualified to ensure that the rejuvenated accommodation met modern day standards for the pony's welfare and, anyway, privately, she fully intended to consult Roz.

Three building firms came at different times to get details for providing an estimate of cost. All of them gave the opinion that the actual structure was sound. However, one advised that the entire roof should be replaced and would quote accordingly, but the other two considered that satisfactory repairs could be affected using local slate. They were asked to provide estimates for converting the existing internal partitioning and adjoining corridor using one entrance, to six individual stables with their own separate stable doors. This would provide more space and light for each animal. The only part that required very little attention was the tack room. Dalmar reckoned his staff could sort out repairs to some of the carpentry.

The Hunter family managed to get time off on Saturday to do a much-needed clothes shopping trip to Windermere town, and then, as a treat, they went for a boat trip on the lake around Belle Island and back, eating a snack tea en-route. Fly did not show much appreciation. He could not go anywhere on the boat and spent most of the time grunting his disapproval, occasionally snuffling the air from the ship's rail.

Dalmar felt frustration and anger the evening before the sponsored swimming event. Everything was ready – everything except the weather. The Lake District had enjoyed an uninterrupted seven days of fine weather. Now – looking at the forecast on the television, he felt cheated. A deep low-pressure system, at this moment over Ireland, would be bringing wet weather to Cumbria. The cold front would pass over during the night with plenty of rain. There would then be a short respite before the warm front would follow bringing heavy downpours. 'Just about the time when the swimmers were due to enter the water,' Dalmar thought to himself.

When Suzanne suggested a few hours postponement

he dismissed the idea immediately. Too much was riding on promptness. "Anyway, what's a bit of rain when we will be immersed in the stuff?" he said emphatically. Suzanne was actually thinking about the backup team and the spectators, but she did not say anything.

In the morning the forecast had, so far, proved to be correct. It had rained a great deal during the night and although it had now abated, there was a grey damp atmosphere in the air. As Dalmar looked out over the lake from his bedroom window he was puzzled by something. Normally, under these conditions, the water would take on a variance of hues from opaque gun-metal to grey. Today, it had a definite slate greenness about it. He shrugged his shoulders, 'light plays tricks,' he considered. He remained there looking at it for quite a while. It had a certain beauty. This lake never ceased to offer surprises. One bonus factor had not escaped him – the air was mild. 'A long swim in September's temperatures would be cold, so with the outside air a little warmer than usual – well – it all helped.'

Having made sure everything was satisfactory at the animal centre and that Jack Twentyman was on hand, as promised, the Hunter's, complete with children and Fly, drove over to the start point for the swim around ten-thirty in the morning.

Frank Maidment had been given time off from his employment, not just to help, but, also, to give a lift to John Precence, the pensioner who was having a go. His wife, some five years older than him, was suffering from a heavy cold and needed to stay at home. Reports indicated that John had more sponsorship money riding on him than anyone else. By the time Dalmar, Suzanne and the children had arrived; Roz and Frank had already set up a table displaying information about the charity. They introduced the extremely agile pensioner to them. The children giggled at him as he joked and played the clown with them.

Collection boxes were at hand to tempt any spectators that might come. Two people from St John's Ambulance had pitched a tent to house first aid items and survival blankets.

Michael and Emma were very excited, but generally spent most of the next half an hour agog at the television crews setting up their equipment before they interviewed Rosalind Maidment. It would be a recording. Highlights of the event would be edited for the evening news programs. It has to be said that they could hardly have had someone more photogenic than Roz. She was quite a discovery and her appearance on the little screen would do wonders for the J.M.Fund. Going out live right now, interspersed with music, was a Cumbrian radio station broadcast, the very one who had volunteered to take listeners card donations by telephone. They had a two-man crew here relaying interviews and information back to the station.

With the arrival of the two rowing club members, Spencer and Toby, everything was ready for the off. It was to be expected, but they were very well built and presented striking torsos in their swimming costumes.

Mike and John were the only two who needed the course pointed out to them. It might seem straightforward to the others, but to them Shimdorie Island was not obvious, nestling half a mile away toward the southern bank of the lake.

The car park had only a few vehicles in it when the Hunters arrived, Dalmar was surprised to see it was now full – or so it looked from his vantage point. He got an even greater shock when he looked along the banks of the lake going away on either side. He could not believe it at first. It looked like the kind of shot often seen in Western films when the Indians first appear on the ridge. The fact was that a handful of swimmers engaged on a sponsored swim were not a major attraction. What had caused this turn out? The answer was because it was here. Because, earlier on this year, nine young men were lost *here*, because three years previously three students from the outward-bound school vanished *here*, and, because twenty-six years ago a scout and scout leader disappeared *here* – Lastwater – that was why. Dalmar started to develop an uncomfortable feeling.

At five minutes to eleven all the swimmers were ready in their swimming attire. John Precence took the starring role. He had dressed for the part in a 1930's style all in one striped costume. With his heavy moustache and full grey hair, he looked the part. He might be seventy-two years old, but his body appeared to belong to a younger person. There was no doubt about it, he looked superbly fit.

Mike Parsons was quite a powerfully built man. This made Dalmar the one with the lightest physique, although hardly unattractive with his square shoulders, height, dark slightly too long hair and litheness. 'Coming in last was now a distinct possibility,' he thought, and, although the object was not to race, but to finish, he was concerned.

Frank sounded a gong, placed on their table, to signify the hour of eleven. Spencer and Toby immediately swept in off the steeply shelving beach to applause from the spectators and straight away, on surfacing, shook the water off their heads, commencing a rhythmic relaxed freestyle stroke. They were twenty-five yards out in no time.

Fortunately, the rain, so far, had held off, although judging by the dark grey clouds looming over the western fells, it would not be for long. At least the spectators looked dressed for the part. Most of the onlookers, especially the children, were wearing rain proof gear.

The Lake District National Park inflatable had already been launched from the rowing club's jetty. Its outboard motor could be heard droning away as it headed out in order to keep in touch with the lead swimmers.

Bray Castle's rowing boat manned by Trevor and a new employee on the estate's ground staff, Pat, were making their way over to Shimdorie Island to meet the first swimmers expected to arrive in under an hour. When they embarked in the boat from the boathouse, Trevor noticed that the water level had risen about four inches up the scale on the post by the jetty. He was sure it had been normal yesterday, when they rowed out to the island to make sure there were no plastic bottles, bags or other litter floating about by the swimmer's landing area. He put it down to the large amount of rain that fell during the night, and now evidenced by the full tumbling gills pouring water into the lake off the fells. Had he thought more about it, he would have realised that heavy overnight rain could not possibly account for that much of a rise in the water level of the lake in such a short time, and he did think to himself 'wasn't there something familiar about this?'

Much to Emma's delight, her father climbed onto a low rocky outcrop at the right-hand side of the beach and stood at the edge now wearing a pair of dark blue trunks. He had spotted this situation while out walking with his dog. He executed a reasonably neat dive, gasping at the sudden chill to his body before rising to commence a measured, almost lazy, breaststroke swim. He could hear Fly barking behind him, held fast on his lead by Suzanne otherwise he would have been sure to have chased after his master.

Mike Parsons followed immediately behind Dalmar in bright red swimming trunks. Like Spencer and Toby, he was wearing goggles. On glancing behind him Dalmar was relieved to see Mike using the breaststroke as well. He trod water for a moment to allow the other man to catch up, so they could swim together side by side.

The two men heard a cheer go up from the watching crowd as John Precence entered the water, and, it seemed only a short while before he came slowly cruising past them. He was using an amazingly effective long action over-arm executed with a half body roll between each stroke, while drawing exaggerated gulps of air every now and again. Dalmar was full of admiration. He was like a machine and looked as though he could keep going for a long time.

After a couple of minutes both Mike and Dalmar had warmed up and it was just a question of keeping going. At the moment, the distant island looked just as far away as when they started. Dalmar turned to look back. They had made some three hundred yards and already the people gathered around the start were beginning to diminish. Before he turned back, he caught a glimpse of Emma and Michael waving after him, standing on the rock from which he had plunged in a short while ago. He put an arm into the air hoping they would see. As he did so, his head went under and he swallowed a small amount of water. He could have sworn he tasted salt.

On the roof of Bray Castle, Brian Cussen and some of the staff had a distant view of the swimmers entering the water. Brian had not gone to the trouble of bringing the big telescope out, especially in view of the inclement weather looming, but he did have a couple of pairs of powerful binoculars. In the mild conditions, with the lack of sunlight, vision was clear. Brian remarked to Edna, one of the volunteer reception staff and the weekday chef Sally Jarvis, that the lake was an unusual colour.

"You know, I thought that," agreed Sally. "Darn me if it don't look like pea soup."

"Bet it doesn't taste like it," laughed Edna.

Shortly after this, the two ladies had to return to their duties.

The large crowd of spectators dispersed considerably during the first leg of the swim. Most of them decided to walk along the northern shore keeping abreast of the last pair of bobbing heads as they made their way diagonally across the lake towards Shimdorie Island. Dalmar and Mike kept up quite a conversation once they had both settled into a rhythm. There did not seem to be a breath of wind and this made talking a lot easier without the odd gulp of unwanted water caused by a disturbed surface.

The inflatable, keeping its distance was always a little way behind them. It was manned by two national park wardens who appeared, from Dalmar's occasional glimpses, to be consuming, between them, an enormous bar of chocolate. It made Dalmar's palette agitate.

It only took Spencer and Toby a little under forty

minutes to reach the island; the distance being just over half a mile, so it was a good effort. They were directed ashore where the rowing boat was tethered, and Trevor and Pat were waiting. Both men accepted a banana and a drink of water pushing their goggles up onto their foreheads as they did so. Although offered a towel each, they waved them aside and started on the return journey after only a short break.

When they met Dalmar and Mike coming in the opposite direction neither of them faltered with their swimming actions. Spencer grinned and Toby gave the breaststroke swimmers a single raised thumb.

By the time Dalmar and Mike arrived they found Trevor leaning over John Precense. He was sitting on the ground in a stony area, away from the wet grass, looking exhausted. Dalmar immediately suggested that he take a ride back in the rowing boat. He was not greeted with any reply, just an exasperated look from the older man. It rather looked as though, this time, John might have exceeded his body's capabilities. He had so far declined any nourishment, but when he witnessed Mike chomping up a banana, he changed his mind.

Just then – it started to rain.

CHAPTER FIFTEEN

... LIKE A CORK IN A FAST-FLOWING STREAM.

To start with it was just a gentle autumnal rain.

Mike Parsons managed to get John Precense into conversation as he sat there under the foil survival blanket. Dalmar and Mike had both been given towels as soon as they waded ashore. The former had not planned to stay long, hoping to make a quick turnaround, but as soon as he saw John's condition, he changed his mind. It soon became apparent that the senior citizen's problem was just an age thing. He merely needed time to recover. The food and drink helped dramatically.

Despite Mike's pleadings to John that he should return in the rowing boat with them, he insisted he would be alright and knew what he was doing. "Be off with you," he said waving a hand to suggest that the other two swimmers get on with it and leave him alone.

Dalmar had a quiet word with Trevor. "Stick with him. Don't let him out of your sight. Okay?"

Trevor completely understood. He had no intention of doing anything else.

As Dalmar and Mike prepared themselves for the return lap – down it came. Some people would call it a cloudburst. Whatever it was – it was torrential. Dalmar threw the towels at Pat and he and Mike launched themselves into the water.

There was no point in hanging about.

Trevor grabbed two golfing style umbrellas from the boat. He opened one and passed it to John who took hold of it gratefully. That rain was cold. The two Bray Castle ground staff sheltered under the other.

On the roof of the castle, Brian, now with Jack Twentyman who had come up for a look, ran for shelter. The other staff had already gone below. The two of them used the observatory intending to stay there until the squall had passed.

With the downpour came turbulence on the water. Conditions were now much more severe for the swimmers – all of them.

While John was sitting it out hoping for a lull, Spencer and Toby already well on their way for the return leg were openly cursing the sudden change in the conditions. They found it difficult to see very far ahead with all the spray and choppiness. Both just gritted their teeth and pressed on, if anything, faster than they had been progressing before despite the extra strain.

For the two breast-stroke swimmers' things were not quite so bad simply because they were pushing ahead with their heads raised. However, their pace had definitely slowed.

Jack and Brian eventually decided to give up their roof observation, especially as visibility over the lake was seriously hampered due to the driving curtains of rain slanting, in frequent intervals, right across the water from west to east.

At the eastern shingle beach, magically, nobody was to be seen; just some media equipment with rainproof covers over them and the charity's table, minus paperwork and promotional material, remained out in the open. All the spectators had retreated to their vehicles for shelter. Suzanne, her children, Roz and Frank plus Fly were steaming up the windows of the Land Rover. They knew that in a while they would have to get out so to assist the swimmers on their return.

John Precense finally rose to his feet and made straight for the water's edge. He was off and into his classic over-arm style before Trevor and Pat had a chance to launch the rowing boat. First, they had to stow the wet towels, survival blankets and remaining food and water before they could do so. Trevor decided to make sure a lifejacket was immediately available in case he needed it by extracting one from the forehead locker. When they got going with an inch of water swishing about in the bottom of the boat, John was already one hundred and sixty yards out.

All went well for about five to seven minutes.

At first Trevor, who was rowing and desperately trying to get up alongside John Precense, put it down to a strong gust of wind. Then he realised it was something more than that. The rain was blowing towards them coming over Shimdorie Island, but the wind was not that strong. Visibility was awful because of the intensity of the downpour but that was all. Why then, did the left-hand oar threaten to be torn from his hand. The unseen force must be coming from under the water. He had to use all his considerable strength just to pull on the oars while remaining virtually stationary; otherwise the boat would be drawn back towards the island. It all happened so fast he did not have time to cry out. It was Pat who shouted. Going past them on their port side was John Precense – in the wrong direction! He was still attempting to swim strongly in the right direction, but it made no difference. His body was being swept backwards in some kind of powerful current. Actually, John did not know it was happening at first. It was not until he felt the power in the current along his body that he stopped swimming and looked about him in alarm. In the sudden heat of panic to his body his goggles misted up and he was swept away from the rowers like a cork in a fast-flowing stream.

Witnessing this, Trevor pulled his oars clear of the water fearing he might catch a crab. The boat seemed to take off after the swimmer. It became obvious, at once, that they were not heading back to the island, but toward its southern bank between it and Bray Castle's shore.

Dalmar and Mike felt the pull in the underwater force at the same time. Mike gulped out the words, "What the hell is going on?" From their position, a good quarter of the way on their return leg and further over towards the northern banks, approximately halfway across the lake as a whole, the power of the force was not anything like as strong as that experienced by the oarsman and John Precense.

Unlike Mike Parsons, Dalmar had a sudden feeling of foreboding. Could this be something to do with Lastwater's feared anomaly? He shouted at Mike above the noise of the wind and the driving rain. "Forget the finishing place Mike! Head for that shore!" He pointed with an outstretched arm at the nearest bank.

As he did so, the strength of his swimming obviously slackened, and he felt himself immediately pulled back. He did not wait for Mike to reply and struck out in the direction he had indicated. At times it seemed that although they were swimming hard, they were not advancing in the direction they wanted to go. There was a panicky feeling that they might be dragged backwards and what that might lead to. Adrenalin powered up their muscles as they pulled with their arms and kicked with their legs. Without knowing why, Mike was fully aware that he must not allow the powerful current to beat him. Both of them experienced the odd coughing fit as the exertion caused them to take unwanted mouthfuls of water not helped by the increased swell. If it was not that, they kept getting temporarily blinded and Dalmar wished fervently that he had worn goggles.

To say that Mike was baffled would be an understatement. He was completely confused. There was this strange current trying to take him in a direction he did not want to go, and Dalmar shouting instructions as though he knew what was going on. Trusting the other man, he followed, but now resorted to the more powerful over-arm stroke. Dalmar did the same.

Both swimmers found themselves making progress in the direction they wished to go, but, at the same time, they were drifting west. Fortunately, this did not last for long and they were finally able to head directly north, but that pull on their legs was still there, and, if anything, getting stronger, or were they getting weaker?

Suzanne felt apprehensive. She tried not to show her concern in front of Roz, Frank and the children. It was due to the fact that she could not see anything out on the lake because of the rainstorm. Every now and then she rubbed a cloth over the misted-up Land Rover's windscreen, but it was no use. A noise cheered her – the sound of an outboard motor out on the lake. If the National Park inflatable was out there, everything should be okay.

Spencer and Toby could just make out their beach destination peering through the miniature rain fountains in front of them, when both men felt a strange force trying to stop them. It was not of any consequence and they were able to shrug it off. Eventually, after another ten minutes, they approached the deep shelve of the beach itself and soon found themselves at waist height. Spencer let his right-hand trail in the water. He was surprised to see it move backwards, almost as though on a seashore as the sea recedes after an incoming wave

There was a ripple of applause to greet them as Frank and a few stalwart spectators greeted them. Both men declined offered survival blankets but accepted towels gratefully.

In the meantime, the men on the inflatable watched the two lead swimmers clamber out of the water from a distance, and then set off to intercept the breaststroke swimmers and John Precense. Despite the poor visibility, they were surprised that they could not see any sign of them. Immediately, they put up full throttle and started back towards the island. To their astonishment they appeared to be going rather fast. This became alarming when they realised how unnatural it was. George, the man on the tiller cut the engine. Even when the continuing propulsion caused had long passed normality, the boat was still travelling back towards the centre of the lake.

At that moment, the rain eased, the wind dropped, and the poor visibility lifted. Greg, the other crewman called out, "Look, over there!" They were just in time to witness Dalmar and Mike clambering up a steep bank on the northern shore, half hidden by the lower branches of a tall Rowan tree. George pulled the cord to start the outboard again. As they made progress across towards the two simmers, they felt the pull of the current, this time, trying to hinder them, although it seemed to be losing its power all the time.

At some stage George began to have doubts about what they were doing. "What about the old guy?" he said out loud. Both men looked over their shoulder towards the island.

It was Greg who said it first. "Where the hell is the rowing dingy?" They could clearly see the little landing area where it had been. It was deserted.

"Let's check that those two are alright first. If they are, we can leave them to make their own way back and go and look for the dingy. Okay?" shouted George.

"Yup – sounds right to me," agreed the other man.

Seeing the inflatable approaching, Dalmar and Mike stayed on the bank. When they got within hailing distance, George cupped his hands together and shouted, "Are you both okay?"

Dalmar gave him the thumbs up. Then, thinking on he shouted back, "Has that undertow gone yet?"

"All but," George yelled back, without really understanding fully. "Where is the dingy?"

"Should be escorting John Precense," Dalmar shouted as loud as he could. "He was very tired. Why?"

George realised what had probably happened. 'Must have gone to Bray Castle,' he thought. He waved, without replying to Dalmar's question, turned the boat around and set off back towards the island at full speed.

"Thanks for the lift," Mike commented ruefully.

"Might as well complete the job then," Dalmar said with a sideways grin. He did not particularly want to get back into the cold water. On the other hand, he did not fancy making it barefoot back along the stony path. Because they had drifted some way down the northern bank; it was quite a way. Mike nodded his agreement and they set off in the water keeping close to the shore at first. The strange current they had experienced – had vanished.

With the abatement of the rain, Suzanne, Emma and little Michael came back to the beach and were disappointed not to see any swimmers approaching. They could see the inflatable heading across the lake towards the island, but nothing else. Roz joined them after helping Mike salvage items on their table they had not had a chance to remove when the downpour started. "Any sign of your husband?" she asked innocently. Suzanne gave her a look that showed concern. Roz caught her mood. 'Surely they must have set off on the return leg by now?' she thought to herself. "Do you think they sat it out on the island," she tried to ask helpfully?"

This thought had not occurred to Suzanne. She brightened and gave Roz a fisted nudge to her arm with a tight-lipped smile indicating gratitude

Emma, meanwhile, had gone back to her lookout post on the rock. "There they are," she shouted, pointing excitedly. The direction of her outstretched arm indicated the north shore.

Suzanne gasped when she saw the tiny heads of two figures swimming, a long way off, but coming towards them. Despite herself, she felt enormous relief.

The National Park inflatable was just rounding the eastern tip of Shimdorie Island. George had scanned the northern shore as they approached. There was no boat beached there. Cloud Point came into view first, and then the foreshore at Bray Castle leading to the jetty.

Apparently alongside the jetty, facing them was the

rowing dinghy.

To start with it looked as though that was that. But as the two men got nearer, they realised that the rowing boat was not tethered. It was just bobbing up against the wooden pier.

"That's odd," said George. "The crew work at Bray Castle. They must have left in a hurry. Can't see them leaving it adrift normally." Greg said nothing, merely wearing a frown on his forehead. Spotting that the water side doors to the boathouse were open, they pulled the dinghy around to the other side of the jetty and shepherded it into the boathouse. "Were the hell are the oars?" George scratched his chin. There did not appear, on a cursory inspection, to be anything else missing. Both rowlocks were in place and the fore and aft storage hatches were closed.

"Taken them with them?" Greg raised both eyebrows as he said this.

"Must have done," was George's brief acknowledgement. They decided to return to the start point and report their findings to the event organisers.

Ten minutes later they approached the little beach. The crowd of spectators had much diminished and there were now just a handful of people, plus the television and radio personnel still in evidence.

Spencer and Toby had departed, presumably to the rowing club. They had both been interviewed by the media who could now function properly, unhindered by rain. Up to now, no one was aware that something strange had happened. Neither of the two freestyle swimmers mentioned the strange undertow. It was hardly significant as far as their experience was concerned.

The inflatable arrived back just as Dalmar and Mike were swimming into the beach. George came alongside them having cut his boat's engine. As the bulbous prow drifted up to Dalmar, he burbled out the question, "Everything okay – how's John?"

"Sorry – no idea," George replied. "Your dinghy was

lying too against the pier at Bray Castle – untethered." He paused as Dalmar placed both arms over the side to allow him purchase while he floated alongside. "Must have taken the oars with them – nowhere to be seen. We put the dinghy inside your boathouse. The doors were open."

From a feeling of pleasure at having finally arrived back at the point where they had started from, and so fulfilling the sponsorship terms, Dalmar's face blanched. Trevor would never leave the boat untied. And he certainly would not take the oars with him. There was a perfectly good purpose-built rack out of the water in the boathouse. "Doesn't make any sense," he said to George and Greg. I'll have to get back pronto. Thanks for all you've done."

"Pleasure," said George. "Is that us done – then?"

"I reckon so. Might as well head back to the rowing club." Dalmar let go of the boat and managed a smile. George started up the engine and they set off at a subdued pace.

Mike was greeted with sporadic applause as was Dalmar when he walked out of the water behind him. When Suzanne handed him a towel and he had properly greeted his children, he said quickly for her ears only. "I am going to be delayed by the media. Get yourself and the children back to the castle quickly. I'll try and cadge a lift with Roz and Frank. There is something wrong." He briefly explained about the boat and John Precense's condition on the island. When she had taken it all in, Suzanne clung to her husband's arm in sheer apprehension. Then she let go and started marshalling her children, as best as possible, without causing a stir.

Before leaving she went up to Roz, who was about to be interviewed with Dalmar and explained that she was needed back at the castle. "Do me a favour, come back for a cup of tea and give my husband a lift – please?"

Roz gave her a smile and said, "Of course – don't worry – see you later."

A few minutes later, the Bray Castle Land Rover quietly

slipped out of the car park with two complaining children inside. They did not want to leave their daddy behind, and Fly seemed to be in sympathy with them.

CHAPTER SIXTEEN

"WHAT ABOUT THAT GASH ON THE BOW?"

"Here we have Dalmar Hunter, the curator of the National Trust's Bray Castle, one of the swimmers in this event." The speaker was Jane Derby, daughter of the rowing club member. She was the outside broadcast news presenter, on this occasion, for Cumbrian Television. "John Precense, the seventy-two-year-old swimmer has not yet returned and there doesn't appear to be any sign of him. Is he okay?" She asked this in a pleasant enough manner.

Dalmar had had a chance to get dressed. He felt a warm glow all over him after his long immersion in a cold September lake. "He reached the halfway point, that island over there in the distance, before Mike Parsons and myself." He pointed in the direction of Shimdorie Island so that the camera could pan out to it. "Unsurprisingly, he looked rather tired, so we suggested he return in one of the standby safety boats. I understand they have gone to Bray Castle."

Two young men and a woman, relations of John

Precense standing looking on, showed concern on their faces.

"You had quite a time out there, by the look of it," Jane carried on passing the microphone back and forth depending on who was speaking at the time. "That was some downpour. Went on for quite a while. It was so heavy we couldn't see anything from here."

"Yes." Dalmar wore a rueful smile. "Maybe we were in the best place."

Jane Derby laughed showing a glorious display of generous teeth against her tanned complexion. "We were puzzled as to why you returned along that far bank. Isn't that rather a long way round?"

"We experienced," Dalmar saw no reason why he should not reveal this, "a strong undercurrent sometime after we had set out on the return leg from the island. In fact, at times, it threatened to drag us back the way we had come it was so powerful. I could feel the pull against my body, particularly the legs. Swimming against it was very tiring and we found ourselves being swept down towards the other end of the lake – so we cut across towards the northern bank. Fortunately, we made it, although the National Park's inflatable was monitoring us."

"Do you think it might have been experienced by John Precense?"

"Possibly." Dalmar was cagey here. Even if John and the two Bray Castle employees had returned in the rowing dingy, they might still have experienced something unusual.

"What do you think caused it? Any ideas at all?"

The curator shrugged his shoulders and pursed his lips. "A freshwater geologist is coming to stay at Bray Castle at our invitation. Let us hope he will come up with an answer."

"Is he going to investigate the reason for the disappearance of the rowing eight earlier this year?"

"Yes – and the other mysterious events involving missing persons on the lake, over the years, where no bodies have ever been recovered."

Sensing an enticing documentary here Jane decided not to progress with this line of questioning right now. "Congratulations on successfully completing the swim – and – Mike is it?" She indicated Mike Parsons standing in the background. He smiled bashfully at the camera. "We will let you go and get some well-deserved refreshment." She moved the microphone towards Rosalind Maidment. "How do you think it all went?"

Roz seemed born for this. During the morning's interview it had been explained who she was, the mother of Jacob Maidment who had died of a rare form of cancer not long ago. She told them that she and her husband had felt drawn to start the charity, which this event's donations were supporting, in order to provide financial assistance for seriously ill children and their parents, so that they could be made as comfortable as possible. "Despite the awful weather," she began, "sponsorship for all five swimmers has been beyond our wildest dreams."

Dalmar left Roz to it and went to help Frank pack up. Mike Parsons came over and he made introductions. "Have you come on your own?" Frank was curious.

"Yes – my fiancée is away on a course with her employers. Some kind of training program," Mike explained. "Don't suppose you could find the time to give me a call later?" he asked looking at Dalmar. "Should like to know if John Precense has recovered."

Dalmar promised he would. Soon after this, Mike said his goodbyes and left, but not before Roz and Frank had had a chance to thank him profusely. He said he would be in touch when his sponsors had paid up.

Dalmar introduced himself to John Presence's relations and asked them if they would like to follow Frank, who had originally given John a lift to the event, back to Bray Castle where they could all meet up? They readily agreed to do so.

On the way back to Bray, Dalmar brought Frank and Roz up to date on the rowing dinghy conundrum.

Roz was shocked. She started to experience a feeling

of impending horror. It was accompanied by dull nausea in the pit of her stomach. She went quiet.

"Only explanation I can come up with," Frank sounded positive, "is that the oars were used to make the frame for a make-shift stretcher, clothing being used for the main support. In their haste they presumably forget to tie up the boat."

Dalmar was impressed. He had not thought of that. "You could well be right," he said gratefully. "Let's hope it isn't serious." He had been very worried about the possible connection to the strong current they had experienced, a diversion which Frank could not really comprehend. But the more he dwelt on Frank's reasoning – the more it made sense.

Roz, however, did not look convinced.

When they arrived at Bray Castle, Jack Twentyman was waiting for them, standing under the archway at the entrance. Looking at his face, Dalmar knew something awful had happened. It was as well the reception and daily catering staff had gone home.

This was the first time either Frank or Roz had seen Dalmar's superior. To start with, they did not know who he was. Jack was aware who was ferrying Dalmar back to the castle, but he decided that he must have a word with his curator first before saying hello.

As soon as Frank parked up, John's relatives arrived and parked alongside. Jack motioned to Dalmar through the car window, making it obvious that he needed to talk to him alone. As soon as his man had extricated himself from the passenger seat, Jack took his arm and led him through the right-hand side of the archway so that they could not be heard. "Suzanne tells me that Trevor brought the elderly swimmer back here because he was unable to continue. Is that correct?"

Dalmar did not have to think about it. "Possibly," he said aware that this was the second time in a short space of time he had made this reply on the same subject. "It was left to

John Precense to come to his own decision. I told Trevor to stick with him because the man was obviously exhausted. By the time I left for the return leg, John was showing signs of recovering."

Jack nodded. "Were they heading here or back to the start?"

"As far as I know - the start. That is where John would have wanted to go, to get a lift back to his home with Frank and Roz." Dalmar casually indicated their presence while they waited in their car. "Those other people are relatives of John Precence. George, in the National Park inflatable, reckons our lads might have given John a ride back here. He saw our boat down at the pier," he pointed towards the lake.

"I see," said Jack, the forefinger of his right hand was resting on his lowered chin; his eyes to the ground. He looked up. "Trevor, Pat and John Precense have vanished."

Dalmar's pallor went ashen. After a long silence, he said, almost stupidly, "They are not here?"

Jack looked at the younger man. "Our rowing boat – down at the jetty?"

"Yes."

"Well – that's it. No oars – nothing. Just the boat."

Dalmar started to get to grips with his responsibilities. "Anyone informed?"

"Yes – the police. They are on their way." The only other person who knows about this, apart from your wife, is Brian. We have asked around, of course, but no one in the castle or the kitchen has seen them. Your family are at home with Fly. Thought it best – the children…"

"Thanks," Dalmar said simply.

All the while this had been going on, Roz had been staring out of the car window trying to lip read or catch something from the two men's lowered tones. Her worst fears were beginning to be realised.

It was Jack who broke off the private conversation. He went straight to the rear of the Maidment's car and opened the door. "I am very pleased to meet you Rosalind, especially as you are going to be favouring us with your expertise in the not too distant future."

Roz was instantly charmed. She had expected to be a little intimidated and was pleasantly surprised. Nevertheless, she sensed the serious undertone. After saying how much she was looking forward to working here, she introduced her husband and then, at once, asked, "Is something wrong?"

Dalmar brought them both up to date with the terrible developments. He then informed Jack about the strange current they had experienced out on the lake.

Meanwhile the three relatives of John, after waiting patiently out of politeness in their car, decided it was time to get out and investigate. The next few minutes were not pleasant.

Although the police were due any moment, Dalmar felt the need to get out onto the water and search the area between the castle grounds and Shimdorie Island. This had to be where the three men had gone missing. Everyone knew this was also the part of the lake, from Cloud Point on, where the nine rowing club members had met their fate. Jack did not object, saying he would stay and meet the police when they arrived. Frank immediately volunteered to go with Dalmar. Roz might have been worried about this, but she said nothing, stating that she would go and help Suzanne with the children.

It was left to Jack to suggest to the distressed relatives that they head home – leaving a telephone number where they could be contacted. John's clothes and personal effects were transferred from the Maidment's Volvo to the relative's vehicle: a most unpleasant happening. It suddenly occurred to Roz that if John had been ferried to Bray – all he would have had to wear was his wet swimming costume. This train of thought ended abruptly, when the girl became overcome with distress, as the reality of the situation hit home. Roz had to spend a while comforting her in the back of their car. She was John Precence's twenty-two-year-old niece.

Frank and Dalmar jogged down the slate fragment path to the boathouse. The shore side door was locked; Dalmar had forgotten the key in his haste, so, instead, he waded into the water ignoring the cold wetness on his jeans and made his way through the lake-side double gate. A spare set of oars were kept in the dry section at the back. They were a bit short but would have to do. He climbed into the boat and coaxed it around with one oar, so that Frank could embark at the pier side. Before they could set off there was a bailing job to do; about two inches of water lying in the bilges. A pot was kept in the rear storage compartment for this purpose. Dalmar made short work of the task.

On the way Dalmar had a look at the water level reading on the marker post. It was normal.

They searched along the bank on the island's south side and went around to the landing area that had been used as the halfway point on the swim. There were no clues there.

While returning, Dalmar said to Frank that he wanted to cross over and look around the promontory known as Cloud Point. He pointed it out.

It was Frank who spotted it first: a bright orange object floating in the water someway out from the point. When they fished it out, it was instantly recognizable as a life jacket, and because it bore the words *BRAY CASTLE*, it was clear to Dalmar where it should belong; the very boat they were in. He immediately checked the forward storage hatch. The normal pair of lifejackets stored there had been reduced to one. "Pity no one was wearing it," he said aloud.

"This strong current you have been referring to," said Frank, "is it unusual?"

"Very," said Dalmar. "In my, admitted layman's opinion, it is the root cause of all the disappearances attributed to this lake going back in history. There are probably others, which we don't know anything about, such as, perhaps, a missing person out walking on the fells; on a hot day, could have chosen to take a dip to cool themselves off, actually more common in days of yore than now – I believe – before we had baths and so on." He finished by open palming his right hand in a, *for instance,* gesture.

As they approached the jetty at the boathouse three men were walking towards them. Jack Twentyman, Brian Cussen and Chief Constable George Lipoce.

When they arrived, Dalmar introduced Frank Maidment to the policeman and the astronomer.

The life jacket was inspected before the Chief Constable asked, "Is the boat damaged at all?"

Dalmar told him about the excess water in the bilges and the missing oars.

"What about that gash on the bow?" It was Brian Cussen speaking.

Dalmar and Frank looked puzzled. It was not, at first glance, immediately obvious, but it was there and definitely fresh. No one could come up with a reason for it, other than some sort of collision against a rock during whatever drama had befallen the crew.

After the two of them had secured the dingy back in the boat house, Dalmar found himself looking out over the water towards Shimdorie Island once again. Everything looked so normal. There was no sign that any trauma had taken place. It was as though the life in the lives' that were – had been transported far, far away. Dalmar shook himself and started to walk with Frank back to the castle turning his back on the lake.

It was now time to inform next of kin. This was Dalmar's direct responsibility.

And there was the media. Jack took charge of this aspect. His demeanour was especially suited to it. Nothing would be done in this direction until all next of kin had been notified.

Trevor Blake had been Head gardener at Bray Castle a little longer than Dalmar had been there. He had been immensely popular and was well thought of. His disappearance caused a lot of wet eyes among the staff when they were informed, some were in considerable distress for both Trevor and Pat.

Roz felt terrible, virtually ignoring Dalmar's attempt to comfort her by stating that it was not her suggestion to hold the sponsored swim and she, therefore, could not be held responsible. She was also informed that Trevor and Pat had volunteered to man the safety boat. They were not instructed to do so. Initially, Dalmar had tried to find helpers who were not employed at the castle.

Dalmar took full responsibility for the tragedy. It had been his idea. Although he was not liable in any way, within half an hour of the fateful tragedy having become apparent, he decided to resign from his position as curator. However, this would be done after his immediate responsibilities had been fulfilled over the next couple of days and the staff had settled. He, himself, was intensely sad about Trevor's disappearance. The two of them had worked well together, each respecting each other in their own fields. Pat Simpson had only recently been employed, but he had showed himself to be a very amiable young man.

As the telephone rang at Trevor's home, Dalmar replaced the receiver almost immediately. This was not the way. "Jack, I know you are anxious to inform the press, but I cannot do this over the telephone. I have to go and see Susan Blake – now." He got to his feet and without informing anyone else left the castle. Jack Twentyman not only understood; he knew the man was right. As there was nothing he could do immediately, he went over to the Dower-house mainly to tell Suzanne where her husband had gone.

It took a full quarter of an hour before the National Trust Land Rover drew up outside Susan Blake's house. One of her daughters was playing in the front garden. She looked at Dalmar as he opened the little white slatted gate. She recognised him, for she had been with her father to Bray

Castle on several occasions, especially at the weekend where she and a friend had been allowed to play in the grounds when her daddy was working there. She smiled at the curator's serious looking face. Dalmar half bent down to her, "Hello Daisy, is your mummy in?"

"Yes. She is cross with me 'cause I shouted at my sister," Daisy replied with a pout.

"Oh dear," said Dalmar, "I'm sure you didn't mean it." He pressed the doorbell.

Trevor's wife opened the door.

Dalmar looked upon a gentle, fair complexioned face with baby blue eyes looking round and wide with questions and felt a rush of sympathy. His voice deserted him – for far too long. In this hesitation Susan read the worst.

The next half an hour was one of life's foul instances: informing a wife that she has lost her husband and witnessing her telling her children – they had lost their father.

Susan, although she was aware that there was no physical evidence, knew enough about Lastwater's history to recognise there was no hope. She told her daughters immediately, practically choking with tears and emotion.

Dalmar realised he should have brought Suzanne with him, or, at least another woman. He had been too tied up with honouring his responsibilities. He made up for it by calling on Susan's mother, who, fortunately, lived nearby.

Pat had lived with his parents in Ambleside. Only his mother was in when he called. How do you tell a mother she has lost her son? He did his best, offering to stay with her until her husband arrived home. But she told him, "To get on." Strangely, there seemed no bitterness.

Jack had to wait until seven o'clock in the evening before he could issue a press release. He and Dalmar had chosen the wording carefully to minimize the distress, as much as possible, for the relatives of the deceased.

Within hours of the news broaching an extraordinary thing happened. The contributions to the J.M. Fund for seriously ill children mushroomed. At nine o'clock Roz Maidment made an announcement to an outside broadcast crew at Bray Castle. An amount from the fund would be made available to the immediate relatives of those tragically drowned during the sponsored swim. Almost immediately, by telephone, this assistance was declined by both John Precence's widow and Pat Simpson's parents.

Shortly after this, Frank and Roz returned to Patterdale. They both had to go to work the next morning. First job on the list for Roz, in the afternoon, would be to acquire a volunteer accountant for the fund management of the charity. It was now too big for them to handle alone.

Suzanne Hunter had not informed her children about the drowning as yet. Michael would be too young to understand; however, Emma must be told before she heard about it from the staff tomorrow. Suzanne decided to leave it until breakfast time the next morning and let her have an undisturbed night's sleep. She gave Jack some supper before he left. He said he would be back after elevenish tomorrow. His handling of the media had been exemplary saving Dalmar, up till now, from having to take part in live broadcasts.

CHAPTER SEVENTEEN

"... SOUNDS LIKE CONFIRMATION TO ME."

At ten minutes passed ten, while watching the second lead item on the B.B.C. news about the day's events at Lastwater, Dalmar remembered he was supposed to telephone Mike Parsons. Suzanne asked him to invite him and his fiancée over for an evening meal while he was at it.

Mike answered the phone and Dalmar apologised for the lateness of the call. "Hardly surprised," Mike commented, "been hearing the lousy news – be more about it on the local broadcast I bet." He said it had come as a great shock to him. The two men talked for a while. They both said how tired they felt physically. Mike wondered if the undertow they had to fight against might be responsible and Dalmar agreed with him. The invitation to dinner was much appreciated and Mike said he would call back later in the week after discussing the matter with his betrothed, mainly to make sure when they could both make it.

The next morning, Saturday, was not so straight forward. Enter the tabloid press. They were all over the place and they knew every trick in the book. The most obvious being to purchase entry tickets posing as tourists, and then straying off the official signed routes, invading offices and kitchens in order to get the inside story interviews from unsuspecting employees and volunteers. Dalmar decided not to create a fuss and let them get on with it. After all, nobody had anything to hide.

Because the telephone was red hot, calls tended to be answered by staff any old where just to stop the incessant ringing tone. One such call was answered by Doris at her reception desk. She took a message and went to find the curator who was giving an impromptu interview to a television station. As soon as she could, she grabbed hold of his left arm and spoke into his ear above the hubbub. "There is a David Fresher waiting at Windermere Station for us to pick him up." Dalmar had not forgotten that the freshwater geologist was arriving today. He just did not know at what time and was certainly expecting him later in the day. He had already informed the media that this expert's arrival was imminent mostly to stop them insistently harping on about it. But now he kept the matter quiet and told Doris to do the same. The last thing they wanted was for his arrival to be made public until he had settled in and had a chance to look at all the evidence.

Having extracted himself from a group of reporters following his session with the T.V. people, he made a run for the Land Rover, but not before asking Doris to tell Brian Cussen what was happening, even if it meant rousing him from his bed. There was a bit more to it than that, such as ensuring David's room was quite ready. He would be using one of the quest rooms reserved for the astronomy students.

David Fresher was waiting outside the station, one foot resting on a suitcase, his back leaning against a lamp post. A hefty backpack lay on the ground beside him. When Dalmar first saw him, he was smoking a cigarette with a rolled-up newspaper tucked under his free arm. This told the curator that he would be fully aware of the latest situation. He was wearing a hat with the brim cast down as though shielding his eyes from the sun, except there was no sun to shield them from. The skies were completely overcast. Dalmar had never seen such a hat. It bore a resemblance to an Australian outback cattleman's, yet it was not. How did Dalmar know this was his man? He just did.

Climbing out of the Land Rover, Dalmar looked upon him and said, "David Fresher I presume?"

He received a complete surprise. "That's me. What kept you?" was said with humour and a highly articulate Geordie accent.

There was no reason why a man from Tyneside should

not be a friend of his brother-in-law's. He just did not expect it. "You've read the news?" Dalmar pointed to the newspaper. "That should enlighten you." He offered his hand with a welcoming smile about his face.

David shook hands. A broad grin showed off a good set of teeth saying a great deal more about his personality. "Hmmm," he said as he took a final draw on his cigarette before crushing it under a heel. "Tell me all about it on route."

After they had loaded up the geologist's bags and were on their way, Dalmar asked him if he had been to the Lakes before. Having removed the hat, he showed off a lengthy hairstyle with a roll of blond hair falling down the back of his neck. His brown eyes were set into a handsomely structured face.

"As a lad on holiday," was the reply. "It is unique in the world: all to do with volcanic activity – long, long ago followed by glacial activity. Gives the area a rare beauty due to the tight scale"

"Huh, huh." Dalmar knew this but he made no comment.

"Anyway," said David, "I am really chuffed to be back." Then he suddenly went serious. "So – you had a fraught time yesterday?"

"Somewhat." First of all, in order to explain the reason why, Dalmar took David Fresher back to the time of Jacob Maidment's terminal illness and how the J.M. Fund came into existence and led to his idea for the sponsored swim. While he said this, David sensed a responsibility problem looming. He wanted to report to one man, Dalmar Hunter, with whom he had made the original arrangement. The idea of a change did not please him.

The curator then told of the tragic happenings yesterday. During this part, David said not a word until he got to the point where the media had been involved in the evening.

This did not interest the geologist and he cut in. "This strong current you mentioned," Tell me – did it feel; as though some massive force was about to take you to extinction?" Although David had a definite north-east accent, his vocabulary held little of the usual Geordie language. Dalmar guessed he had lost it during his further education years – probably mostly at university.

"Beautifully put," commented Dalmar. "It was exactly like that."

Just at this moment they were entering the town of Ambleside. "Oh, I remember this town," said David. "Is there still a mountain clothes shop at the top of this street?"

"Yup – still there in the same place."

"Canny ! Must get a look in there sometime." David then returned to the subject. "Okay, let's leave it there for now. Perhaps we can have a parley tomorrow?"

"Agreed," said Dalmar. "We'll get you settled in today. There are people you have to meet. My wife, the Regional Director, Jack Twentyman and other members of staff. Number one priority is to hide you from the press."

"I would appreciate that. It will only hamper things if they know what I am about. I know from previous experience. Have you a back entrance?"

"Sort of. First of all, I'm going to take you to my family's residence. No one will suspect anything there and it's on the estate."

"I am in your hands." David trusted this man instinctively. After leaving Ambleside, he made the comment, "First we come to Rydal water and then Grasmere, is that right?

"Yes, and shortly after that we turn off the road to head towards Lastwater. What I will do, if it's alright with you, is stop at a viewpoint over-looking the lake so that you can have a good look. It's on the way to Bray Castle."

"Fine."

As the Land Rover negotiated the road above Grasmere, David let out a sigh. "Canny. This is what the poet's raved about – aye?"

"Never get tired of it," agreed Dalmar. "Like to take my

dog up Loughrigg fell when I can. Some people reckon it's the best view in the world." He paused before saying, "Mind you, with all your experience, travelling across the globe, you probably know some better?"

"Not necessarily." The Tyneside dialect was good with that word. "I reckon it has more to do with roots, childhood memories and so on. Someone from New Zealand would say Milford Sound; the States – Grand Canyon and so on. Me – I am always ready to see something else."

Dalmar smiled at this. It was a good philosophy.

Soon, they turned off the A595 for Lastwater. As they did so the sun came out for the first time in several days. It had its usual effect of lifting the spirit by bringing out all the colours in the landscape.

Dalmar parked the vehicle under White Crag. Now - there was hardly a cloud in the sky over to the west. A complete change from the dull light at Windermere. David Fresher gasped at the sight of the notorious lake, which he had only seen glimpses of up till now. "Where the hell does that colour come from!?" he exclaimed.

"That's the Lastwater blue," said Dalmar. "Mind you, it only shows itself when the sun is out."

"It would," said David. "Only thing I know that could cause that – is something called sodium chloride."

"Salt!" Dalmar said incredulously.

The geologist jumped out of the Land Rover after first extracting his Olympus OM1 camera from his backpack and starting taking photographs of the entire lake at different settings.

Dalmar kept quiet while this was going on. Out of nowhere David said, "You mentioned a dog – what breed?"

"Oh – a tri-colour collie – male."

"Not the same fella that helped tackle a certain notorious snake?" And then he added with that grin, "Tim told me."

Dalmar smiled back. "The very same. He is nine years old now."

"Looking forward to meeting him – very much." Secretly, he was hoping he might be allowed to take him for walks. He changed the subject. "That colour – the royal blue hue in the water – if it is caused by salt, it must come off the hills somehow, which, quite frankly is a geological nonsense."

"I think you should know something," interjected Dalmar. "When I was out there taking part in the sponsored swim yesterday – on several occasions when accidently taking an unwanted mouthful of water ... well – it tasted salty. Not as bad as sea water – but it did have a salty tang to it. The chap I was swimming with mentioned it as well."

"That sounds like confirmation to me," David remarked. "Is it always like that?"

"No. I have swum in the lake before and never noticed. One of the lads who lost his life in the rowing boat tragedy, earlier in the year, used to fill-up bottles of the water to use at home – said it was better than most mineral waters you have to pay for."

"Well, I will have to look into it." David dismissed the subject for the time being. "Let's go and see this castle of yours."

On the way Dalmar told him about the estate's short history.

Thankfully, there was no press activity at the entrance drive, but there were much comings and goings of private cars. Dalmar suspected, correctly, that most of them were curious tourists. Added to this was the fact that it was the weekend when visitor numbers naturally increased.

Because the Dower-house was situated just before the castle itself, it gave them the opportunity to park outside without attracting attention. The first to say hello was Fly who had taken up his usual station on the lawn. There was plenty of activity to watch today. David bent down to the magnificent collie and spent some time stroking his glorious ruff. Dalmar reckoned he might be rather fond of dogs.

"I see what you mean," David commented looking across to the castle forecourt and the driveway by the big lawns. That is some media entourage: never seen anything like it. Mind you, judging by the coverage in the papers, I am not surprised."

Suzanne opened the front door to say hello and welcome their guest. Emma stood behind her.

During the introductions, Dalmar could sense his wife's interest in the Geordie tongue. Her ability to mimic all kinds of accents and dialects was quite amazing. He hoped she would not attempt to do it in front of David. Suzanne was quite open about this trait of hers. The whole thing fascinated her. "It makes life more interesting," was her usual brief comment. She did not realise it but her interest was actually linguistic.

While David was enjoying Suzanne's percolated coffee, Dalmar went across to the castle to see how things were going. He took the geologist's luggage with him intending to deposit it in the room allocated. It should make it easier later when David Fresher came over. The bags might attract curious questions from the waiting reporters. As it was, Dalmar was hindered twice. The first reporter recognised him and let him pass, the other asked about the luggage. Dalmar explained that they had astronomy students staying at the castle. And in response to inevitable queries, it gave him the opportunity to give the observatory programme a good plug.

Once inside the sombre mood was still very evident and seemed to have infected all those working there. This could not fail to be passed on to the abnormal number of visitors. Replacing Trevor and Pat was not very high on Dalmar's list of priorities. He wanted to wait until a suitable period of mourning had passed, out of respect, and it might well be one of the first jobs for his successor.

Dalmar made his way up to his office where he found Jack Twentyman and Brian Cussen hiding. They freely admitted it. Brain informed the curator that the geologist's room was all ready for him. The part time lady who usually prepared the rooms was not here, Friday being the changeover day for students, she had made sure the room was prepared last week.

A television crew, taking advantage of the sudden fine weather, were currently down at the lakeside taking pictures of the infamous Shimdorie Island. Jane Derby, the presenter for this particular slot, put this open question to her viewers, "What is it's dark secret?" while the film camera stayed focused on the island, with just the sound of water gently lapping up against the side of the jetty. Then the picture and the program – faded out.

The majority of the press contingents were now hanging around awaiting the arrival of the police diving unit, which was on its way up from Barrow-in-Furness. Otherwise there was little they could do.

Dalmar, Jack and Brian got on with the running of Bray Castle whose facilities, particularly, in the restaurant were stretched to breaking point. At some stage during the day one or all of them had to turn to and help, especially at the entrance. Doris was on her own taking money for entrance fees or checking National Trust membership. The car park situated below the castle adjacent to the woods had overflowed onto the gravel drive and forecourt area. As soon as he decently could, Dalmar went to see how his guest at the Dower-house was getting on.

In view of the situation, Suzanne had asked David to stay for some luncheon. Roz was due to arrive early in the afternoon principally to answer any further queries from the media concerning the progress of the J.M. Fund.

As David Fresher was comfortable for the moment, Dalmar returned to further assist Doris at the entrance only to find that Edna had arrived to help during the extraordinary circumstances. He could tell from the state of her eyes that she had been crying. It was well known that she had thought a lot of Trevor and knew all his family who lived at Grasmere village. It might be small comfort, but it was important that people like her knew of the arrival of the geologist. Something was being done. Doris and Edna understood as did most of the staff here.

The worst affected was Bea in the animal centre. Brian had already asked her if she wanted to go home, however, she insisted on staying with her charges and coping with the extra visitors, especially as Suzanne was otherwise engaged. "Someone who knows what they are doing has to be here," she said emphatically. "And anyway, I would rather be busy – better than moping at home." No one seemed to be aware that it was supposed to be her day off.

It was Jack who finally prompted matters. At his suggestion, he and Brian went over to the Dower-house to meet David Fresher leaving Dalmar to cope at the castle. They were just in time to witness the arrival of the police diving unit. Two of the officers had been involved the last time, earlier in the year.

Emma and Michael wanted to come out and have a look, so Suzanne left the men to it, and took her charges outside for some fresh air, where they could watch from a safe distance on the front lawn. It was not long before two inflatable boats, engines, aqua-lungs and other equipment were carried off on their way down to the jetty. The pathway would be just about wide enough for the task with the occasional lift over protruding bushes. Some of the media contingent went with them, but the bulk of the entourage packed up and left. Roz Maidment arrived soon afterwards, to find Suzanne talking to Doris and Edna at the castle entrance while her children played with Fly nearby. She was relieved to find out that no one wished to see her, for the moment, that is.

Taking advantage, Jack, Brian and the geologist made their away over to the castle while there was nobody about to intercept them. Some of the reporters were aware that he was due to arrive imminently, and, therefore, he was their next major target for an interview.

In order to give David the right atmosphere they went through the front entrance archway and introduced him to Doris and Edna. Then it was off on the rounds of all the facilities. They found Dalmar helping at the check-out counter in the restaurant. He was able to extricate himself almost immediately and the four men made their way back to the office on the first floor. They only had a brief discussion because a meeting was scheduled for the following day when the whole morning would be made available. There would only be two people present, the curator and the geologist with Suzanne contributing at some time during the morning. The agenda was to lay before David all the information that had been gathered in the past few months. Also, he would be made au fait with the history of the lake in terms of its anomaly over the past seven hundred years.

Jack Twentyman, who, by now, had formally welcomed David, assured him that all the facilities of Bray Castle and beyond, if necessary, would be at his disposal during his investigation. A little later, before going home, he offered his hand to the two words, "Good luck." David took it with a very unsure smile. He was beginning to realise the extent of the expectations they were all placing on his shoulders.

CHAPTER EIGHTEEN

"LAST IS AN ANAGRAM OF SALT."

Following another sad evening of news bulletins on the television, with David Fresher retiring to his bed early, Bray Castle finally settled after a fraught day with the promise of more to come.

Sunday dawned without a cloud in the sky. When the geologist rose in his new surroundings and looked out of the window, his eyes were greeted with a view over the estate's woodland area. A strip of blue signified the extreme north-eastern end of the lake and stretching up, the lower fells of the Helvelyn range hid from view the summit ridges which lay some way beyond. It was a stunning outlook. David got washed, dressed and made his way down to the canteen for breakfast. Brian Cussen and his students had been up half the night, taking advantage of the clear skies, so there was only himself and the weekend chef, Trishia, on hand. She was normally a cheerful soul, but not today. She tried to hide the tell-tale grief in her eyes by keeping her head lowered while relying on spectacles to do the rest.

At nine o'clock, as arranged, David found Dalmar in his office setting up a coffee percolator. In response to the question as to how he had slept, David replied, "Like a log. Amazingly comfortable bed, I must say man."

"One of the originals, apparently. Goes back to the days when wealth occupied the place." Then he quickly added, "Relatively new mattress, of course." He caught David grinning at him.

Soon – they got down to the matter in hand. Dalmar had already given the geologist a history of Bray Castle, now it was time to go farther back to the occupation of the Dread family, here, at Bray House; as it was then called, and, also, to tell him about the near six hundred years of sheep and poultry husbandry carried out at Lastwater Farm. He

185

informed him about the flood of 1512 and various other events leading up to the Posselthwaite's emigration to Virginia, supposedly due to the Dread Curse in the eighteenth century.

David's natural query about the so called Dread Curse enabled Dalmar to return the story to that particular family. Of greatest interest here, as far as David was concerned, was the claim made by Professor James Dread that he discovered the secret of Lastwater during his lifetime in the mid 1700's. To David's obvious disappointment, but not surprise, Dalmar informed him of the vandalism to his papers and loss of a certain box that ended up with the Posselthwaite's in the United States. David was particularly fascinated to find out that it was the professor who had given the name to the lake and other local geographical points.

"What arouses your curiosity here?" Dalmar asked him.

"Well – you know I mentioned that salt was the most likely reason for your lake's unusual colour."

"Yes."

"Last is an anagram of salt."

To say that Dalmar was taken aback was an understatement. After gaping at David stupidly, his mind gradually calmed. "Could be a coincidence," he commented.

"Could be."

Dalmar had the distinct feeling that David did not think so.

It was now time to go through the drowning incidents of which there was some detail available. He started with the origins of The Dread Curse, which required some further explanation and the disappearance of the Posselthwaite young man and the girl from Bray at the turn of the fifteenth century. Then he went forward to the disastrous loss of a mother and two children belonging to the Legg family living at Lastwater farm in 1851. Dalmar did not mention vague happenings such as lost walkers and a sheep dog, preferring to stick to more relevant occurrences. Therefore, he advanced to 1956 when the scout and master lost their lives and on to the three missing students from the outward bound school at Bray Castle in 1979 and, finally, the rowing club tragedy in March of this year followed by the recent loss of three men the day before yesterday.

The geologist wanted to know a lot of detail: time of year if known, possible location on the lake when last scene, weather conditions, and the single fact that interested him the most when Dalmar mentioned the water level rise on the morning of the rowing boat disappearance. "You are absolutely sure that the level had increased by a few inches?" he asked sitting forward in his seat attentively.

"I remember thinking we must have had a lot of rain over the fells to cause that. It seemed freakish to me." Unfortunately, Dalmar could not recall exactly how much the level had risen.

"And then – you say the level went back to normal later – after the accident?"

"According to the marker post – yes."

It was almost exactly eleven o'clock. There was a knock on the door and Suzanne entered carrying two carrier bags. David virtually leapt out of his seat to assist her. Unfortunately, his travel style tan trousers possessed rather too many pockets and one of them caught on the arm of the chair he was trying to vacate. The unmistakable noise of tearing fabric assailed all their ears. David momentarily forgot the presence of Suzanne. "Shit!" he said. And then allowed one hand to shoot up and cover his mouth, eyes bulging in horror.

Suzanne's reaction was to let forth a soft string of giggly laughter; something that had not been heard in Bray Castle for a couple of days. "You will need a needle and cotton for that," she chortled at the embarrassed geologist.

He muttered something about being prepared with his kit, when he caught sight of a large smirk, Dalmar was trying to hide on his face. "Amusing is it?" he challenged him.

"Not at all. Most unfortunate," Dalmar said suddenly

straight-faced, but still with a twinkle in his eyes.

David studied him suspiciously. "Humpff," he uttered, glowering, before inspecting the damage minutely.

"I'll be back in a mo'," said Suzanne; "just going to get us some biscuits from Sally in the canteen." She smiled at her husband, put the two bags on his desk and left.

"I'll wait for her to get back," Dalmar half suggested to David. "Let's have a break. Is your room okay?"

"Brilliant. Really comfortable." David brightened, forgetting the recent annoyance. Compared with the rooms he often had to use abroad; this one was luxurious. "Fabulous view from the window," he added.

"Anything you want to do or see while you are in the area?" asked the curator. He got up from his desk to check the coffee supply. "Refill?" he said holding the black bulbous container up.

"Canny," David offered up his cup; "if we are to get some biscuits. I'm a dunking man," and then answering the first question. "Nah – just the task in hand."

When Suzanne returned the first thing, she asked David was to do with his family. Having learnt yesterday that he was one of five children, she wanted to know more. "Did you say you had four sisters?" she asked.

"Yes," he answered her. "It can get a bit overpowering at times, I can tell you.

"What ages?" asked Suzanne.

"One older – the rest younger. David himself was the same age as Tim Westward, 31. "My kid sister is only 23. She is after an invite – I warn you."

"Tell her she is very welcome," immediately answered Suzanne. "She can stay at the Dower-house. What's her name?"

"Jodie." David glanced at Suzanne. "It ain't me she wants to see – it's your animal rescue centre." While saying this he immersed half a digestive biscuit in his coffee before offering the wet half to his mouth with a grunt of pleasure.

"Really," Suzanne was surprised. "How did she get to

hear about it?"

"Don't ask me," the geologist replied, mouth also engaged in another activity. "Appears your fame has travelled. Anyway. the point is she is very keen on that sort of thing – always tending to some unfortunate damaged bird when she was a little-un."

"Well – you tell her she is most welcome. Could always do with a helping hand. She can earn her keep." It was also revealed that two of his sisters, including Jodie, still lived with his parents in Newcastle while the eldest was working in Australia and the other had moved down to London with her husband.

When they had finished their refreshments, Dalmar explained that since returning from the States, he had gone through all the documents contained in one of the bags. They were tied together with ribbon and placed in an acid free folder. David could still not believe they had gone to so much trouble, nonetheless, he was grateful and spared no one's blushes saying so.

"Look – most of these papers relate to farming matters – some of which, especially the earlier ones are very simple. Obviously, they are going to be of more interest to farm historians – but the diaries, or should I say, diary type references – well – they are not always calendar based and vary from person to person through the generations. They could be a different matter. Quite often, it is mentioned that the lake level had gone up or down, almost as though it was a common observation. This was taken seriously for an unknown reason." Dalmar was immediately interrupted when he mentioned this.

"Ah – where do I find those?" David Fresher reached towards the bundle. Dalmar put up a hand. "I have put markers in. Do you see?" he said pointing to slips of green paper showing every now and then. "You may study them at your leisure."

"Canny," said the geologist and withdrew his outstretched hand.

"Now for the box. Suzanne is going to talk you through this one." As he said this, he withdrew the small wooden article from its bag; rose from his seat and handed it across the desk to his wife.

Suzanne balanced it on the palm of her right hand and addressed David. "This," she said, "is supposed to contain the secret of Lastwater. It went with the Posselthwaite family when they emigrated to North America. Now – considering that was in the later part of the eighteenth century it may connect to a robbery, apparently carried out here – or rather – Bray House, the old building, before the castle was built. Anyway, that is what the Dread family claimed."

She was unaware that she was repeating details which her husband had already covered, but no one said anything. "It would have been when Professor James Dread was alive," her husband added.

"Are you saying this Prof Dread made it?" asked David with raised eyebrows.

Suzanne answered him. "That – we don't know – could be." She handed the box over so that David could study it.

He did much the same thing as Dalmar and Suzanne had done in Virginia. Looked at the lid closely, the sides, the base, opened it and peered inside. Then he closed the lid and studied the map on the lid more intently. "Even got that strange blue in the water accurately," he observed.

"Yes," said Suzanne. "Dalmar tells me you think that is caused by salt."

"Yup. Thing is I've got to prove it." The geologist hesitated for a moment. "You see it isn't just a case of taking a sample and analysing it. We have to know its source." He sighed. "Look – no matter. That is my problem. Anything else?"

"Just one thing," said Dalmar, almost succinctly. Then he motioned to his wife. "You spotted it darling. So – go ahead, tell the man."

Suzanne's brow furrowed. "Pardon."

Dalmar smiled before saying. "No river?"

"Oh." Suzanne partially gaped in recognition. "Yes. Again – this happened on our visit to the States. We were at a gospel choir concert. It was when they were doing a beautiful rendition of the song, 'Oh Shenendoah.' David looked at her face in puzzlement wondering what was coming. "Well – it occurred to me that our lake has no river." She left it at that.

David immediately nodded his head enthusiastically. "Ah – now you're talking. I spotted that on a map – and, as far as I know there is no other inland waterway of its size in the U.K. without one. In fact," he looked at them both in turn, "there are not that many examples in the world. The best known are in northwest Canada." He looked at Suzanne with his eyes cast down. "This means – there must be one below the waterline." It was the next remark that had his small audience rapt in attention. "I believe – that is probably, somehow or other, the cause of the Lastwater anomaly." But he did not add anything further.

Dalmar could not resist it. "And?"

David raised a single finger. "You have provided the information. I shall now go to work. May I use your boat this afternoon?"

This caught Dalmar somewhat by surprise. "Ah – yes – of course. You know we have lost the proper oars. Only got a short pair."

"They'll do." 'That was what I learnt to row with, as a kid - on a boating lake,' David thought to himself. "Only want to go as far as the island for now. This afternoon I aim to verify that *there is* salt in your lake and then start the process of finding out why, or, if you like eliminating certain possibilities." Neither Dalmar or Suzanne were sure as to what he meant by that. Wisely they both decided to ignore it for the moment.

With that David Fresher went off to join Brian Cussen before having lunch in the canteen. He and Dalmar arranged to meet at two o'clock.

The Hunters found their family in good spirits. Fly

greeted them in front of the Dower-house and Emma and Michael were being entertained by Rosalind Maidment. She called, by arrangement, to spend some time with Suzanne after her baby-sitting stint and not to talk about the tragedy, or not intentionally. The main purpose was to start preparing outline plans for the actual operation of Bray Castle's riding school. She was due to stay and have lunch with them.

It was about this time that the police divers called an end to their underwater search having found nothing, which might have explained further the disappearance of the three men. One diver reported a localised underwater current near a rocky outcrop by Shimdorie Island, but he said that he could swim against it without any difficulty. There were no media people about when they brought their equipment up to the castle car park, and they were soon on their way without hindrance. An announcement would be made via a press release later in the day.

This meant that David Fresher had the lake to himself during the afternoon. After Dalmar had left him to it, he made straight for Shimdorie Island where he took a sample of the water close in shore, then further out in the lake and another near to Cloud Point. He had a little box with corked glass phials that he used for the purpose. Once satisfied, he returned the rowing dinghy to the boat house and immediately took the sample case to his room. It was there that he absolutely confirmed his suspicion. All three samples contained a small quantity of salt. A great deal less than, for example, seawater, but, nevertheless, it was there.

When he went downstairs his mind was in a fog. The samples had contained salt certainly, but it was not what he had expected. Dismissing the matter for the moment he went across to the Dower-house hoping to find Dalmar. He had a sudden urge to get out and think, and it occurred to him that the best thing he could do − would be to take Fly for a walk.

Suzanne answered the door. She readily agreed to let David take Fly out for some exercise and suggested a route through the woodland area, which would be easy for him to follow and find his way back. Dalmar, at the time, was speaking on the telephone, but Suzanne explained that he would be free when he returned.

Fly did not seem to mind going off with David, Suzanne explained that there would be no need for a lead, he would respond to basic instructions.

They took the path down to the jetty. As Fly walked on ahead, the geologist could not help admiring the magnificent animal. He might be getting old, but he still held his head up and walked with a spring in his legs. They followed the path along the water's edge, the dog leading the way until they came to Cloud Point. David could not resist climbing out onto the very end. Here, he gazed long and hard at the lake's vista before him. The weather today would be termed changeable. There were plenty of light cumuli scudding about in the sky. Right now, the sun was shining and, with clear visibility during a time approaching the changing of the season, little tinges of yellow and gold had started to creep into the leaves of the deciduous trees. It was very beautiful.

The collie, in the meantime, prowled around while keeping close by. David Fresher allowed his thoughts to dwell. He reached into his light-weight cotton outdoor style jacket. It had even more pockets than his trousers. Locating the one containing a packet of Rothman's filter-tipped cigarettes, he withdrew the pack and took out the last remaining one. Placing the empty packet back into its pocket he lit what was to be his last ever cigarette. From what he could tell he was the only smoker in this place. It, therefore, occurred to him that it was a golden opportunity to kick the habit. He took a long draw into his lungs and blew it almost aggressively out over the water.

An analysis of the water samples taken from this lake should have been straightforward. The greater content had been exactly what he would have expected, rainwater mixed with traces of peat and minerals from the fells. The small sodium chloride part was a mystery as to its origination. But when he came to check, by means of dipping various spatulas coated in the appropriate chemicals to ascertain what other substances existed in the water, he rapidly came to the conclusion, that this small part of the water content was exactly what one would expect – if ...

He left his thoughts there and decided to spend the rest of his walk enjoying the dog's company – thinking only of him.

Dalmar greeted him on his return and invited him in for a pre-dinner drink. Nothing much was said between the two men about David's work that afternoon, simply because there was really no opportunity. The time was taken up with an introduction to Roz Maidment and engaging in play chat with the children. Before David left, he informed Dalmar that tomorrow he would be carrying out the task of taking water samples in all the streams coming off the fells, which discharged rainwater into the lake. It would take most of the day, and as he would be on foot he wondered if Fly would like to come? Dalmar and Suzanne were both delighted. Suzanne said she would arrange a packed lunch for him from the canteen plus a flask of tea or coffee. He turned the latter down explaining that there was perfectly good drinking water at hand whenever he felt thirsty.

CHAPTER NINETEEN

"NOW – I HAVE TO FIND OUT WHY?"

During the Monday morning, long after David and the Collie had set out on their expedition, Dalmar had an unexpected phone call. He answered the instrument himself, "Good morning – Bray Castle." This was his standard greeting depending on the time of day.

"Hello, Mr Curator. How's it going?" He knew instantly who the soft toned, but strong girl's voice belonged to. It was Adred Dread.

"Well – hello. We're okay. What about you."

"Good." Adred ignored his enquiry after her wellbeing and ploughed straight in. "Look – after the terrible news, I decided that I should try and help a bit more. Think I may have found something useful in some old papers. Can you meet me in Keswick?"

Dalmar was a bit apprehensive. "Sure," he said hesitantly. "When?"

"Tomorrow afternoon?"

At first, the curator felt annoyed at the urgency; then, he realised, that if it was important regarding the safety of other people on the lake, he should comply and be grateful. "Okay. Where and when?"

"The Two C's tearooms near the Lake Road car park." Adred paused before suggesting, "About three?"

Suddenly Dalmar had an idea. "Would you mind if I bring along a colleague, David Fresher, a geologist. He is working with us right now trying to solve Lastwater's dark secret."

Adred went quiet for a moment. "Sounds good," was all she said.

And so, it was arranged. Dalmar had not even glanced at his diary and he hoped he had not double booked. There was an entry for the 28th, 'meeting with heating engineer.'

He telephoned their office and left a message.

Soon after this another phone call came through. It was from an uncle of Trevor Blake's, to inform him that a remembrance service would be held at St Oswald's church in Grasmere village on Friday 1st October – at eleven o'clock. Following this, a similar arrangement had been made for Pat Simpson's relatives and friends. Although Pat's family hailed from Ambleside, it had been considered that this might be the best arrangement so that Bray Castle staff and others could stay on for the two services. Dalmar naturally enquired if there was to be any kind of event to be held on the lake comparable to the rowing club's in March. Would they like the National Trust to organise something appropriate? He was told quite succinctly that it had been mentioned, but as far as he could tell nobody wanted to go out on the water.

Dalmar wasted no time. He contacted Jack Twentyman and arranged, as a mark of respect, for Bray castle to be closed to the public next Friday. Jack would issue a press release to this effect during the afternoon.

Suzanne took Emma and Michael over to the animal centre as soon as possible. Bea was having the morning off, so there were only the two sixth-form students working on from an extended summer stint. They were both very keen and obliging, so Suzanne only had to keep a good check on things. She had heard that the centre might be getting two donkeys in the very near future. These animals, when recovering from an injury or illness, usually went to a specialist donkey sanctuary, but they were rather full up at present and had asked Bray Castle if they could help out. This gave Suzanne the motivation to move the sheep on the grazing meadow below the castle, to join the others on the other side of the woodland in preparation for the arrival of the first ponies sometime early next year. The donkeys would be constantly visible from the Dower-house.

There seemed to be no let-up in ticket admission sales at the entrance. Doris was very glad when one of the new volunteer receptionists arrived to lend a hand. It appeared that many of the visitors were attracted by the ghoulish aspect of things. So many of them made their way down to the lakeside to stare at the waters, in case something awful might happen, which they could witness.

Meanwhile David and Fly had finished their exploration of the southern side of Lastwater. He called into the farm but only managed to meet the shepherd lad who was working in one of the winter shelter barns. The lad told him that the t'ol lass was in town and the t'ol fella was out on the fells with the dogs.

Right now, man and dog were having lunch alongside Salmon gill at the start of the northern bank's set of streams. David used the same simple system at each gill to collect his samples. He took one tube-full of fast running water over rock formations, and another from a still pool usually lying to one side of the main descent. At first Fly had cocked his head on one side to study the actions, but after the second gill he sensed there was nothing in this for him and went sniffing off on his own quests.

Since the announcement to the media that the police divers had failed to find anything, the press appeared to lose interest. They literally vanished in the physical sense and there were only a couple of follow-up cursory phone calls from reporters

After lunch, Dalmar turned to with the ride on mower to give the big lawns a trim. It was important to keep the exterior appearance up to scratch. The rain kept off for him.

That evening, Mike Parsons telephoned just to get an update on everything. It was arranged that he and his fiancée Susan would come over in about a month's time for an evening meal. Suzanne planned to invite Roz and Frank as well.

When David returned late in the afternoon with Fly, both man and dog looked tired. Fly went off to the living room and fell sound asleep in his favourite corner. The geologist found the curator in his office exuding a pungent aroma of newly cut grass. He guessed what he had been doing and tactfully made no comment.

"Well – I have got several samples of water to have a look at. That will keep me busy tomorrow morning," he said.

"Are you able to come with me to Keswick in the afternoon," Dalmar quickly cut in. "One of the Dread ancestors thinks she may have found something of use for us."

"Alreet –count me in." David was too hungry to stay and talk now. He went off to get himself some dinner and was in his bed reading by eight o'clock, not overly tired, just pleasantly so.

Emma Hunter waylaid her father the next morning before he had a chance to have his breakfast. "I'm going to school very soon," she said.

"Yes Darling – I know. Are you looking forward to it?"

Emma ignored the question. "You promised me a treat before I went." Her appealing blue eyes were full on his as she said this.

Dalmar remembered that he had. Because of recent events, sadly, he had not exactly forgotten – but he had been lapsed in suggesting something – especially – when. He thought quickly. "I shall have to talk to your mother, but this Sunday looks good," he said, hoping this would appease her.

No such luck. "Where are we going?" For this was what a treat meant to her. It would be a day out – not a present or anything like that.

"Have a chat with mummy. I will try and think of somewhere as well." This reply got him off the hook for the time being, but she still gave him a suspicious look before he managed to make his escape.

On the way to Keswick, David and Dalmar managed to discuss how his water sampling had been going. David was non-committal at this stage, but he did confirm that Lastwater contained a small percentage of sodium chloride in its overall make-up. "Now – I have to find out why." The geologist added with finality.

"Yes – but that *is* progress," Dalmar encouraged him.

David and Dalmar found the Two Cs tea rooms by asking the car park attendant after they had parked up the Land Rover. Looking at the frontage, Dalmar thought the contemporary design strange for a tearoom. They usually tried to be the opposite. Once inside the theme carried on. Everything was white. White walls, white counters, white tables and chairs with white tablecloths. The only splashes of colour were the bright blue curtains draped down the sides of the two windows and two Greek style, bright translucent blue, pots set in their own individual alcoves on the back wall. Dalmar wondered if the design might be ahead of its time.

Adred was already seated at a table with a young man. She looked different to the last time Dalmar had seen her.

After she had been introduced to David Fresher, Adred, almost coyly introduced her *fiancé*, Henry. He appeared shy as well, half hiding his small bespectacled head in the folds of an oversize anorak.

Dalmar had to stop himself from gaping in astonishment. "Congratulations," he said and then unable to resist the temptation. "When did this happen?"

"Well – last week – but we have been seeing each other for a while. Actually, we share a flat not far from here."

So that was why she looked different. She had become civilized. Dalmar felt relieved, if he were honest. David added his good wishes, and then they ordered a pot of tea and cakes. Dalmar explained to Adred and Henry about David's profession. They were both very interested, although only basic details could be divulged to them. The possibility of an underground river seemed to excite Adred's imagination.

After tea had been poured, she started to explain the reason for the meeting.

"Henry persuaded me to look through all the old family documents and we found this; a letter from James Dread of

Bray House dated 1753. It was addressed to a cousin, by the sound of it, who lived at Morecambe. She produced a rather tatty ochre coloured sheet of paper folded in half. Opening it out, she handed it across the table for the two men to see.

The writing was so appalling that neither man could decipher a word. Seeing their hesitation, Adred got to her feet and came around to Dalmar's side. Her scent surprised him. It was cosmetic. When she had been close to him last time, he distinctly remembered a perfume of something totally natural: kind of homemade. Placing her finger on some script about a quarter of the way down the page she read out, "Folk often refer to an irregularity on this lake, which causes death by drowning. I believe I may have discovered the origin. It will never be proven because no man could swim far enough underwater. It must, therefore, remain a theory. As you know cousin Gerald has made a box. I have added a clue to the secret of Lastwater within. The bottom of the box must be espied from every angle. And when you repair to your bed, do likewise. I will tell you further, there is, I believe, a connection to the ocean. This may'st be proven satis, if thou fishest with the long line … I could not read this at first," added Adred. "Henry taught me how to translate the old script." She went back to her seat next to her fiancé.

David Fresher immediately asked her if the author was the same gentleman who had given names to various topographical points of interest around the lake, including that of *Lastwater* itself. She nodded at him. "Then – this information is of paramount importance. Canny. Thank you." He was obviously delighted and wore his broadest smile.

After they had finished their tea and eaten a slice of walnut and coffee icing cake, Dalmar wished the couple well and thanked them. He then paid the bill and he and David got ready to leave. Before doing so, Adred informed them that, officially, she had changed her first name to Andrea. "Good," said Dalmar and he smiled his approval at her. It also occurred to him, at the same time, that once she and Henry were married, the family name of Dread would cease to be.

Before going to the car, the geologist asked if there was a fishing equipment supplier in town. "If it's a fishing rod you are after, we have a couple of sea angling types at the castle," said Dalmar.

"Canny. That'll cope with the long line referred to. Now all we have to do is decipher what the hell this mazer was on about." At this David grimaced. He did not consider himself a solver of riddles. Dalmar was not much better either.

"I *presume* he has a voice," commented David.

"You mean young Henry – I take it?" Dalmar guessed that David was referring to the fact that he did not utter a single word the whole time they were there. He received a nod. But they left it at that.

As soon as they got back to the castle, the two men went up to the office. Dalmar retrieved the Lastwater box from its resting place on a shelf, and for the next half an hour they looked at the bottom of it from every conceivable angle. At the end – they were none the wiser. David took the box with him when he left. Perhaps Brian Cussen might have some ideas.

Dalmar found his wife in the animal centre attending to the needs of a wild rabbit with a back leg in a splint. "Emma and Michael want to go to the seaside on Sunday. Is that okay?"

"Sure," affirmed her husband. "Any chance of an early start to beat the traffic?"

Suzanne giggled at him. "I doubt it," she said. Dalmar shrugged his shoulders. He knew from past experience that it was unlikely. "Let's look at the weather on the day," he suggested. He then told her about Andrea's discovery. He thought it strange that she never queried her change of name. 'Perhaps she already knew.'

Later, when he put his daughter to bed, she waited until

the good night kiss before saying, "You won't forget Sunday will you dad?" Her father thought to himself, 'he had better not!' and assured her so.

Dalmar could not sleep. David Fresher could not sleep. Both men turned the riddle over and over in their brains. Brian Cussen was the only one not bothered about it. He was working.

It must have been about one o'clock in the morning when Dalmar finally blurted out, "I've been lying in my bed for an hour and a half – thinking – over and over in my mind. It just makes no sense."

Suzanne ignored him. She was in a twilight sleep and although the riddle played on her mind as well, she just let the whole thing take its course. 'If the solution came to her – so be it,' she considered.

At this time of year, the first dawn light started to creep into the Hunter's bedroom at a quarter passed seven. The National Trust provided furniture was not over basic. Her dressing table was a little hotel-like but served its purpose. *She* had a double wardrobe and *he* a single. Suzanne found the bed very comfortable. Apparently, it was a very good make of mattress. They had just started getting used to the new fashion of duvets, alleviating the need for an over sheet and blanket with eiderdown. At first, Dalmar had found the duvet too hot, especially on warm summer nights, but he had become accustomed. Suzanne supposed she had better think about acquiring winter duvets for all the family. Autumn was nearly on them.

It would shortly be time for the household to rise. Suzanne awoke and lay in bed thinking. The radio alarm clock was due to start up at half past the hour. Her husband had tuned it to a news program. Every now and then she altered it to a light music station, really, just to annoy him. She had clandestinely changed it for this morning, except that she had not selected light music. It was full-bore popular.

Right now, her mind had returned to the Lastwater box.

It had done so, off and on, for the last hour or so, as though pre-set by her brain. At twenty-five minutes after seven she banged her right arm hard down on the duvet beside her, once, and then twice and then three times. Dalmar, who was lying partially on his stomach, rose arching his back upwards bringing the duvet with him. He started blinking, trying to get his eyes working. "What the...!" he eventually mouthed.

"Got it!" Suzanne – yelled out loud. "I've got it!"

"You certainly have," commented her frustrated husband, "first degree insanity – I would say." And then as his brain began to awake, he asked, "Got what – exactly?"

"When Professor Dread wrote about the bottom of the box, he wants us to think about the bottom of the lake! Look at it from every angle. Lateral thinking. And the same applies to our bed. Again- lateral thinking. The bed of the lake!"

Her husband gaped at her. She was a woman who could get away without cosmetics to her face, although she usually applied some sparsely, but seeing her now, as nature intended, her eyes sparkling even more than usual with the tousled dark hair falling against the stark white pillow case; he loved her and showed it with an ecstatic kiss. "You bloody genius!" he exclaimed and leapt out of bed.

And then he started to think clearly. "Just a minute." He said nothing for a while as his wife studied him with an amused expression, as he first rubbed his hair and then pulled his dark blue night shorts further up onto his waist. "Okay – but – well what does that tell us? I mean – the bottom of the box represents the bottom of the lake." He opened palmed both hands at chest height. "So?"

"And what is on the bottom of the box?" said Suzanne dryly.

Again, Dalmar studied her face which now wore an irksome expression of mild impatience. And then he said, "A hole...." The dawning hit him. They had naturally thought this hole had been caused accidently at some point in the box's history. It would appear that this was not so.

Just then the radio alarm burst into life. "I am the god of hell fire!" Very loud lyrics blasted into the room. At this Suzanne burst into uncontrollable hysterics as she reached for the volume control to turn down the band Wizard's popular music song, which had so rudely assailed her husband's ears. Emma came in and flung herself on the bed. From somewhere the voice of a toddler started crying.

The curator found David Fresher finishing off his breakfast with toast and marmalade. Dalmar located a cup in the kitchen and helped himself to some of his coffee. "I have news," he opened.

"Morning," said David. "About the box?" It was sitting in front of him on the table.

"Yes. Suzanne has come up with something. You and Brian have any luck?"

"Nope. Go on. Spill it," David encouraged him enthusiastically.

As Dalmar relayed his wife's discovery, David's face broke out into his broad smile. He pushed his plate to one side, grabbed the box and got hastily to his feet. "Have you a ruler in your office?"

"I have indeed, why?"

"Show you when we get there." And he led the way.

Once up on the first floor and safely inside the office, Dalmar produced a wooden twelve-inch ruler from a draw in his desk.

David grabbed it and started taking measurements on the back of the box of length to hole and width to hole. He memorized them and turned the box over. He placed the ruler across the painting on the lid, first lengthwise and then for the width. "As I thought," he said with a confident air. "There should be an opening to an underground river just off the southern bank of Shimdorie Island."

"The very place," said Dalmar, "where the Rowing Club's boat and crew were last seen." He spoke those words slowly and softly in a revered tone.

CHAPTER TWENTY

'SAD ANGELS BY A POET'S GRAVE.'

Early the next morning, Dalmar received a call from an executor handling the John Precence estate, informing him that a service of remembrance would be held at Keswick a week on Saturday. Dalmar assured him that a representative from Bray Castle would attend. Secretly, he was hoping that Jack Twentyman would go. His office was only just around the corner from the church.

David Fresher had been spending some time going through the old records from Lastwater Farm, which the Hunters had brought back from the United States. He was quite pleased. It was not without success as far as he was concerned. What he needed to do now was get to Shimdorie Island with one of the castle's sea angling rods.

He found the Hunters, with young Michael, in their office and asked if he could have a word. He explained his need and requirements, asking, at the same time, if Dalmar had the time to accompany him. "I need a witness – you see."

"Definitely," he answered. "Your program has top priority."

"Good. I need a rod and basic tackle – no hooks though. Plan to get out to the island this afternoon. Weather looks good."

"I am at your service."

Suzanne had abruptly developed a wan expression. When the geologist had made his solo trip out on the lake, she had kept her thoughts to herself. Now that it involved her husband, she was developing strong concerns. "Is this wise?" she simply asked, albeit, with a deep furrow on her brow.

This was the first time David had seen Mrs Hunter with anything other than an unfriendly face. "I assure you Suzanne, I am pretty certain there is no danger. We know now that the time to avoid the lake is when the water level rises. History tells us that is when the drowning incidents have occurred. So – if we spot this – we wont go – okay?"

Suzanne answered him with a question, "Pretty certain?"

"Alreet. As certain as I can be."

Dalmar cut in. "I promise you; David knows what he is talking about," he attempted to reassure her.

She accepted this, although she sensed that behind David Fresher's disarming smile lurked a man of adventure, and, he might, of necessity, entice others to join him. Knowing that her husband was a man who might not turn down a challenge for honourable reasons – she feared for the future. Suzanne raised her head, smiled, although somewhat without enthusiasm, and said, "Okay."

"Actually, while I'm at it – spoke to my kid sister on the phone." David hesitated and chewed his lower lip thoughtfully. "I won't be here of course, but she would like to come in the autumn if that is okay?"

Suzanne looked pleased. She knew she would be requiring an extra pair of hands at that time. A lot of new patients were due in soon. It usually occurred at this time of year: young birds and animals finding out about life the hard way. "Yes please!" she replied. "Give me her details and I'll contact her. Will save you the trouble."

David looked relieved. "Thanks," he said smiling. "I'm due to join Brian for a coffee. I'll give him the good news about your clever solution, Suzanne." She blushed. Michael gurgled at David, looking up from his early learning game, where the idea was to find the right whole and push a matching shape through. Michael had just completed the task for the first time. He looked very pleased with himself.

"Look David – I don't know whether this is important, but – since my husband mentioned to me about you saying –

that last was an anagram of salt." This remark, out of the blue, caught the two men by surprise.

David looked at her. "Go on pet," he said.

"Well – I have been doing some doodle stuff with some of the other names around our lake. Didn't come up with much except – sounds silly really," she looked coy. Her husband, while studying her face, made encouraging come on signs with both hands. "Thing is – if you take *cloud* from Cloud Point and *shimdorie* from Shimdorie Island – those two words are an anagram of sodium chloride."

Dalmar and David looked at her open mouthed. David spoke first. "Not just a pretty face, is she?" He turned with an impressed expression on his countenance. "I would say our Professor Dread definitely was on to something." He hesitated a second or two before adding, "Pity he wasn't more forthcoming. All these riddles." He slapped a hand against his thigh in disapproval.

Dalmar Hunter found the two sea-angling rods in the cellar. He selected what appeared to be the better of the two, then changed his mind, and brought them both up to the ground floor. David wanted to know what sort of tackle was available. "Look – all we need is something like a coned weight. Nothing else. No floats, hooks or anything like that. We are not after fish – man." Dalmar was not sure what they were after. He just went along with it.

They got everything ready and then went off to have lunch together. Brian Cussen was intensely curious. David tried to explain. "This mazer professor fella from way back reckons he found the answer to the Lastwater anomaly with a long line fishing rod. Presumably he found the entrance to an underground river source. Not sure how he did it. Will just have to experiment. Personally, I think there is more to it than just an underground river. The Proff mentioned a connection to the ocean..." David stopped speaking. He privately wondered whether he was going too far. Divulging an idea before it was properly theorized was something he had learnt not to do.

Brian was about to say *"and"* when Dalmar added his thoughts. "Is that because he reckoned our lake has some strange comparison to the seas. You have established that Lastwater has a small content of salt in the water for instance?"

This let David off the hook nicely. "Perhaps," he said. "Look – let's carry out these experiments from the island first – alright?" The other two sensed they should let the matter drop and set about their meal of bangers and mash with generous helpings of onion gravy.

The lake was calm; ideal conditions for the two men to set off in the small rowing boat. Dalmar found the short oars difficult to control. He made a mental note to order a pair of the correct size.

Due to the *clue* offered by the box, it would only be necessary for them to cast their lines from the southern bank of Shimdorie Island, so they started at the end almost opposite Cloud Point.

David separated from Dalmar by twenty feet and let him make the first cast. They came across a snag straight away, for to cast the line needing a travel from the spool of 150 feet, the trees behind them got in the way. They did not have hooks to worry about, but the domed lead weights kept snagging on the branches. These weights were necessary to make the line reach the bottom of the lake. It became obvious, after the first few attempts, that it was virtually impossible. Normally, sea anglers using a long line would have a vast expanse of empty beach behind them. Both men realised that the only way to do this was from the boat, facing the island, and casting back behind them over open water. After some discussion, David asked Dalmar if he would do this from the rowing dinghy. David said he would stay on the island and attempt to direct the spot where he wanted the weight to sink.

"I'll do my best," said Dalmar. He had actually had experience of sea angling down in the south-west of

England many years ago. However, standing up in a small rowing boat was a different matter from doing it on a sturdy beach. David had worked out that this must be done with a long, long cast. There would be no big fish on the end to drag the line out. If they were going to catch an underwater current leading to a river mouth, the line should be extended as much as possible to start with.

Well, Dalmar cast and cast up and down the south bank area for nearly an hour and a half, and all that ever happened was the line kept falling dead to the lakebed, a mere twenty to thirty feet down. After each go Dalmar had to laboriously rewind the line to the spoil manually.

They were about to give up when the geologist decided to try one last thing. He asked Dalmar to bring the boat back to the island, and then he took his rod, prepared the line, and asked Dalmar to pass it up to him when he had scaled a stumpy pine tree growing near the water's edge, above an extremely rocky part of the southern bank. It was the only tree suitable; however, that was not what had attracted David to it. He had spotted something and cursed himself for not having done so earlier. "Call yourself a geologist," he sneered at himself out loud.

"Pardon?" said Dalmar confused.

"Ah – no matter. Will explain later if this works." At this he climbed about fifteen feet up with ease – got himself secure in footing – and put his right hand out to receive the rod. Dalmar climbed a little of the way and holding it in the centre stretched his arm out to give David the reel end to grab hold of.

David inched his way along a sturdy branch over the water holding on with one hand to another branch slightly above his head. He cursed at foliage getting in his way. When he was satisfied, he was in the right position, he managed to achieve a balanced *no hands* position and held the rod out. Then he started to wind out the spoil. It took a little while for the coned weight to enter the water. David kept on unwinding.

Dalmar expected the line to come to rest almost immediately. It did not. It kept on going ... and going. The weight had entered the water between a hard, sharp volcanic rock edge, and, another, similar, but not so sharp and considerably longer ridge projecting from the lake. It travelled for about six yards or more before disappearing below the surface. The gap between the two ridges was about six feet at its narrowest, widening to double that.

All of a sudden, the reel started to play out, not aggressively as though a large fish had been hooked; just a steady travel. David had half expected it, so it caused him little concern. He did not try to stop it either.

To Dalmar's growing amazement, the entire line was pulled out over a period of several minutes before it ran out coming to a halt when the rod started to bend slightly. David made a sign to the other man indicating that he should take hold as he passed it down rather awkwardly.

"If it is okay with you, can we leave this here? It will take an age to reel in and might be more useful to our research if it remained," suggested the highly articulate Geordie.

"Right," replied the curator, and then when he thought about it added, "Don't we need to secure it somehow?"

"Yes. Look – if we put a rock over the rod for the time being, I'll bring some rope out tomorrow morning, or later today, and tie it to this tree – okay?"

Dalmar nodded his agreement. He could see the logic even if it meant, in the end, the loss of the rod. "Mind you, don't know why you are asking me. This island comes under the administration of the National Park." After he thought about it, he offered, "I'll let them know if you like?" David just gave him a quick nod.

On their way back, he intimated to the curator that he was close to coming to a conclusion. Dalmar was surprised. He had formulated the idea in his mind that David would be around for quite a while yet. He decided not to say anything for the time being and await events.

"To be honest," explained David, "I should have spotted

that ridge formation on the bank where we left the rod. It would have saved a lot of time. Classic mini-harbour indicating the birth of an outflow – man." Dalmar said nothing. He did not know what he was talking about.

David Fresher did return to Shimdorie Island in the early evening alone. He lashed the fishing rod securely to the tree with the man-made fibre rope he had brought with him, and left the line suspended into the water. As the spool was empty, the line had travelled its full length – three hundred yards.

During the remainder of the evening, the geologist returned to studying the historical farming documents. The following morning, he made arrangements by telephone to visit Chris Legg at Lastwater Farm. Dalmar gave him an introduction. He was curious to know what, if anything, David had discovered, though he resisted the temptation to ask. The man would communicate when he was ready.

It was also arranged to leave the documents with the Legg family so that they could be sorted through and a decision made on what they might wish to retain.

David enjoyed his time with Chris Legg. The two men discussed matters while the geologist spent most of the time cradling the two border collies; one in each arm. There was certain information that David had already ascertained from the documents, which he needed some sort of family historical background to. He got it – emphatically. His theory as to the *Lastwater Anomaly* was now clear in his mind.

On his return to Bray Castle David Fresher found Dalmar talking to Brian Cussen outside the restaurant. "I shall be leaving on Saturday morning. My work is done – for now." David sort of threw this at them.

Both men were astounded, especially Brian. "You're joking?" And then noticing David's slightly annoyed expression – clarified matters, "I mean you have come to a conclusion?"

"Definitely. Of course, it will remain a theory until proven – but that could be as early as next spring. And – in the meantime – I could be more usefully employed elsewhere. Can we have a meeting Friday morning?" He directed the question at the curator.

"I have to attend the remembrance services for Trevor and Pat during the morning and early afternoon. Can't speak for Jack – have to give him a call." Then Dalmar hesitated. "If this is what I think it is. A final explanation of the lake's anomaly. Then we must invite someone from The Lake District National Park. They are paying half your fee after all."

"Alright. I'll get to work to prepare my case. Perhaps we could get something organised for late Friday afternoon?" David seemed to want to get the matter finalised. This had far less to do with the fact that he was anxious to leave, and far more to do with the excitement of getting the job done, especially, as he earnestly believed ... there was more to come of far greater geographic importance.

What had not escaped Dalmar's attention was that David did not challenge the intimation that the matter would be concluded. Once more he resisted the urge to ask for details right now – but he was intensely curious and bit his tongue in frustration.

Jack Twentyman could not attend either the commemorative services for the two deceased Bray Castle employees or the meeting with David Fresher. He had to go to London on urgent Trust business. However, he readily agreed to represent the castle at the John Precence memorial service in Keswick the following week. Dalmar managed to get a senior director from The Lake District National Park to meet them tomorrow at four o'clock in the afternoon.

Suzanne was determined to accompany her husband on Friday morning. She managed to arrange a babysitter in the shape of Beatrice from the animal rescue centre. As the castle was closed to the public, she could arrange things so that the animals would be able to be left for three hours.

However, she would be making a check around mid-day with her charges in tow. She had another reason for volunteering. She knew the service of remembrance for Trevor Blake would be far too upsetting for her.

At ten thirty in the morning, Dalmar, Suzanne and Brian Cussen set off in the Land Rover for Grasmere. Other members of staff would be making their own way from their respective homes.

As though prearranged, dark clouds descended low over Grasmere village. It did not rain; however, it was enough to add to the sombre atmosphere. The little church was crammed with mourners, many of them representatives from all walks of life, marking their respect over the tragedy on Lastwater resulting in the loss of Trevor Blake and Pat Simpson. No one who attended the service for Trevor would ever forget the sight of his two young daughters walking up the aisle on either side of their mother. They were not dressed in black. They wore white, almost in defiance of the fate that had befallen father and husband. While it made them stand out against the rest of the congregation, it also gave stark pictorial emphasis to their loss. The press used this to great effect for the next day's papers, photographing them walking away from the church as they passed by the grave of the bard, William Wordsworth. The overcast skies increased the contrast between the lace covered pale dresses of the mother and daughters to the dark background of yew trees growing among the gravestones. One headline read, 'Sad Angels by a Poet's Grave.'

Meanwhile, David Fresher had been busy putting together his case for his theory as to the cause of the Lastwater anomaly. He raided the deserted kitchens to try and build a model out of empty plastic food containers, so that he could further illustrate his point, however, he gave up on the basis that it would be too amateur and might make a fool of him by simply not working. He would be building a far more professional affair once he could get to use the facilities at the Royal Geographical Society in

London. Part of his agreement with the National Trust and the Lake District National Park was that the result would be published through the Geographical Society, with copies provided for both concerns.

CHAPTER TWENTY-ONE

"WHAT ABOUT THE FISH?"

At 16:05 in the afternoon, four men and a dog walked down the slate fragment path towards the lake shore from Bray Castle. They were Brian Cussen, Dalmar Hunter, David Fresher and Donald Altringham, Senior Director of the Lake District National Park, and Fly who had insisted on accompanying them as though it was his divine right. He padded out ahead of them looking magnificent. Emma and Dalmar, together, had given him a good grooming yesterday.

Donald was a balding, portly man in his late fifties. He looked a little out of place in his light grey suit, white shirt and tie of some club recognition. However, he had expected a meeting in an office, not a draughty lakeside, and, secondly, he had been attired correctly for the rest of the preceding day. But still he bore the matter in good humour. "Thank Christ it isn't raining," he muttered.

"You will appreciate why it is best to do this on site," said David striding out ahead of the rest. He had no paperwork with him preferring a verbal explanation right where it happens. "I promise you. The whole thing will be laid out before us, and, actually – well ... you will see – man."

"By the sound of things," Donald started to remark: he was puffing a bit trying to maintain David's fast walking pace, "you seem to have come to a definite conclusion?"

"No doubt about it." David did not add a phrase such as, 'in my mind.' He felt no need. "Of course, will have to make a return visit to provide positive proof. Next spring would be a good time: a safe distance after the event." Not one of the other men had a notion as to what he was talking about.

"Will this require further funding?" If the others required any evidence as to Donald's suitability for his post, they had just received it. Straight to the point.

David turned his head to look at him without faltering in his stride. "I will certainly require the permission of the Lake District National Park as it is your patch. As to funding? No promises but think this one might be the turn of the private sector. Have an idea – man," he finished with one of his disarming smiles. He received an equally affable one in return.

Once down by the dry-wall style boathouse, David led them out onto the jetty. He did not have to ask them to gather around him: the narrowness of the little pier guaranteed that. "All you have to do now – is listen and absorb," he said. His shoulder length blond hair flicked about in the breeze. His eyes were alert with concentration as he appealed to his audience to believe in him.

"As you will probably know," he waved an arm over the length of the water from west to east, "our lake has no visible outflow."

Donald looked taken aback. "Pardon?" he said.

"No river," said David, looking at him in surprise.

"Bloody hell! – you're kidding," said the senior director.

Dalmar joined in. "Don't worry. It took my wife to point it out to me. I hadn't realised either."

"Well – where the blazes does all the water go?" asked Donald – reasonably.

"In various other situations like this – in other parts of the world – there is an underground river outflow. In some cases, there is a massive seepage over a large area through porous rock. This would hardly be applicable here. Hard volcanic rock."

"So – does Lastwater have an underground river? In the mid-18th Century Professor James Dread reckoned there was, and it was his information that led us to find it." He pointed to Shimdorie Island. "You will see – just about – a white painted ring on that pine over on the bank facing us." 'Should have made it bigger,' he thought to himself. However, all three of them could make it out. Brian with ease. "Just below that tree, about twenty-five feet down, we have a fishing line trailing into the opening of an underground stream for some three hundred yards. So – has to be. It is my opinion that the water erosion caused over millions of years is considerable – far more than a usual river outflow for a lake of this size, because it is the only one." He went on to explain, "Take Elterwater lake, to the south of here. It is an inland waterway of a similar scale to Lastwater, which has a heavy water volume in the shape of the river Brathay flowing out of it down to lake Windermere.

No one argued with him. "Well – I'll be," said Donald placing a hand on his smooth head, partly to stop the wispy bits of side hair billowing about.

The white ringed pine was over-shadowed by a group of rowan trees with a full harvest of scarlet berries. They cast a facsimile picture into the water beneath them. It was one of those seasonal cameo pictures on Lastwater that was particularly appealing.

David carried on. "The next factor we have to take into account is that this lake is salinated."

Donald interjected. "Really – like a salt-lake? The Dead Sea?"

"Not quite to that degree," David answered him with a grin. "In fact, nothing like it. The saline content in this water," he pointed into the lake by the jetty without looking at it, "is considerably less than it would be for sea water in any part of the planet's oceans, but what there is – has come from the sea."

Donald was starting to get a little worried. "Are you saying from; he stretched an arm over to what he thought might be a westerly direction, "the Irish Sea."

"Or – the North Sea. Can't be certain yet." David's answer caused Donald's brow to furrow even further.

Brian Cussen rarely swore. "How the fuck?" he said.

Donald spluttered wanting to laugh, "Hururumph," he said. "My thoughts exactly."

Dalmar was amazed and looked it. He had assumed all along that Lastwater's salt content, when first brought to recognition by David Fresher, was similar to an inland salt-lake. 'What could the sea have to do with it?' was the question that rushed into his brain. 'Surely a reverse flow from sea to lake was impossible.'

"So – there you go – how?" David concurred grinning. He held up a hand. "All will be explained – man. As you know this lake is known for its unusual royal blue hue, particularly when seen in sunny conditions."

"Much photographed for that very reason," added Donald. "Or rather was – tends to be photographed for rather more sombre reasons nowadays."

"Yes," – agreed David. "The colour is what gave me the clue as to its salt content, subsequently analysed conclusively. In fact, if it had the same salt content as sea water it would be a great deal greener, but it doesn't – so – it has its own unique palette. It appears that Professor James Dread, who lived at Bray House in the eighteenth century, discovered this. It was he who apparently gave the name to this lake which is an anagram of salt and, courtesy, of Mrs Hunter's discovery," he made a small wave in Dalmar's direction, "Sodium Chloride may be formed from an anagram of," again he pointed to the island, "Shimdorie," and moving his outstretched finger along to come to rest over the promontory a few hundred yards away, "Cloud."

"What – that is Cloud Point?" asked the senior director.

"Huh huh," David replied acknowledging with a movement of one hand that not everyone would know that.

"How extraordinary," Donald enthused. You guys have been doing your homework. He turned to Dalmar. "I understand you and your wife went to see the original ancestors of the local farm over there." It was his turn to wave an arm in the general direction. "They live in the States – yes?"

Dalmar gave him a nod. "And what they brought back was of paramount importance," David immediately interrupted. "The Posselthawite family in Virginia have let us have papers and an artefact which, not only have led us to discover the source of the underground river – but, also, enabled me to come up with a theory, that I have no doubt will prove to be fact in due course. In short, therefore, you will be able to publish, with confidence, exactly when this lake should be avoided. At all other times, it will be as safe as deep water can be – provided it is treated with adequate caution."

Donald was impressed with the geologist's articulation. He invited him to explain further. Dalmar and Brian, both with eyes practically bulging, were intense with anticipation.

"What no one seems to have spotted is actually rather obvious," David continued after an exaggerated demur. "But then – without the sea water connection – why should they?" He glanced at his small audience. The wind had dropped and the lake water, with its current slate grey under the overcast sky, was utterly calm. "Let us take this year's misfortunes. Both the disappearance of the rowing team and, more recently, those that vanished during the charity swim occurred roughly twelve hours after the seasonal equinoxes. Spring in the case of the rowing club and autumn for..." He did not have to explain further.

"Never!" exclaimed Brian and Donald together. It was Brian who arrived there first, "Spring Tides!" he virtually shouted.

David raised a hand, "Got it in one Brian. Spring Tides. Or to put it correctly Equinoctial Spring Tides."

It was the astronomer who raised the obvious. "But an inland waterway isn't tidal – is it?" He looked confused.

"No. You are quite right. It is only the oceans that are influenced by our moon and the Earth's movements." David started to explain. "Just a sec though, I need to explain this further. The documents you brought back from America mentioned, several times over the years, an abnormal rise in the level of the lake's water at particular times by means of a diary entry or farm record observation. Dalmar, you saw this with your own eyes on this very marker post just before the racing eight vanished." David went over to the post affixed to the jetty and placed a hand on it. "My visit to see Chris Legg at Lastwater farm gave me the final confirmation I needed. It turns out his family have kept records of the lake's level changes over the last one hundred and fifty years. Rather like an amateur meteorologist keeps his barometer recordings. And guess what, immediately after each and every equinox, the water level dramatically rose – more than at any other time during the year. At other times, a rise of perhaps half an inch occurred following a period of particularly heavy and prolonged rainfall. Let's face it that is normal around here. The wettest place in England is only a few miles away. This explains why the abnormal increase in the water level after the equinoxes went unnoticed for its regularity. Not only that, but that level always subsided back to normal after a few hours. This showed up in the farm's records – the day following an entry indicating a big increase."

David took a deep breath. "All of the recorded loss of life that has occurred on this lake, throughout history, has happened, as near as we can tell, on the day following the spring or autumn equinox." David stopped and looked at the three men in turn. To observe that their attention was rapt would be an understatement. Not even the squawking and wing flapping of two Mallard ducks suddenly taking to flight across the water in Tadpole Bay could distract either one of them.

"Now – you may well ask. How does all this cause the kind of drowning accidents where no bodies are ever found?" David held out both hands, with the left higher than the right. Imagine my left hand to be Lastwater and my right hand is the sea. Normally, water flows from Lastwater underground to the sea. What I believe is happening is this. When a spring tide comes in to the shore, a massively increased pressure due to weight caused by the extra volume of water and – now this is important because it would not happen without the additional extra force – the sheer power of the mammoth equinoctial tide – causes a blow back in the river's course all the way to this lake – man. Hence the injection of neat sea water and a sudden water level rise over all of the lake. I appreciate this is difficult to take in. It does tell us that the river's outflow is also under the sea. It could not happen otherwise as, say, our underground river joining a surface river somewhere else. We don't know where our river comes out – or on which coast. Therefore, calculations as to volume, power required, and time involved are impossible. We simply must go by historical records. However, you will know that when you siphon petrol from a fuel tank – all that is required is a certain sucking force. On a much greater scale, this is the same, except that the power exerted to cause the temporary reversal of the river's flow is caused by pressure, due to increased weight of water above the underground mouth of the river – together with the tidal force."

"These equinox tides vary according to meteorological situations in force at the time, which accounts for the fluctuation in the abnormal water level rises recorded. Sometimes it has only been a couple of inches – others as much as six! The crucial factor is this. When the spring tide subsides – goes out – it causes a sudden discharge back down the river's water course all the way to the sea, and everything is balanced back to normal as far as this lake is concerned– probably within half an hour or so. For obvious gravitational reasons the force of sea water infusion is gentle, taking place over some hours, whereas, the force of discharge is considerable."

Nobody on that jetty moved a muscle.

So," David said, "our victims – boats and all were caught in an all-consuming whirlpool. We know that it happens in the same place every time; very near where we have discovered the opening of the underwater river to be. Why the Bray Castle dingy survived the latest trauma, quite frankly, is a mystery to me. If there was loss of life – then the boat should have gone with them. The only possible cause I can think of is that it capsized early on, righted itself, unfortunately, without the crew and drifted away from the main current – so avoiding the same fate as the men."

The astronomer, the curator and the senior executive all let out low whistles of expelled air.

"Of course, because the danger only occurs twice a year, accidents have been infrequent. More often than not, there was no one on the lake when the whirlpool and its accompanying powerful current occurred. This year has been something of a freak. But now we can stop all disasters permanently." He said with an air of triumph.

After a suitable spell during which the information could penetrate everyone's minds, Donald Altringham spoke up. "My congratulations. This is superb. Absolutely superb!"

All three men shook hands with the geologist. After which as they started back towards the castle, in the approaching gloom of the late afternoon, David went on to explain that he would be building a model to illustrate the anomaly and would carry out a demonstration at the Royal Geographical Society's headquarters in London. The media would be invited. He would now go home and prepare a report outlining what had just been divulged. A copy would be sent to both the National Trust and the Lake District National Park together with his account.

"What about the fish? Aren't they affected by this intrusion of sea water?" This question came from Brian.

"No. Fish possess osmotic regulators which control any fluctuations in salt content. They are unaffected," explained David. "Although I do not know what happens to those who are drawn out at the time of the whirlpool, or, for that matter, those that are sucked in at the sea end. The spring equinox next year occurs on March 21st. The evidence should occur sometime the next day. Anyhow, I plan to be here – invited or not – on or before the 20th."

"A helicopter shot would be ideal," said Dalmar. It was then the curator recalled something. "You know   –   I remember... The day before the L.R.C. disaster, on my way back from Ambleside, I stopped to give my dog a run on White Crag ... and while there I noticed an odd change in colour out on the lake..." Dalmar put a hand to his forehead pushing back a dark lock of hair. "It was this side of the island ... the water became – it seemed to me – pale green. Then it dispersed or appeared to and returned to normal."

David looked at him intently. "The day before the loss of the boat and its crew ... so we are talking about the 20th March?"

"If you say so – a Saturday," replied Dalmar.

David spoke slowly. "The 20th March was the date of the spring equinox for this year. What you saw was new sea water entering the lake."

"I can lay up an observation post on the castle roof next year," said Brian. "Damn it – this is exciting!"

Donald agreed with him.

"But," said David Fresher. "This is well and good – but hardly sufficient evidence for a concrete theory. I have in mind organising an underwater exploration of this here river." He looked pointedly at Dalmar. "Would need to be a two-man operation. Thinking around April," he finished off with one of his smiles.

The intonation that he wanted Dalmar to accompany him on this exploration did not escape anybody's attention. Donald merely noted it. Brian was curious and Dalmar's thoughts were split in two; part alarm – part excitement, although, there was a third element, which, just now, he was unsure of. He said nothing. It was too early for that.

CHAPTER TWENTY-TWO

"CAN WE DEAL WITH THIS LATER?"

Brian and David volunteered to take the impatient collie for a longer walk. They both said their goodbyes to Donald Altringham with David promising something in the post very soon. In the meantime, he suggested that a press release be drafted, keeping the information low key, until, at such time as underwater exploration could be arranged next year, after the spring equinox. There would certainly be media interest at the time of the equinox, and David was quite confident that they would get the evidence of both the water rise and the sudden drain of vast quantities of water twelve hours later. Meantime the public could be informed, and National Park rangers would be on hand to warn away would be adventurers over the *risk* period.

Before Donald left, Dalmar invited him for a drink at the Dower-house. He declined stating that he was expected at home. In a brief chat, before he drove off, it was agreed that the National Park would take charge of the press release as it was their responsibility. Bray Castle would have the job of informing visitors to their estate.

When Dalmar, with Fly aboard, drove David Fresher to Windermere station the next morning he could not help remarking, "When you arrived – you smoked cigarettes. Haven't seen you do it for a while. Given up – or having a break?"

"Kicked the habit ... I hope. You guys don't smoke – so

made use of the opportunity."

Dalmar inclined his head saying, "Well done. I jacked it in about – hey – must be seven years or so ago. Remember having to run some distance in a hurry and my chest was on fire. That was it for me." For the first time since he arrived, David was sporting his strange Aussie style hat. Dalmar wondered why he only used it when travelling but refrained from asking.

"Will let you know when things are ready to roll at the Geographical Society; shouldn't be too long. Just now – when saying bye to your family, Suzanne looked pleased about my kid sister coming over to work next month?"

"She is; said something to me about her sounding really nice over the phone."

"Oh – she's okay. Bit intense sometimes," and then thinking about what he said, corrected himself. "I'm sure she'll do a good job." Dalmar smiled knowingly. "Oh ... by the way. I meant what I said yesterday. I shall need a team mate to come with me when I have a look at that river: Safety in numbers and all that. Hope you will consider joining me? Can't think of anyone better suited."

Dalmar did not cough with embarrassment. "He merely said, "Of course," and smiled. Anyone who knew the man would have expected nothing less. The geologist looked pleased. He decided not to explain further right now.

The two men said goodbye outside the station and Dalmar thanked his new colleague enthusiastically. David was equally complimentary, explaining that without his and Suzanne's thorough research, the conclusion would have taken a great deal longer to arrive at.

As promised, Dalmar took his family out for the day on Sunday leaving the running of the castle to Brian and other members of staff. They went to Brown Robin nature reserve, which was not exactly the seaside but certainly on the coast with views of the sea. It was explained to Emma that this time of year was hardly appropriate for buckets and spades on the beach. She seemed to accept it, partly because of the magical place she found herself in. A lot of the reserve was woodland, and Suzanne had a bit of a torrid time making sure Michael kept his fingers of the poisonous autumnal spindle berries. She eventually placed him into his push chair and strapped him in for his own safety.

They saw several roe deer, which delighted both children. It was widely thought this was where the nuthatches found at Bray, earlier in the year, might have migrated from ... their parents that is.

On Monday morning the curator wrote his letter of resignation and handed it to Jack Twentyman on his arrival.

Jack had come over to hear all about David Fresher's conclusions and talk about other matters. Dalmar had telephoned him at his home on Friday evening to let him in on the amazing results David had come up with, so he was aware.

"What's this?" Jack said looking extremely worried. Dalmar's letter was laid out before him on the front of the curator's desk. Jack always sat here when he visited, so that he could easily reach the telephone. The envelope gave everything away, written in Dalmar's familiar hand. It simply read, 'J. Twentyman.,Esq.' And on the second line,' The National Trust, North West Region,' and low down in the right-hand corner, 'By Hand."

The regional director opened it. He read with his face now poker blank. Once mind digested, he refolded the paper and placed it back in the envelope. Then he tucked it into the inside pocket of his suit jacket. "Right," he said. "Can we deal with that later?" Dalmar made a suitable sign of acquiescence.

He poured a coffee into Jack's cup and saucer and placed it on the desk in front of him. "Well – I've had the chance to chew over this equinox theory of David's. Although somewhat fantastic – can't see anything wrong. Neither can Donald I can tell you. Spoke to him yesterday."

Jack looked a little apprehensive about what he had to say next, simply because he was in the place where the latest loss of life had personally affected many of those who worked there. "We are of the opinion that this little lot is going to become something of a tourist attraction?" It was put to Dalmar with a questioning tone.

The curator, a little chagrined that his resignation had been treated with such disdain commented. "That thought had occurred to me. Our big telescope might be useful." Sentiment had been thrown aside. Dalmar put his curator's hat on. So be it.

Jack was agreeably surprised. The two men went on to discuss the implications at some length before moving on to the question of replacing the two-ground staff. It was decided that Jack would instigate an internal advertisement throughout the National Trust, together with county wide local advertising for a head groundsman. Dalmar suggested doing away with the title head gardener, it was not appropriate. The estate had hardly any formal gardens; just the big lawns to the right-hand side backing onto woodland. Bray Castle would canvas locally for an assistant and hold interviews. When they had finished, Jack told his curator that he would be back at six o'clock when the estate closed to the public. "Does your wife know about your resignation?" he reasonably asked.

"No," thought it best at this stage. "Presumably she will want to carry on with the running of the animal rescue centre."

"I sincerely hope so," said Jack. He could see an entirely fruitful situation going belly up. He supposed he should have expected this from Dalmar, after the recent tragedy, and blamed himself for not saying anything earlier. 'The trouble with men of honour was that they could be too darn sensitive,' he thought to himself.

After supposedly taking his leave, he shot downstairs and, in between welcoming visitors, asked Doris for a word. He told her bluntly what was afoot and asked her to ensure all members of staff gathered in the main hall at six o'clock this afternoon. He pleaded with her to impress upon them not to leave until after he had addressed all of them. He also asked Doris to keep Dalmar's resignation to herself until then.

Suzanne took her daughter to primary school for the first time that day. For the rest of the week she would be attending for the morning only, and after that she was scheduled to start going full time. Suzanne's own private opinion was that children under six years old were not ready for the time discipline required at junior school. She thought they would be better educated by carrying out reception school curriculum classes at an extended playgroup until six years old. Emma, on the other hand, probably did not agree. She was more than ready and entered into her first morning's attendance with real enthusiasm. There were no tears.

Meantime, Michael was getting on at his playschool and could now be left alone until noon at the end of the session. This left Suzanne free to go about her work at the animal centre. When she went to see Bea at around ten-thirty she was immediately asked why Jack Twentyman had asked to see all members of staff, on duty today, at six o'clock before they went home, especially as some of them finished work half an hour earlier.

"Sorry – don't have a clue," replied Suzanne completely puzzled. She suspected it had something to do with the fact that they would shortly be advertising for new ground staff. 'But surely, that was her husband's responsibility,' her mind was in a whirl. So – off she went to track down Dalmar and ask him.

She found him putting fuel into the grass cutter before taking it out to give the lawns a final cut before winter set in. He told her of his resignation letter. "What! ... Why? She asked looking miserable and completely surprised at the same time. She appeared very demure in her working N.T. clothes and, therefore, vulnerable with such a sad expression on her face. She knew Dalmar would not have done this lightly. Before he could reply, she threw another remark at him, "And why – oh why – didn't you talk to me about it?"

"Because I didn't want to involve you: it is important that you stay on." The answer seemed obvious to him. "Look," he carried on; "there is no way I can stay here. That charity swim was my idea and it led to the deaths of two of our employees." This was said as though there could not possibly be any doubt as to the decision.

Suzanne was about to splutter a protest when she stopped herself. It dawned on her, in a rush, that she should have seen this coming. Any honourable person would have done the same and for Dalmar not to – was unthinkable. She walked over to him as he rose to his full height having put the screw cap back on the mower's fuel tank. She put her arms around his chest and buried her head under his chin – saying nothing. For the time being, there was nothing to be said. She would have to wait to see what Jack had to say. She did, however, make the comment, "Think you are being too hard on yourself," but she knew it would not be heeded. "Anyway, you should know that Jack has asked all members of staff to attend a meeting in the hall at six." Dalmar nodded, he had expected something of the sort; they had to be informed as soon as possible. He decided that he would be well away from the building at that time.

As the instruction for this assembly had emanated from Doris, Suzanne went straight to see her. Once both women became aware that they were the only ones in the know, Suzanne asked Doris for her opinion. She told her that she understood the reasons why, but sincerely hoped her husband would change his mind. "It'll be a tragedy. Everyone has such high regard for him. Why should we suffer two tragedies? – one's quite enough."

'What glorious common sense,' thought Suzanne and she told Doris so.

During the afternoon while Suzanne was with her two

children back at the Dower-house she, also, decided she would give the meeting a wide berth. She had not been asked after all. She would be able to go and do her evening tour of duty with the animals later, after Bea had departed.

Emma's first attendance at school was the success expected. Her father went to see her at lunch time and hear all about it.

Jack Twentyman drove into his usual parking place over by the main ramparts so as to be well away from the castle entrance. He could see that Doris had done her job well. Several staff members were milling around inside the entrance hallway.

He did not waist anyone's time holding aloft Dalmar's envelope containing the resignation letter as he entered. The gathering consisted of Brian Cussen, the weekday chef and assistant, plus two waitresses and, of course, Bea. Also present were cleaners and guest bedroom attendants; Doris and one of the volunteer tour guides, plus two part-time site maintenance men.

When he had all their attention and Doris had shut the big doors behind them, he, initially, thanked them all for staying on and then said, raising his voice a little. "I received this letter this morning. It was given to me by the writer himself. I shall read it to you. It will not take very long." Jack took a piece of paper out of the envelope and unfolded it. Having stated who it was addressed to, namely himself, he read the text. "It is with great sadness that I must tender my resignation as curator of Bray Castle, as soon as it may decently be achieved. Yours sincerely, John Dalmar Hunter."

There followed an awful silence before Jack spoke again. "I would assume that Mr Hunter, having muted the idea for the charity swim, feels responsible for the tragic loss of Trevor and Pat. We all know that it was rank bad luck and that both those men volunteered to take part willingly, without any form of suggestion coming from management. You will have all heard by now of David

Fresher's conclusion that during the year there were only two days in which people out on the lake were at risk. Two days out of three-hundred and sixty-five. You see what I mean by bad luck." The regional director then pulled a folded sheet of paper from his jacket inside pocket. "I am going to leave this," he opened it out, "on the reception table over there." Jack pointed to the table Doris and others used just inside the entrance. "It is addressed to Dalmar and states at the top; the following persons, while understanding your concern, wish it to be known that we would like you to reconsider your decision to resign from your position as Curator of Bray Castle. I have taken the liberty of signing it myself following on from the signatures of Susan Blake and Joy and William Simpson." Without another word he went over, laid the paper on the table, put a convenient paper weight on the top right-hand corner, opened one of the huge doors soundlessly, and departed.

Dalmar returned to the castle just before seven o'clock having spent most of the last hour and a quarter gazing out over Lastwater at the extreme end of Cloud Point. The lake was in gentle mode but without any sunshine – looked sombre. Even the autumn colours over on Shimdorie Island and beyond to the far northern bank did nothing to improve his state of mind. It was at times like this that he took great comfort from the proximity of Fly, who sat right by his side the whole time. Usually he would be off snuffling about, but not this evening. He could sense distress in his master.

Dalmar cursed himself for wallowing in self-pity and rose to his feet with a resolve to check that all was locked up at the castle, and then to attend to his children. 'The pity lies with certain loved ones inhabiting the village of Grasmere and the town of Keswick,' he thought determinedly.

He entered the vast building via the kitchen rear entrance and went about his business. Brian Cussen waylaid him before he went on duty at the observatory. Although the nights were drawing in, tonight would be too overcast for his students to indulge in scanning the skies. "Glad I caught you," he lied. He had actually been lying in wait. Without ceremony he took Dalmar by the elbow and led him firmly across the main hall. "There is something you should see," he said.

When Dalmar had taken in the signatures on Jack's deputation – particularly those of the deceased relatives, he picked up one of the ball point pens on the desk and wrote on the bottom, 'O.K.' Then he put his second name alongside.

Some people would think that he had changed his mind. Brian read it the right way. Dalmar had agreed to reconsider.

"I certainly put my name to that piece of paper," said the astronomer, "but I should like you to have my thoughts on the matter. He carried straight on before Dalmar could interrupt him. He did not mince his words either. "Okay – you have done the honourable thing – now it is time to really face up to your responsibilities, which are considerable when you think about it. We don't have to worry about Lastwater's notoriety anymore, and it will be up to you to get that message across in the coming months. Your wife needs support particularly with the new equestrian centre starting up next year. I speak with respect – you understand?" Brian did not actually accuse Dalmar of running away, but he got dangerously close to it, so he decided to add a softener. "Oh – and it goes without saying – we are all here to help you."

Brian's words went straight to Dalmar's heart. "Yes Brian – I understand – believe me – I do understand." He put an arm on the older man's shoulder and gave him a wan smile before going to see his family.

Suzanne had a plate of food keeping hot in the oven. Dalmar brought her up to date about Jack's petition. His wife nodded. "Good. So, you are reconsidering?"

"Yes." Suzanne thought that was all she was going to get, but he told her about Brian's pep talk. "It seems that if I did stay on, I shall have some serious absolution to perform."

Suzanne had not the slightest idea what he meant by that, merely agreeing whole heartedly with Brian Cussen, and, at the same time, crossing her fingers behind her back.

"I will go and see Susan Blake in the morning and make my decision afterwards – immediately afterwards," he said. "It won't be fair to keep everyone waiting." And then he looked directly at her, "Especially you." They embraced and kissed and with perfect timing Emma came bustling into the kitchen to ask her daddy to run her bath.

Michael was already fast asleep and so while Dalmar attended to Emma's bath time, followed by a story in her bed, Suzanne went over to the castle to see to all the animal's needs before the night set in. While she was there, she stole silently across the great hall, looked at the petition on the reception desk with a strong emotional feeling and signed her name at the end.

When Dalmar drove into Grasmere village on Tuesday morning the sun came out. The brilliant light transformed the look of the village. The dry-stone buildings lost their dour greyness to be replaced by attractive variegated textures all over the volcanic stone.

Susan Blake was at home having just taken her daughters to school for the first time since the loss of their father. It was, naturally, a head-reeling sorry time for her – alone. She was just getting ready to go and visit her mother – when the doorbell rang.

Dalmar was impressed for she instantly recognised him and even managed a small smile of greeting. "Susan – I'm really sorry about this. Do you have a moment?" This was difficult enough as it was, so he decided to get straight to the point as tactfully as possible.

Susan did it for him. "How do, just goin' to see my mum. She won't mind waiting ... especially for you's – when I tell's her," she said all in a jumble.

Dalmar adored her soft Cumbrian accent. 'I could fall in love with that voice without seeing the face,' he thought privately. "Right – I'll keep it short." He made to start his appeal to her at the doorway.

Susan hushed him with a finger to her lips. Dressed in a simple plum dress with a light, darker coloured woollen top, the gentle features of her face could not hide the crying tones in her eyes. She ushered him into her sitting room and invited him to take a seat. He accepted gratefully but declined any refreshment at her suggestion.

Before he could start, she said, "I think I know what this is about. You's aren't goin' to give up your job over Trevor are you? Cause us all more grief."

That simple questioning sentence from her was the end of the matter. He no longer had to make any kind of roundabout statement about his position. There was a silence for perhaps twenty seconds while she looked into his eyes with genuine appeal. "I came to tell you that I shall be facing up to my responsibilities to see this matter through to its conclusion. Yes, I will be staying on. And, incidentally – thanks for your support." This was said in reference to her signature on Jack's deputation, which he must have obtained by a personal visit. Dalmar was not lying. He had already made up his mind.

"Oh good." She looked puzzled. "What conclusion is that?"

Dalmar bit into his lower lip. "Well – David Fresher and I will be taking a look at that underground river next year. Would appreciate it if you could keep that to yourself until it's official. It was just ... well, I wanted you to know."

Susan looked pleased. "Thank you. I'll do as you please." The widow looked at the denim clad National Trust man. She wondered if his casual attire would be frowned upon by his seniors.

On his way out Dalmar bent his head close to hers. "Susan, I know you have family nearby – but if you ever need us – please telephone. My wife has asked me to tell you that she wants to maintain your daughters' visits to the castle, just as they used to when Trevor was alive; if they would like – on a regular basis."

"Okay," she said.

As Dalmar greeted his waiting dog in the back of the Land Rover, he could not help harbouring the feeling that this heralded the start of a great challenge in his life. He was unaware of his sister in law's strange premonition when she and her family left the castle at the end of their summer visit. It was as well, for, usually, these futuristic calms of hers – came into being.

A little later, as Dalmar crested the hilltop before the pull-in below White Crag, he decided to forgo the usual stop. It was time to get on.

OCTOBER EVENING

Sky of yellow bold
Are you beauty or setting gloom?
Kindle our fires and close the doors.
Hold onto precious things.
Keep not your secrets from us.
Help our fragile souls
Before you chill our bones.

Herald you the passing of warmth.
Remember the summer.
The last summer?
And yet you display such splendour:
The coming of something better?

We do not know,
But it seems so.

All those that take your signal
And burrow down for winter.
The final light;
A splendid sight.
Being the last they will see,
Until another day
Brings forth the new-born May.

PART TWO

1983

CHAPTER TWENTY-THREE

1st JANUARY 1983

John Dalmar Hunter's head was sore, and his eyes were bloodshot. It had been a good New Year 's Eve party at the McLennan farm in Langdale, the night before, and now he was paying for it. When the invitation came about a month ago, he had agreed to go even though he did not know most of the guests. It had been a case of being a dutiful husband. And, as often happens, when meeting new people, he had really enjoyed himself. Trouble was the beer was somewhat more-ish. Now – early on a Saturday morning, there was a likely-hood of a good turnout of visitors to Bray Castle during the forthcoming day and he had to be with it. Much to his surprise there seemed to be a hundred percent staff attendance. Most of them would have been celebrating last night, especially as it was still holiday time for many of their husband's or wives', so he had expected some late arrivals at least.

John Fisher, the newly appointed head groundsman was the first to arrive, but he would only be putting in half a day. Two volunteer women were manning reception and the kitchen was up and running.

Both Dalmar and Suzanne were now a year older. All the family were enjoying excellent health. Even Michael seemed to be coping with the frequent knocks toddlers had to put up with.

The old stable conversion had been completed by the builders in time for Christmas and a new desk had been added to Dalmar and Suzanne's office ready for Rosalind Maidment to start work on Monday morning. In the early days she would have to spend quite a bit of time at her desk organising pony acquisition, tack and so on. Later on, when the riding school actually started to operate, visits to the office would become less frequent.

The David Fresher demonstration showing his theory of The Lastwater Anomoly at the Royal Geographical Society's London headquarters went well, except that it was delayed until late November. It had proved extremely difficult to demonstrate equinox tidal power off the British Coast in a small model. Lastwater was interpreted as a shallow glass container about eighteen by ten inches. It really needed to be connected to an Olympic sized swimming pool to illustrate the scale of the sea, so, instead, David constructed a wind machine to blow intermittently across the surface of a three-foot aquarium. When the water in the aquarium rose to simulate a spring tide, no blow-back occurred up the tube to the smaller container until the wind generator had been switched on for a couple of minutes, thus, exactly illustrating what he was trying to convince others would happen when an excessive tidal surge caused a current reversal up Lastwater's underground river, whatever its distance might be: the fact being that once in motion the tidal bore would be self-perpetuating. When the wind generator was switched off the increased water level in the small container did not immediately go back to its previous level – not until the water level in the large container had been reduced – and then it did so in a rush. David had, through this experiment, illustrated his point. Now, all that had to done was to wait until the next spring equinox when the anomaly would, for the first time, be seen by people who would live to tell the tale.

It was strange but the most dramatic and rewarding happening at the animal rescue centre occurred in late October. Two children found a very small hedgehog hiding in a bush at Grasmere village. As it was in obvious distress, they bought it to the attention of Bea at her home. Naturally, she took it with her to work the very next morning. While the animal was far too small to undergo a season of hibernation and needed feeding up, there was also something else that required urgent attention. While it was unknown how the baby hedgehog, christened immediately by Emma as Spikey, had come to be orphaned, it was quite likely that it had been abandoned due to its size and, presumably, a late in the season birth, or, the mother simply might not have survived. The problem was a serious number of maggot eggs that lay clustered about his ears. Suzanne spent most of the morning patiently getting them off with tweezers. It was important to remove every last one before they hatched out and started burrowing and eating their way under the skin. To her great credit Suzanne was completely successful. Now they could start feeding him up with the type of milk usually fed to kittens. After a week, he started taking slugs and other tasty morsels found in the castle grounds. Within a month he had gained enough weight to be allowed to go free and seek a suitable nesting area for his hibernation. Both Emma and Michael were hopeful that he might reappear in the spring of the coming year and would be recognised.

The Hunter family Christmas had been wonderful. Primarily, this had not actually been due to gifts and indulgent food, but more especially because of the heavy snowfall a couple of days before, giving them their first white Christmas at Bray.   Suzanne's mother and father had managed to make the long journey up from the West Country before the snow depth had become excessive. Tim and Christine decided to have a family holiday season at home for a change, so they did not join them. They and their children were missed but there was always next year. It had been debateable who had enjoyed the wintry landscape the most – the children or Fly. The dog took on a new lease of life bounding around in the snow like a two-year old. For the first time in ages, Dalmar had to control his barking with sharp commands, mostly for fear of disturbing the sheep munching their hay.

The curator had been approached by Ambleside

Mountain Rescue during the autumn wondering if he might like to consider becoming a reserve member of the team. He had agreed to do so, which had involved going out on training exercises so that he could become proficient at using climbing equipment, stretcher handling, and other survival matters to do with the injured or incapacitated. He had found some of the work arduous, but he persevered until they appeared satisfied that he was ready, although he would only to be called out if a regular member was unavailable. To date, it had not happened, although the main team had been called out on several occasions especially during the recent wintry weather.

And so the big day arrived, at least, it was very important for Suzanne, in particular. She took great delight in welcoming Roz early on the Monday morning. The new riding instructor/general equestrian manager arrived clad in a dark green winter weight skirt and National Trust emblemed sports shirt. No jodhpurs or jeans were required just yet. After an inspection of the newly completed stable area where all seemed to be satisfactory even down to running water and electricity, they made their way to the office to start arranging for the acquisition of the first horses. There was also the not inconsiderable task of getting together tack, saddles and feeding accoutrements, all at competitive pricing so as to stay within the allotted budget for the agenda.

All was well with the animals and bird inmates at the castle; even though it had been hard work getting sufficient quantities of hay to the sheep while the snow was lying. Things had eased temporarily due to a thaw, but more snow was expected soon. This was one of those tasks when anybody and everybody volunteered a stint no matter what their duties. It made things considerably easier for Suzanne and Bea.

The two donkeys they had looked after during the autumn had been repatriated to their sanctuary. The owners had been very grateful for the help and they were impressed with the level of care provided.

Rosalind's husband, Frank, Dalmar and Mike Parsons, the teacher from Carlisle, had started a lad's get together on a weekday lunchtime at a pub near Keswick, about once every two to three months. They had only achieved the one meet so far, back at the end of October last year. All three were keen to organise another. This was proving difficult as they were all working men. Mike would be on a half term break in February and this looked like being the best chance for all of them. After the last session, they returned home satisfied that the country's politics had been sorted and the national teams for football, rugby and cricket were on the up, after their thoughts and ideas had been thoroughly voiced over a couple of pints of real ale and good English pub grub.

Emma and Michael were due to return to school and playgroup in a week's time, but while they were at home there was no longer any problem with child minding because Jodie Fresher, David's young sister had taken up duties as an au pair, doubling as an extra hand at the animal rescue centre. She kept her thoughts to herself, but she generally preferred the animal centre tasks, although she fitted in well with all the Hunter family. Little Michael adored her. This meant that Suzanne could devote more time to her duties; something that was becoming more and more necessary. Jodie had come back from spending Christmas with her family in Newcastle before the weekend, simply because she wanted to. It was this incidence that enabled Dalmar and Suzanne to go to the New Year's Eve party.

While Roz and Suzanne were discussing horses with information already gathered from Roz's knowledge and contacts, Dalmar was introducing a young man to John Fisher. His name was Nick Jordan and he had arrived through an arrangement with Jack Twentyman, to work as John's assistant for a while as part of his studies with the

National Trust. Something that Dalmar, himself, had undergone, although a shortened version, on a different estate several years ago. John Fisher was short in stature but made up for it with an incredibly strong, wiry physique. The effect was added to by his dark complexion and an abundance of black hair showing on his limbs when exposed. Nick, in contrast, was fair skinned with blue eyes and a reddish tint to his hair, but that was not the stark difference between the two men: the fact that Nick was six foot four inches tall might have something to do with it. Even Dalmar felt dwarfed by him, although there was nothing threatening about Nick. He was naturally gentle in his demeanour.

About mid-morning Dalmar brought the two ground staff back to the castle. It turned out they were the only two members of the Bray Castle staff Roz had not met, so they were introduced, after all they would often see each other round and about the estate and would frequently have to confer.

Neither Suzanne nor Dalmar were sufficiently au fait with Roz's marketing talents. In fact, she was not fully aware of it herself, even though the evidence lay with her part in promoting her late son's charity. It was one of the prime reasons why it had been so successful. Therefore, it did not take her long to persuade Suzanne to start the stable with a Palomino. Initial results would have to be achieved with photographic images. They had the scenery. What they required was the horse to go with it. In terms of attracting parents to entrust their children for riding lessons, it was further important to have the right mounts for that as well. So they decided to go for a three year old Welsh mountain pony that was up for sale in Lancashire. This breed was well known for its trustworthy behaviour with juniours. To complete the start-up plan, the purchase of one more ponies was further required. They had arrived at this point a day later. It was early in the afternoon and the women decided to leave it at that fearing they might be moving too fast. Suzanne went off to the animal centre and left Roz looking at tack brochures.

Brian Cussen's astronomy courses were still going well. It never ceased to amaze Jack Twentyman. He had not been all that enthusiastic about the project at the start. People would come and stay at the castle for the specific purpose of studying the sky at night, only to return home a few days later having seen none of it due to adverse weather conditions. It was quite usual, when this happened, that the person involved would book another time hoping their luck would change. The truth was that visitors loved the ambience of the place, and, if there were no clear skies forecast, instead, they would get a good night's sleep and go walking on the fells the next day.

Roz Maidment learnt something about Bray Castle during her second week working there. Fortunately for her the first few days had been very mild, and she had come dressed mostly for office work. The heating system was archaic. The cost of creating a satisfactory system was prohibitive due to the size of many of the rooms and the great space from floor to ceiling in the entrance hallway. Dalmar's office and some of the other smaller rooms possessed small convector heaters but that was all. The guest bedrooms were still using sheets, an eiderdown and blankets. At night, it could get very cold. And it invariably stayed like that during the day. Low pressure systems frequently swept in off the North Atlantic providing copious quantities of rainfall and mild conditions. This accounted for the lush greens in the grasses along the valleys. Although the Lake District had enjoyed a white Christmas at the end of last year, usually, the really cold weather would arrive in early January, heralded by a dusting of snow on the mountain tops. In fine weather this looked enchanting and in dull conditions the icing on the cake effect took place. A depression coming down from the north and the Arctic was forecast to arrive in the middle of the month. This was when the quilted jackets, deep pile woollen sweaters and thick wool socks would become general wear all the time. The rain-proof hooded cagoules would be hung up to dry to await the next change in the local climate.

The great entrance doors to the castle were closed off in the winter season and access to the castle interior was gained via a side entrance adjacent to the restaurant. This was less welcoming, but it was simply impractical to have the huge entrance opened up allowing all the cold air in.

Dalmar's favourite wintry indoor item was an Arran sweater. It gave him all the extra warmth he required. If he did anything exerting it was quickly pulled off over his head causing ruffling in his thick dark hair. Suzanne, by now, had a collection of cuddly woollen jumpers to choose from, but her favourite was still the hand knitted blue number, Dalmar had bought her on their first trip to the Lakes together back in 1975, two years before they were married.

On Monday, January the 17th, John and Nick, both wearing working gloves in the chill morning air, were helping Roz prepare and hang all the new riding tack in the room to the right-hand side of the awaiting horse stalls. The first horse, a beautiful Palomino by the name of Stargazer was due to arrive on Thursday. The groundsmen and general estate caretakers had set aside all other tasks to make sure everything would be ready. There was quite a bit of carpentry still do in the shape of shelving and cupboard provision. They had the tools, wood and hardware so it was just a matter of getting on with it.

Jack Twentyman phoned to remind Dalmar that the wearing of seat belts in the front seats of road vehicles would be a legal requirement from the 31st January. Dalmar cursed, not because he did not agree with it; he knew it would take him some adjustment time before the action of putting the seat belt on when driving off became a habit. Jack had reminded him, so that he, Suzanne and other staff members who were permitted to use the Land Rover could get accustomed before the new law came into effect.

The arrival of the mare, Stargazer had to be delayed. A

blizzard hit Cumbria on Tuesday afternoon and Roz preferred to be clear of such weather, just in case it caused any problems at the newly restored stables. Things had seemed alright over the Christmas period but there were no occupants. It was thought prudent to wait a week when more settled conditions were expected.

Significant snow falls were not uncommon in the area but every now and again they exceeded expectations in the sheer quantity of the stuff that fell gently from the skies. In the grey twilight of the late afternoon on Tuesday, Dalmar could be seen with his wool lined parka obliterating his face, only allowing one eye to peer through the hood, as he huddled his way from the castle to the Dower-house. After leaving the bright lights of the canteen area, as soon as the heavy door closed behind him, everything went ultra-still and silent. There was just a steady falling curtain of big snowflakes. Unless you knew your ground, driveway and lawns were all one. Behind him the solid mass of the castle walls soon disappeared. Somewhere ahead of him over to his left he could make out a dim light coming from his family's dwelling. It was shining through a small glass panel set into the front door. As he approached, using the light to guide his way, he noticed the familiar view down to the lake had gone. It might as well be the middle of the night as far as visibility was concerned.

On entering the porch, he untied the laces on his walking boots and kicked them into a corner before tapping a knuckle of the frosted glass. He was greeted by an exuberant Emma closely followed by Michael. Both of them wanted to go out and play in the snow. One look at the grey and white exterior, before Dalmar shut the door, made them both think again without anyone having to say anything. Fly came shuffling up – made a grunt like bark of welcome, turned around and went off back to his corner under the table by the window in the front room. Dalmar took off his coat and went through to join him. There were three women there: Suzanne, Roz and Jodie. They all looked up and smiled at him. He accepted the offer of a hot drink and sat down. While his wife poured him a cup of tea, Roz sat quietly showing disappointment all over her face.

"It can't be helped Roz." Dalmar opened, "I know you are frustrated and want to get on – but a few days?"

"Yea – I know," she said in that soft but clear way of speaking she possessed. "It's just that I wanted to get things ship-shape with mounts in situ – right here – so that we can get on with the marketing. Until that is under way, we won't get any bookings."

Dalmar shrugged both shoulders. "Yes – but better safe than sorry. You know it's right."

Jodie decided to join in. She had her brother's features. It was easy to see the family connection. Her blonde hair was cut to medium length. She had hazel eyes together with an absolutely charming smile that looked like the sun shining out of a chill blue sky due to her slightly pinched features. She always wore washed denim jeans. Some people would say she was still tomboyish, but it was just because of what she did – children and animals. There was little point in being smart. She could dress girly when she wanted. "Will I be able to help out – later – when you get things going?" And then she threw in the important matter saying it in an offhand way. "I have ridden quite a lot. Da used to be involved in a circus." Roz nearly fell off her chair and Suzanne stared at her. Jodie spoke with the same north-eastern dialect as David, her brother. However, instead of it being further education which had given him good diction – her style was definitely the exclusive province of the Geordie female. Top notch enunciation – as clear as sparkling ice.

"I didn't know that," said Suzanne. "What did he do?"

"He was the main acrobat trick rider."

"No kidding," said Roz. "Don't tell me you got involved in that?"

"Yeah. Leotard, sequins and all. I was only thirteen when I first performed in the ring."

Dalmar was speechless until he could see the funny side of it. "That could be useful in your marketing campaign Roz," he said dryly. Both of the other two women looked at him appalled. He burst out laughing.

Jodie giggled openly before saying the single word, "Canny," accompanied by a glittering smile as though to add emphasis to the suggestion.

CHAPTER TWENTY-FOUR

– "YOU ARE THE TEAM LEADER" –

The telephone call came through at 07.45 the following morning. Dalmar was caught with a mouthful of toast and marmalade. Ambleside Mountain Rescue wanted him. The main team had been out half the night. 'What - in those conditions?' he thought to himself. Apparently, a woman had gone walking on Bowfell mountain at the top end of the Langdale valley, yesterday morning, and must have got caught in the blizzard. Anyway, she had not returned to her hotel that evening. This looked like a classic case of someone not checking on the weather forecast before they set out.

Mountain rescue required him and three other reservists to go out this morning and continue the search, the night team having returned without any sighting. The heavy snow fall had ceased in the early hours of the night and the skies had cleared. With the snow lying everywhere, together with moonlight, visibility had been good, but getting to the head of the valley, even in the rescue four-wheel drive vehicle, had proved very difficult. After that, making headway on the fells was not only arduous, due to the deep lying snow, but, also, extremely tiring.

Brian Cussen had been on duty for part of the night in his observatory so Suzanne would have to man the show until her husband returned. This was where Jodie would prove invaluable. She could drive, and Dalmar needed someone to drop him off at the rescue centre just outside Ambleside.

Suzanne wished him luck. "I hope you find the poor lady," and then she added, "alive."

As they drove on their way, it being the first time, the

volunteer worried if he had remembered to gather together all his personal equipment and get himself togged out correctly. He had planned this several times, but, because he had not heard anything had rather forgotten all that was required. He was aware of a nagging feeling that he had not brought something vital. He knew he had his pocketknife, a whistle, a small metal drinking bottle, an ice axe and two pairs of lined gloves. Other necessities would be already on board the mountain rescue vehicle.

Passing by White Crag, the view over Lastwater and the surrounding land was breath-taking. The snow laden lower fells, with the big hills behind stretching away to the north, west and east, now over laden by a deep blue sky and not a cloud to be seen was enough, but the addition of the lake's royal blue, several shades darker than the sky looked almost surreal.

His wife had been full of curiosity as to what her husband was about and the purpose of the rescue itself. She could not believe a lone woman had gone out yesterday with all the warnings of the snow falls to come. This sounded crazy enough, and to choose one of the longest treks in the Lake District to undertake, that of the peaks of Crinkle Crags and Bowfell from Great Langdale, made it doubly daft. It was not until he and Jodie departed while trying to hang onto Emma and Michael, who were desperate to go along as well, that she suddenly felt concern over the safety of Dalmar himself. She was morose for a while before she pulled herself out of the worry to attend to the children and get them to their respective schooling.

When Dalmar and Jodie arrived at the mountain rescue station they were immediately introduced to the other three members of the team who were gathered around a white, extended wheelbase, Land Rover 90. This was the rescue team's spare vehicle. One of the men Dalmar vaguely knew as a friend of Frank Maidment, John Templeton. The other two were Torry, short for Torrant, and Paul, both of whom worked for the tourist board and indulged in rock climbing as a recreational pursuit. All three were younger than Dalmar. After saying a brief 'hello', Jodie was able to get on her way back to the castle. Her boss would not be requiring a lift back for quite some time.

Jock Shoreman was the regular member of the rescue team left behind to give these reservists their instructions. At forty-two years of age he was still very fit and took a pride in being so. Right now, he was jaded having been up most of the night on the fells. His deep black eyebrows added to the effect hooding his tired looking dark brown eyes. "Okay lads," he said as though it was a pre-match talk before a game of football. "You've got everything on board you need. Stretcher, ropes, climbing hardware and crampons. There is another team coming over from Patterdale to give assistance. Hopefully you will all meet up at the rescue station at the top end of the valley. If not," Jock leaned his head in toward the group of men as though he wanted to be more confidential, "just get on your way. Your route will be up the Band and straight onto Bowfell. If two of you go round the Climber's Traverse and the other two over the summit ridge – that will be best. There is no need to bother with the Crinkle Crags – our lot scoured them in the early hours of today. Concentrate on this side of the Bowfell summit mass which includes the buttresses." This was a reference to the rock formations favoured by climbers under the summit ridge of the mountain on its north side. "Your short-wave radio has been tested."

Suddenly Jock went back to an upright posture. "Now – here's the important thing. If you find her – we only know she was wearing black trousers and a dark blue anorak. She may have carried waterproof leggings which could be any colour. She does have a red – dull red – small rucksack. Do not attempt to bring her back if she is still alive. She will – by now – be very weak. There isn't time. We have air-sea rescue standing by on the west coast. Call us and we'll have a chopper out in no time. So – it will be a five-strap secured stretcher with the four-loop attachment to the helicopters line. Okay?" All three men remembered the training practice for this operation. "The Patterdale team will be going up Rossett Gill to look at the western end of the mountain." Jock looked at his volunteer rookies in a fairly hard manner before saying, "Everything clear?" Nobody said anything. "Right – Dalmar you are the team leader and the driver. Good luck gentlemen." What Jock did not tell them was the little matter that really, they should not be going out without an experienced member of the mountain rescue team. Due to a flu virus having laid low two of their regular lads, this was not possible.

As they drove away, Dalmar remembered what he had forgotten – his compass. He hoped that the weather would stay as it was, then he would hardly need one. No one spoke for probably the first mile until they reached the Skelwith Bridge junction. "I hate to say this," said John, who was sitting in the front next to the Dalmar, but I am glad you're driving – I've never been out this way before."

"What – never been to Langdale," said Torry, a short powerfully built, slightly balding man in his mid-twenties, never had a session in the Dungeon – you haven't lived man." He spoke with a mild Cumbrian dialect as did his companion Paul. The 'Dungeon' he referred to would be the bar of a hostelry known as the Dungeon Gill hotel often frequented by rock climbers.

John laughed. "Don't suppose I'll get much of a chance today," he said. John had the slightest build of all of them, but he was superbly fit. He did not brag about it, but he could run for long distances over these fells. Paul looked all muscle like Torry, however, he sported a great main of black hair that fell all over his eyes.

Considering Dalmar had not done any rock climbing since his training for the rescue team, he felt embarrassed about being chosen as the leader knowing how experienced Paul and Torry were in mountain craft. He presumed it must be because he was the eldest. 'Anyhow,' he considered, 'just accept it.'

The drive was not particularly arduous for Dalmar, simply because he had had plenty of experience handling a four-wheel drive vehicle in these conditions. The Land Rover made short work of any snow lying on the road until, that is, they got past Elterwater, and then things started to get interesting. On two or three occasions, because the snow had had a chance to freeze, in the cold hours before dawn, when the cloud cover had completely dispersed, all four wheels spun in the deeper lying snow, causing the driver to have to continually correct skidding and keep the speed right down, despite the emergency.

Eventually, after forty-five minutes they got to the mountain rescue post at Middlefell Place. The Patterdale team had not yet arrived, which was hardly surprising considering they had much farther to come, probably, over even move hazardous roads.

From the back of the Rover 90 they extracted ropes, climbing equipment and the all-aluminium stretcher complete with all its patient retaining straps and helicopter rescue harness. It was decided by consultation, rather than instructions from the leader, that Paul and Tory would carry the stretcher, while John and Dalmar would take all the climbing hardware in their rucksacks, and, also, carry a coiled nylon rope by putting it over their head to lie from shoulder to waist. All of them had bright orange hard hats attached to their belts in case of the need for some more serious climbing. For the time being, Dalmar would have to carry the radio. Fortunately, it was one of the new Sony light-weight models. They made a huge difference to this kind of operation. The very first item the climbers put on was a pair of snow goggles. They would be essential today with the bright sunlight on an ample covering of snow. They each wore a pair of waterproof over-trousers together with their parka jackets, lined under trousers, two pairs of woollen socks and the latest man-made fibre gloves. Because of the presence of sunshine, it was expected that some disrobing would take place after the exertion of walking uphill while carrying their equipment took effect. Before setting off they fitted crampons to their boots.

The Great Langdale valley looked completely different this morning. Gone were the lush green pastures by the becks of Mickleden and Oxendale. Gone was the soft pink of the heather on the fells and standing out starkly against the brilliant white snow, especially that exposed to sunlight, were the black volcanic outcrops. Everything, apart from the sky, looked to be in shades of black and white. Even the becks were hidden by overhanging snow drifts.

The hour had just passed ten when the team were on the move making their way to Stool End farm, before crossing the foot bridge over the becks and starting on the steep ascent of the Band.

The four men were feeling excited although a little apprehensive. This was not due to fear of the mountain in these wintry conditions. It was due to worry about carrying out their task properly. It became clear after a short while that John and Dalmar were going to be the fleeter walkers. The other two, being stocky in build would naturally find it more tiring, and they were not used to moving over the fells in a hurry. Dalmar suggested that he and John move out ahead as they had the furthest to go. Paul and Torry were to take the stretcher to the start of the Climbers Traverse at the base of the first crag under the summit dome of Bowfell, while John was going all the way up to look out on each side of the summit ridge. If he did not spot anything, he would move onto the Great Slab, an enormous sloping escarpment of volcanic spillage coming away from the mountain's top on the western side. Meanwhile Dalmar had the rather hazardous job of securing a rope at key points so that he could get a look from the top of Flat Crag, Hard Crag and the infamous Bowfell Buttress itself.

The so-called team leader kept something to himself. This was the first time he had ever worn crampons and they took some getting used to. They slowed you down for a start. It was necessary to exaggeratedly raise your foot on each step. Of course, the extra grip obtained would be invaluable once they reached the icier heights, however, on the lower slopes they helped prevent the boots sinking into the deep snow, which greatly alleviated effort. Dalmar noticed one more advantage. He found it considerably easier to keep up with John, who, in normal weather conditions, unhampered by what he had to carry today, would be able to run up the Band in no time: a fifteen-hundred-foot climb over two miles. All four men carried ice axes in the walking position using the head as a handle.

Perhaps it was not a time to admire scenery, but it was difficult not to appreciate the wild beauty around them. Everything was snow and rock, but because it was such clear weather – unbelievably beautiful. Halfway up the Band both pairs, at different points, took off their over trousers and gloves, and, using the arms, tied their parka's around their waists. The advancing day in the sun and the breathless exertion made it necessary. They all wore brushed cotton shirts with either a sweatshirt or thermal vest underneath. The discarded clothing was carefully placed in their individual back packs. For, if the conditions changed, it could do so very quickly.

Dalmar and John eventually arrived at a path junction by Earing Crag. Their way was to the left towards Red Tarn. Torry and Paul would be going off to the right to take the Climber's Traverse and have a look at the lower parts of the steep, rock formations descending from the summit of Bowfell. Dalmar looked behind him. He could see the following pair, with the stretcher, not more than a thousand yards away. He waved to attract their attention, and when he received an answering raised hand from Paul, signalled that they were about to turn off by moving a pointing finger, high above his head, in repeated movements to the left. Paul acknowledged him with the thumbs up sign.

When they on their way again, John asked, "What's this woman's name? Do you know?"

"Only her first name: Hazel. Come to think of it – know very little about her – But isn't it strange for a woman of any age to be walking out here alone?"

"Not nowadays," replied John. "I often see them when I'm fell running. They usually stand and stare at me – as though I'm completely bonkers."

"Perhaps they're right," said Dalmar in his usual succinct way. He thought so anyway but said nothing. 'Anybody who wanted to run up a mountain had to be. Cycling up a hill was bad enough.'

"Thanks very much." John gave his colleague a cast down look until he saw the smirk on Dalmar's face. "Yea – you're probably right," and he grinned back. Nevertheless, it was noticeable that whenever Dalmar spoke, he frequently had to pause to take breath, whereas John never did.

Within half-an-hour they had crested the high valley between Bowfell and Crinkle Crags at 200 feet above sea level. With it came a chilling strong wind – a north-westerly. Both men immediately replaced their over trousers, jacket and gloves. Now the parka hoods went up to, and they had to clear some snow deposits off their dark goggles. The sun was still shining full bore but at this altitude, with the strong wind, it made little difference.

Red Tarn looked like a huge glistening flat cut sapphire in a giant white porcelain soup bowl. They turned their back on it and headed up towards the summit ridge of Bowfell. It would shortly be time to give serious attention to their task. Due to the wind and the icy conditions, Dalmar tapped John on the shoulder. They had a short discussion having to raise their voices against the blustery weather. Dalmar had decided it would be best if they kept together instead of searching on their own, so they would both look above the rock buttresses before moving onto the Great Slab.

Frequently, Paul and Torry were spotted, still without the all-weather clothing, moving below them and often obscured from view as they rounded the base of a crag.

When the ridge searchers had climbed another four

hundred feet, they were right above the first of the rock climbers' buttress crags. It was time for John to take charge of the radio. Dalmar took a piton from his backpack and drove it into a suitable cleft just off the ridge itself. Then he played out a rope and inched his way towards the cliff edge. John, meanwhile, his rope secured to his partner with a karabiner looped into the same rope around his waist, took up a safe stance against a boulder acting as a safety line.

Once on the cliff edge, Dalmar had a really good view down a succession of steep gullies. Things were made a great deal easier due to the lack of cloud, which, at this height would have been swirling around them. Nothing untoward could be seen from this vantage point, but before moving onto the next, Hard Crag, Dalmar shouted "Hazel!" several times. His strong masculine voice echoed down into the valley. If she was there and conscious, she would certainly hear it.

For the first time they spotted the team from Patterdale, far below, moving in line down in the valley. Dalmar wondered if Frank Maidment was among them, for he knew he was a reserve member of that team.

Hard Crag was a more sprawling affair and they would rely on the other two's viewpoint to properly execute a thorough scan. Dalmar drew another blank so they now had to go up to the very summit of the mountain, and a little way past, so that they could see over the infamous Bowfell Buttress.

The two men were now looking the part. Hooded and covered in parts by spumes of snow, blown at them constantly off the mountain's ridge. Paul and Tory would be able to see this spume drifting over the summit set against the blue sky. The ridge team got into their now familiar position and Dalmar gingerly let himself down towards the lip of the buttress. He would not have liked to have done this without crampons, for in order to give good attention to the ropes he had had to leave his ice axe behind.

Looking over the fierce cliff he could see Paul and Torry

having a good look at the lower buttresses of Hard Crag below him and to his right.

Dalmar gave Bowfell Buttress some considerable attention before calling out the lady's name a few times. Because of the size of the buttress cliffs he decided he should make another sortie a little further over.

He was just about to make his way back towards John – when he saw it.

CHAPTER TWENTY-FIVE

A THIN FILM OF DEW BEGAN TO FORM.

What had caught Dalmar's eye was a small flash of silver in the sunlight – nothing more. But it was too bright to be a discarded inner paper from a cigarette packet or something similar. There was a significant item that it could be. Dalmar knew he had to check it out. He shouted up at John, "Need to have a look at something." He puffed, "I am going to lean back over the edge. Tell me when you are ready?" He was giving a preparation warning. The man at the other end of the rope would have to hold him.

However, John was ready anyway. While his partner made his way down the inclines, John was always ready. "Go ahead," he said.

Dalmar let the rope tighten until it took the full weight of his torso, then he turned his head and looked out and over as far out as he safely could. Just then a gust of powdery snow blew all over him. He spluttered; staying where he was and waited until it was over. As the wind abated enough, he brushed some fine snow off his goggles, as best he could, and looked in the direction where he thought he had spotted the silver fragment. As his eyes focused – he could definitely see something. About twenty feet down protruding around the corner of a hidden fissure in the rock face, a thin strip of what looked like chrome tape was showing. Dalmar realised it could be larger but the rest of it would be obscured from sight. He stared at the oddity for a while before realising that it would have to be investigated. That strip of silver might be a miniscule part of a winter strength survival blanket. On the other hand, it could be litter and probably was. Of necessity, it must be verified. "I'm coming back," he shouted to John who had been taking his strain all the while.

When he came up to his team-mate; he explained. This now meant that John would be carrying out a similar exercise except that Dalmar would be taking the other rope with him together with some climbing hardware. It was time to put his hard hat on, for he would have to climb down twenty feet of rock face by means of an abseil.

Once in position, he placed a piton into a small crack in the rock at the very lip of the cliff and made sure it was utterly fast. The sound of his hammering attracted the attention of Torry and Paul who looked up from the base of Hard Crag. Seeing what Dalmar was doing, they decided to make their way over to the base of the Bowfell Buttress in case it might prove necessary to assist.

Dalmar secured his rope in the abseil position, using a karabiner. He then removed his crampons, cursing to himself at the fiddly task, and left them on the edge. He signalled to John, who still had him secure on the other rope as a safeguard and started his descent swinging out in short pendulum movements against the rock face. There was another reason why John still secured him to the rope, which he had to pay out rapidly as Dalmar swung out and down away from the rock face; if he found someone, the second rope would prove invaluable.

In a very short space of time Dalmar arrived with only a few feet separating him from the silver oddity and he was able to peer around the corner of rock formation to enable him to see under the overhang. What he saw – made him gasp in disbelief. Curled up on a narrow ledge, completely encased in an aluminium foil survival blanket, was, what looked like – a body. At first, it was hard to see how it had got there, then Dalmar realised that if someone had fallen from the cliff top a little further on from where he had started his descent, they would drop down a vertical gulley and, at the bottom, due to a slanting base, slide out onto this ledge – or fail to stop and career over it.

Dalmar lowered himself down some more. He looked

around the corner of the right angle in the rock formation and noticed a foothold lying beneath the ledge. It was not particularly ample but would have to do. He inched his right arm around the corner, followed by a leg, and managed to secure the side of his boot into the crevice. Then he made the move to bring his whole body around so that he was in line with the encased object with his head well above it. With one hand holding onto a prominent knobble in the rock he was able, with his free hand, to fold back the blanket at one end to reveal the face of a woman and a tangle of blonde hair. Her eyes were closed and the pallor in the skin was very pale. Her lips looked more blue than pink. Dalmar managed to remove the glove on his right hand by using his teeth, and then he searched in his jacket pocket. His hand closed over a metal spoon which he brought out into the open air and let it get colder holding it out to and away from him. Satisfied that it had achieved the right degree of chill, he placed the bowl of the spoon against the woman's partially open lips and waited. Quite discernible, a thin film of dew began to form. Quickly, Dalmar put the spoon back in his pocket and fumbled under the zip of the parka. He brought out a whistle which was secured by a thin cord around his neck. He took a deep breath and blew as loudly as his lungs would allow – giving three lengthy blasts.

Everybody on that mountain, with the possible exception of the casualty, heard it, and, as they were all connected with mountain rescue knew exactly what it meant. The lady had been found – alive!

Dalmar heard John shout, "Bloody hell!" Paul and Torry immediately turned around and started to scramble their way back along the traverse to where they had left the stretcher. It would be their job to bring it up to where John was waiting and would take them around twenty minutes to half an hour. They both knew that time was probably vital. Neither of them could hide a feeling of elation.

Four other men heard those whistle blasts: the team from Patterdale. They stopped their ascent of the western flank of the mountain. One of them got the radio set up and they then sat down to wait for instructions.

Meanwhile Dalmar was trying to get some life out of Hazel. However, if the whistle blasts had not wakened her; nothing else would, so his gentle calling to her produced not a whimper. She was obviously in a coma. There was no way of knowing what her injuries were, except that there were no abrasions or bruising showing on her head, or, at least, the front of it. Her rescuer did not want to poke her about too much.

Somehow, she must have been conscious long enough to have been able to struggle and get the lined survival blanket out of her backpack, which was nowhere to be seen, and wrap it around her on this confined space. There was no more than eighteen inches of shelf width on the ledge, and that was at its widest point.

'Poor John,' thought Dalmar. He had better let him know what was going on. "John," he called out, "can you hear me?"

"Loud and clear," came back a voice from above, surprisingly audible due to a lull in the wind. "You've found her then?"

Dalmar lowered the volume with his reply. "Yes, and she *is* alive." He did not add 'just' or other suitable comment in case she heard him. John would have to work that out for himself. Someone who had been out on this mountain all night, in these conditions, would hardly be in the best of health. "Look – you are going to have to let me use your rope. There is no way I can put her on a stretcher here – just not enough room – even with help. I'll put a tie around her chest and under the arms and sort of follow her up when you haul away. About ten feet further up there is a gulley which looks as though it goes all the way to the summit crest. Okay?"

"Sounds good," replied John. "Are the others on their way up with the stretcher?"

"Should be. But I tell you what. Can you get on the radio

before doing anything else. Tell our people we will be above Bowfell Buttress. They'll inform air-sea rescue."

"Right you are."

Dalmar undid the first safety rope around his waist and gave one pull to signify it was free. It slithered away from him around the cornice in the rock as John pulled it up. Now he would have to wait while their base was informed on the radio. He debated whether to put the glove back on his right hand; it was beginning to suffer with all the contact on cold objects. He would certainly have to take it off again when the serious business of tying a rope securely to Hazel took place. Then it suddenly occurred to him that he had further work to do at his end. His own rope, secured by a piton from the top of his abseil descent, would hardly suffice if he were going to get behind Hazel when the others pulled her up. Thinking hard he realised he would need to assist the ascent so as to prevent the woman swaying about and adding to her injuries. He must rig up a new piton hold for the rope on the face above Hazel's position. He would then be able to play out slack as he climbed up behind her. The gulley presented far more holds than the rock face itself, so there should not be any difficulty. He raised his voice a little to attract John's attention. "Hello – can you hear me?"

John was in the process of setting up the radio. "Yes," he answered.

"Sorry John, could you release my rope where it is tied to the piton. I am going to set up a point further over above us."

"Got you. Won't be a sec." It took him a little longer than that to free the knots but soon the rope was free.

Dalmar meanwhile had started to drive a piton into an enticing slit in the rock face. The hammering rang out down the big buttress. Hazel did not stir. This operation should have taken a minute or two but her rescuer had to manage it one handed. Consequently, it took quite a while longer before he was satisfied that the rope was now re-secured in its new position. He could hear John at the radio telling someone that they had found the missing person and exactly where they were. His voice faded in and out with the wind.

As the Patterdale team where on the same frequency they were able to listen in. There seemed little point in them going up to the summit themselves, so they waited patiently to receive instructions to return.

It seemed to Dalmar that he had only just finished his latest task before the other rope came snaking down the gully. This meant that John was now in his new position to act as lift man, although he would wait until his partner gave him the signal.

Unfortunately, the rope stopped well short of the ledge and despite John's attempts at flicking it loose, it just coiled up on itself in a little hollow. There was only one thing to do, Dalmar would have to climb up and bring the rope down the last few yards. He hoped that the helicopter would not get here just yet. There was still a lot to do and nothing could be rushed. Giving himself some slack on his rope he started to climb. One of the blights in climbing in these conditions was that nearly every nook and cranny was full of snow. The rock face itself was completely clear but this hardly helped. Before any hold could be trusted it had to be scooped out by hand or foot to ensure it was not only deep or hard enough but, also, free of ice which often lurked beneath the snow. Dalmar carried a spare piton in his right hand to act as a tool on the climb.

When he got clear of the ledge about six feet up the incline towards the base of the gulley – he fell. Amazingly he stopped himself from crying out. It happened as his left foot failed to make contact with its intended purchase, a small hump of rock protruding from the buttress face. The sudden jarring it caused as his foot slid violently down loosened the grip on his one and only hand hold. His body went right back down to the right side of the ledge, where Hazel's body lay prone still wrapped in its silver cocoon, and then, blessedly, came to a sudden halt as the rope tightened before holding fast against the piton embedded in the rock. He swung in a grazing momentum against the cliff. He could see right over the overhang of the main buttress formation. There was nothing between him and a four-hundred-foot drop to the valley below.

Shaking somewhat Dalmar found the smallest of foot holds and, more out of desperation, managed to scrabble and haul himself back up to a position almost on top of the injured woman's head. He lay there breathing hard. His goggles had gone askew, so he straightened them while trying to control his breathing. This woman did not want a panicky rescuer helping her.

John witnessed the majority of the trauma. "Dalmar ... are you okay?"

He answered immediately, surprisingly, in a very calm manner. "Yes – coming up again. Try and do better this time." John said nothing.

On the second attempt, Dalmar made sure that the coil of the rope hung well clear of Hazel's head. It occurred to him, with some horror, what might have happened, if, when he fell, the rope had snagged her.

It was not long before he was back into the rhythm of the climb again. This time, he treated the knob of rock, where he had come to grief on the last attempt with severe respect. He discovered why it had let him down – the spot immediately above it was not rock but solid ice in a shallow indentation. He managed to chip away with his improvised tool and break it up. After that, he had no more trouble and was able to bring the rope end down clamped in his teeth. It did not taste very nice but that was the least of his concerns.

Now came the difficult task of attaching the rope suspended from the gulley, safely, to Hazel's torso. Quite obviously he could not carry out the operation one handed. With a couple of good foot holds, he would have to rely on his safety rope to hold him in position above the casualty, so that he could use both hands. He removed his gloves and pushed them down behind the invalid's legs and the rock face. Then he tried out balancing just supported at his feet. It took a bit of getting used to. At first, he kept grabbing the ledge edge with his hands because of the swinging motion against the tightly drawn rope, which he had deliberately arranged. Soon he managed to trust the rope to such an extent that he could stomach it when one or other of his feet lifted off their positions.

He became aware of voices above him. 'Good – the other two must have arrived with the stretcher,' he reckoned.

"You alreat down there?" Dalmar looked up to see the hooded, goggled, grinning visage of Torry looking down at him.

"Yup. Should be okay now. Just give us as minute."

"Sure you don't want me to come down and give a hand?"

"It's possible," Dalmar conceded. "Just let me have a try by myself first – okay?"

"Sure. Just yell up if you want me. I'll shin down this rope."

'All very well,' thought the team leader. 'That would mean Torry would not have a belay to a safety rope. Not a good idea.' "Tell you what," he said with raised voice, "I think John could do with a hand once she's ready to be pulled up."

"Paul has already swapped with him." This was said as though it was an obvious requirement. Dalmar had to admit that Paul's physique would be much better suited. He felt relieved. It would make his task of following Hazel up considerably easier.

Dalmar had to get the upper part of the survival blanket well down below the woman's chest so that he could free her arms. It proved difficult. He did not realise it, but he grunted a lot in the process. Something happened then that cheered him, even though it might have meant he was aggravating an injury. Hazel moaned.

Taking the end of the rope right around her, under her arms and tying it to itself behind her back actually was less of a trial than he had presumed it would be. He was able to get her torso into an upright position without any great effort. When he was satisfied all was secure, he rewrapped the blanket, as much as possible completely around her like a mummy. The last jobs were to transfer his hard hat to her head and put his gloves back on. This done he gave two solid pulls on the rope. "Away you go!" he said loudly.

With one hand cushioning her head for as long as he could, Dalmar watched as her body began to be hauled up. He admired the smoothness. There seemed to be no jerking at all. Quickly he gave himself some slack on his rope and started up after her. The early moves were already familiar to him and once in the gulley itself, he found it easy as long as he avoided the small areas where there was lying snow. It was with utter relief he saw Hazel's silver body disappear over the cliff edge against a brilliant blue sky. She would have a little way to go yet, as John and Torry manoeuvred her up the slanting rock face that led to the summit ridge.

CHAPTER TWENTY-SIX

"SHE WOULD PROBABLY STILL BE THERE."

It was not long before a snow-dusted hood framing an anxious goggle-eyed face crested the buttress edge. Already, there was a rope waiting for him and he could clearly see Paul at the very top, looking down. "Come on then - I've got you," he said. Dalmar thought he could make out a smirk on his partially hidden face. "First things first though – stick those crampons back on."

'Bless them,' thought Dalmar, 'they've brought them along for me.' Without these, his ascent up the final slope of snow and ice would have been somewhat hazardous, even with Paul on the other end of the rope. "Thanks," he said in between getting his breath back. He had to take both gloves off to execute the fiddly task.

Soon he was up alongside Paul. They exchanged welfare queries and set about coiling one of the ropes. The other one was still tied to a piton in the rock face twenty odd feet down. Both men were distracted by a voice emanating from their radio. "Ambleside to team B – over."

John was on it. "Go ahead," he answered flicking the appropriate switch. Dalmar was impressed with the little miniature shelter he had built for the radio from fragments of slate.

"Chopper will be with you in about twenty-minutes. Are you ready?" It was only just audible over the incessant noise of the wind. Whenever they spoke between them it was necessary to raise their voices.

"Will be by then – over." John gave Dalmar a look to get his approval – who waved a hand indicating he knew best.

"Well done. Look out for it. Will be approaching from the south-west. A line man will be coming down on their winch to give you a hand and to support the casualty on her way up. Over and out."

"Thanks." John closed the transmission.

Dalmar made his way over to where Torry was fastening the last of the straps around Hazel's body pinning her securely to the stretcher. They then just had to make sure the four straps up to the lifting hook were properly aligned and fixed in place.

"You okay," Torry asked Dalmar, "heard you had a tumble."

"Yea, just skinned a leg a bit. I'm fine. My own stupid fault." He gave the questioner a smile and cast a rueful eye at his torn over-trousers. "Look, may I suggest we move her over to that point over there. The helicopter will have a clearer sight and more room to manoeuvre the line." He pointed through the low swirling snow at a part of the summit ridge that was considerably wider than the part they were on right now.

"Right you are," acknowledged Torry. "Going to take the other side Paul?" The two men brought the laden stretcher over. Carrying a stretcher wearing crampons was hard work. All four men were glad they would not have to carry the casualty back down to the valley.

"Did you get any I.D.?" Paul asked Dalmar.

He had forgotten to do this. It did occur to him at some stage, but he thought her description matched even down to the dark blue anorak he had spotted under the foil blanket. "No," he replied. "To be honest – didn't want to poke about too much. Don't know what her injuries are." He shrugged his shoulders.

"Aye – hardly likely to be two women out here in a snowstorm," but then he thought about it, "although, I don't know. They all seem to turn left when they want the right." It was Paul speaking and he seemed perfectly serious. Tory chortled, then he pointed way out towards the coast. There was a black shape in the air coming fast towards them.

Quickly, before the noise of the advancing helicopter

prevented him, Dalmar asked all of them to stand between the stretcher and the westward sky. This would mean their bodies would shield Hazel from the massively increased blown snow that would shortly encompass them when the rotor blades of the aircraft drew near. It was good thinking on his part. This would, very soon, be born out.

The dark shape of the distant helicopter soon transformed into a red colour and then as it made its final approach proved to be scarlet. The distinctive thuk – thuk – thuk – staccato noise of the rotor blades began to get louder and louder. All four men, standing with their backs to the stretcher, waved at the aircraft to indicate to the pilot that they were the party they were looking for. Soon the machine was overhead with the high frequency, sizzling sound of the engine, plus that of the rotor blades, together with a whirring sound from the rear rotor causing a stupendous racket. A great cloud of additional snow was blown off the summit ridge of Bowfell practically swamping the climbers. In a very short while, the air sea rescue helicopter hovered over their heads before a large hook-ending line appeared descending towards them, with a man standing on a small platform above it. The waiting team never even saw the side door of the passenger cabin open.

What impressed Dalmar most about the whole operation was its speed. In no time the winch-man, kitted out in a weather proof ensemble in sympathy with the bright red of the helicopter, was down and by various gloved hand and finger indications the stretcher was lifted onto the waiting hook to hang suspended a couple of feet off the ground: a quick verification of the general roping around the stretcher to make sure everything was in order, then the winch-man jumped back onto his platform, and, with a thumbs up sign to the line operator in the chopper, up they went. Afterwards, if any member of the mountain rescue team had been asked to give a description of the winchman, it would have been very vague.

The pilot seemed to be coping very well with the high

winds. Dalmar had half doubted that the operation could be carried out because of this. Within, it seemed, seconds the stretcher was alongside the chopper before being pulled in by waiting hands, the winchman climbed back in and they were gone in a further enormous spume of snow, banking hard away towards the Lancashire coast.

As the noise died rapidly away, they watched the helicopter diminish in size. There was one job to do before they could head home. While John packed up the radio after reporting a successful lift and Dalmar busied himself generally making sure all their equipment was packed away, Paul and Torry set about retrieving the rope still attached to the buttress cliff. Paul got back into his anchor man position and Torry quickly abseiled down over the edge. He undid the knot on the piton, while suspended by Paul's rope, his crampons firmly gripping the rock face some five hundred feet above level ground. What would daunt most men hardly bothered Torry. The piton would be left in place. Perhaps it would aid another climber someday.

Once the two men were back on the ridge coiling both ropes, Dalmar could not resist wandering aside. Despite the chilling wind and the bothersome snow spume he had heard so much about the magnificent view from the summit of this mountain, he wanted a chance to take it in. He had never climbed Bowfell before. There was a glorious vista of the Scafell group, but what entranced him mainly was the sight of the Irish Sea and, in the distance, Morecambe Bay. Whether it was the effect caused by snow lying in the foreground and on down into the valleys together with the clear blue sky fading away to a pale cerulean on the horizon, he did not know, but that distant sea was like a sheet of pure silver.

"Great isn't it?" Dalmar's concentration was distracted by John's voice by his side. I have run up this beast a view times. Never get tired of that view." His partner could see why.

After a brief discussion, it was decided that they would

stop and take some refreshment once off the ridge and away from the biting wind. After the helicopter visit, they all looked a sight, their clothing covered in sticky deposits of powdery snow even around their goggles, nose and mouth. They took it in turn to brush each other down.

Back down by Red Tarn they soon made their way through the high valley between Bowfell and Crinkle Crags to descend towards the Band. Getting out of that wind was a transformation. Off came outer clothing and they sat down on a rocky outcrop to eat mint cake and drink from the mountain streams running, quite often, under a canopy of pure white snow. They could make out the Patterdale team almost at journey's end.

"When thew were looking over the Buttress," asked Torry, "was the lass easy to spot in her foil blanket?"

"No," replied Dalmar and then he explained.

Torry whistled escaping breath. "In that case," he commented, "as we could see nothing from below – I know we hadn't actually reached the base of the Buttress, but I can promise you she was not visible – if you hadn't spotted that itsy bitsy teeny bit of silver – she would probably still be there." As though emphasising some important point, he pointed to the west and Scafell. The sun was going down.

Dalmar could not believe it – where had the time gone. "I had no idea it was that late," he said looking at his watch under the cuff of his patterned blue shirt. It was half past four.

"Amazing in't it," said Paul. "It's the searching time that does it – always is – apparently," he added suddenly realising he was talking as though very experienced instead of being on his first rescue mission.

Once they had finished their sparse refreshment, they set off on the long descent to the valley below. By the time they reached Stool End farm another hour had gone by and it was dark. Due to the snow and moonlight there was no difficulty finding their way along the path by Oxendale Beck to the mountain rescue post and their vehicle. All four men abruptly felt very tired.

Dalmar drove back practically in silence. This was more out of courtesy when he noticed Paul nodding off in the back.

On their arrival at Ambleside they were warmly welcomed by a waiting member of the main team who had been on Crinkle Crags and part of Bowfell in the early hours. Since then he had some sleep. Jack Shoreman had gone home immediately after Hazel Down, the rescued lady's full name, had been taken off in the helicopter. He must have been very tired. They were informed that Hazel had arrived at hospital in Lancaster but had heard nothing further.

Dalmar borrowed the rescue station's phone and called the castle. Suzanne answered; she was at the Dowerhouse. "Hi darling. How'd it go? We heard on local radio that the woman has been found alive." She, at this stage, would not have known which rescue team had discovered her.

"Went really well," Dalmar told her. We found her unconscious near the summit. Thankfully, at some stage, she must have managed to struggle into her survival blanket – otherwise don't think she would have made it."

"Wow – was it your team that found her?"

"Yes. It was on our route." Typically, Dalmar played it down. "Any chance Jodie could pick me up or shall I get on a bus?"

"She will shortly be on her way. Catch a bus! That would mean you would have to walk all the way from the main road. Don't be silly. And you must be tired!"

"Yea – well," he said. Nevertheless, he was relieved. "Children okay?" He remembered to ask just in time.

"Yup – you won't be getting out of the bedtime story."

"Alright." Dalmar gave a little laugh of acknowledgement. "Looking forward to supper – I'm famished."

"Casserole with dumplings – that do you." As it was unquestionably Dalmar's favourite dish, his taste buds started reacting at once.

"Thanks. I'll look out for Jodie."

While he was waiting, Dalmar went into the office at the station and filled out the details required on the operation report, and then he gathered together his own belongings, said "cheerio" to John, Paul and Torry who were just off to the nearest pub for a well-earned pint of beer.

Jodie was very tactful on the way back to the castle. She refrained from asking too much about the rescue because she knew his family would want the first information, especially Emma. Instead she told him about the new arrivals at the animal centre. "It's a pair of very young roe deer. Apparently, they were born two to three months early! Something to do with the fertilised eggs failing to remain in a state of suspension in the doe and, as a consequence, not only were the little ones born too early, the mother, due to weakness having to cope with the full pregnancy in the winter, did not survive. So, we have two orphans being bottle fed."

"Uh oh. We won't be seeing much of you lot for a while." Dalmar gave her a knowing smile.

When they arrived at the Dower-house there was a distinct aroma of something nice in the slow cooker but not a sign of anybody. "Guess they are over at the castle," suggested Jodie.

She was right. After Dalmar had pacified the welcome from an unusually exuberant collie, he left Jodie in charge and made his way toward the rescue centre. Emma and Michael spotted him coming from a window and rushed out to meet him. It was not a greeting for a returning hero however, it was very much, "Come and look daddy! Look what we've got." Neither of them asked one question about his day, excitedly showing off the two fawns who were being fed after stirring for their evening spell of activity.

"Hello darling, we've got twins," Suzanne greeted him with a startling smile.

"What have you done to yourself?" she asked, suddenly

spotting dried blood on his walking trousers.

Dalmar looked down. "Oh, just a stumble. Looks far worse than it is." How he could know that without removing his trousers, his wife and children did not query. There were far more important matters in the shape of two impossibly cute, spotted backed fawns guzzling teated bottles of special milk provided by Ursula, the vet. Bea held one and Suzanne the other. Emma had already been told that her turn would come in a few days' time. Bea should have gone home over an hour ago, but she was keen to stay on and help Suzanne with their new arrivals. They had only just woken up having been fast asleep since their arrival. This explained why the Dower-house had been deserted, Bea having summoned them on the internal phone as soon as they woke.

Emma was given something useful to do. There were plenty of other animals and birds to feed and she was, by now, able to be trusted to give the right feed to a particular species. She had been told over and over that if she was not sure – to ask. She really enjoyed helping out when she was able. Something was being very noisy while complaining in one of the pens.

The fawns would have to be suckled morning and evening for up to two to three months so even with Jodie's help, Emma would definitely get plenty of turns – even little Michael.

"Where were they found?" asked Dalmar entranced by the spectacle before him.

"Grisedale Forest," answered Bea this time. "Ursula told us their mother had died a good day or two before they were found – weak and undernourished. Poor little mites."

'Well, they would be alright now,' thought Dalmar. 'That was certain – with this lot looking after them.'

It was not until they were all sat down at the big kitchen table enjoying the stew that Suzanne thought to ask her husband about the day's mountain rescue expedition. "Did they find out why that woman was out alone on Bowfell in those conditions?"

"Haven't a clue," said Dalmar. "One of the guys I was with reckoned it was quite common nowadays. "Probably missed out on a weather forecast. She was prepared – survival blanket and all that. Just as well."

"Where was she?"

"Right near the summit. She had fallen down a gulley. Very hard to spot, but, fortunately, we did." Dalmar went on to tell them about the big bright red helicopter that took the lady off the mountain in a stretcher. Michael, in particular, was agog. "She was still unconscious at the time. Hope she has recovered by now – have to watch the news later. What we were not able to ascertain was the actual extent of her injuries. She had fallen some way."

"What uncosos?" asked his son.

"Asleep," his mother quickly told him knowing that is all he would be able to understand.

"She won't die will she?" asked his daughter now all attention on the matter.

"Oh no, but she will be in hospital for a while, I expect." When the children had finished with their questions he added, "Fantastic panoramic view from up there, especially, on a day like this."

This irritated Suzanne.' That's my man,' she mused. 'We want to know the details about the rescue, and he talks about the view.'

After the children had gone to bed, supper had been cleared away, Jodie, Suzanne and Dalmar finally got to watch the local news broadcast on the television. Hazel Down had regained conscience and she was off the danger list and declared to be comfortable. Someone had found a picture of her taken outside the hotel she had been staying at, but there was no film of the actual rescue, just a short account stating that she had been found injured high up on the mountain by Ambleside Mountain Rescue.

The sheer fact that she had survived gave Dalmar a feeling of pleasure: his first and successful rescue op.

CHAPTER TWENTY-SEVEN

"HE HASN'T GOT TO SWIM – I HOPE?"

Everything was going according to plan, more or less, for the launch of Bray Castle's riding and trekking school. Riding lessons, together with horse care sessions would be first on the list. The lessons would commence, due to advance bookings already received, in a week's time, the 7th March.

As well as the Palomino, Stargazer, four other ponies had been purchased and it would be these that would be used for the tuition. Stargazer would only be ridden by Roz or Josie Fresher. The breeds had been especially chosen for temperament and their general suitability for teaching: an Irish Cob and Gypsy Cob for older children and adults, plus two Welsh Mountain ponies for the younger children. The Irish mare was black and white; the Gypsy all black and the two Welsh pony's chestnut. All of them were outstandingly handsome in their own way. They were constantly well groomed and being tender in years, not one was older than four; Roz had got them to really look the part. Other horses, possibly, a retired hunter would be added later, and it was planned to erect a jumping course to pony club standards at the top end of the meadow just below the castle. This could lead to gymkhana days but that was for next year.

However, today, Monday 28th February, was official launch day for the local press. Bray Castle was already preparing for the initial media activity because in just under four weeks' time it was the spring equinox. David Fresher was due to arrive a few days before to get the scientific program started.

Rarely, at this time, did the sunshine. Most days were either snowy or, like last week, mild and rainy, but not today.

It was just what the photographers wanted, crisp and cold with a heavy frost, although bright and cheerful. At ten-thirty, thankfully with the Hunter children out of the way at school, Roz Maidment brought Stargazer out onto the big side lawn by the castle main entrance.

Suzanne distinctly heard one or two male reporters gasp. This tall, well-proportioned woman with her Nordic good looks, suddenly and effortlessly mounted the Palomino. Her pale blonde hair, hanging down below her shoulders almost exactly matched the tone of the pony's mane and long flowing tail. Even her riding kit looked the part; dark chocolate brown top and stretched jodhpurs with tan riding boots made her figure stand out, with compatibility, against the light chestnut colour of Stargazer's body. Many of the pictures taken that morning were considered almost capable of becoming iconic. Of course, transposed to black and white for the newspapers they did not have quite so much appeal, however, those that made it into the county magazine and especially on local television were, without a doubt, an amazing piece of publicity. Suzanne had arranged for a National Trust photographer to be there for this picture session. Horse and rider, set against the background of the castle entrance, would be extensively used not just to adorn equestrian brochures, but, also when promoting the castle and its grounds as well.

Many members of staff were out there looking on. Doris and Edna could see most of the action from just inside the entrance. They had opened the main doors despite the time of year, although, the number of people and the sunshine kept things comfortable. The kitchen staff took it in turns to pop out and have a look. All of them were intensely proud of this new addition to the castle's attractions.

After the photography session, the press were invited into the castle interior where one of the reception rooms had been laid up with coffee, biscuits and other refreshments. Roz would give them all a run down on the various activities that were going to be on offer this year, plus planned projects for the following spring onwards. Jodie took Stargazer back to his stable, so that he could be unsaddled before returning him to his grazing in the meadow with the other ponies, and Roz could get started and introduce herself. Everything went really well. She tended to move from group to group rather than make some cold general announcement.

One of the female reporters recognised her from television appearances last year. "Aren't you the lady who lost a son to cancer and started the charity for seriously ill children in his name?"

This was what Roz did not want. She needed to publicise the Bray Castle equestrian centre in its own right and not on the back of a personal tragedy. However, the reporter's next comment, said almost as an aside, as though in confidence, really surprised her. Certain of her facts and observation she did not wait for Roz to confirm anything. "You see, I am full of admiration – especially at the success of the charity itself. I hear it is doing great things. Would it be possible to see you on this matter alone? My readers would love to catch up with its progress – I'm sure."

"Yes – of course," replied Roz, you would need my husband present as well. He does a lot of the admin – well – most of it actually."

"Sure, I will give you a ring to arrange things. Evening I guess?"

"Yes – fine."

"Right, enough of that – let's hear more about *this* venture. It sounds very exciting." The reporter seemed to sense her inappropriate timing. Although, Roz would probably have been disappointed if no one had mentioned anything, especially for the sake of Jacob's memory.

At the weekend it was Emma's turn. Jodie took her on a lead reign down the drive to the castle estate's entrance and back. She was mounted on Trudie, one of the Welsh ponies. Because of a wide grass verge between the tarmac and the iron rail fence up against the meadow land, they were able to avoid hindering traffic. This would serve well when the riding lessons got into full swing with all the ponies in line. Michael was allowed to sit up with Emma when they returned and have his picture taken with her. Jodie thought Emma did very well showing no apprehension whatsoever. This came as no surprise to her mother.

Roz and Jodie had arranged to do alternate weekends so that Roz could have some time off. They might have to make other arrangements when the trekking started in the summer. It did not bother Roz too much; she was quite prepared to take her days off during the week. Before the daily schedules got too busy, Roz spent some time giving Jodie a good grounding in pony care so that she could be an instructor on the stable husbandry day courses. Everything was progressing well without any hitches entirely due to Roz Maidment's expertise. Bray Castle was very fortunate. Mind you, as Roz herself said, "It was a lovely place to work with nice people," and now that the lake held no more fear, everyone could enjoy it to the full. Many of the staff still grieved for Trevor and Pat and would do so for some time to come.

It was towards the end of the week that a telephone call came through for Dalmar: one he had been expecting. Jack Twentyman had warned him to stand by. However, he was secretly glad this person got in ahead of the others. Jane Derby, the Cumbrian television local news presenter caught him when he was about to go off duty late on Friday afternoon. "When's it all going to happen?" she drove straight in, referring to the much-heralded events that would take place on Lastwater at the end of next week.

"Hello. How are you?" Dalmar ignored her question to start with preferring to enquire after her wellbeing and that of her father's. Having been assured that all was well, he continued. "David Fresher, the geologist is very much in charge for this. He is due with us some time on Wednesday.

It has been forecast that during the early hours of Monday, the 21st, the first event, not expected to be particularly dramatic will occur. That is, the lake will receive a vast quantity of sea water solution, which will raise its level by somewhere between two to four inches. However, apparently, that will probably take several hours. The most spectacular event will be the exodus of this excess at around four o'clock in the afternoon of the same day."

"How?" Dalmar admired her succinctness.

"We don't know ... But a massive amount of water will leave the lake in around fifteen minutes or less ... so expect something like a whirlpool just this side of Shimdorie Island – that is the shore nearest Bray Castle."

"Don't know whether you know but the Air Ministry has banned all but one official helicopter flight in the area, so the only pictures we will get, ourselves, will be from the shore. Can we get to the island?"

"That is the Lake District National Park's province, but I can tell you that the answer to that is 'no'. Only David Fresher and those assisting him will be allowed out there."

"Surprise, surprise," commented Jane. "We aren't going to see much from the shore below the castle; are we?"

"Right ... the BBC and one other camera crew on the castle roof. Interested?"

"Yea!" there was a pause as she thought this through. "What's the fee?"

"One million pounds."

Jane spluttered. "I hope you're joking?"

Dalmar chuckled. "Usual thing – make a donation to the charity."

"The National Trust?"

"Yup – and don't be stingy."

"Okay. Can I take that as booked?"

"Yes. Liase with our astronomer Brian Cussen."

"You're what-er? Didn't know you had one."

"Yes. That odd-looking construction on our roof is an observatory. Instead of the telescope being trained on the sky; Monday week, it will be pointing towards the lake just over the tops of the trees at the strip of water between them and Shimdorie."

"Brill." Realising there was nothing more to be gone over for now, Jane thanked Dalmar profusely and rang off promising to contact Brian at the start of the week.

The B.B.C. was next, actually, within five minutes. Dalmar gave them the same information.

Suzanne told her husband that everywhere, locally, was buzzing about what might happen in a week's time. Even the teachers at Emma's school were doing a special session for the pupils about it. However, she did raise one point that many people seemed to have forgotten. "March 21st would be the first anniversary of the Lastwater Rowing club tragedy." Dalmar gasped, he had, much to his chagrin allowed the matter to be taken from his mind in the crush of everything else.

He put through a call to the club that evening and managed to get Jim Derby. They had a lengthy conversation in which he was told that it had already been decided to hold a memorial service for the lost crew of the racing boat, on the water near the scene the next day, Tuesday 22nd. There were two reasons for this, 12 noon, the time of last year's disaster, was too close to the estimated time of this year's equinox outflow and therefore far too dangerous. Also, it was hoped, that the media circus would have gone leaving relatives and friends of the deceased to remember their loved ones in peace. Dalmar promised to pay his part and keep quiet about it. However, he did say, his family and some of the staff would be watching from the shore in order to pay their respects.

David Fresher contacted them the next day. It was an overcast and very wet Saturday morning, so all the Hunter family were in the Dower-house except David's sister, Josie, who was on stable duty. An extraordinary thing happened when he came on the phone. Fly must have picked up the sound of his voice tinkling out of the telephone mouthpiece for he suddenly jumped up and came to investigate, obviously remembering good vibes concerning the Northumbrian man. Naturally, David was told that Fly wanted to speak to him.

When they got to serious matters David dropped his first bombshell. "Press conference arranged for Wednesday morning ... okay?"

"What?" replied Dalmar. "Where?"

"Well, there of course. Surely you were expecting it?"

"Right. What time?"

"Told everyone 1100 at the castle. Expect around twenty to thirty media bods. It will be outside broadcast cameras *only* for the TV people, so they'll want to talk to me outside after the official conference. I don't know – allow an hour. Just water, coffee and biccies will do." David paused. "That okay?"

Dalmar's diary was in his office. He said, "Yes," realising that it was too late to alter anything.

"Canny. I will be with you on Tuesday. No need to pick me up from the station. I'm coming by car. By the way have you still got a tent?"

"Yes, two, two-man jobs. Why?"

"I shall be camping on the island from Sunday afternoon until after the main event on Monday. Can you join me?"

Dalmar drew air threw his teeth. "No way. Far too much going on here. What do you want – assistance?"

"More of a witness, actually. Anyone will do as long as she has big tits."

Dalmar nearly choked. This came right out of the blue and he had difficulty controlling the urge to belly laugh. Eventually he told him he would see what he could do.

"Canny. Oh – tell my kid sister I'll see her next Tuesday – bye."

Over a late brunch style breakfast with Emma and Michael enjoying some scrambled egg which kept them reasonably quiet, Suzanne asked her husband if anything had been seen of the otters and their pups recently. He told her that Chris Legg had – towards the end of last year. He had spotted them in the western part of the lake opposite his farm, so they were able to establish that they had survived the outflow of the autumn equinox.

"Apparently they have taken up permanent residence off Lastwater farm's shores," her husband answered her, "and have never been seen farther east than Tadpole Bay's western border. I wondered if the mother had learnt her lesson since her trauma at last year's spring equinox and kept down that end deliberately. Chris reckoned that fish stocks are better down there as well... It figures."

"Oh good. It suddenly occurred to me during the night that I had not heard anything. You know – I think we will have to forget all about our water bird sanctuary down at the boat house. It is just too near Shimdorie Island. Don't you think?"

This thought had also occurred to Dalmar but he was very glad the suggestion came from her. He looked across the table at her pretty face with those twinkling enquiring eyes that he loved so much. "You are right," he agreed. "Never mind, you have plenty to occupy you. How are the fawns doing?"

"You mean Archie and Matilda," said Suzanne illuminating her face with a broad smile. "What do you think Emma?" Before breakfast they had been to the animal rescue centre where Emma had taken her turn bottle feeding.

"Mummy says they are weaning well," was her comment with a mouthful of toast that she scrunched in between words.

Her parents smiled while her brother joined in by giggling. Even Fly grumbled from his ensconced position in his bed in the corner. Normally he would have been outside at this time. It was too wet right now.

There came the sound of horses' hooves on the gravel by the castle. They all looked out of the kitchen window to see Jodie on Stargazer leading two eight-year-old girls on the Welsh ponies, and two older children on the cobs. It was a very appealing sight despite the inclement weather. Suzanne knew that Jodie would take the easy route today alongside the drystone wall and down the meadow to the lake shore, before following the path through the woodland and back.

By Monday midday, Dalmar had begun to realise, hopefully not too late, just quite what a huge amount of attention for this coming week, Lastwater was creating. It probably had a great deal to do with the two tragic occurrences at last year's seasonal equinoxes. The media attention was showing signs of becoming international as well as nationwide; such was the infamous renown of the lake. No one really had any idea quite what the visitor numbers might be, but judging by the casual enquiries coming over the phone and through the National Trust network, together with a great number of requests for information at Tourist Information centres and The Lake District National Park office itself, things could get pretty clogged up in the vicinity. Clearly the National park must assist on the approach roads many of which were single carriageway. Jack Twentyman would be drafting in additional personnel from other N.T. attractions in the wider area.

Suzanne refused to be fazed. She sensibly concentrated on her animal centre and the wellbeing of her own children. Roz picked this up from her and adopted the same attitude for the riding school. On the other hand, Bray Castle was beginning to hum with preparation activity. It was amazing how it had all seemed to mushroom beyond expectation. Extra provisions had to be ordered for just about everything. The normally placid Brian Cussen was actually showing signs of irritability, which, unfortunately for him, rather amused his colleagues.

The most important endeavour had to be to ensure everything was ready for David Fresher. Dalmar approached the assistant groundsman Nick Jordan when he caught him leaving the canteen after his lunch break. "Nick – any chance of a word," he asked, allowing John Fisher to overhear.

"Sure thing," answered Nick as he bent his head to go under a pillar support, something other people would never have to do. He looked at his employer wondering what was coming.

"David Fresher, the geologist in charge of matters on the lake over the weekend will be camping out on Shimdorie Island – Sunday night. He needs someone to stay with him – give assistance and act as a witness to the events that are expected to transpire. Would you be interested in being that person?"

John said it as a joke, but it had a large ring of black humour. "He hasn't got to swim – I hope?"

"No way," immediately answered Dalmar, albeit with a small smile. "You would have to go over in our boat on Sunday afternoon and stay until Monday evening or even Tuesday morning. Any chance? Have you got anything important on at the weekend?" Dalmar asked this out of courtesy because Nick would be officially off duty at least one day over the period in question.

The tall young man beamed all over his rather angular face. "You bet!" he said enthusiastically. "Wow! Can't believe it." He did not even answer the query about previous commitments.

"Okay. Thought you might say something like that. It is a great opportunity to witness, at first hand, an event which has never been seen before – or, not by anyone who lived to tell the tale. However, I must make it clear, that as long as you do everything David tells you, there is no danger to either of you."

"Fine. Count me in," the young man confirmed.

"Right, I'll introduce you to him when he arrives on Tuesday."

After that the two-ground staff went off about their business. Dalmar heard John distinctly say, supposedly in a hushed tone, "Lucky bastard."

CHAPTER TWENTY-EIGHT

"YOU WOULD SEE A HOLE."

David Fresher arrived on a bright sunlit Tuesday morning in an M.G. sports car that had lost the appeal of its yesterdays. Once, the body colour had been a glorious scarlet. It now possessed a dull, unpolished brick tone. He came roaring up the drive in the early afternoon. The roar had more to do with a faulty silencer than a powerful engine.

Jodie had felt a great deal of pleasure over the last two days. Although she would always be pleased to welcome him when he visited the family home, this was different. Firstly, he was a very important person in this situation, and, secondly, it would be just so nice to have him here for a week or more. When she heard the car, she rightly guessed it would be her brother and came charging out of the stable area to meet him; long blonde hair billowing about and a face with a gleeful smile. She jumped up at him as he tried to climb out of the low-slung car with the sheen of expectancy in her eyes.

"Give us a chance – our kid!" he exclaimed as she practically pushed him back in the driving seat. He was eventually rescued by the appearance of Suzanne who had come to welcome him as well.

"Great to see you," she said and plonked a kiss on his left cheek. Nobody had a chance to say anything else before a tail wagging Collie suddenly jumped up at him having made a traverse from the Dower-house lawn at a fast trot.

Jodie laughed. "Somebody thinks they are going to get lots of walkies," she commented patting the animals glorious furry back.

Together the two women took him up to his old room in the castle. He had only brought a back pack with him this time, and that seemed fairly light. The young man was in a chatty mood and the sound of his clear Geordie voice brought Dalmar out of his office. He spoke loudly from the first-floor interior balcony. "Oh god, we've got two Tynesiders in the place now. No mimicking Suzanne, they might take offence."

"Why – does she?" David seemed surprised as he looked up to see where Dalmar was speaking from.

"Ever since you left the place, we've had *canny* this and *canny* that. Back me up Jodie."

"That's right," the sister confirmed.

Suzanne looked acutely embarrassed; she shrugged her shoulders, "Can't resist it," she said. "Sorry."

"Right," said David, "two can play at that." He said this in a remarkably upper crust Oxford accent. Everyone laughed.

Dalmar met them at the top of the stairs and warmly shook the geologist's hand. "How was the traffic?"

"Just driven up from Liverpool – not that bad – quiet time of year I guess." David looked to be in the peak of health as he said this. "How's it all going? Really looking forward to this stay. Seems to be a lot of interest?"

"Probably too much," Dalmar informed him, although in a light-hearted manner. "Anyhow, go and get yourself settled in and then come and join me in the office for a coffee. I'll bring you up to date this end."

David allowed himself to be led off by Jodie and Suzanne. His sister was still pumping him with questions as they disappeared along the far corridor at the back of the castle.

Later Dalmar, David and Brian Cussen got down to the business of sorting out a program for the rest of the week. The press conference was in the morning for which all preparations had been made. David wanted to visit the rowing club and Lastwater farm on Thursday leaving him free to make his camping arrangements for the end of the week, plus numerous other tasks involving measuring instruments and radio-controlled photography.

There was a knock on the office door during this meeting. At Dalmar's invitation Nick Jordan entered. He had been asked to call in so that David could meet his camping partner. The two men seemed to get on all right although David could not resist asking if they had a tent long enough to fit Nick. "He will be useful with that height. I'll send him up a tree so that he can lean out over the whirlpool and take photographs man." While they were all laughing at this, Nick had a distinct partial grin on his face as though he doubted that David might be joking.

Brian would have to contend with the two television camera crews on the castle roof, as well as a full contingent of astronomy students who were coming for quite a different reason from the normal sky at night. This had more to do with the lake's water during the day. All of them were either geology students, or just plain interested, and had reserved their accommodation months ago.

Suzanne insisted that although David Fresher had his accommodation at the castle, he should take dinner with her and the family in the evening, especially as his sister was living with them.

While they were all enjoying a pre-meal beer the telephone rang in the hall and Dalmar discovered Mike Parsons on the end of the line. "I might have something interesting for you," he opened, "and talk about perfect timing!"

"Oh," said Dalmar, listening carefully. The two men had recently met up with Frank Maidment for one of their pub lunch sessions, so there was no need for well-wishing at the start of the conversation.

"When we were talking, at the Fox and Goose the other day, a little bell kept jarring in my brain. You were telling us about the preparations for this coming weekend's events and it was that which started me on it. Last night I realised what it was. As you know my fiancé and I are avid fell walkers, and one of the bible's we consult are a series of books written and illustrated by a man in the fifties and sixties, detailing his extensive fell climbing trips all over the mountains of Lakeland." Mike paused – "still there?"

"Ye-es carry on. I haven't gone away."

"Oh – it just seemed very quiet. Right, well I dug out the book on the walks that touched on your lake and it wasn't long before I found what I was looking for – written in 1959. Listen – I'll read some of it. *My plan was to take the path over White Crag up above the western flank of Lastwater and proceed along the ridge, not descending until the very end so as to bring me down at Lastwater Farm. It was a beautiful day and I was able to take in the grandeur of this lake showing off its unique deep blue colour while surrounded by new growth starting to emerge at the very zenith of the Spring Equinox.* Mike broke off from the script at this point. "I should explain that he had set out fairly early in the morning to walk all the way over to the southern end of Borrowdale, by a scenic path, from the bus stop on the Keswick-Ambleside road. I'll skip a bit. When he reaches the top of Pelm Crag he turns and looks back along the way he has come. Listen. *I could not believe my eyes at first. I could now see into the strip of water between Shimdorie Island and the shore at Bray; whereas before it had been hidden by trees, or I was simply not high enough to see over them. Just this side of the island there appeared to be a hole in the water. There is no other description that applies to what I saw. It was quite a large hole with what looked like a circular, extremely fast current around the edge. I sat down and stared at it for quite some time wondering what it might be. Then, all at once, it vanished.*" Mike stopped reading before making the comment, "Unfortunately he did not do one of his excellent drawings. I guess he couldn't trust his memory of the scene. Still I thought you would like to know."

Dalmar was agog. "You do realise Mike that what you have told me is the only sighting of this anomaly ever recorded. It has been assumed that it can only be seen from the air and that is why. But – it appears Pelm Crag might be the one vantage point from which it can be witnessed." Dalmar thought for a while – his mind racing. "Tell you what – apart from David Fresher, let's keep this to ourselves. See if you can get Monday afternoon off and shin up the crag and see if it is true. If we don't say anything about it – you should have the place to yourself. Got a camera?"

"What a bloody good idea – and yes I have – a Pentax SLR."

"Perfect. Right you're on." They discussed the details for a little while before Dalmar thanked his friend profusely and went back to join his family. He would tell David later when they were alone.

The press conference went well, mostly because Dalmar and Suzanne had prepared things, and David Fresher's articulate speech with his tempered Geordie accent, spoken confidently, could easily be understood. Everyone picked up on his enthusiasm and there were many questions after his address. The only negative side was the chorus of disappointment on being told that no one was allowed on Shimdorie Island. Dalmar took note of this; he would have to have a word with Donald Altringham concerning security. He could foresee an attempt or two at getting a boat out there during the dark hours, especially if Sunday night/Monday morning produced an overcast sky deleting moonlight. Judging by the groans, it was quite obvious that some of the tabloid reporters had made plans which had just been thwarted.

After they had gone, over lunch in the busy canteen, Dalmar told David and Brian about Mike Parson's discovery.

"Canny!" came the predictable response from David. "What a stroke of luck. It gives us hard evidence of what to expect. I think Nick and I will climb a tree, not just to get a good view, but for our safety as well."

"Don't get it," Brian looked doubtful about something. "A hole in the lake. How?"

"Aye," David cut in. "Now – if you watch a white enamel bath after the plug has been pulled, you will see a spiral tube of water going down towards the plug hole. What you have to imagine is a bath coloured a dirty dark brown containing blue not very transparent water. Then, instead of a spiral of clear water – you would see a hole. Now amplify that up to the scale of our lake and you have a sizable black hole. Not sure how big yet – but, probably in the region of a twenty-five to thirty-foot diameter." He looked grave, "Anyway – enough to swallow a sleek rowing boat with nine seats." The other two went silent for a while – remembering.

The Roe deer twins had reached the stage when they needed to start on their adult diet of woodland vegetation. There was plenty near at hand, but it would be mostly grassing, lichen and bark to start with. John and Nick had started preparing a small area in the woodland near the castle with high fencing so that Archie and Matilda could be released once the warmer weather arrived in late May. It was still too early to let them out, and, by then the more succulent young shoots would start appearing to aid their diet. Suzanne and Bea's plan was to establish them permanently in the woods. They would then be let out of the enclosure which would be maintained for other similar eventualities. Emma loved enticing them with their new food at the centre.

When Miss Hunter returned home from school on Friday afternoon, the lift share parent having dropped her at the castle entrance, she could not believe the amount of activity going on as she made her way quickly up the drive. Jodie usually met her by the bus stop, but she was nowhere to be seen, just, it seemed to her bewildered young mind, hundreds of people, trucks and cars, some of whom were festooned with cable and things poking out of roofs, windows and doorways. At last she spotted Jodie running along the grass verge towards her. She too had been held up with all the traffic. This was set-up time for the two television crews, together with establishing arrangements at ground level for international film crews and newspaper reporter teams. There hardly seemed to be a square foot of space left available at the castle forecourt and the gravelled drive around the big sloping lawn by the smaller of the two wooded areas.

John Fisher was getting seriously worried about damage to his cared after lawn-edging. The two girls managed to fight their way through to the Dower-house unscathed. Emma had started to develop a childlike excitement over the whole thing. Her mother was still at the animal rescue centre helping Bea, and her father was rather busy trying to appease everyone with all their requests and queries. Brian Cussen was helping out and Jack Twentyman, after unsuccessfully trying to get back to his office at Keswick to close off the working week, gave up and stayed put considering he would be more useful where he was. He was right. It did not end there; a coach arrived in the middle of everything taking up valuable space. Apparently, the operator had added the stop to their tour agenda because of the topical interest without checking ahead that it would be wise. Quite clearly, it was not, and the unfortunate driver had a bad time. After a while Dalmar put Brian onto them exuding a suave charm. It worked and the hapless tourists, after managing to get a cup of tea in the crowded restaurant went smiling on their way even though they had seen absolutely nothing relevant to their curiosity.

The one person most people wanted to see had executed a crafty exit. David Fresher was somewhere outside the castle grounds ostensibly taking Fly for a walk. However, even here he had to be careful for the surrounding fells were attracting far more attention from the walking fraternity than usual, so David had borrowed the castle Land Rover and driven off with Fly on board. Currently, he was on the homeward leg of an extended stroll around Grasmere lake. It gave him much needed time to think things out. This was his excuse and he was sticking to it. Anyway, Fly enjoyed the outing; a nice level walk for a dog approaching his senior years. He was now ten years old; although, normally, a casual glance would not detect it. Thanks to an abundance of grooming attention at home and a constant healthy diet with exercise, he looked magnificent. David felt proud of him even though he was not the animal's owner. A lot of the attention the dog received came from Jodie. If she decided to leave Bray Castle there would be some tears, of which, a considerable amount would be due to her adoration of Fly. Her appointment had only been supposed to be for a short while, and she had already stayed far longer than she had originally intended.

The weather forecast for the next few days was rather dubious. Everyone involved had been hoping that an anticyclone would develop over the U.K. this weekend, but it was not to be. While torrential rain was not expected, nevertheless, a low-pressure system was approaching from the Atlantic Ocean and would start to make its way over Ireland on Sunday. The television people were not too disappointed for no sunlight meant no glare on the water; their pictures should be the better for it, although Lastwater's famous royal blue hue might not be evident especially with the expected new intake of salt water during the early hours of Monday morning, when the spring tide river course reversal was due to take place. The actual infusion of the saltwater into the lake would occur during night time. There would be no point in trying to capture any evidence until after dawn, which at this time of year was around six o'clock in the morning. Fortunately, the main visual happening, when the excess water was due to leave the lake, was expected to take place during daylight hours between two to four o'clock in the afternoon of the same day.

Saturday brought the expected increase in visitor numbers to the National Trust property, although it was nothing extraordinary, and the British Broadcast Corporation and Cumbria television were able to finish off their preparation on the castle roof under the watchful eye of Brian Cussen, who had already moved the observatory's big telescope to its mounting point overlooking the battlements facing lake-wards. Additionally, a still camera facility had been connected with assistance provided by the Royal Geographical Society. By Saturday everything was ready, a full twenty-four hours in advance. For the media this provided plenty of scope to set the scene in general for news broadcasts and current affairs programmes.

Jack Twentyman and Dalmar were both anxious about a possible overload of tourists on Monday morning. It was not a holiday time, and this would help, but there was always the possibility that many people might take the day off to come and visit the area. Donald Altringham of the Lake District National Park was contacted, and between them, they came up with a plan to monitor traffic levels ready to put into place temporary road closures backed with the authority of the Cumbrian police force. While such action might prove unpopular it was considered necessary, otherwise vital routes in the event of emergency service access could become inaccessible.

CHAPTER TWENTY-NINE

'UNPARALLED IN HUMAN HISTORY.'

David Fresher and Nick Jordan had to make a preparatory trip out to Shimdorie Island on Saturday afternoon. It was just a question of getting camping paraphernalia out there, so that, the next day, they could devote all the space in the rowing boat, now replenished with the proper oars, to photographic and film equipment. David also wanted to have a look at the line he and Dalmar had left in place last year. This was still suspended from a rod tied to a tree with its weighted end lying somewhere along the underground riverbed.

The weather was kind and although overcast and threatening - there was no rain. After loading the tents and other camping equipment into the little boat, they set off with Nick making short work of the crossing with his powerful strokes expertly executed. It prompted David to ask, "Have you done this before?"

"Yes – quite a bit of sculling," he said with a smile. Actually, he was a Cambridge University Blue but he said nothing further.

The rod and line had survived the winter months unscathed, in fact it looked as though it had been placed there yesterday. They pitched their tents, one for themselves and the other to act as shelter for the expensive filming apparatus that would be brought out tomorrow. Finding space for the tents was not that easy. They had to be on the highest ground to allow for the increased water level, and as all of that was covered in a dense area of young birch trees, they would have to contend with some uncomfortable surface roots beneath their bodies. Anyway, they managed to make camp and sort out the cooking utensils. One more trip to the beached boat brought back a fairly long coiled rope among other items. Coming back to the shore David pointed out two substantial Rowan trees.

"They will do for our perches when the big moment comes, so that we can get up above the whirlpool, which ought to be visible about there." His outstretched finger seemed to indicate a part of the lake about fifteen yards from the water's edge next to the rocky ridge sticking out all along this part of the shore. "So that is what the rope is for. Are we going to rig some sort of cradle on each tree?" asked Nick standing to his full height and gazing at a suitable branch jutting out over the water from one of the trees.

"Yes," replied David scratching at his locks of straw-coloured hair above his forehead. "Mind you – not quite sure how. But we'll work something out man." He grinned at his companion. "That reminds me, have you got a knife?"

"Sorry – no." Nick shrugged his shoulders.

"Oh well – someone will at the castle I guess."

They were soon on their way back in a little while. David made a point of studying the water level all along this side of the island's shore and making mental notes.

Sally Jarvis, the senior cook at Bray Castle, together with Dalmar had taken a chance and ordered far more supplies for the restaurant than would be normal for a weekend at this time of year. When Trishia was on duty on the Saturday, she thought they might have gone over the top, however, by eleven o'clock on Sunday morning, she started to worry that they might run out. Talk about standing room only. The combination of the strong media presence, most of whom had nothing to do at the present time, and a huge increase in visitor activity, even though there would be nothing out of the ordinary to see yet, gave the venue its biggest trading day to date.

At two in the afternoon the police closed the road to Bray Castle, and, inconveniently, Lastwater Farm, but it had to be done until traffic started rolling out from the opposite direction.

Many people had brought their own sustenance and just wandered through the grounds, although a lot more than usual paid their entrance fee and looked around the castle itself. There were cars parked along the verges on the drive leading into the estate and several found space alongside the access road from below White Crag.

Any ambitious newspaper reporter, television presenter or freelance cameraman could not see any point in trespassing out onto the lake during the night – the main event was not due until the Monday afternoon and even then, no one in their right mind would venture on the water. There had been too much evidence and loss of life to convince one and all that it would be a foolish thing to do, even in a powerful motorboat. And then there was the problem of launching such a boat onto the lake anyway. Security was so much in evidence that it would be virtually impossible. Due to the no-fly ruling over the general area of Lastwater things were pretty well sewn up. It looked as though the only photography that would take place would be David Fresher's efforts from Shimdorie Island, the official Royal Air Force helicopter and that achieved from the roof of Bray Castle both by Brian Cussen and the television crews.

Unofficially, Mike Parsons would be having a go from Pelm Crag, above the south-western end of the lake. There was, however, something that everyone had overlooked. A senior photographer who worked for one of the broad sheet daily newspapers practised a sport that took up a considerable amount of his free time. His name was Duke Peterson and he was an experienced hang glider pilot – a member of Lewes hang Gliding Club, in Southern England, for the past five years.

Making a successful flight from the cliff tops on the West Sussex coast where air currents could be accurately forecast, and dangerous down-draughts were well known was one thing. Hang gliding in the valleys of the Lake

District was quite another. Wind direction could change in seconds. It was not an area to be seriously considered for the sport let alone guaranteeing a flight direction for a one off. Over the last two months Duke had carried out a great deal of research into the matter. He had concluded that there was only one flight possibility which could end in a low-level run over Lastwater, and that was to carry out the launch from the western upper slopes of the Helvelyn mountain range.

During Sunday afternoon quite an audience assembled to see David and Nick off on their camping expedition. It included the entire Hunter family and David's sister, Jodie. Emma held onto Fly, who, naturally, was under the impression that he was going with them, while Suzanne held little Michael up so that he could wave goodbye. The little boat had ample space to stow all the photographic equipment. It had been covered over with a tarpaulin in case of accidental splashing. The rain held off and looked like continuing to do so, which would be enormously helpful when they arrived on the island and started setting up the cameras for remote control operation. The video filming would be carried out by David, and, considering the weight of the camera, he would have quite a job on, especially when perched up a tree for the final act.

Dalmar added one last item, a round life saver ring. "Just in case," he Indicated to David who gave him a nod.

The media contingent at the boat house had been kept to a minimum in the interest of safety for all, so there were only two camera crews allowed, plus half a dozen photographers.

On arrival at the island David, among other tasks, had a very important one to accomplish – the taking of a sample of lake water. It was essential that samples were taken at key times during the next day or two to illustrate the salinity changes that would presumably take place. He had debated to himself whether to give this job to someone at the castle, but decided, on reflection, to trust no one, especially considering how busy they would probably be with visitors.

Later, when everyone at Bray had settled down for the night, the last tourist had long gone; the birds and animals at the rescue centre were quiet and even the astronomer students were more interested in the daytime activities on the morrow, Dalmar was contemplating retiring himself when an alarming thought occurred to him. 'If something serious happened on the island and the two men were unable to get away in their boat, how would anyone over here get over there?' He reached for the short-wave radio handset, which would be accompanying him everywhere for the next twenty-four hours and switched on the transmit button. "Shimdorie – this is base – over."

For quite a few seconds nothing happened – then there was a low crackling noise followed by David Fresher's voice – very loud. "And who is this disturbing our tranquillity?"

Dalmar frantically adjusted the volume before it woke everyone in the house. "Are you settled?" he asked.

"If you call settled – lying in a sleeping bag with a tree root up my arse – then – yes, I suppose so," replied David.

Dalmar detected a minor slurring about the voice. He chuckled. "Had a few, have we?"

"If – having a few is a couple of Newcastle Brown's – then yes – we have had a few man."

"Oh yes?" Dalmar laughed – "Look just wanted to check everything was alright before I go to bed. You see – you have our only boat, so if the level rises a little too much there could be problems."

"I assure you the boat is secure, plus with the rock bank around most of the island at the water edge we wouldn't have a problem even if the level rose by six inches, which is not very likely. That would need a coincidental tropical style downpour at the same time and there is no sign of that in the current weather conditions – even in Cumbria." There was a short pause before David added. "Anyway, I am way ahead of you. We are watch keeping here. Nick is taking the first until three am and I am on for the remainder, so enjoy your full night's kip."

"Okay," said Dalmar with a further chuckle. "Talk to you in the morning. You can call me early if you like. Need to be up and about by six. Good night."

Nick Jordan woke David from his fretful slumber at 3am on Monday morning. The air was damp, although, it was not raining. There was no wind and everywhere was pitch black. For the last hour Nick had sat by the water's edge adjacent to the fishing line. Periodically, he had shone his torch to check the water level against a mark David had scratched onto the side of a boulder where the water lay up against it. There had, as yet, been no alteration. It had remained obstinately the same. The eerie mournful hoot from the long-eared owl had been his only conscious companion during this time, apart from the occasional splashing from, perhaps, a large fish. He was glad his stint was finally over.

David grumbled and struggled out of his sleeping bag. He became suddenly alert. While his body wanted to carry on sleeping. His brain did not. Having heard the negative report from his colleague he set about brewing up a pot of tea. Nick declined a beverage and opted for a quick release into the world of sleep. He had become very tired over the last couple of hours and had had difficulty avoiding nodding off, frequently making himself stand up until the heavy eyelid syndrome wore off.

David had consumed two mugs of sweet tea in the same location Nick had been sitting – when he heard it – the sound of a large bubble bursting a few yards away. BLUPP. To another person it would have seemed an unreal noise in the dead of night. David knew exactly what it was. He had been expecting it. His thoughts were confirmed, almost instantly, when he switched on his powerful twenty-inch Mag-Lite and let the beam play out over the water. BLUPP – BLUPP – BLUPP – three more giant bubbles burst forth: the convex shape rising three feet above the surface of the water. To David this happening was extremely important, for it told him that the underground river was not a tunnel filled with water, but a great deal of it could be expected to be cavernous. And, furthermore, because there was no pungent aroma coming from the bursting bubbles – it must be air. The caves should, therefore, possess breathable air and there was, in all probability, several stretches like this along the subterranean river's course. The breadth and formation would depend on the geological rock structure encountered.

It became obvious, very soon, that the water level in the lake was rising. Immediately David grabbed his sample case and procured another to line up with the tubes slotted in their racks in the wooden box. It took a good hour for the first inch and a half of extra water to show and then, fairly rapidly, two further inches were added. During this time the geologist acquired a couple more samples of the lake water. He had taken a photograph yesterday afternoon to show the level at that time, and he would take another shot as soon after dawn as light would allow.

Dalmar would be doing the same at the level marker post by Bray Castle's jetty. It was not possible to measure how much trapped air had escaped through the lake surface, but David knew that the area in which it would be evident was right in front of him, and even after two and a half hours there was still the odd bubble, sometimes several in rapid succession. He had privately thought; it was highly probable that the area of coast where the mouth of the river was most likely to be would lie over towards Whitehaven on the Cumbria coast. However, there was no guarantee of that. It was the shortest distance from here to the sea. He had based his thoughts on geological structure as well as general gradient.

Because of the amount of air escaping, he was beginning to revise that theory. He did not for one moment entertain the idea that the whole course of the river would be cavernous. For the phenomena of the tidal theory to be valid, a section must be totally full of water as the course neared the coast. And there was no doubt that a mile or so must be completely immersed at the lake end. David was beginning to feel a buzz of excitement. 'The forthcoming exploration of this river course in a couple of months time looked as though it might reveal something wonderful: scary yes, but the experience was shaping up to have all the promise of an adventure, of its kind, unparalleled in human history.'

He decided he would not confide his thoughts to Dalmar just yet. Since returning to Bray, the trip had not been mentioned due to the concentration on the matter in hand.

One thing puzzled the geologist. Given the amount of giant air bubbles he had witnessed, even with just the aid of a torch at night, surely someone, over the centuries, must have seen the phenomenon when it occurred during daylight hours. 'Okay,' he thought to himself, 'the thin membrane of the bubble might not be that visible under some conditions from the shore, but, again, at some moment in time, a person in a boat would have been near enough to witness it. After all, in the outflow, human beings had lost their lives, so why had there never ever been any reports of this – the inflow? Could it have been put down to escaping methane as witnessed in marshy areas?' He came to the conclusion that he would probably never know.

Curiosity brought Nick out of his sleep without the helping hand of David. He came to at five minutes to six; half an hour before sunrise.

"So far we've got an eighty-five mill' rise in the water level. That is a hell of a lot!" exclaimed David in reply to Nick's questioning look. "You imagine that spread all over this lake. I'm telling you it would fill an Olympic sized swimming pool thrice over and we ain't finished yet."

Nick scratched at the dishevelled hair on his head. He found it difficult to take the information in. "Shall I brew up?" he suggested.

"Great idea," David responded. "But before you do that – give your face a douse in the water. Tell me what you think."

Nick was not at all sure why he had received this instruction, but not wishing to show ignorance, he got down on his hands and knees by the nearest spot at the water's edge and scooped up two palms full of water until they brimmed over. He applied the remainder to his face spluttering away as he did so. He did not know what to expect, perhaps there might be a significant temperature change. He got a surprise. "Urgh," he uttered with a grimace. "That is disgustingly salty."

David laughed. "Good job I filled up a spare pot of water yesterday – huh man."

"Oh Christ!" Nick looked at the pot in wonder. "Wow – thanks," was all he could think of saying.

"It'll disperse and dilute later. Won't notice it by mid-morning. But there ain't no doubt - that there is sea water – huh man?" Nick nodded his head in complete agreement.

The short-wave radio handset suddenly burst into life. "Morning campers." This was followed by a gruff low-level bark from a dog.

David grabbed the handset and switched it to transmit. "High – are you at the jetty?" He did not bother with greetings; he had an urgent need for information.

"Yes – and the answer to your next question is 3.5 inches. How about you?" Dalmar had already seen the water level rise on the marker post. It was just light enough to do this without the aid of a torch.

"Snap. Still a bit more to go I reckon. It's been blowing bubbles since four o'clock this morning."

"Pardon?" It was not only Dalmar that appeared confused, Nick had a questioning look on his face as well.

"Oh – never mind, I'll explain later. I expect you need to get back to the castle. Reckon you are going to be busy today. Talk later. Nick and I are going to feast on bacon sarnies man.

"Okay – enjoy them – over and out." Dalmar felt a little envious. 'Bacon sandwiches and a mug of coffee or tea by a campfire.' The thought appealed to him, just at that moment, instead of what he had to face that day.

CHAPTER THIRTY

COMPLETELY IMPENETRABLE.

Even though it was a normal working day, a great many people seemed to have managed to find the time to visit Lastwater on Monday 21st March. The authorities had to close the access road by eleven o'clock. Initial interest was invoked from news broadcast announcements that the lake had received its expected top-up of saltwater during the night. This was beautifully backed up visually, when, by a fortunate chance, in opposition to the weather predictions, the clouds parted, and glorious vibrant sunshine showed off Lastwater's new infusion of spectacular blue colours. The television cameras from Bray Castle roof captured the scene perfectly which only lasted for about twenty minutes just after eight o'clock. Unbeknown to anyone a lone amateur photographer in the guise of Mike Parsons having decided to set up camp early on Pelm Cragg took several shots. He was not to know yet that the results, after processing, would become the standard when illustrating the phenomenon of Lastwater, because the coincidence of sunlight on a strong new tidal surge had not been witnessed for some time. This was coupled with the fact that he had been led to the best viewing platform for the event thanks to the writings of a fell walker and no one else had thought of it.

David and Nick had attended to strengthening up their respective harnesses on the Rowan trees. Of great help was the fact that new leaf growth was yet to happen, so that they were able to arrange for good sight lines onto the area where the whirlpool would probably form later in the day. There were several conversations between them and Bray Castle with Brian Cussen joining in, because nearly all the questions being fired at him by the B.B.C. and Cumbrian Television personnel could only be answered by those on the island.

Dalmar and his staff were kept constantly busy trying to please tourists and the press, mainly due to overcrowding in the restaurant and too much congestion both inside and outside the castle. Thankfully, many visitors took the hint and dispersed throughout the grounds, particularly to the lakeside areas. Nobody who worked there could ever recall experiencing anything like it. Privately, Suzanne looked forward to the end of these days; it was too much for the animals, and Roz feared for the comfort of her horses, although, in truth, they coped well with all the hustle and bustle, because they were secure with their welfare at Bray Castle. Over a sandwich at the Dower-house at lunchtime with Jodie and Michael, just home from his playschool, all three women confessed to their distaste for the current goings on. Even Jodie moaned that she had hardly seen her brother since he had been here. However, they did conclude that it must be worth it in order to rid every one of the terrible fear over the lake itself. This weekend should end in satisfying all that there were only two days or nights in a year when the lake was dangerous.

Dalmar and Jack Twentyman did get a chance to sneak up onto the roof of the castle and have a chat with Brian and the film crews. They had all been well looked after having been supplied with numerous hot drinks and biscuits from the canteen. There was only one major worry, and that was that the main event might occur later than thought and encroach into the twilight time, when it would be difficult to film with the departing light.

Meanwhile Duke Peterson and three helpers had parked their Volvo 245 estate, with its large fibreglass container affixed to the roof rack. Inside this, neatly folded onto its frame, lurked the latest Canadian Birdman lightweight hang glider. They had used a lay-by under a forest canopy by the side of the Keswick road just south of the Thirlmere reservoir. After gathering all their equipment together, they set off up a steep little used pathway by the side of Birksdale Gill and its tumbling waterfalls. The idea was to ascend up over Willie Wife Moor onto the heights of Dollywagon Pike. It would be hard work carrying the glider and they would be taking it in turns to share the weight.

Duke was a very tall man at something over six foot four. Kitted out in his black leather flying suit alongside his rather diminutive companions he looked a striking figure. Nevertheless, the task he had set himself made him feel quietly nervous about this afternoon's adventure, and he was not looking forward to it. The higher they climbed on the moor, the more apprehensive he became, something, in recent years, he never experienced on the south coast. He was committed and had been for some time, but he was now ardently wishing that he had never had the idea in the first place. All four men were breathing hard with the exertion. On reaching a rocky outcrop they decided to rest and have their lunch. It was the upper legs that ached the most. The sunshine they had experienced earlier in the day, when travelling up from the south coast, had vanished. It was now still dry, but grey and quiet. Duke new that as they climbed higher the wind strength would increase. He also knew that if it increased too much, then that would be that, and he would have to call the whole thing off. 'So far – so good,' he thought to himself.

He suddenly remembered an important matter he was supposed to have carried out. Unhitching his backpack, he quickly set up the radio communications transmitter and receiver. "Completely forgot," he said to one of his colleagues. "Need to test this. Hope Jock is in place." After raising the aerial, he switched on. "Jock – can you hear me?"

Immediately after he had switched over to receive, the soft dialect of south Edinburgh came on loud and clear. "Are – there ye are. Got a good view of proceedings at the lakeside. You guys okay?" Duke established that Jock was sitting right on the end of a promontory opposite Shimdorie Island and satisfied that the radio was working properly he said, "Next time we hear from you, I'll be ready. Keep your eyes peeled over the next hour or so."

"I will," replied Jock and closed the transmission. In his exposed position on the end of Cloud Point he was thankful it was not raining. He had a long wait in store.

Mike Parsons was enjoying his ham sandwiches sitting on a lump of volcanic rock over-looking the whole north-south vista of Lastwater. He was regretting not having bought a paper back or, at least, a magazine with him. Boredom had set in despite the fact that he had been for a walk across to White Crag and back. He had beaten a hasty retreat from there due to the number of people who had set up tripods for cameras and other film making equipment. Some of them were obviously from press and television, but others; indeed, the vast majority were definitely amateur photographers or the just plain curious. Mike managed to pass himself off as one of the later. His camera was hidden inside his rucksack and no one spoke to him before he turned around and headed back towards Pelm Crag, although taking a different route lower down towards the lake on his return. Of one thing he became certain. Providing you had a telephoto lens, Pelm Crag provided the better viewpoint for the waters this side of Shimdorie Island.

A substantial drystone wall, four to five feet in height, was prominent from the left-hand side of Mike's current situation hidden amongst the rocky summit of the crag. It meandered and undulated steeply downwards with a bank of browned bracken alongside the path on which he had made his ascent. Lower down it wound around a stumpy yew tree copse, disappearing over the crest of a hill before reappearing further down. Eventually, almost in the centre of his picture it met another wall coming from farther over to the left. The two joined as one and continued down into the valley. Mike practised a telephoto shot with his camera using his two-hundred-millimetre lens. It looked as though the triangle formed at the joining of the walls would be his marker towards the point in the lake where the illustration in the book had shown the black whirlpool to be. It would also act as a good scale reference with the walls ending suddenly and the lake surface appearing, in focus, but distant thus emphasising the phenomenon.

Looking at these waters were David Fresher and Nick Jordan. It was two o'clock. The calmness looked innocent as though nothing could disturb its tranquillity. David knew that the reality was that any fish territorially locked into this part of the lake would perish. Even he noticed though, that in all the time he and Nick had been on the island, there had be no sign of the resident otters or, for that matter, any waterfowl such as swans or ducks. They could be heard but not seen, except for fleeting moments in the distance.

At three o'clock in the afternoon Jane Derby was in place on the roof of the castle. While she was waiting to do her presentation bit she got talking to Brian Cussen. "Can't help thinking – this is going to be some let down if nothing happens?" The truth was that she had not been able to get her brain around the scientific theory of all this.

"That isn't very likely," replied Brian. The air was still calm, and the absence of any wind made things quite comfortable in their exposed position despite the time of year. "We've had the first event after all: a substantial rise in the water level of the lake."

"Yes – but does it always go back down in a rush. Sometimes it could be gradual – yes?"

"No way – sorry. It's called gravity." Brian was trying to be patient here. Her doubts were understandable. One of the camera crew came over and joined in the discussion before Jane threw out the obvious statement that there was only an hour left to prove Mr Fresher right or wrong.

At half past three, Suzanne brought Michael and Emma up onto the roof with Jodie as well. The children were told to keep well away from the two camera crews, who, initially, would be concentrating on the photographic aspect; any voice over presentation would be carried out later.

Dalmar and Jack Twentyman had to remain in the office to take telephone calls, and deal with any operational difficulties inside and outside the castle. Assisting staff, from reception to restaurant, was virtually constant and would remain so for the rest of the afternoon.

At 3.44 Greenwich Mean Time, David Fresher, from his position some twenty-five feet off the ground in the rowan tree called across to Nick just fifteen yards away in the other tree, "Something is happening. Look out on all sides away from the fishing line." He was referring to a wide arc extending beyond the island by a hundred yards or more. A disturbance in the water was causing a very slow anti-clockwise circular current. He pressed the transmit button on his radio and spoke the single word. "Standby."

Two camera men on different television cameras went straight into action. They were already focused on the right spot in the lake. At the same time a signal was sent to the Royal Air Force helicopter base responsible for providing the aerial photography. The crew took off almost at once and would be over Lastwater within twenty minutes.

Nick Jordan abruptly started to feel fearful. He was not aware of it but his hearing seemed to have become affected. All outside sound away from his immediate vicinity vanished causing an unreal atmosphere. His fear was compounded by the enormous swirl of water before him that possessed a noise, the like of which he had never experienced before. It built, gradually at first, and then in a rush to a massive storm sound in reverse. Imagine a high wind following the sound of its power. Impossible – yes – but now witnessed. Even David was perplexed.

Jock from his position on the end of Cloud Point saw the disturbance in the water near Shimdorie Island over to his left, as did all the other onlookers lining the shore. A buzz of excitement, in general, went up. Jock immediately alerted Duke Peterson high up on the Helvelyn mountain slopes. He was ready.

Mike Parsons had trouble realising that the sketch he had seen in the book, far from showing any exaggeration might even have understated. The black hole in the lake shot into view from his distant platform and his camera started clicking.

From their tree perches David and Nick became gripped within a world that was supremely foreign to them. They could not see the side of the now fully developed whirlpool nearest to them, but they could see the rest of it. From the grey-blue crest down into a disappearing funnel of black depths slowly spinning in an anti-clockwise direction vast walls of water made them feel miniscule, and irrelevant in the scale of the circumstances they were witness to. There was also a feeling of trespass about it as though they should not be there at all. The constant revelations had a dangerous hypnotic effect and threatened to plunge them into an unconscious state and – disaster. They were both in positions on branches that overlapped the lake's edge. The near edge of the chasm of water was too near for there to be any escape if one of them fell. And then there was that continuous noise. It would have been impossible for one of them to shout to the other. They would not be heard. It was the sound of pressure waves blocking all else. Completely impenetrable. It left the watching humans in a state of weak isolation. But – they had their sight, although, certainly in Nick's case, to add to his fear, an atmosphere of mounting dread came on.

David brought himself back to reality. There was filming

to do. He had a camera rigged up from the branch above his head. It was already loaded with film and focused. It was just a matter of reaching out – pointing the lens in the right direction and switching on. At last he did so. He was using a VHS video camera and he kept filming for quite a while

It was with some surprise that Nick became aware of the underside of a grey helicopter hovering over them. He knew enough about them to immediately find it odd that the rotors caused no detectable disturbance in the water, and the noise which would normally have been deafening was inaudible. The thing was like a giant mosquito waiting to strike.

They talk about it today – when the man with the black wings flew down off the mountain.

Duke Peterson had already carried out a thorough pre-flight check before he received the signal from Jock. Not only that but he had made sure his photographic equipment was functioning. This was something untried. At great expense, he had persuaded the newspaper he worked for to fund it. Housed inside his crash helmet was a sophisticated 35mm lens camera with motor drive. All Duke had to do was look at the target for a photograph and press the shutter release which was conveniently strapped onto the inside of his right wrist, enabling him to reach it with a fingertip, so when he arrived over the target area on Lastwater he could keep the motor drive engaged. It would then take a rapid sequence of pictures using a very fast shutter speed. Focus was automatic. Just in case, measures had been taken to make sure that the camera itself was set in a waterproof housing. There was no knowing what weather conditions might occur during the flight and there was always the chance of a crash landing in the lake itself. Instead of his usual warm protective clothing, Duke was wearing a wet suit with full head protection. For dexterity reasons he had chosen skin-tight rubber gloves.

Due to the steepness of his take-off position, Duke

stood upright in his harness and let the sail dip down from vertical to horizontal. He gave a nod to his back up team who were waiting nearby in silent anticipation. With his feet, he pushed off. He was held by a full strap harness so there was no need to carry out the tricky acrobatics of getting his legs into a bag harness on the glider. He let the black sail glide effortlessly down into the valley levelling off well before he arrived over the forest area near Thirlmere reservoir. This was an utterly thrilling sensation as the ground rushed past him. The great scale of the mountain slope took him along as a large bird of prey might do using an air current. Gone was his fear. As always, adrenalin flooded into his brain exciting him to a heightened tension.

He needed to get into a position where he was flying plum in the middle of the valley leading down towards Grasmere. Duke had to admit that, so far, he had been lucky. There were no high winds. The rain had held off. Everything was in his favour for a successful flight. All he had to worry about was the sheer fact that he had never flown in this kind of geographical terrain before. Unfortunately, the Lake District mountains and valleys were all so compact increasing the likelihood of dangerous rogue gusts of wind. This, naturally, made him alert.

Cars having travelled down on the main road from Kirkstone Pass were amazed to see a man dressed in black, under what appeared to be a giant kite, glide over their heads. A travelling salesman, going in the opposite direction, alarmed that he might be being attacked by aliens, nearly drove off the road.

CHAPTER THIRTY-ONE

LIKE A BROKEN BUTTERFLY

All too soon, Duke Peterson found himself approaching the first vital change of direction he had to negotiate. Down below him, he could see the course of the river Brothay approaching with the eastern slope of Helm Crag over to his right. He must not get too close to the steep crags of this fell, which being on the lee side, could well be harbouring dangerous air currents. At the same time, he had to manage a steep turn to the right, in order to bring himself on a flight lying between Helm Crag and White Crag. This heralded the beginning of the valley in which lay the deep waters of Lastwater.

Unfortunately, he was too late and too low. An unseen thermal caught him as he was leaning his body to start his turn. The big twelve metre sail gripped the current and started to spiral upwards in long lazy curves. Fortunately, he had been far enough out from the slopes of Helm Crag to avoid a possible fatal crash. There was nothing he could do but go with the ascent until the thermal petered out. It was important to fly as naturally as possible, like a bird with its wings outstretched, and not try any counter manoeuvres. This could cause a disastrous out of control spin from which there would be no going back. He would plunge all the way to the ground. As he climbed higher and higher, he was glad he had his thicker flying suit on. The temperature fell rapidly. The great valley housing Windermere, the largest waterway in the Lake District opened up to the south. But he had no time to admire the view. Duke concentrated on planning his descent so as to attempt another try at aligning himself with the entrance to Lastwater's valley. The thermal ran out at three and a half thousand feet above sea level – higher than the tallest mountain in Cumbria. Duke piloted the craft in a wide anticlockwise curve before starting the downward trajectory with circular flight ever decreasing in diameter. All the while he edged over towards Grasmere Common and the great bulk of Rydal Fell to keep clear of the air current that took him aloft to start with. With a great deal of patience and skill he managed to get down to the required height for his approach. He had started to get anxious in case the phenomenon now happening on the lake should abate and be over. This whole effort would then be wasted.

It was with plenty of satisfaction that he managed to execute the final circular movement so as to bring him opposite the entrance to the valley leading to his destination. He straightened out the glider's flight and headed on between White and Helm Crags. New Bridge lay directly below him, with the narrow waters of Easedale Beck winding its way at the very depth of the valley.

Very soon – there it was. Lastwater lay calm and steely blue, dead ahead of him. Carefully he dipped the front part of his body to bring the craft lower on a definite path to fly between Shimdorie Island and the southern Bray shore. He had planned this, by observation on foot, from both sides of the lake, several times in the last few weeks. Then he saw the helicopter, but with immediate relief noticed that it was flying a long way off his path going west along the northern shore of the lake.

Quickly, he fired off a couple of test shots by pressing the release trigger for the camera housed in his helmet. The cable, taped to his right arm, ended within reach of his index finger. He heard the distinct clunk of the shutter operation resonate inside the helmet.

Duke Peterson's launch team were well on their way back down the mountain. They had to get to the estimated landing site as quickly as possible – Lastwater Farm.

On Bray Castle's rooftop, Emma Hunter saw the hang glider first. She had no idea what it was, "Look!" she shouted, at the same time tugging at her mother's coat sleeve. "What's that?" Her other hand pointed towards the eastern end of the lake. The glider was approaching over the unseen rowing club building hidden by treetops. Suzanne had no idea what she was looking at. At first, she thought it was a giant bird.

Jane Derby enlightened her. "Good grief! That's a hang glider." For a moment the flying sail disappeared behind a group of trees obscuring their vision before reappearing again headed, apparently, towards the island.

Jock, from his position on the end of Cloud Point got a magnificent view of Duke Peterson as he flew low over the water, and so did everyone else who had chosen this vantage point. It looked so dramatic – like some prehistoric flying dinosaur heading in to land.

Duke had the presence of mind to put the camera operation onto motor drive as he approached what looked to be a black hole in the lake by Shimdorie Island. As he flew over, first he was conscious of a complete loss of sound, even from the camera shutter operating inside his helmet. Secondly, although he saw it only fleetingly, a sense of shocking trepidation at the sight of the powerful whirlpool, with precipitous ultra-blue sides leading to a sinister looking black depth now directly below him. But he had no time to dwell on this. He ceased taking pictures so that he could look ahead and concentrate on keeping his craft in the air.

Nick Jordan was the first to see the piloted hang glider

as it loomed almost immediately in front of him passing over the whirlpool. David was peering, fascinated, into the depths of the giant swirling motion when a pair of black suited legs and boots flew above his eye-line. As it progressed over and passed on down the lake, David stared after the huge black sail in disbelief. The event was so unexpected. He guessed the reason straight away – 'an enterprising press photographer no doubt.' Nevertheless, he admired the gall and, indeed, the bravery.

From his vantage point he could see the glider fly on, perhaps twenty-five feet above the water, an amazing feat in itself. David's knowledge of thermal air currents was not that great; however, he guessed correctly, that the pilot would be expecting a lift once passed the island on exposure to the more open water beyond.

It was the watchers on the castle roof, especially the adults, who saw the danger first. The helicopter had been making a wide arc out over the northern shore of the lake and the pilot was now well into his turn to make a last run over the whirlpool.

It was extremely unlucky that the helicopter should be making its turn at exactly the same time as Duke Peterson's fly past. They were both on the same mission and, therefore, must be on the same flight trajectory, fortunately at slightly different altitudes, but, nevertheless, approaching each other very fast in opposite directions.

Duke saw the approaching helicopter undercarriage far too late. Although, painted out in camouflage, as far he was concerned it was big, black, suddenly loud and utterly threatening. It was on and just above him without warning. Instantly – he knew with a panicky feeling of horror that there was no way out. He had no chance of flying straight through or manoeuvring around in any way. His glider was pushed by a giant hand: the downdraft from the chopper's rotor blades. He was in the water in seconds.

Considering the speed he was travelling, the actual entry, as his body hit the surface of the lake with the big sail immediately following and covering him, seemed remarkably calm. He just came to a sudden stop. All was darkness and the icy temperature of the water did not immediately penetrate through his flying suit. He became concerned about keeping his head above water, fearing a leak through the helmet into the camera and so ruining all the effort with the destruction of the film.

The pilot's harness to the glider had been especially fitted with a quick release aircraft pin for just this type of emergency. He pulled the pin. At first, he tried to lift the glider over his head as he frantically trod water to stay on the surface, but it was simply too heavy. There was no way out other than to duck dive and swim clear under water. He would have to trust to the waterproof seal to the camera. Taking a deep breath, he went under. After a couple of strokes downwards, he swam away from the sail before surfacing. He found himself still alongside the glider, the whole of which was lying flat on the water with hardly a trace of the harness visible. Duke pushed himself clear. Now he was able to look about him.

At first, he was glad to make out the proximity of the island: he ought to be able to get there without too much physical stress – and then cold horror gripped him from head to toe. He was moving backwards very fast ... towards that terrifying whirlpool. Caught in that would mean certain death. The likelihood – given how fast the island shore was moving past him and the not so far away jaws of that black hole – of this happening – within seconds – was all too obvious.

As soon as David saw the glider hit the surface of the water he was down from his perch in the tree in no time. He called to Nick to do the same and that man did not question the reason, he was on the ground by David's side shortly afterwards. David had left the unused section of the rope they had brought with them coiled up by the edge of the water. One end was tied firmly with a bowline knot to a stout tree trunk ready for this type of emergency, although it had been primarily designed for their safety. David seemed to sense the importance of Nick Jordan's physique now and immediately passed the coil of rope to him. The distressed hang glider pilot preceded by the glider was approaching them and would soon plunge down into the whirlpool. David merely pointed in the direction of the bobbing black helmet. Nick understood at once, and quickly made his way onto the rocky edge by the underwater shelf leading to the mouth of the underground river far below. He had no time to prepare fully, but simply flung the coil, with all his strength, so that it opened out on trajectory across the water. He had had the presence of mind to aim some way in front of the terrified looking eyes peering at him through the glass visor of the helmet.

Duke saw the rope snaking out in front of him. He literally hurled his body towards it even though he was actually propelling himself towards the now visible lip of the outflow. He felt the rope's presence somewhere under his body and groping wildly managed to not only catch hold on with his gloved hand, but, also, to loop his right arm around it giving him extra holding power. Bringing his left hand to bear on the already tightening rope he waited – hoping – desperately – that the people on the island would be able to haul him in.

David and Nick; pleased that the rope seemed to have been taken up by the pilot had their wishes confirmed at the sudden tightening of the rope against the tree, as it held out straight and rigid. Both men quickly found ground hugging positions with their feet near the edge, in order to give them purchase, so that they could start heaving. David knew that it would not be easy. It was not just the man's weight they had to contend with – there was another force, which was far more of a threat to his survival. The two men watched incredulously as the floating glider's sail and frame folded like a broken butterfly over the edge of the whirlpool and disappeared into the depths of that incredible giant sucking vortex.   Not being in their lofty perches they were only unable to see it being pulled down as though a giant piece of sodden paper crumpling on itself.

When Duke reached the whirlpool itself, he became aghast with fear. Immediately his hands started to burn, even though his gloves, as he hung on with all his strength. As his body sunk below the swirling cataract, he felt an enormous pressure on his shoulders. It was as though he was holding up a vast quantity of water beyond his imagination, while another force was trying to propel him round. And – he knew he would not be able to hold on for long, let alone prevent himself from drowning. He could no longer breathe, being, effectively underwater. Added to this, the searing pain he was experiencing in the palms of his hands and where the rope held tight against his right arm was something that he was totally aware must be born. The whole thing seemed impossible – but – was it wild hope, or was he being pulled up – inch by – unbearably long in time – inch.

David had to yell out a time count so that the two men's pulling power was consolidated into simultaneous effort. "One – Two – Three!" He called out for the fifth time. It was getting increasingly harder to hold their balance between pulls, and more than once both men feared that they might be catapulted into the raging – no coming back – whirlpool immediately adjacent to the jagged rocky edge of their island. 'Time must be running out for the drowning man,' thought David.

The reality was that the tremendous pressure exerted by the weight of water out flowing through the whirlpool was too great. Far ... far too great. There was no way that the two men could pull the drowning man out. But, somehow, miraculously, Duke's helmeted head suddenly broke through the surface just near the lip and, within seconds, after one more valiant effort from the two men on shore, he was up and over – and free.

The exhausted bleeding pilot was pulled ashore somewhat roughly over the rocks. He would not have cared.

He had survived.

Nick, also, could feel rope burn on his hands. Both men were shattered from their efforts.

It soon became obvious why they had succeeded. Within inside a minute, the whirlpool had gone to be replaced by a weak tumbling eddy, and soon this dwindled to nothing more than an isolated area of rough water. Normality of sound from the outside world returned – welcomingly – like an old friend, even though radically impaired by the racket from a hovering helicopter immediately above them.

From his position on Pelm Crag, Mike Parsons saw it all with the aid of the telephoto lens on his camera. He fired off a few shots but due to the distance had no real hope of any clarity in the developed photographs, especially with speed factor setting being unavailable at that distance.

Dalmar Hunter had finally managed to extricate himself from duties at the castle without being rude to anybody and made it onto the roof just before the accident. He pulled rank and demanded the castle telescope to watch the drama.

The R.A.F. helicopter's pilot had not witnessed the actual dunking of the hang glider in the lake; however, he had seen it pass beneath him and guessed the result correctly. Immediately, he forgot the photographic element of his final pass and banked hard over the island so as to come back for a look. The crew saw the sail disappear into the whirlpool, and, from a hovering position, it was with some relief that they were able to watch the dramatic rescue of the pilot, although to start with, they were unsure what was happening.

Once Duke was safely on dry land, all three men did nothing for at least a full minute apart from find reasonably comfortable sitting situations. They needed to gather breath and alleviate aching muscles.

Before Duke could remove his helmet, he needed to take off his gloves. That was when the pain re-started. He stared in disbelief and mild horror at the sight of the palm on his right hand. It was a bloody mess. The left one was not a lot better. Neither David nor Nick wanted to remove their gloves just yet, and, as they did not have to, elected to keep whatever rope burn there might be left hidden. One thing was certain their wounds would be nothing like as bad as Duke's. Added to which this man, also, felt searing discomfort on his right lower arm where he had wrapped the rope around to give extra holding power. The burn marks were hidden under his flying suit and they could stay like that for the time being. Ignoring all his injuries, Duke set about the tricky task of removing his helmet. He could feel wetness inside and feared for the condition of the exposed film in the camera. The other two men did not try to communicate with him in the meantime. There would be little point. He would have difficulty hearing them.

When Duke finally exposed his head and face, he looked at his two seated rescuers who were studying him and wondering about his condition. He half raised his bloodied hand. As a prelude to saying, "That rope – it saved my life." His speech faltered as though still out of breath – which he was. "Thanks."

David pointed to his companion. "That is the man who threw the rope. Not many men would have been able to reach you." This was said just to make sure that the hang-glider pilot understood how fortunate he had been. But it was not necessary, before he grabbed that life-saving rope Duke had already decided he was about to end his days. As a result, his dramatic salvation had left him feeling extremely lightheaded. This helped combat the pain of the rope burns. "Are you with a media organisation?" David asked the obvious question.

"Yes – I am photographer attached to a national, Duke Peterson", he simply replied. As Duke did not know who his rescuers were, he prudently did not mention the paper's name.

David introduced himself and Nick. After a brief

discussion of what each man had been about, Duke asked how long it would be before he could get back to the mainland. The answer was as soon as they had packed up camp. Nick hardly said a word during this conversation. Privately, he rather held the pilot of the hang glider in awe and was delighted he had managed to get the rope to reach him when the time came.

While Nick went off to the tent to get the first aid box to attend to Duke's hand injuries, David took a final sample of water. The lake had now completely returned to its former calm state as though the dramatic occurrence of the last hour or so had never happened.

Jock, from his vantage point, had witnessed the event and radioed the glider recovery team to inform them. They were now on their way to Bray Castle.

It took David and Nick, between them, fifteen minutes to break camp. David then asked Nick to row over to the pier with Duke. They put the tent and some of the equipment in the dinghy and set off leaving David to take care of dismantling his photographic gear. He decided to leave the rope harnesses on the trees in situation for the present. He would need to return in a couple of days.

CHAPTER THIRTY-TWO

IT WAS SHEER TREPIDATION.

On the roof of Bray Castle, Dalmar, Suzanne and their children had departed together with all the other non-television personnel. The broadcasting companies wanted to conduct a presenter's news item using the lake as a background. They had plenty of earlier footage concerning the whirlpool. The hang glider incident required editing in, and the film from the helicopter would not be available until the later news broadcasts.

Duke Peterson had been dispatched to hospital. His hands and right arm needed immediate attention. David and Nick got away without requiring any treatment other than minor care.

The Lake District National Park went into consultation with the Royal Air Force to decide whether to prosecute the national newspaper that employed Duke. However, they got away with it because the no flying order had been in force for powered flight machines and using a hang glider would not contravene that order. The paper had a scoop, although, only for Duke's story, unfortunately the photographs from the helmet camera had been contaminated by water. The seal had not been able to withstand the extreme pressure exerted on it in the whirlpool.

The distant shots taken by Mike Parsons from Pelm Crag, when they became available, were much sort after by colour supplements and magazines for their quality and natural viewpoint origin. Mike, generously, donated all the fees to the J.M. Fund for seriously ill children. Roz and Frank Maidment were delighted. This gave the fund a much-needed boost in a lean time.

Nick Jordan found his new status as a hero very

embarrassing. The popular press, in particular, pounced on him. His sporty good looks and impressive physique added to the appeal. He kept repeating that he had done nothing more than throw a rope. "Ah but what a throw," folk were saying. All over the country, young boys re-enacted the drama from lakesides and ponds, using a swimmer who sometimes jumped into the water wearing wings made of all sorts of objects and materials as a make-believe Duke Petersen, while another boy threw a rope to him.

The hang glider pilot himself became a celebrity much promoted by his employers. He did not know then that it would set the scene for him to establish a hang glider school in his beloved Sussex within five years; press photography becoming an occupation of his past.

Tuesday, March 22nd was a sombre but pleasing day. The rain kept a respectable distance from Lastwater when the rowing club held their memorial service on the lake, at noon, to commemorate the dreadful loss of life a year ago. Bray Castle staff and Grasmere village inhabitants turned out in numbers to line the shore. Those wearing headgear removed them when the oars were raised in salute from the boats carrying relatives and club members. It was a similar scene to that of last year with white tulip petals being cast onto the water. Media attention was localised with Cumbrian television being most in evidence.

Although Jodie was sad to see her brother depart, she did agree with Suzanne and Roz that it was nice to get back to normal, with all the hustle and bustle from the media and extra visitor numbers out of the way.

Fortunately, the animal and bird centre had not suffered from lack of attention or, for that matter, too much. Suzanne and Bea made sure of that. It was, however, a quiet time with no new residents. That would be about to change with the new breeding season almost on them, especially in the shepherd department. Emma was really looking forward to her first lambing assistance. Three pregnant ewes could give birth any day now.

Daily observation of Matilda and Archie, the Roe deer twins, in their new enclosed sanctuary at a quiet area of the woodland at Bray showed them to be continuing their recovery. They would be repatriated back to Grisedale Forest when strong enough as they could not, sensibly, be released into Bray Castle's wooded area. It was just not naturally quiet enough for them. Recent activity had persuaded Suzanne of this. No one disagreed with her, although, there would be two very disappointed young children

At the beginning of April, Cumbria received one of its frequent deluges. For four days it rained heavily nonstop. Outside, work in the grounds of the estate was kept to a minimum. Immediately following this, an anticyclone developed near Iceland and gradually drifted down to show off the Lake District at a wonderful time of year.

During his recent stay at Bray Castle, David Fresher never mentioned the underwater exploration of the river that he had talked about last year when he had hinted at Dalmar accompanying him. And that man did not remind him. As we shall see later this was not because he hoped it had been forgotten – quite the contrary – it was sheer trepidation.

After David had left Cumbria, he was not about to be engaged on some other commission or project – his mind was still firmly on Lastwater and the greater geographical implications. From his modest home near Newcastle, he set about researching the world of underwater submersible craft – particularly two-man craft. It was with great delight he discovered that one of the best, by reputation, was manufactured at Barrow-in-Furness situated just south of the Lake District.

After an exploratory letter to the company's chief executive and engineer, he was invited to visit the engineering laboratory and works. Although the craft were primarily designed for the offshore oil industry, they did not see why one could not be adapted for the specific task in mind. David expected a lot of the journey to take place on the surface in cavernous structures, many with breathable air. This would probably be crucial otherwise oxygen supplies might run out.

At the source and for most of the upper course of the river, it was expected that the way would be narrow; however, David did not envisage that being unmanageable in a submersible. He was certain that two million years or more of erosion, especially from tidal activity would have taken care of that. This also meant that there should be no jagged edges in the rock formations, which could cause serious damage to the craft from minor impacts. On the other hand, just what to expect was largely unknown. Where would the river outflow? It must be connected directly to the open sea for the tidal anomaly to occur, not to mention the presence of saltwater. But – at which coast? West or East? Just because the shortest distance to the sea was to the West did not mean that would be the way the river travelled. Geological factors would govern this. These could not be ascertained from above ground. What David feared was a detour north or south which could prolong the journey even more. Anyhow, all this made it imperative that he had a craft that could carry enough fuel for several days allowing about two hundred miles of travel. The different geological structures that they would pass through should be interesting, and in order to observe them they must have good lighting.

The mini submarine, a two-man submersible craft, 'was shaped like a fat torpedo,' David thought when he first saw it in its dry shed at the manufacturer's works. Coloured a striking British racing green, it certainly looked capable of carrying out the task the geologist envisaged. There was a confident aura about the obvious engineering skills. The low flat elongated cockpit designed for two men to sit with legs out straight, one behind the other, provided plenty of storage room; a necessity for this expedition. The cover was made of six-millimetre-thick acrylic. It had two opening methods. One, where the whole thing went up and over to allow the crew to disembark, and the other using two sliding panels each side, one fore and one aft so that the two men would be able to sit completely upright and use paddles like a canoe. This facility was extremely important to allow them to conserve power whenever possible. Although the submersible was considerably heavier than a canoe, with the current always favouring their direction, this should not cause too much difficulty, except in areas of turbulent water when the problem would have to be dealt with at the time, perhaps using engine power.

The craft had a single encased propeller connected to a battery-operated engine situated at the stern behind a further storage area. On each side of the unit where located the ballast tanks: these doubled as floats when on the surface. It only had an operational depth of thirty metres. This should be sufficient for their purpose, even allowing for the mouth of the underground river being under the sea. The short time the submersible would be at an excess depth should be minimal. The pilot's controls and light switching operation were located at the front of the cockpit. This later consisted of two main headlights fitted under the canopy on each side, and a further smaller unit, mounted centrally, which could run on low power where absolute visibility was considered unnecessary.

Dalmar and David might not see daylight from the moment they left the surface of Lastwater until they reached the open sea – however long in time or miles that might turn out to be. Therefore, the power available to the craft needed to be increased to double its present accumulator capacity to give extra recourse, in general, for the entire journey. This had nothing to do with more power being available at any one time, it was for duration purposes, and would be achieved by enlarging the battery compartment so that an additional unit could be fitted. Then, when one set of accumulators were exhausted, power could be switched to the reserve.

The only other adaption considered necessary would be

concerned with the increased weight of the craft. This might affect the level propulsion when the hydroplanes, fitted behind the ballast tanks were in the horizontal position. Any adjustment required would come to light under trial, probably on Lastwater itself.

Freshwater supplies would be paramount. It was known that the river contained a small amount of sea salt; however, this might become more so the further they progressed towards the sea. David planned to take along a mobile desalination kit to do the job of keeping them well supplied with drinking water.

Whenever the acrylic canopy was in the closed position, air quality could be maintained by removing carbon dioxide as the occupants, using a chemical device known as the scrubber, breathed it out. By means of a humidifier, excess moisture would be neutralised. Air quality in the caverns was largely unknown but David, from experience, knew that there would be many areas where air either found its way through rock crevices and fissures, or, literally, permeated through the less dense rock. Additionally, they would be carrying scuba diving equipment with air tanks for emergency use.

The major problem they would have to face was temperature. It would be very cold, at times, and they might have to endure it for a few days. It would not be a problem with the submersible closed up, as in diving conditions, because as well as air quality being automatically regulated, so too would temperature. A problem would arise when they were paddling the craft on the surface. Clothing suitable for a polar expedition would have to be available as well as thermal wet suits for use underwater. Storing everything they needed was going to take some working out.

Bray Castle had a happy atmosphere during the month of April. The riding school was developing very well. Everything seemed in order with regard to the ponies' health and well-being under the stewardship of Roz Maidment. Already, the venture was showing a reasonable profit helped by a highly successful Easter holiday period. Jodie was still enjoying her dual role of helping out with the riding tuition and stable management, while working with Suzanne to assist her with the children.

In early May, on one of those glorious days in the Lakes when the sun shone at the most beautiful time of year, Dalmar was trying to make a low-key entrance through the main doorway at the castle, when Edna, who had just finished attending to a group of visitors on a coach trip from Manchester, arrested him. The tourists were quite noisy with their chatter and Edna had to raise her voice. She could do so very effectively when she wanted to. "David Fresher has been trying to get hold of you! He's very persistent, I must say, even though I told him you would be out all morning!"

Dalmar suddenly developed a quizzical look. "Did he leave a number?" he asked. He was very much aware this could be the phone call that he was not so much dreading – but, certainly, apprehensive about.

Edna gave him a piece of paper with a telephone number written across it in large letters. The actual number was heralded by the Newcastle area code.

As soon as the curator had settled himself at his desk, he dialled the number. Greeting him was a rather flat woman's voice, who advised him that David Fresher was not available and could he leave a message. Dalmar said that he hoped he was well – just adding that he was returning his call.

Later in the evening, at the Dower-house, long after Emma and Michael's bedtime, Dalmar decided to broach the subject with his wife. They had both just sat down in the sitting room with a mug of coffee. Jodie was upstairs having a bath so they were alone. "David called earlier today while I was out," he said. "I phoned him back, but he wasn't at the number he left me. I am wondering if it is about his plan for both of us to have a look at that underground river."

"What?" At first, Suzanne could not believe what she thought she had heard. However, one look at her husband's face with its attempted matter of fact expression did not fool her. "Look at the underground river. Are you telling me that you and David are going to dive down there?"

"No." Dalmar lowered his eyes. He decided to go for the bull's eye. "You misunderstand. I mean – a full exploration."

"What! You must be joking?" Her face had frozen in a mask of horror. "I mean David's theory has been proved... so why?"

"Ah. The thing has been seen to happen and chemical analysis backs it all up, but there is the question of authentication. You see we need to know that physically an underground river, going all the way to the coast, does actually exist."

Suzanne's eyes opened out even more. "All the way to the coast. You are actually going to explore this ..." She waved her right hand up and down in exasperation as she searched for the right words ... "what must be a small underground stream winding its way through the depths of the earth ...?"

"Look. Why don't we wait for David to explain further? I'm talking in the dark here ..." It suddenly occurred to him that the man might not want to reach him for this reason after all.

Suddenly, Suzanne sat bolt upright and glared at her husband. This was something she very rarely did. "I don't care!" she exclaimed vehemently. "You have responsibilities. There is no way you can risk your life like that."

Dalmar went very quiet. Unfortunately, Jodie came down the stairs in her robe at that very moment. Her long-tousled hair showed signs of having suffered a good shampoo. At first, she was completely oblivious to the scene.

"Well?" Suzanne was still looking fierce – or – as fierce as she could look. Jodie came to a halt looking from one to the other. "My husband is under the impression that he is going off with your brother to explore the underground river."

Suzanne turned her face towards the Geordie girl, although with a much-softened expression, but with a distinct hint of sarcasm.

Jodie said nothing. She did not really understand. It never occurred to her that there was actually anything to explore.

When Dalmar spoke, it was with an equal firmness. "When I agreed to stay on here, after failing in my responsibility last year – with the deaths of two members of staff .... I knew that there would be this possibility of redeeming myself. A physical exploration needs to be carried out to prove the theory, so that Lastwater can be used – safely – for ever more."

Suzanne looked at him open mouthed. He did not return her gaze. Jodie decided it was time for her to speak. "Should I talk to David?"

Unfortunately, this was probably the worst thing she could have said because it took away one of Suzanne's lifelines.

"Definitely not." Dalmar's voice was not in the least bit harsh, but it was full of authority. Then he softened the whole thing for the time being by adding. "Anyway, the trip has not, to my knowledge, been confirmed, so let's not get all wound up about it." That statement might have pacified things for the moment, but it had started an emotive train inside his wife's brain, which would only stop at one place. The name of that place was called *Cancellation*.

CHAPTER THIRTY-THREE

"I STILL HAVE A TRUMP CARD TO PLAY."

David Fresher finally got hold of Dalmar at his office the next morning. Although he should have been expecting the call, it caught the curator by surprise. He was heavily involved in N.T. matters. Suzanne was at her desk, and, when she heard David's name mentioned, raised her head, at the same time flicking a strand or two of dark hair from across her eyes. "Hello David. How's your luck? "said her husband down the telephone mouthpiece.

"Pretty damn good, that's why I'm ringing. We've got a top-notch submersible to explore that river with, and – wait for it – free of charge!"

Dalmar was amazed. Firstly, he had no idea things had progressed that far, and, secondly, he could not imagine anyone owning an expensive piece of equipment like that wanting to take the risk of its loss, without some form of pre-arranged compensation. "You're joking?" was his comment.

"Nope. The M.D. of the firm who makes them reckons he will quadruple sales from the publicity – and this is the only bit I didn't like – whatever!"

"Ah – I see." Dalmar could not resist a glance in Suzanne's direction. He was arrested by a pair of sparkling eyes looking intensely at him. Despite the dramatic questioning look from her, he felt a sudden pang of deep love. The kind that only time can create. He brought himself back to concentrate on the telephone conversation.

"Anyhow reference our forthcoming expedition." David paused as though a thought had quickly occurred to him. "Still keen?"

The question left Dalmar in a dilemma. 'Was he? - or was he apprehensive?' Silently he pondered the thoughts and decided to be careful. "Yes." It was the simplest of answers uttered without enthusiasm.

David immediately picked it up. "You know – if you'd rather not?"

"Oh no – got to be done." Dalmar tried to sound more positive.

"Canny. Right well. – the modifications to the craft for our specific journey should be complete by the end of this month. That will mean we can carry out trials on Lastwater during the early part of June, and – I reckon we will be able to set off about three weeks later. That suit you?"

"Don't see why not. I intend taking a couple of days leave – owed to me." Dalmar had already worked this one out. He did not want the National Trust involved in any way. We will need permission from The National Park, I reckon."

"Already granted. Although there are some conditions, but nothing that need worry us. So, it's all systems go." This was not said as a question – it was a statement of intention.

"Just one thing?" Dalmar had to ask this. "Who is funding you and what about equipment? Must be all sorts of things."

"The National Geographical Society." David answered him in a matter of fact tone.

"Really. They must think it important then?"

"You could say that. You see it is unique. Never been done before."

This added even more pressure to Dalmar's honour situation. He changed the subject. "I'll have a chat with Suzanne, but I am sure you will be welcome to stay at the Dower-house."

Despite the circumstances, Suzanne liked that idea. She understood what her husband was implying even though she could only hear one side of the conversation. With both recalcitrants under her roof, plus an obvious ally in Jodie, she stood a better chance of stopping the whole thing.

David replied that that would be fine. He had assumed

he would be staying at the castle, but, of course, he was not going to be on National Trust business. "So, I'll be in contact soon to arrange things with regard to the submersible's accommodation. Does the rowing club have any facilities which would be more secure than your boat house?"

"That's a point. I'll make enquiries. Give Jim Derby a call. Look, sorry to be ignorant but what is this submersible? A two-man sub?"

"Sort of. I'll send you some pics and drawings. We're having a standard two-man submersible especially converted for our purpose. I'll be able to explain more later."

Dalmar thanked him before they said their goodbyes. "Did you gather what that was about?" he asked of his wife.

She nodded at him with a bland expression on her face – at least – as bland as she could muster. "David wants to stay at the Dower-house while you and he are planning your expedition?"

"Yea – that okay?" One thing they were not short of at the Dower-house was spare bedrooms. There were three.

"Okay. When is he coming?" After a brief discussion, this was left at that, Suzanne changing the subject as soon as possible wishing to talk about the animal sanctuary and its immediate needs. The equestrian school was fine. All the ponies were well and in good shape and bookings were quite adequate. The first pony trekking outings were scheduled for next month.

While discussing all this there was a polite knock on the door. On being invited to enter, John Fisher stuck his wiry head around the door with a big grin on his rugged face. "Guess what we've found in the woodland – below the castle?"

Suzanne immediately sensed something requiring her attention, although by the look on John's face it did not appear to be urgent. "Come in John – what's up?"

"Don't worry – not a rescue problem – more of a security situation", said John, moving into the office and closing the door behind him. He brought with him the scent of arboreal work.

Dalmar got hold of the wrong meaning here. "Do you need me?"

"No, no – not that kind of security. We have a rare animal, or, I should say, animals – in the woods", clarified the head groundsman.

Suzanne visibly brightened. Her eyes shone out of her appealing face with keen interest. "What?" she simply asked leaving her mouth slightly open.

"A pine martin with four young ... Their eyes have just opened, so they must be about four to five weeks old. The nest is in a hole about three feet off the ground in one of the oaks, fortunately well away from the pathways."

Suzanne did not need to doubt John's identification; it would be spot on. "Wow!" she exclaimed. "Are they all okay?"

"Yup – in really good health by the look of them. Haven't seen much of the mother. But it was a fleeting glance of her climbing the tree that led me to them." John paused briefly feeling that what he was about to say might be ticklish. "Thing is – we need to keep inquisitive little hands and eyes away from them, don't you think?"

Dalmar laughed softly; much to John's relief, Suzanne was right with him. "Particularly Emma and Michael," she confirmed. "There are some things you just don't tell the under twelves. What about visitors. It is off the beaten track?"

"Yes – very much so. And I would suggest we don't draw attention to the tree by roping off – or anything like that." John gave out a rueful smile as he finished.

"Okay," agreed Suzanne, "but there is one curious person who insists on being shown to them right now." She put on a fake spoilt brat look. Somehow, it did not come across quite right, but John got the message. He opened the office door and made a beckoning movement with his right arm.

Dalmar said he would get a "looksee" later and left them

to it.

When Jodie Fresher heard about her brother's forthcoming stay, she had mixed feelings about it. She was joyous that he would be here again for a while, but full of fearful doubts. It was not just the dangerous exploration he and Dalmar were going to undertake, but, also, Suzanne's feelings about the matter. It might be very difficult. She did not want to give up her job because she loved it, however, privately; she was wondering whether it might be tactful to look for something else. She decided to consult Jack Twentyman and see if there were any vacancies elsewhere in the National Trust organisation. She did not intend to say anything to anyone else, for the time being, including the one person she *should* talk to – her brother.

Dalmar contacted Jim Derby that evening at his home. When he heard all about the forthcoming exploration, Jim promised to raise the matter of accommodating the submersible securely at the next meeting. While Dalmar was on the phone, Jim thanked him for helping his daughter during the filming of the equinox events.

It is time we caught up on the situation at the castle in general. Everything appeared to be on the up. The publicity generated by events over the past year or more had increased general awareness among tourists to The Lake District that Bray Castle was well worth a visit, and they came in ever increasing numbers. There was even talk of opening a National Trust style gift shop, which would have to be purpose built, probably behind the lower battlements of the castle, where a screen of ash trees could help hide the new building. However, it was only being talked about for now.

Currently, Brian Cussen was on leave and, therefore, there were no astronomer students staying at the castle. This was actually overdue. Brian had planned to go away in February, student bookings being non-existent, but, due to the spring equinox preparations, he had postponed it. Anyhow, as there was a gap before the summer season, he took advantage, and was now visiting relatives in New Zealand. He was not due back for another ten days.

Both Emma and Michael were another year older. Michael had yet to appreciate his surroundings at Bray Castle, but Emma was old enough, at five, to start comparing her home with her friends at school. Due to everything she enjoyed, good sized house, ample gardens and grounds, not to mention the attraction, especially for girls, of the ponies and the bird and animal shelter, invitations by her play mates to come to her were commonly sought rather more than the other way round. Because Suzanne had Josie to help, she did not mind. It was more often the case that Emma would spend the weekday afternoons with a school friend at the castle. Mind you, her mother made it a rule that they were never to leave little Michael out of it. Being girls, this was not a problem. Emma adored her young brother and loved attending on him. His cheeky smile would frequently accompany bossy elder sister's cajoling.

Mountain rescue duties were quiet for Dalmar. This was just as well, considering how busy he was kept in his day job. He had managed to sneak in a lunch time session with Frank and Mike, which, on this occasion, had been ruined by the unfortunate occurrence of an elderly man, obviously unwell, who, in the act of passing them on his way to the toilets, vomited, fully, over their table. The three friends had been enjoying fish and chips accompanied by a pint of ale. The enjoyment came to a sudden halt.

Rumours were abounding at the Castle of romance in the air. Suzanne had noticed it but decided to pretend ignorance because she had a great deal to do with the employment of both parties. Roz confirmed her thoughts one afternoon when the two women were alone at the stables. "Is there something going on between Josie and young Nick?" she asked with a conspiratorial expression on her fair features.

"Oh – you've noticed as well have you? Why, what do

you know?" answered Suzanne, her face alight with interest.

Roz stroked the underside of her chin before saying, "Nothing obvious – just longing glances between the two of them, and Nick taking every opportunity to visit us at the stables whenever Jodie is working here."

"And that – in different situations is exactly what I have seen." Suzanne grinned hugely. "Wonder when Nick will summon up the courage to ask her out?"

"Think he already has – actually. They both looked very excited about something this morning when they appeared from behind those bushes over there." Roz pointed in the direction of a bank of rhododendrons backing onto the woods behind the big front lawn.

"Oooh!" exclaimed Suzanne.

Emma, in particular, and Michael frequently enjoyed helping out with the lambing in the sheep meadow. It had become an after-school exercise whenever the weather was fine. They did not have much to do regarding the lamb's welfare. It was more about observation as they gambolled about in the spring's late afternoon air.

As soon as the opportunity arose, Suzanne, while she had the office to herself one morning, placed a call to her sister-in-law, Christine, at her home in Hampshire. After they had discussed everyone in their respective family's wellbeing, Suzanne told Chris something that made that person's heart chill losing any joy and humour from their conversation like a dire newsflash. "Dalmar and David Fresher are going ahead with an underwater exploration of Lastwater's river," Suzanne announced.

Christine was silent for too long. Immediately, the memory of the doom-blanket style premonition she had experienced when leaving Bray Castle, last August, came back to her. Not even bothering to ask when. She blurted out, "Don't let them. They must not ... do you hear? Absolutely not!"

Suzanne read what she thought was desperation in Chris's tone. Before she replied, she could hear the urgency in her sister-in-law's breathing. "Oh – don't think I haven't tried. Trouble is Dalmar thinks he is under some kind of honourable obligation because of the loss of life during the sponsored swim."

"What! That's ridiculous. Why do they want to explore the damn thing anyway? David has proved it exists – so what's the point?"

Suzanne knew exactly what she was doing here. She was secretly delighted Christine was so anti - for, naturally, she would talk to her husband about it, with strict instructions for him to telephone David. The rest of the conversation went pretty much that way. Christine did not ask for any details. They seemed superfluous to her. The principle matter was to get the whole thing squashed and quickly. She promised to call back after she had spoken to Tim.

Later that day, quite late in the evening, after settling the children and during an appropriate moment between programs on television, Christine casually broached the subject with her husband. "Have you been in contact with David Fresher lately?"

Tim immediately recognised an investigative tone about her voice. They had been married for twelve years and he was very familiar with this one. He let the infectious grin develop on his features. "Why do you ask?"

"Oh." Christine deliberately pushed her abundant blonde hair back with a flourish. "It seems he and Dalmar are planning some quite crazy underwater exploration of that odd river at Lastwater. Just wondered if you knew anything about it."

The grin on the side of Tim's face vanished. This was no laughing matter. "No. Haven't spoken to him since last year. News to me. Tell me more."

"Suz is very worried. I suggest you have a word with David. I know no more than that."

"When do they plan to do it? Have they got a submersible?" He lent forward in his chair trying to break his wife out of her relaxed air.

This was put on. She knew that if she sounded interfering it would put Tim on guard. "No idea. A sub what? I don't know – frogman suits probably." She genuinely believed this to be the case. Why don't you give David a call? Find out. And while you're at it – tell him just how worried your sister is." Cleverly, she hoped, she left it at that.

Tim managed to track down David the very next day. He was at his home in the north-east of England. They brought themselves up to date on each other's activities, during which David said how much he was looking forward to his exploratory trip with Dalmar, and how lucky they were to have acquired a really modern submersible, especially prepared for trials due to take place on Lastwater very soon. Tim learnt enough to realise that the adventure was no more dangerous than an extended scuba dive into the lake itself, provided they both took the proper precautions. During the course of the conversation, it became obvious to Tim that David was well aware that training Dalmar up in all this was of paramount importance, and he was gratified to find out, without asking, that, actually, David was taking this more seriously than anyone else. He was surprised that Suzanne did not appear to be aware of this. The truth was that nobody had told her because the one person, who should have done, her husband, had not done so. Tim knew Dalmar well enough to know that, probably, to admit ignorance would be misinterpreted as a valid reason for him to be an unsuitable candidate for the task. This would only add to Suzanne's concern.

And so, it was that Christine received something of a shock. When it came to the professionalism of two colleagues involved in their expertise, there was no way that one would condescendingly advise, or request a biased favour from the other. Tim informed her, that, as far as he was concerned, David was handling the whole thing in a highly professional manner, and Dalmar would not have got involved if he did not want to. She was dumbfounded, calling her sister-in-law at the first available opportunity. After telling her all she now knew, she said, "You know the answer, don't you? Get that David's sister, Jodie is it? to have a word with her brother. What does she think about the crackers idea anyway?"

"Bit dodgy that Chris. Don't want to cause an atmosphere. She is very welcome here. We get on really well. No point in upsetting the apple cart."

"Would you like me to talk to her?"

"No!" Suzanne suddenly realised that would not help at all. "No – look thanks for your concern Chris. I still have a trump card to play. Didn't want to use it. But I think it is time for me to contact our regional director. Somehow I don't think the N.T. are going to be too impressed with my husband's little jaunt."

"Ah – good one Suz. Let me know how you get on."

In the next few days Jack Twentyman received one phone call and one letter, both of which caused him, at first, great concern.

CHAPTER THIRTY-FOUR

"ITS NAME IS CHARLIE – BY THE WAY."

The first item that Jack received was not the telephone call; it was a letter from Jodie Fresher asking for a transfer if there was a suitable vacancy elsewhere. Unfortunately, for Jodie, she was under the misunderstanding that the National Trust paid all her wages. In reality, they only paid for the time when she worked at the stables, her childcare duties being directly paid by Dalmar and Suzanne. She was one of those people who instinctively trusted others, where money was concerned, and stuffed her payslips into a draw without looking at them. Jack thought that he would wait until he could talk to the girl, rather than send her a formal letter just yet.

Then came the phone call from Suzanne. His first reaction was that the whole matter was a shame. After solving the riddle of Lastwater's tragic past, everything was going well at Bray Castle. The financial side was very encouraging. They had a very good curator with a superb back up – his wife. With able staff running it, the new equestrian centre could not be expected to be doing better than it was. Now a bomb had been placed under the whole thing because of that damned lake ... again. Jack was angry. Not with anyone in particular – with fate. "Bloody typical," he mouthed out loud. "Just when things were going really well!"

Because he was the least needed at Bray, at the time, Dalmar had to take Fly to see the vet in Ambleside. It was early on a Tuesday morning. Suzanne had urgent duties in the animal rescue centre and Jodie had the school run to carry out with Emma and Michael at their respective educational establishments. The day had followed a bad night. Suzanne had first become aware that all was not well with Fly, when she spotted him excessively panting late in the evening on his bed in the kitchen. She and Dalmar took it in turns throughout the night until the small hours to go and check him out. He did sleep, fitfully, but it was obvious he was far from comfortable.

It had come as a shock to them all. Fly, although older and slower, still showed good health generally. Dalmar regularly groomed him. Feeling washed out through lack of sleep, Dalmar cursed when he found the veterinary practice crowded with people and their pets. He had to calm the Collie repeatedly by stroking his head while they waited for his appointment with Ursula, the vet who usually attended at the rescue centre. She seemed extraordinarily fit and strong for a slightly built woman.

Ursula diagnosed Fly's problem almost too quickly. "I'm afraid it's his heart," she said placing her stethoscope down on a sideboard. She looked Dalmar in the eye. "Just age you know." She was implying this for the breed, but tactfully did not mention it. "Medication should sort him out for now." Fly responded to her gentle touches as though sensing relief would come soon.

Indeed, the medicine worked almost at once. By the time Fly had been driven home and Dalmar let him wander over to his favourite patch on the front lawn at the Dower-house, his breathing seemed completely relaxed and normal.

However, the dog would have to stay on medication, probably, for the rest of his life. What was obvious to Dalmar was that that life had been radically shortened. Ursula had made it clear; Fly should be kept clear of unnecessary stress – not physically – mentally: in other words, a secure environment.

When Dalmar told Suzanne, she gave him a deliberate pointed look and merely said, "Absolutely." The obtuse meaning behind that look struck home. He knew, instinctively, that she was thinking about the approaching exploration that he and David Fresher were undertaking. In the end though, this did not cause him much concern simply because he had no thoughts about a prolonged absence. Due to attending courses on N.T. business, at least twice per year, he did not consider the couple of days, at the most, he might be away likely to cause Fly undue stress. If, on the other hand, members of his family showed anxiety – then – yes, the dog's senses would pick it up. He knew he would have to explain this to Suzanne – tactfully – as soon as possible, but, for now, he cried off.

Michael was visiting a playschool friend for tea when Emily came home with Jodie. After Suzanne told her about Fly, she went and sat beside him in the afternoon sunshine, often bending her head to run up against the soft mane of fur around his neck. Fly always responded with an affectionate whimper. He had always been with her during her life so far, even on holidays, and she could not bear the thought that, one day, he would no longer be there.

Jim Derby called on Dalmar after his stint at the club one afternoon to let him know that they could provide a safe berth for the submersible when it arrived – on one condition – there must be no publicity. As, in this case, both David and Dalmar would prefer not to have the press aware of where the craft would be moored, he readily agreed. The owners of the craft naturally wanted maximum publicity, but it had been agreed that until David had carried out his initial solo dive to establish the feasibility of entry for a two-man submersible, no press release would be made. David Fresher planned to execute at least one dive using compressed air sub-aqua equipment, mainly to look at the actual opening to the underground river itself.

It could be that it was deliberate – only Jack Twentyman knew the answer to that, but Dalmar, together with John Fisher, had been asked to go and have a look at a new forestry management scheme applicable to deciduous woodland over at Grisedale Forest. Jack had arranged everything with regard to the people they would be meeting. This gave the regional director the opportunity to go and have a quiet word with Suzanne, and, also, Jodie, should she be available.

He found the curator's wife helping Bea in the birdhouse at a quarter to eleven in the morning. As a general cage and enclosure clean-up was taking place, the inmates were keeping up their usual squawks and high-pitched alarm calls in disapproval. Bea went quiet when Jack Twentyman was present. To her, he was the big boss man and the less you said, or, for that matter, were noticed – the better. She was relieved when he asked Suzanne for a private word, and after an apologetic glance in her direction, they left.

Jack took Suzanne out into the garden area. There were only a few visitors wandering about at the time. They walked far enough across the front lawn so as not to be heard from the stables' entrance. All the while Suzanne studied Jack's features trying to read something from his various facial expressions. She instinctively knew they were negative to her wishes, and, by now, half expected it. However, she did not intend to accede to his authority just yet.

"I have given your problem with Dalmar's imminent exploratory trip in the underground river some considerable thought. At the end of the day, the National Trust cannot intervene. Your husband is entitled to a couple of days off, and David Fresher has obtained permission from the Lake District National Park authority. The island is there domain you see."

They had come to a large overhanging branch belonging to the cedar tree. "That's as may be," replied Suzanne looking at Jack directly, her big dark brown eyes fairly sizzling at him. "But he does have a responsibility to his family – doesn't he? Can't you say something to him? Tell him this whole jaunt is completely crackers!"

Jack's shoulders sagged a little. A lot of men would at

this stage have mumbled something about 'having a word' or another suitable phrase. However, his reply was not in that direction. "Sorry. Not the National Trust's concern. Look – you know the man you married. And you must know Dalmar has to do this?" He could have added that, according to reports, it was not that dangerous an undertaking provided the two equinox times of year were given a wide berth, but he knew that if he did, he might land himself in trouble later.

Suzanne was visibly taken aback. The finality of it caught her out and wrecked her last line of attack. Her lips tightened in defeat like a small child losing an appeal to a parent. She said nothing, mostly out of fear that she might start crying. Jack sighed. He had been carrying a small package around with him in his left hand. "Do you have a video recorder?"

"Yes," Suzanne replied. Actually, they had only just acquired one.

"If you get the chance – this might help. The film itself is probably not your cup of tea, but the underlying message is appropriate." Jack knew a change of subject was necessary. "Think I'll wander over to see the ladies at the stables – just out of courtesy – and let you get on. That okay?"

Suzanne came to from her despair. "Err – yes I think so – although Roz might be out on Stargazer with a student. She is due to go any moment now."

"Right I'll go straight over. Tell your husband I'll catch him next time." They walked together off the lawn before Jack made his way around to the stables and Suzanne re-entered the castle by the back entrance. Before returning to Bea at the bird sanctuary, she quickly went to her office to leave the package in a draw of her desk. She did not want to have to explain it to anyone.

Jodie Fresher was, it appeared at first sight, to be liberally covered in bits of hay, several strands of which were stuck in her hair. She was engaged in mucking out while Stargazer and one of the Welsh mountain ponies were out trekking. Jack was glad to find Jodie alone apart from the other horses. The stable girl was startled to see him. She had expected a letter – not a personal visit.

After generally enquiring after her and her family's well being, Jack came to the point. "Jodie – concerning your letter, are you looking for full time employment with the National Trust somewhere else?"

Jodie found this question strange, until it was explained to her that she was currently a casual employee for the N.T., while working for Mr and Mrs Hunter as a child carer as well. "Well – I guess so," was her eventual reply. "Is there anything?"

Jack ignored her query. "Is that why you wish to relocate – to find a more permanent job perhaps where we have an equestrian centre." Jack suddenly had a thought. 'Perhaps there weren't any. They might be the first.'

"Sort of," Jodie lowered her head. All of a sudden, a horse raised its head and gave a little whinny. "You know – this business – my brother and Mr Hunter going on their jaunt – it's upset Mrs Hunter." She paused and cast her head down before saying, "Well – it's difficult." She held her broom tightly: the knuckles of both hands showing white.

So, Jack had guessed correctly. "I see," he said. He paused before saying, "It is natural and understandable that Mrs Hunter should be worried. But let's look at the other side. Your brother is engaged on a professional matter. There can be no shadow of doubt about that. Mr Hunter is just ..." Suddenly, Jack was very unsure of his next words. He had had this prepared, but what he had been going to say seemed inappropriate for this girl.

Jodie said it for him, – "Just Dalmar?" She was smiling.

Jack nodded – grinning despite himself. "You know I should cool it for a while. Might find it'll all sort itself out. If it doesn't – then yes – I will certainly look around for you. Okay?"

"Okay," replied Jodie.

After Jack had left, Jodie thought to herself, 'might be all right for you – but it sure doesn't help me.' Then she cheered up. 'I'll see what Nick thinks about it all later.' The realisation that she now had someone whom she could confide in on this matter, made her feel a lot better. That, in itself, was just one more reason to stay put.

David Fresher arrived during the first week in June. The school half-term and Spring Bank Holiday weekend was over, so on a sun-bright, pleasant early summer's morning, David's M.G. sports car made its way up the long drive towards Bray Castle. The occupant felt relaxed at being here again. He had been to some of the world's most dramatic and awe-inspiring geographical places, but the initial sight of Lastwater always gave him a thrill. It was difficult to explain. Perhaps, like the appeal of a woman with an especially endearing personality, over the classically beautiful lady.

His sister was waiting to greet him. Knowing, in advance, of his impending arrival, she had stationed herself on the lawn by the Dower-house keeping Fly company. Roz had let her off stabling duty half an hour ago. With the grass, unusually dry, she and Fly were ensconced alongside each other gazing peacefully out over the lake. A low-level toot from a car horn made her turn her head to look up the lane. A small red open-top sports car was approaching with her brother's head grinning at her from the driving position. She leapt to her feet and ran to meet him. Fly rose casually to his four feet – only out of curiosity.

"Hello our kid!" David said with raised voice, as he drew to a stop and switched off the now quietly throbbing engine. Jodie went around to his car door and, bending over, gave him a kiss and a sisterly hug. When David had extricated himself, he noticed the obvious slowness with which Fly approached them, albeit, with a furious tail wagging. "What's up with the Collie," he asked looking concerned.

Jodie explained bringing him up to date. In a flash David

was out of the car and almost ran over to meet Fly, who responded by even faster tail wagging and low grunts of welcoming affection.

When Jodie got the chance, she immediately had a serious word with her brother. She was pleasantly surprised at the attention he gave her. "I think I should warn you – you are not exactly Suzanne's favourite person at the moment. She probably won't say anything directly to you, but she is not at all happy about her husband going on this canoe trip of yours."

David did not challenge her description of the expedition, instead he asked his sister to explain further, particularly as to when this dissention first arose. Jodie brought him back to the night when she had, inadvertently, interrupted Dalmar and his wife's fraught conversation. This dialogue finished with a promise from her brother that he would make the matter his first priority. And that is exactly what he did.

Having enquired as to the whereabouts of the Hunters, he abandoned car and luggage, and went at a fast pace towards the stable area leaving his sister in trepidation wishing she had not said anything – just yet.

When he found them, they were in deep conversation with Roz next to the stall housing Stargazer. All three tried to greet him warmly – but – rather rudely he acknowledged only cursorily, especially Roz, and demanded an immediate private word with Dalmar and Suzanne beckoning them outside.

He made his way out onto the lawn area under the big cedar. "Suzanne – I want you to tell me honestly if you would prefer it, if your husband didn't join me in the exploration of the underground river?" At the same time, he gave her a very serious, although, an appealing look.

Suzanne's big round eyes were wide, and her mouth was a little too open. Dalmar did not give her a chance to say anything. It was as though he had been waiting for this. "Of course, she would. Most wives would. But Suzanne knows this is important to me, and I am sure she will give me her support." Before David could say anything, he held up his right hand slightly cupped. "Can I ask you something though? While we are being frank. Why me?"

"Because I know no one better. No one I would rather have in support." He looked as though he meant it too. However, he was not going to leave it there. Without any further comment he said, "Suzanne?"

There was a long pause before the poor girl faintly asked. "How dangerous is it going to be – really?"

David immediately replied. "If I thought it was reckless, I wouldn't be going. While I do not consider myself cowardly, I am not over brave either. If you are agreeable, I will take you both out to dinner tonight and explain."

When Suzanne just nodded, mostly with head bent, David asked, "Well?"

She knew she must say something. She knew that she must support Dalmar. "Okay then." She gave him a smile. And that was exactly what he wanted to see.

"Canny." And he gave one of his broadest in return before adding, "Just as well really. The submersible is arriving on Friday. Its name is Charlie – by the way."

Suzanne looked puzzled. "I thought boats had female names?" At this David just gave a shrug saying nothing. Both Dalmar and Suzanne kept quiet as well, sensing this was the north- east Englander asserting some kind of non-conformity with tradition.

CHAPTER THIRTY-FIVE

'EVERYTHING WAS FINE.'

Our freshwater geologist had given himself a couple of days in which to carry out his diving exploration from Shimdorie Island. If all went well, he would call the Barrow-in-Furness manufacturers of the submersible to give the all clear for its transportation to Lastwater on Friday morning. Therefore, on an overcast, but calm morning with hardly a flicker of movement on the surface of the lake, David busied himself preparing the scuba diving equipment outside the Dower-house. It was half past eight and Nick Jordan would be joining him soon. The two of them would then carry the gear down to the jetty prior to loading up the dingy.

The meal with the Hunters, the evening before, had been good humoured and Suzanne had showed no signs of her anxiety. She, naturally, was inwardly worried, but David's thoroughly articulate expectations of what they would be likely to come across on their no more than a two day exploration; possibly even less, if they got away at first light on the day of departure had considerably lessened her negative attitude.

Over a plate of gammon, egg and chips at The Drunken Duck, an inn near Hawkshead over on the less populated west side of lake Windermere, David's Geordie tongue fuelled by a pint of Workington Golden Bitter held forth. "Should be a doddle. Just a matter of following a river course in the pitch dark, freezing cold, sometimes completely submerged – nothing to it." Despite herself, Suzanne had to laugh.

Prompted, particularly by Dalmar, David did go into some detail of what he expected from his considerable knowledge, and experience for he had undertaken two underwater river explorations in Western Canada, although on almost certainly larger courses. He said he was hoping to come across caverns once they had descended clear of the mountainous terrain they would be travelling under.

"Stalactites and stalagmites? Never could remember which goes up and which comes down," said Suzanne.

"I know that," answered her husband deciding to get some minor contribution in. "Tights down. Mites up." Suzanne looked blank. David chuckled as the subtle innuendo registered in his brain. Suzanne frowned.

Nick arrived punctually. He had been looking forward to this morning's trip to the island, although his part was primarily concerned with the safety aspect in case David got into trouble on his dive.

Once they had loaded up the dingy and were on their way with Nick pulling his long seemingly effortless strokes on the oars, David could not resist asking the obvious question. "So, what's this I hear about you and our kid?" David had to turn his face side on to hide a smile from the rower's gaze.

"Yea," replied the tall young man, trying to look Jodie's brother in the eye. "Afraid I'm smitten."

The frankness of the reply caught David out. He felt a flush of pleasure within him. "Ha – yup – she can do that to a guy. Good on you though, I'm as pleased as a pony covered in rosettes." And he let the younger man see his beaming smile. "Our kid going out with a Cambridge man. Wha!"

Nick chuckled; delighted David was on their side. "I may have been to a top university, but I come from quite lowly stock you know. My mother had to bring me and my younger brother up alone. Our father cleared off to ... don't know actually. Some foreign place. Christ knows how she managed. I was not very bright at school. One year before taking 'O' levels, I suddenly woke up and got down to the studying. Much to everyone's amazement, I was accepted at Cambridge – eventually."

"Canny. That's some achievement." David paused before asking his next question. "Where does your mum live?"

"Illfracombe – in Devon. We have moved about a lot in her constant quest for suitable work. Reckon that's why I don't have a dialect."

"Yea, you sound quite posh." They both laughed at this. Nick had a smile almost as big as David's, although not quite. Probably, nobody did. In England anyway.

The two men talked all the way across. There was already a bond between them from their experience on the island at the autumn equinox without this latest development.

Once landed, David got on with the task they were engaged on. They carried the diving gear over to the shore area above the underground river. The place brought back the memory of the intense drama while rescuing the hang glider, Duke Petersen. He could almost feel the rope burns on his hands.

David laid out his equipment; a single steel cylinder containing compressed air, hose regulator, dark blue flippers and facemask. Satisfied that everything was in order he stripped off his shirt and jeans exposing a pair of bright blue swimming trunks. His skin had not yet had time to develop a tan, it being early summer, so the starkness of his white skin against everything else was not very flattering. Nick tied the nylon safety rope around his waist and tied the other end to himself. David turned on the regulator, tested his breathing, and, giving a thumbs up to Nick moved off over the granite ridge by the water's edge and lowered himself in, trying not to gasp at the chill of the water.

He was expecting poor visibility. Immediately, he regretted not having brought an underwater light. He had dived in enough lakes to know that some areas, especially when there was no bright sun light could be extremely murky. This was one of those days for Lastwater. A lot of sediment floating about in front of his facemask made things difficult. No matter, he did not expect to have to go down more than thirty feet. 'Let's get on with it,' he said to himself.

Surprisingly, as he descended headfirst down the underwater cliff face the visibility improved simply because the sediment floating near the surface had vanished.

Important matters happened faster than he expected. The rock face in front of him started to shelve inwards at an acute angle. The whole thing appeared to be approaching a black hole, and, all at once, he became aware of a current pulling him into it. It was not fierce enough to alarm him, although it would have caused others to possibly panic. David just kept a steady pull on his safety rope without causing Nick, waiting up above, any cause for concern.

Once again, he regretted not bringing a waterproof torch. He realised he would not be able to enter too far into the cave like structure appearing before him. There was, however, a highly positive realisation to this. The opening to the underground river was no small affair. Millions of years of erosion had created something far greater than the start of a mountain stream. This had to be due to the bi-annual bore that came through in the opposite direction. Where the shelving commenced, there were some jagged rock edges, but, once inside, the sides and roof of the beginning of the cave were as smooth as the bodywork of a motor car. David reached out and felt quite a large area just to make sure. Again, he had expected this, but it all just added weight to his theory that there would be no risk of dangerous collision in the submersible. What he had not expected was just how big the opening to the river was. He knew it was the entrance because of the current that kept trying to drag him in. He had to exert backward swimming movements to counter the force. To determine how wide the opening was he swam to the far side. It was this distance that surprised him. Some twenty-five feet, he reckoned. And the distance between the top of the cave and its floor was possibly the same again. 'Well – that was fine... Everything was fine.' David gave one pull on the line to signal to Nick that he was coming up.

As soon as he hit the surface, David gave Nick the thumbs up with his right hand. This meant there would be no need for a second dive. They could pack up and return to the castle. David had an important telephone call to make.

A chunky, heavy package arrived for David Fresher the next day, and, as a result, he dragged Dalmar off down to the jetty in the early afternoon. Dalmar had had some experience with underwater breathing apparatus, although most of his diving amongst coral reefs had been of the snorkel and mask variety, nevertheless, he considered himself competent with scuba diving equipment. What he had not bargained for was a three-millimetre-thick wet suit, which might well be very useful where they were going, but not on Lastwater in June. He found the whole experience very uncomfortable and complained constantly. David ignored him. His concern was that both suits were watertight and did their job. After an extensive dive from the jetty to the middle of the lake and back again he was finally satisfied. Dalmar could not wait to get out of his. Mind you, they had an amused audience when Jodie brought little Michael down to watch. The little chap went into an elongated giggling fit at the sight of his daddy trying to clamber out of his black rubber shroud.

The next morning, Friday; David, Dalmar and Brian Cussen, who had insisted on rising earlier than usual to accompany them were present at Lastwater Rowing Club, in plenty of time before the expected arrival of Charlie.

It was not a particularly nice day being overcast with frequent drizzly showers. However, this did not matter much. The vessel was going to put into the water anyway. When the small flat-bed truck arrived, a man got out of the passenger seat in the cab whom David was familiar with. He was Dursden Meadows, the firm's chief executive, in fact, only executive. He managed all the senior tasks for Marine Submersibles Ltd. After introductions with Jim Derby included in the welcoming party, Jim had a bit of a joke with Dursden suggesting he might have to consider altering the business name relative to this particular job taking place in *fresh* water.

When the protective covering was removed, Charlie was revealed as a glass domed, squashed saucer shaped object, on elongated floats, having lost its original deep green colour to be replaced by a glorious bright orange. This had been elected as the most suitable for its use, purely so that it could be spotted easily if it arrived off the coast in need of assistance. It was certainly a very bright orange and did something to cheer up the dullness of the day.

With the assistance of the truck driver, making a total of six able bodied men, they were able to lift the craft off the flatbed and carry it through the club's side gate down to the jetty. This was without the two large accumulator sets installed. It would have been extremely difficult otherwise. Dalmar and the driver making six trips each, off loaded the batteries and carried them down to join the others, before they all set about getting Charlie into the water. They were blessed by a calm day.

"Compact little chap," Jim Derby commented as it floated lazily by the jetty.

Dursden agreed with him adding, "Once we've installed the batteries – let you have a sit in it, if you like? You'll be surprised how much room each passenger has actually."

"Cheers, thanks," answered Jim. "I'd like that. Never been in one."

This, of course, turned out to be everyone except Dursden, the driver and David Fresher. Brian was particularly interested. "Got to the stage in life when I never thought I would get a chance at this," he said as he lowered himself into the driving position.

"Don't get any ideas," uttered David in his serious tone. "That's all you're going to get. No fare ground rides under water. Not at this stage anyway."

"Oh pooh," said the astronomer.

While it lay there moored by the small pier, Dalmar took advantage of the situation to enter into a conversation with David and Dursden requesting many details.

David let the builder of the craft hold forth. "She is actually some two and a half feet longer than our standard model and at least fifteen inches wider. This is to give you extra storage space in case your journey is prolonged. You will need ample food storage capacity plus extra for survival rations, which, hopefully, you won't have to use – but" ... he waved an arm lazily in explanation, "then there is the extra accumulator space underneath it all. David here," he jerked a thumb in the geologist's direction, "requested internal storage space for your paddles. Normally they are mounted on each side just below the cockpit. What we have done is to provide you with two of a collapsible variety, although assembled and ready for use right now. They are made from a good strength fibreglass."

"I was worried that the externally mounted type might get brushed off if we get too close to the side of the tunnel at any time," explained David. "It just isn't the same as a normal river." Dalmar nodded in appreciation.

Many more features were explained. Brian Cussen was particularly interested in how air quality was maintained plus the filtration to provide drinking water. They would not be taking any with them to keep the weight down.

At last, it was time for David to get in and press the start button. Charlie fired up with a low growl almost at once, the rear propeller churned away at low revolutions. It seemed placid and calm. After his trials down at Barrow he looked quite proficient and expertly manoeuvred the craft towards its secure mooring in the rowing club's boat house.

Following lunch in the club Durseden and his driver departed, although, not before they had been thanked profusely by David. Charlie's creator told them to call his office if there were any problems during the trials. He seemed utterly confident there would not be.

During the weekend the weather became a bit wild and although the lake surface was only mildly choppy, they decided not to take any risks and postponed the first trials until Monday when the weather was expected to improve, due to an anticyclone currently out in mid Atlantic. This gave the opportunity for Dalmar and Suzanne to take advantage of an invitation from Frank and Roz to go to their house for dinner on Saturday night, so leaving the Fresher's in charge of babysitting, also, they escaped for a few hours from all the talk of the imminent expedition.

Roz had made a point of asking Frank not to talk about the underwater river exploration in front of Suzanne, and during the meal it was not mentioned once. Most of the conversation tended towards the ongoing success of the J.M.Fund. It seemed to have matured into its own self-propelled production and there was no need, currently, for any extra fund raising. As a result, parents and carers of terminally ill children, mainly in the north of England, were often supplied with additional funds to help them with their general expenditure.

Monday morning was glorious: a pale blue sky with a few isolated miniature, shock white cumulus clumps drifting very slowly from west to east. Lastwater's blue water was glorious. It promised to be one of early summer's bright, cheerful and emotionally pleasurable days.

Dalmar was busy with duties at the castle, so David took Charlie out alone for a surface trial. From the roof of Bray Castle, the tiny bright orange craft could be seen clearly making its way to circumnavigate Shimdorie Island.

David loved the soft purr of the electric engine. It was a satisfying, almost secure sound from inside the acrylic bubble. He felt the craft could go on like this forever. Before they left on the actual excursion, it would be essential to ensure all the accumulators were fully charged. This should give them enough power, including that required for lighting for three days travel, which should be ample considering he envisaged three days as being the outside length of time required before they reached the coast. Plus, they would be spending a lot of the time paddling the craft on the service in cavernous situations. The only power then being used would be for lighting. Additionally, they would be carrying six powerful rubber cased torches, all with long life batteries installed.

With the exception of all day on Wednesday when the weather was too unfriendly for them to go out on the lake, David, and, sometimes, Dalmar went out in the submersible. Dalmar, very soon, got the hang of surface piloting and it only took him the Friday morning to get used to doing it underwater. David would be the main pilot, but it was vital that Dalmar would be able to handle the craft in an emergency situation on his own.

Because, in all probability, the most miles covered on their journey would be on the surface, the submersible, in the standard manufactured model would not be suitable. Extra carbon fibre had been moulded to give Charlie a proper arrowed bow so that when paddled it did not just waddle forwards. It was now possible to keep up a steady glide through the water.

Essentially the controls were simple. David had learned everything during his training at Barrow, and he was able to demonstrate in a way that made it easy for Dalmar to understand and put into practice. He carried out his first dive in the deepest part of the lake well to the north away from the island. The actual depth was about two hundred and ten feet, but they only went down about a hundred. It was unlikely that they would have to go any deeper than this when they reached the sea.

Dalmar found it an exhilarating feeling leaving the surface of the lake behind and entering a strange quiet world. Far quieter than his experiences in the Virgin Islands where the sound of small boats always seemed to be apparent. He did, privately, hope that the two of them would not be cooped up in the small craft for too long. It was fairly claustrophobic especially when the strong light on the surface vanished and became all the more muted the deeper they went. What it would be like in complete blackness with only artificial light secretly filled him with dread.

The pilot's controls in the cockpit were basically very simple. A lever, with gauge for ballast in and out read up and down for diving and surfacing, a straightforward electric engine on/off button and a central joystick for steerage and minor depth adjustment. A set-back right foot pedal provided acceleration to around 3 to 4 knots, ample for what was required. Dalmar had no trouble with any of it, and David piloted the craft as though he had been doing it every day for months.

Thankfully, Charlie's handling did not seem affected by the increased weight due to the doubling of the battery power capacity. True, David had not had a great deal of experience driving the standard model, but he felt nothing untoward about this one's manoeuvrability.

Throughout the underwater trials air quality using the scrubber to remove carbon dioxide worked well and neither occupant felt any discomfort.

Due to a reasonable fine Saturday afternoon, Suzanne brought her children down to the lake. David, tactfully, had suggested a quick ride for all three of them, one at a time. His ruse worked, although Michael's excitement was so intense, it was a sheer joy to witness. Suzanne said not a thing after her go – not a thing.

That evening David found Dalmar on his own locking up the office in the castle. "How about Wednesday?" he said without a 'hello' or other greeting.

"What for?" asked Dalmar in all innocence.

"The off, of course. I can get the rest of the provisions ready by then. Gives you time to okay everything with Jack."

Dalmar gaped at him. "Christ – that soon?"

CHAPTER THIRTY-SIX

THERE WAS NO WAY BACK.

Other members of staff at Bray Castle had been fascinated by Charlie's coming and goings on the lake from the rowing club's boathouse, but they had deliberately kept conversation on the subject at a low profile, out of regard for Suzanne Hunter's feelings. This was initially prompted by Jack Twentyman on his last visit. The underwater exploration had also been deliberately talked about as though there was no real danger – just like a normal sub aqua dive; accept that this one could have great significance.

Naturally, there was a great deal of technical interest shown by Brian Cussen. While having a morning cup of coffee in the canteen with John and Nick on the day before the scheduled departure, Brian raised the subject. "How are you two assisting the commencement of tomorrow's adventure?"

"Same as you, I guess," John quickly answered clattering a spoon in his saucer as he caught the end of it while moving an arm across the table. "We've been told to carry on as normal. All the launch stuff is being carried out down at the rowing club." John paused here and gave Brian a direct look. "Are you in charge with the boss absent?"

Brian did not look in the least uncomfortable about this. It was well known that he was the sort of unofficial number two, however, a great deal of the day to day running was handled by Suzanne. "Well, perhaps. Depends what's required. If there was a prolonged absence, I would suggest you contact Jack Twentyman if there is something you need authority on. Otherwise I'll be glad to help."

John gave him a nod. He seemed to understand.

"Prolonged absence?" Nick chipped in here. "We were told no more than a couple of days."

"Yes. All being well." Brian looked a little uncomfortable. "Worse scenario. You know..." He shrugged his shoulders. All three men cast their heads down suddenly deep in thought before Brian added. "Can't really see our geologist taking unnecessary risks. He knows what he's doing." This seemed to bring on a more positive atmosphere.

"Yea – wonder if they'll go all the way to the sea? Fantastic - wish I was going," said Nick. "David reckons they might see some amazing caves."

"I'll bet you they don't get anywhere near the sea. It's all too fanciful. Probably come to the surface in the Derwent lower down." This reference to the nearby river was made by John who had not the slightest desire to be involved. He hated caves.

Getting together the last of the provisions, a three-day supply of foodstuffs, very much in the survival mode in order to contain storage space, necessitated David making a last-minute trip to Lancaster to visit a retailer who could provide him with all the essentials. These had been pre-ordered, so it was mostly a pick-up situation, but while there David could not resist a last-minute look around. Dalmar's task, shopping elsewhere, involved things like spare torch batteries and some of the niceties such as chocolate covered Kendal mint cake. They would be taking an outdoor gas appliance with two small additional gas canisters. The prime purpose for this would be to get a brew of tea or some hot soup when, and if they came across any caverns with an air supply.

Both men met up in the evening after dinner at the Dower-house to make a trip over to the rowing club and load up most of the provisions; spare clothing and other essentials. The craft had a fitted radio, which would be totally useless underground, never mind under water, but it might have its uses when they reached the open sea. There was, also, the possibility that a cavern not too far down might give some reception – but unlikely.

Jodie gave her brother a hug before they both retired to their respective rooms that night. The mood in Dalmar and Suzanne's bedroom could only be described as sombre with neither of them saying much. In mutual response they both cuddled tighter than usual, although, Dalmar was anxious not to give the wrong impression. He avoided making any promissory statements about what they might look forward to, trying to give the impression that the whole thing was really rather straight forward. He did not fool his wife. She could feel the tenseness in his body. There would be little sleep for either of them.

David, on the other hand, slept soundly and he was the first to rise in the morning causing two children to vent themselves on the household. They had not been told about the day's forthcoming departure of their father. The submersible would be gone before Michael returned from his playgroup late in the morning. Both parents had decided to let Emma know when she came home from school, and her brother when appropriate, so as not to attach too much importance to it.

Several phone calls were received from friends and family after breakfast and Jack Twentyman made an appearance to wish them well. He had decided to spend the morning at the castle anyway.

Brian Cussen rose early after the night's star gazing. He had volunteered to drive the Land Rover over to the rowing club and bring it back again. The two explorers took their highly able wet suits with them. They would be putting them on just before leaving. All the kit was already at the club ready to be loaded into Charlie. This would not be an easy task due to the amount of equipment required, most of it in case of a prolonged exploration or emergency.

Roz, Jodie, Jack and Edna made up the small group who had assembled on the Dower-house lawn. Dalmar and Suzanne said goodbye from the office. "I hope you understand," she whispered into his ear. "I don't want to make an exhibition of myself. You see ... I don't care what you all say with your reassurances. There is no doubt in my mind... I may not see you again."

Dalmar had been dreading this far more than the forthcoming submersion on the lake. He knew he had to do it, but despite himself he did understand Suzanne's feelings. And so, to his credit, he did not make light of the moment. Instead, he said, "Alright. Just in case it is the last time." And then he kissed her, fully, on her lips making it last for however many seconds it needed to be. Immediately on release, he lowered her arms, looked into her eyes ... smiled, and said softly, "Actually ... I think I'll have to come back to see your face ... again;" before walking out of the door, leaving the poor girl sobbing quietly at first, until, with the sound of his footsteps having receded; she let herself go with the tears flowing uncontrollably.

When Brian, Dalmar and David arrived at Lastwater Rowing Club there were already a few people gathered to assist the two explorers and see them off. Durseden Meadows was very excited, not just because his submersible might soon be receiving a great deal of attention in the media but because of what had happened yesterday. Having received information, he had jumped into his car at Barrow-in-Furness and driven fast down the M6 motorway to visit a firm in Preston who had just announced a new miner's safety lamp and helmet. He had returned proudly bearing two of them and they were still on the back seat of his Volvo. He lost no time in telling Dalmar and David the good news. They were the very latest thing with rechargeable NiCad batteries, and had been easily adapted so as to be able to be charged from Charlie's accumulators. This meant that they would be able to make their way, with both hands free when on foot in the caves. Also, the rechargeable operation gave them almost unlimited capacity as long as they were able to keep the submersibles power sufficiently conserved.

When Charlie was brought out alongside the little pier,

Jim Derby and two other members of the club joined in giving a hand to load up all the provisions and equipment. Included among the items already known was a twenty-metre length of 10mm caving rope with a quantity of screw gate karabiners, pitons and a rock hammer in case they had to make an attempt at escaping from underground.

David tried on one of the cavers headlamps. It was affixed to a deep yellow fibreglass safety helmet with the battery compartment at the back. Even in daylight the light seemed very bright. Both men were delighted with these last-minute innovative arrivals. They decided to take along only one of the four torches they were going to use in order to make some space.

When they had finished and everything was ready, Jane Derby arrived with her Cumbrian television film crew. This had deliberately been kept low key and was, ostensibly just to record the *off.* However, Jane had other ideas and kept David on camera discussing at some length what they hoped to achieve – namely to establish, beyond doubt, a geographical back-up to his tidal bore theory.

Disappearing into the changing rooms of the club house, the two men got kitted out in their wet suits. Although, before putting them on they both made sure their bladders were as empty as possible, for it might be several hours before they could next, comfortably, relieve themselves. They had both chosen to wear light boots similar to those used by rock climbers. The contrast between these and the wet suit leggings looked totally out of place, being joined at the ankle by thickish woollen grey socks. Their spare clothing was stored in the submersible. There was just no knowing if it would be necessary, though to Dalmar, the thought of having to make a long trip home in the wet suit in mid-summer was just not an option. He even threatened to wear underpants only, if that was all that was available. With the wet suits unzipped down to the waist to allow the cool, but, nevertheless, summer temperatures to be born without too much discomfort, they made their way back to the jetty.

At 1.00pm they embarked. Because, they had by now, spent some time in the craft they were well used to the tight conditions and had even become comfortable with them. Now – especially for Dalmar, with everything piled at the sides and to the back of him, it was not quite the same. He shrugged his shoulders and muttered in the affirmative when asked if he was okay. Their compressed air tank, face mask, hose regulator and fins were laid out immediately at hand for both of them, in case they were needed in an emergency such as a serious collision with a rock or unforeseen obstacle. David had good reason to suppose this to be very unlikely.

The geologist brought the situation to finality. He looked up at the waiting men, Jane and her camera man. "Right. That's it. See you guys in a couple of days. Be good." And with that Dalmar pulled the canopy over their heads for David to secure it in the bow end. Dalmar had only time to make a cursory wave. The engine quietly came to life. Durseden gave Charlie a push off the jetty and David steered her away to the left. They were on their way.

Some members of Bray Castle staff had been let off duty to go down to the small pier by the lakeside and watch out for the approaching submersible. Jack Twentyman had made sure of it. Alerted by Brian's telephone call at the rowing club, they had all made it before Charlie had reached the southern end of Shimdorie Island. Roz was busy and not able to be present, but Jodie was there to give a final wave to her brother. She had Fly by her side, although the dog would be unaware as to the real goings on. Doris made an appearance during her lunch hour, also Sally Jarvis, leaving the kitchen to her assistant, and, of course, John and Nick who had been on the end of the jetty with binoculars for a quite a while.

Nobody was watching from the castle roof and if they had been, they would not have seen much. The craft looked so small from up there: a bright orange elongated oval shape, with a glass-like bubble at its centre and it soon disappeared behind the tops of the trees at the foreshore.

For today it was essential that there were no high winds churning up the lake water, otherwise, the whole thing would have had to be postponed. During the morning, the local weather had been typical for Lakeland – overcast skies with rain showers. Now, however, it had suddenly changed. The water was very calm, like a giant sheet of glass, and although there was no sunlight – really, these were perfect conditions.

Approaching the point near the island immediately above the opening to the underground river, the front man, without turning his head, spoke the single word, "Ready?"

"Yes," replied his companion.

David opened the ballast tanks to let in water and so they started their short descent. As the water closed over their heads both men had very different thoughts. David was full of anticipation to indulge his professional knowledge, while Dalmar just kind of hoped for the best in his emersion into an unnatural world. As they submerged, it felt as though his entire body was yelling at him with a giant, 'No!'

As Charlie descended, the light from the surface grew less and David switched on the main headlight. The hard rock ridge forming the island's bulk could be seen quite clearly through the murky water with the exception of one area. That area was dead ahead. It was the mouth of the underground river and David steered straight towards it.

As they entered under the faintly welcoming canopy of the river itself, the diminishing natural light they were still able to see behind them felt to Dalmar like the impending loss of everything he had ever known. Even in his wetsuit he was aware of a sudden drop in temperature. They were now being propelled towards a large dark hole. For, without the craft's front lights showing some sort of way in front of them – pitch black is what it would be. Immediately, David switched off the electric engine. There was sufficient flow in the river to give them all the propulsion they needed at this stage.

That first introduction to their new environment was most uninspiring. They were in a tunnel of black rock filled with cold, cloudy water and that was it. And nothing changed as they drifted along in the slow methodical current, occasionally getting too close to one side or another before David tweaked the joystick. This went on for half an hour. "If it's like this all the way, I'll think I'll have a kip," commented Dalmar at one point.

David gave one of his low chuckles. "Oh – I think there will be more interesting things to see yet," he merely commented.

It happened gradually – a quickening in their speed of travel. At first, David was not concerned, but when he realised, they were being propelled by a current that was, simply, too strong for this sort of geological situation, he began to show concern with a tautening of his limbs' muscles.

Dalmar did not need David's reaction to become alarmed; he instinctively knew things were not right. Charlie was suddenly propelled into a fast-moving tunnel of water – like a giant flume. Even the rock encasing them was ultra-smooth. This was just as well because now and again the craft bumped, with an accompanying audible squeal, up against either, the sides, roof or bottom. The overall effect of this and the speed was terrifying. How long it went on for was, in reality, only about forty-five seconds, but to both men it seemed impossibly long, as though there would soon plummet into the hot fires at the centre of the earth. Both men put hands out to feel for their air canisters and face masks – fearing the worst.

Instead, with a horrendous belly flop, the submersible crashed down into what, at first, with their limited vision, appeared to be a basin of still water apart from the disturbance caused by the deluge behind them, which they had just been a part of. They were now floating on the surface and no longer submerged.

It became obvious that they had tumbled down an underground waterfall, fortunately, with a not too acute angle of descent, in fact, a very gentle gradient like the side of a chalk-down slope. Shaken but incredibly relieved that Charlie seemed to have not suffered any damage, the two men blinked and looked about them. Even the sub's light was still functioning well.

As they drifted away from the fall, David could not resist pushing open the rear sliding acrylic window, gingerly at first, until he was able to ascertain that the air was breathable. From a drop-down box he extracted a meter to measure the level of carbon in case there were any dangerous gases present. There was not. The air had a stale aroma about it like a room full of five-day old worn socks. Both men wrinkled their noses in distaste. However, their initial conversation was not about that.

"What the hell happened?" asked Dalmar. His voice echoed and reverberated like the sound effect from a suitable scene in a horror movie. Taking in some of their new surroundings, he instantly thought it appropriate.

"Reet at this moment – I dunno ," replied David his voice having the same effect but with the strange twist of the Tynesider dialect, which had temporarily returned to his speech pattern. "Thing is – how far have we descended? And – where are we now?"

Dalmar reached for his headlamp helmet, placed it over his polypropylene encased head and switched on. With the extra illumination over the submersible's and at a greater height, Dalmar was visibly shocked and even David let out a low whistle, which seemed to go on and on echoing into a black abyss. They looked ahead and to both sides of them, David now adding his headlamp illumination as well. "What we have here – is an underground lake. Bye the looks of it – in all likelihood, larger than Lastwater itself."

As Dalmar took this in, he began to realise the scale of the geography they were involved in. Add to this an almost desperate, dreadful awareness that was now numbing his

brain – a certainty in the knowledge. There was no way
back.

CHAPTER THIRTY-SEVEN

'FOUR HUNDRED MILLION YEARS ... RIGHT.'

David and Dalmar stared about them silently and despite the possible acres of space either side of them, they both felt claustrophobic. This was due, without a doubt, to the huge sheets of rock only some eight feet above them. Because of undulations in the slabs, at times, the distance between their submersible and the subterranean lake ceiling was even less.

"*You* ought to be able to touch those rocks above us in places," David turned his head to look at Dalmar when he said this, being conscious not to shine his head torch directly into his eyes. "If you do – you will be the first human being to do so – even if our species has been around for over four-hundred million years."

As Dalmar took this in, the information hardly made him feel any more secure, if not quite the opposite. His only comment was, "Right."

He heard David mutter to himself, 'right – that it? ... right. Four hundred million years ... right.' The curator of Bray Castle grinned.

They had no time to think about it anymore. There was a sudden bump underneath Charlie and the craft bucked a little. Dalmar just looked puzzled, but both of David's hands involuntarily grabbed at the side rims of the mini-sub. "What ee!"

Almost at once, a ghostly white half-moon shape appeared slightly submerged on the starboard side. It rolled over towards them; a sickly, ultra-pale tubby fish-like body, nearly a metre in length with no visible eyes and a trumpet shaped fat lipped mouth. The scales had a most unattractive pearlescent appearance. It approached them very slowly – trumpet extended. Before the two men realised what it was about, it had fastened its mouth on the submersibles casing. Suddenly two more of the strangely sinister looking beings came up on the port side and there were probably more, but David had already sprung into action. "Quick, grab a paddle," he shouted, sending loud resonances of his voice into the depths.

As Dalmar caught hold of his paddle, David already had one in his hands. Without bothering to extend it, indeed, if he had, he would probably have crashed the end into the upper rock face in its upward arc. The agile Tynesider brought the blade down flat onto the first creature's head just as it started to wriggle its body to exert more force with its suction technique. The result was instant. The fishlike being disappeared as did all the others about them... Gone into the depths. Vanished. Just the ripples of their disturbance on the surface of the water remaining. "Bloody hell!" where did they come from?" he shouted.

"What are they?" Dalmar asked, amazed and bewildered.

David did not answer his question immediately, as though he too needed time to think about it. "Well – seems that might have been the first time they, or their ancestors, have ever known anything fight back. They didn't like it one bit – did they?" He was asking himself the question really and carried on speaking. "No idea. Could be a first I'd say. Canny."

"Okay – But what the blazes do they live off in this god forsaken pit?"

"I would reckon their food source is provided precisely twice per year."

Dalmar thought for a while grappling in his mind for the meaning behind his companion's comment. Then it dawned on him. "You mean the equinox events. Yes? What? ... fish from the lake?"

"Yes. Although, I doubt they'd be too fussy."

The implications of what David was saying sent a new

chill through Dalmar's mind. Judging by the way they went for their craft: he was probably right.

"Must have thought they had received an unexpected bonus. You know I reckon the suction power in those jaws could have broken up Charlie. Where would that have left us? Don't mind telling you – I never expected anything like that. Didn't reckon on this lake for that matter. Wonder what other surprises we have in store?"

Dalmar was uncomfortable in his wet suit. "Do you think we could get changed yet?" Cold it might be, but he would far rather have been in his polar clothing than this skin of rubber. It was not Dalmar's scene, preferring the feel of wool or cotton.

"Need to get past this lot first if you can bear it. I don't know how big this lake is but the sooner we are through, the happier I shall be. Gives me the creeps man. Okay?"

Dalmar had to agree. "Right – what do we do? Start paddling?"

"You got it. I'll take the port. You alright on the starboard?"

"Sure. But in which direction?" He had this feeling that finding the way out would be nothing like as easy as it would be on a surface lake.

"We'll let the little current there is tell us that. Have you noticed we are drifting?" Dalmar concurred. They were now some way from the waterfall entry area and although they could still hear it, the sound was getting fainter all the time. "All we need to do is give Charlie some gentle encouragement. Better watch out in case our welcoming committee returns. Somehow, I don't think they will. Probably as far away from us as they can get. Will be relieved to see the back of us."

As they started paddling, Dalmar let his mind think about the strange fish. "Don't you find it amazing? The only reason they can exist is by some completely freakish tidal bore, and, according to your discovery, even freakier water repatriation to supply them with their food." It was at this point that he began to dwell on the human life that had been lost not just last year but, periodically, in preceding years.

David gave him his thoughts on the matter. "On our planet, and, I daresay, throughout the universe life can become sustainable in the most inhospitable situations. Can't say I would relish being one of those trumpet snout creatures. But, perhaps, they think it's marvellous: easy supply of nourishment. Their guts are obviously capable of handling five-month-old fish meat. Or perhaps they have some sneaky freezer hidden away somewhere. Tell you what the salt content in the water may help, I reckon. There is another reason for their suction power man."

Dalmar, for once, was ahead of him. "To hang onto something when the tidal bore comes in and – goes out."

"You got it."

After a while David suggested they conserve energy and switch off the craft's main bow light. Their own helmet headlamps were extremely efficient. They even found that Dalmar could extinguish his with David's providing the sole light source. It became, instantly, even gloomier if that were possible.

One of the factors that puzzled Dalmar was the lack of any water droplets coming down from the roof. It was absolutely dry. Considering the whole thing must have filled up in the latest bore about a month ago, not to mention the damp atmosphere, he was surprised. He kept his thoughts on this to himself however, not wanting to show ignorance.

The air quality seemed surprisingly good for neither of them were suffering any untoward effects. Dalmar did not exactly feel like embarking on a sub four-minute mile but – still – he felt okay in the lung compartment

It was a full hour before David asked his partner to stop paddling. As Charlie settled into its own rhythm with the current, both men instantly became aware that the rate of movement in that current was increasing. David reckoned he could make out a narrowing in the lake's boundaries. Dalmar noticed no difference at first but he was soon to realise that it was, indeed, so.

The decision was whether to close the side windows of the canopy in case they became submerged suddenly. It did not feel likely, so they elected to carry on as they were; paddles at the ready in case they needed to prevent Charlie hitting the side of the approaching continuation of the underground river.

Without uttering a word between them, they left Lake Depression, as David had nicknamed it, and found themselves in much the same geographical situation as when they first started. The roof line was now higher and more undulating. The width of the river varied but nowhere exceeded twenty-five feet. The rocks were ultra-smooth. Frankly, it was plain boring.

This situation continued for the next two and a half hours, so much so that both men had been glad they had put gloves on before they started using the paddles earlier in the afternoon, not just because of the cold temperatures but to ward off blisters, especially this early in their exploration.

"Time for a tea break, don't you reckon Dalmar?" who agreed at once. Finding a suitable landing site with a good-sized flat bank, they set about brewing up with their Butane camping gas equipment which appeared to work very well. Perhaps the flame was a little less obvious than above ground, suggesting slightly less oxygen in the cave air, although nothing to worry about. Dalmar took the opportunity to get out of his wet suit. He did not ask for David's opinion. He had just had enough. Anyhow, David did the same and they both got kitted out in their new fleece lined and thermal clothing. It was certainly easy to distinguish between them; David was all red and Dalmar a striking blue. David could not resist a jibe. "Bloody Tory," he said.

Dalmar gave him a look and immediately came back with a quite ghastly rendition of the first few bars of, "We'll keep the Red Flag flying ... *down* here ..." They both chuckled.

Refreshed by a large mug of sweet tea, courtesy of a small amount of fresh water they had brought with them, and a couple of *dead fly* biscuits, they continued on their way. It would be necessary, at some stage, to purify some of the river water for consumption, using the on-board lab supplied with the craft, which, if required, could go to full desalination.

David Fresher, as well as taking advantage of Charlie's nautical miles metering, used his own instrument which gave him the distance in imperial miles. By seven o'clock in the evening they had covered some twenty-two of those miles. Between them they decided to have a drink and continue for another hour and a half or so, depending on what they came across. Dalmar was already convinced there would be no caverns, just this interminable scenery of the same rock and black water with not even the sight of any plant growth to provide interest – just a lifeless eternity.

It was certainly true that when light from their torches was brought to bear on the underground river's make-up, the rocky casing did have varying tones of brown and the water was not quite so black, in fact, in reality it was just clear water with a slight mid-green cast. What made it look black was its transparency showing the rock bed over which it flowed.

With the interminable paddling, occasionally changing sides so that they could give their arms a different use, Dalmar had time to think. Despite the presence of his knowledgeable companion, he already missed his family; however, he was still confident that he would be reunited with them, possibly by late tomorrow.

At some stage in the evening hours, at least, evening up above, the two men decided to find a place to make camp for the night. They had already planned this in advance. By pushing back the front seat in the submersible and collapsing the rear seat's back, one person would be able to recline and get a reasonable night's sleep. David, effectively being the pilot would take this position tonight, while Dalmar would try out the rather sparsely bodied duvet on a rock bed.

At a fairly acute bend in the river, they found a suitable place. The water on the short side kind of doubled back on itself to form a minute harbour – Charlie size. In the centre was a wide flat bank of slate like volcanic rock. This would be there dining table and later, Dalmar's bed.

Suzanne knew it was not very likely, but she was disappointed nobody had heard anything from the two men since their submergence. Somehow, she felt that if they were going to survive at all it would be fairly soon – popping up into a river on the land surface not too far away. Of course, this would disprove David's underground tidal bore theory but, right now, she could not care less. She just wanted to know her husband was alright.

After the six o'clock news broadcast on local television showing the small orange mini-sub setting off from the rowing club earlier in the day, the telephone at the Dower-house starting ringing. Jodie took the first calls. She had been asked to say that Mrs Hunter was not at home if they were from the press. She suggested that they contact Bray Castle tomorrow morning when Jack Twentyman would be on hand. However, the calls started to get too frequent and so they disconnected the phone unit from the wall socket. It was too disturbing for the children, the sound travelling up into their bedrooms, and Fly became quite agitated.

Emma and Michael having both been told that their father and David would be away for a couple of days seemed to accept this. When Emma spoke to her friends at school the next day, following the television piece, it might be quite a different matter.

Even though Suzanne had a bad night's sleep twenty-four hours ago, she still slept fitfully tonight. The trouble was – non-existent communication. If her husband had gone way on a business trip, he would have telephoned her when he got there. She thought how distressing it must have been for sailor's wives, in times past, who would be gone for months on end before they heard any news.

Dalmar could not be said to have passed a bad night really. Considering the hardness of his bed, apart from waking with aching limbs requiring frequent readjustment to his position, he actually slept quite well and so did David in the submersible. The discomfort that Dalmar found the most difficult was not due to this, or the cold, for his thermal clothing topped off with his beloved Arran jumper served him well; it was actually psychological: the fact that there was no dawn light – nothing to herald the start of a new day. They were both astir by six o'clock and a little numb with chill, but nothing that some vigorous exercise could not put right. Being out in the open, Dalmar had gone to sleep with a dark blue balaclava on his head. It served the purpose keeping his head and ears relatively warm. After ablutions they attacked a breakfast of some delicious nutty cereal that David had procured. There was no point in trying to ration their milk supply. Despite the low temperature in their surroundings, it would soon go off.

When they resumed the journey, it might just as well have been a repeat of yesterday afternoon's trip. There were times when Dalmar felt sure they had passed the same place before. He began to think they were going around in circles and, at one point, he mentioned this to David.

"Yea, I know," agreed the other man. "If it were not for the steady flow of water in one direction I could sympathize." Dalmar knew this really, but it was nice to have reassurance, nevertheless.

They were in the process of discussing when to stop for a mid-morning coffee when all thoughts of it vanished. Rounding what seemed like a long bend their headlights, which they had charged up overnight, gradually at first, and then with absolute definiteness picked up such a complete change in the colours of their surroundings that Dalmar audibly gasped. It was a not an expression of displeasure either.

David, on the other hand, kept quiet. He had quite different thoughts.

As Dalmar looked above his head and all around as far as he could, he let out a strange comment for him. It was just the word, "Wow!" said like an over excited schoolboy.

What had caused all this was, exposed by their lights, was a fantastic world of shades of blue. The continuous turgid browns they had encountered for mile after mile had gone, and, in their place rock formations, still very smooth, like giant pebbles on a sea shore all stuck together, of pale, mid, and dark tones of blues interspersed with undulating veins and streaks of a dull white to a sky blue. In order to appreciate this fully, David switched on the two main sidelights in the front of the submersible.

Now, they had to be careful with their steerage for sometimes the roof line would come down quite close to them and others, as right now, they would stare up amazed. To Dalmar it felt as though he was looking into the arched height of a cathedral in natural stone. David just appreciated the natural majesty of it all. Added to this, the brackish colouring of the river water, picking up the same rock formation below it, took on a vivid deep, almost navy blue. To anyone who had never seen anything like it before – it was beautiful. And when they stopped their gentle and infrequent paddle strokes, loosing even that sound of wood against water, the silence brought an amazing feeling of peace upon the two gazing men.

"Did you expect this?" asked Dalmar.

"To be honest – no. I have seen something similar before but not as rich. I am afraid it means Bad news."

Instantly, Dalmar lost his enthusiasm. "What do you mean?"

"This has to be limestone rock or a blend off." David straightened up and pushed back his shoulders. A habit of his when disturbed by something. "Trouble is there isn't any to the west of the Lake District's mountains. This little lot here means we are; quite definitely, heading east man."

CHAPTER THIRTY-EIGHT

"IN WHAT WAY COULD YOU BE WRONG?"

"So ... our journey may take somewhat longer?" Dalmar made the obvious remark.

"Yea. Probably only another day provided there are no deviations. Trouble is we have to go under the northern Pennines. Could be a bit rough."

"Rough?" Dalmar looked quizzically at David's back.

"Yea – rocky – don't think rapids 'cause the boulders will be very smooth – but turbulent certainly. Might be fun."

"Right," was his companion's only remark. He preferred to wait and see.

Meanwhile, they had the present scenery to admire – and Dalmar did, although, it was rather a long time; perhaps two- and a-bit hours before they noticed a significant change. They floated through cavern after cavern of immense proportions all in shades of blue. Their pace of progress remained effortlessly constant as one or the other of them occasionally exerted a paddle through the water to keep going with the lazy current.

In one particularly atmospheric chamber where the blue tones seemed even more somnolent, perhaps darker and going into French ultramarine on the lower roof lines, Dalmar made the following comment. "Blue ... on blue ... on blue ... on ... blue."

"David turned his head to look at him, almost in mid paddle stroke, "Going all poetic, are we?"

"Well – yes," was the reply. But he did not explain further. And David being unaware of Dalmar's sometimes hobby of writing poetry did not pursue it. As a down to earth Geordie he had no interest in the art form.

"Oh God," said David with an exasperated air. Then with

an urgent start he said, "Jesus, I forgot the camera." He laid down his paddle.

"No you didn't, I saw you put it onboard. Over in that corner somewhere." Dalmar indicated an area to David's left side.

"No – you daft wassus. I've forgotten to *use* it."

"Ah." Dalmar thought briefly before saying, "Well you haven't missed much, especially Lake Depression. The rest of it was all the same."

"Yeah. But we want this lot though." He then proceeded to set up the expensive looking photographic equipment and shot off a few studies. "Sorry – can't agree – missing Lake Depression was a big mistake. We will have to go back." As his face was turned away from him, Dalmar could not see the huge grin on his face.

"You have to be joking!" was the abrupt comment he received.

The change came gradually. The blue hues in the rock formations began to diminish and the water flow started to increase in intensity. Nothing alarming but their progress quickened. This meant they both had to be more alert to afford collisions, for their speed was now fast enough for a bump against the river's unforgiving bank to cause serious damage. This meant that they had to keep one of the submersible's lights on as well as their helmet lights.

They decided to tie up at the very next available situation; a wider basin with slower moving water.

It did not happen. For the next three and a half hours two increasingly tiring men had to constantly look out for the safety of their craft. They progressed for mile after mile along a narrow fast flowing subterranean river, mercifully, free of any jagged rocks. They hardly noticed the scenery, which, really, was as drab as most of what they had encountered earlier and might be described as a dirty brown meandering tunnel.

David Fresher so marvelled at the distance they were covering that he began to hope they might make the east coast of Britain by tonight, or early tomorrow morning.

They had no lunch, although they took it in turns to munch on energy giving dark chocolate covered mint cake.

At last, on rounding a long, long bend, the river suddenly widened, the current subsided and they entered an enormous cave. Despite their lights, the water became almost black and virtually still. Immediately, David switched off the light on Charlie and they continued with just the light from their hard hats. Resisting the urge to stop and rest they meandered from one large cavern to another until, as they negotiated a tighter bend than normal, a huge stalactite loomed down straight ahead of them and both men had to duck to avoid colliding with it.

The large calcium coated needle measuring, something like five feet in diameter where it joined the cavern roof before tapering down some eight feet in length to a sharp point, with what looked like a small amount of milky moisture waiting at the very tip to drop. The strange thing being it appeared to be the only stalactite in the vicinity. "Must be a tiny lonely rivulet up above causing that deposit to grow over the centuries," David explained.

The area looked good for the nights camping, so they berthed Charlie by tying fore and aft lines around pitons, which Dalmar hammered into the rock face at suitable points.

After they had both enjoyed a good brew of tea, David broached the subject of rationing. "I am hoping, as you know that we will reach journey's end sometime tomorrow; in which case, we have enough food to last us. But – just in case I am wrong – well – what do you think?"

"In what way could you be wrong?" Dalmar asked him. He was preparing soup at the time. The single burner gas cooker was purring away on a low flame emitting a warmish glow to their surroundings.

"Well, you see there is no way of knowing. The compass is unreliable down here and, although, geologically everything looks good we might have made a diversion to the south. I sincerely hope not. We could run out of battery power for our lights, let alone have sufficient to start the engine when we finally need it. Add to that, the fact that we would starve before we got to Lands End..."

"Well, let's look on the bright side, shall we? Tomorrow it is – but, just in case, perhaps we should be a little sparse with our nosh. We can always have a beano if we arrive at the seaside in time for breakfast." As he finished saying this, Dalmar gave David, who was obviously worried, an encouraging smile.

Anyway, they enjoyed their meal not because it was especially delicious but because they were ravenously hungry and packet soup with some crusty bread plus pasta with a tangy cheese sauce might not sound too wonderful, but to them it was very satisfying. They decided to finish off with the bananas. No point in leaving them to go black.

Michael Hunter, during his drink and cake time in the afternoon, unexpectedly announced to both Emma and Josie that daddy was coming home soon.

"Is he," asked Josie, quite believing the child knew something.

"Yes," he answered. Emma looked at her brother with hooded eyes and a bit of a pout.

"How do you know," his sister said, sounding a little annoyed.

"Two days," said Michael between munching.

Emma immediately came back at him, "Two days – what?"

"Mummy said daddy would be away for two days." Michael said this matter-of-factly.

"Ah," Josie quickly realised that the boy had heard nothing. He had just worked it out for himself that his dad would be home today. She got around the problem by telling him that it was about two days, but it might be tomorrow before he saw his father. Emma tutted, although, she had the grace to keep further thoughts to herself.

As the second night of absence became increasingly obvious into the evening, Suzanne was now getting really anxious. Matters were not helped when her sister-in-law, after she had finally got both her children to sleep phoned her around eight-thirty. Like Suzanne, Christine was anxious for information and simply had to ring, especially after watching the slot on the main news at six o'clock, which went into some detail about the expedition and what they hoped to achieve. Possibly due to the dramatic events on Lastwater last year, there were signs of intense public interest nationwide. The very thought that the two explorers and their submersible might appear on the coast from under the sea had a unique feel about it. It was rumoured that quite a few hotel rooms on the north-west coast were occupied by media employees and some freelance journalists.

Christine left off mentioning her awful premonition concerning Dalmar which she had experienced last summer, although it certainly worried her. She was not a superstitious person; however, she had not been able to come up with an explanation for the dark feelings she had had on that occasion. It took a long while for Suzanne to get it across to her sister-in-law that it was just not possible for them to have radio communication with Dalmar and David. She finally rang off after obtaining a promise that she would be the first person to be told if there was any news.

In the morning, Jack Twentyman made a big point of informing everyone that they were about to commence only the second full day of exploration and it was therefore more than likely they would hear something later on. Privately, he fervently hoped so because, if not, there would be a lot of distress going on.

Somewhere underground, in the north of England, Dalmar had a much warmer night, it being his turn to bed down in Charlie. David groaned stretching aching and numb muscles over his breakfast, a tasty bacon sandwich. Dalmar found it odd they were sending fried bacon aromas into the far corners of their surroundings. He felt they were polluting the atmosphere, although, to him, it was a vast improvement to the usual damp lankness. Before igniting their gas burner, on each and every occasion, David tested the atmosphere in case there was any methane present, otherwise there was a possibility they could be blown to extinction. So far there had not been a sign of the gas, either by instrument measurement or odour detection.

By seven a.m. they were on the move again having broken camp and cast off into the gentle current, not forgetting to remove the two pitons. They might need them again.

And so, they continued until well into the morning hours. The safety helmet lights that Dursden had procured were proving invaluable. Both men could not imagine any alternative now, especially David who had been forced to use traditional lamps when travelling on an underground river in Canada. The dark river wound on and on, sometimes becoming quite narrow with a consequential quickening in the speed of the current, and sometimes ballooning wide and bringing them almost to a standstill. At such times they used their paddles to keep up momentum.

David was constantly on the lookout for a sudden change in the roofline that might herald the need to submerge, because, before entering the open ocean they would be bound to have to navigate some way under power in a tunnel full of water. They must, therefore, be ready to close up the hatch canopy and, if there was time, change into their wet suits.

Neither man knew quite how it came upon them. All of a Suddenly, the scenery changed into the most incredibly large cave structure absolutely stacked from top down to base up with stalactites and stalagmites of varying sizes. In fact, they had to be very careful how they navigated. The reason for the abundance of stalagmites was due to the river splitting into a multitude of channels were the bed of the river rose up into protuberances of islands. The stalactites had no such hindrance to their layout and, consequently, David and Dalmar had to continually duck out of the way if one loomed up upon them. They could not risk a head injury. Their hard hats would give them some protection but there was still considerable risk.

After a few minutes of this they decided to pull alongside one of the islands so that, primarily, David could take some photographs, but, also, for some much-needed rest. After the photography, Dalmar made a pot of coffee. For some reason he could not explain he wanted a cigarette, a habit he had given up some seven years ago. He mentioned it to David.

"Canny." David looked uncertain. And then he said, "So do I." And after pausing expectantly he said, "Crash the ash then man."

Dalmar knew this to be an expression requesting an open packet of cigarettes be offered to him. He grinned. "I haven't got any. Anyway, we could hardly smoke down here ..." Pausing he asked, "Could we?"

"Why not. Air gets in somehow – so fag smoke should go out. Might be interesting."

"I guess the fumes from the gas thingy we cook on disperse somehow." Dalmar shrugged his shoulders.

David made no comment. It was not important at the time. Something very disconcerting was troubling him. That was why *he* wanted a cigarette. "Where do you think we are?" he casually asked.

Dalmar looked at him. "Well if you don't know – I certainly don't.

David waved a lazy arm at the surroundings. "This little lot couldn't be on the East coast of the U.K."

"Oh." Dalmar suddenly felt huge disappointment. He had had enough of this dungeon existence.

"Yea." David was sitting crossed legged on his rocky perch, pretending to be comfortable with one hand under his chin. "I know the compass can't tell us – but – it seems to me – geologically – apropos this limestone formation, we are either going north or south – give or take a few degrees."

Dalmar knew the implications. They could be stuck underground for days. He was not, at this stage concerned about his own wellbeing. With no news of them, by tomorrow certainly, Suzanne would become increasingly distraught. And there was nothing he could do about it. It was desperate concern he felt – not guilt.

It was time to seriously discuss rationing of their food supplies. There was nothing much they could do about battery power except use one head torch as often as possible. David estimated that progressing like this should give them sufficient power for seven days use, importantly conserving enough to get the engine started when necessary.

They used their last slices of fresh bread over lunch. This had been kept moist wrapped in foil and David regretted not having brought more because they would now be on a primary carbohydrate diet of sweet and savoury biscuits. Vitamin C was still available for some time mostly in cordial drinks. They had eaten the last of their fresh fruit simply because there was no point in rationing a food stock that would soon perish. Protein would still be enjoyed in the shape of eggs, tinned meat and fish. They also had a considerable quantity of freeze-dried packet soups, milk powder and potato. It would, however, be soon necessary to desalinate some water to replenish dwindling stocks of the fresh water they had brought with them in two four litre clear plastic bottles.

Another factor that had to be discussed and acted on was their physical condition in terms of their entrapped habitat and existence, which limited exercise to the lower body. The upper body was getting plenty with all the paddling but their legs – very little. Before they set off again both men carried out different exercises of their choice. David executed an extremely rigorous sequence of squats until he felt it had achieved the desired effect. Dalmar preferred to lie on his back, with his legs in the air, partially supported on his hips by both hands. He used a cycling action to stimulate his leg muscles starting at a gradual rotation and building up the speed, not to a sprint, but attempting to maintain a longish ride. He had to cut it shorter than intended because of the discomfort on his back caused by the hard rock. They both realised it would be best to carry out exercise perhaps little and often.

Their clothes would increasingly develop a feeling of lankness. Laundry facilities were obviously available, but not the drying of, and therefore any form of washing was out. Dalmar had already left a pair of drawers behind at last night's camp site. He amused himself by thinking that they might be propelled back into Lastwater on the next tidal bore. Some poor soul might come across them on one of the numerous little beaches. The two men could, of course, wash themselves and frequently did using a mild hair shampoo for everything.

During the afternoon they continued working their way through the massive conglomerate of limestone caves. David Fresher came to the conclusion that it must be the largest such geological structure in the world and sometimes unbelievably spectacular. There was one particular cave whose stalactite and stalagmite population became smaller in individual size but not in quantity. There were literally hundreds, if not thousands, of them depending on how wide the actual cave was. The two men could not see far enough into the depths on each side of them to discern this. When Dalmar shone one of their powerful spare torches above them, the encrusted roof, some thirty to fifty feet in varying height looked like giant spiky macaroni cheese, which threatened to drip molten sauce upon them at any moment.

At frequent intervals David used the camera to record as much as possible. It had been suggested by the National Geographic Society that they take along filming equipment, but there was just not enough space to carry it unfortunately.

The caves started to get small and the limestone geology began to diminish back to that they had known during most of the journey so far, but not before an occurrence that cheered both men up considerably, especially Dalmar. He became almost childishly cheerful afterwards.

Neither traveller could quite believe what they were seeing. In the far recesses of one of the last of the caves and high up into the left-hand corner there appeared a glow. At first, Dalmar thought they were looking at an area of starkly paler rock, although a translucent spread rather than a block.

"Daylight!" shouted David, his voice deafening both of them accompanied by discordant echoing.

Indeed, it was daylight. Very small and very narrow but definitely daylight – even quite bright – suggesting that the sun was shining up above ground.

Any thoughts about reaching it were very soon discounted. The climb involved scaling difficult walls of very smooth rock ending in a long-curved traverse under the giant cavern's ceiling. Although not impossible, it would certainly use up all of their climbing equipment, which might well be required for more important matters. Were one of them to make it to the top there was no guarantee that access above ground would be possible. The actual aperture was not visible and might be very small.

They moved on but the minor event cheered Dalmar, in particular, a great deal, although he was well aware that is was mainly psychological. Having spent almost two days without seeing daylight it had that effect.

That evening Emma Hunter could be heard singing, in her five-year old's tones, the first few lines of the new popular music song, *Every Breath You Take.* It was quite sweet, although, when sung over and over again – perhaps not.

Suzanne's brother, Tim Westward knew he would have to clear it with his employer's, although, he did not envisage a problem: instead of his wife going up to The Lakes, as she was threatening, he decided to pull rank by virtue of the fact that Suzanne was his sister and it would be better if Christine stayed behind and looked after their two children. To take them up to Lastwater at what could be a sad time was not advisable. Having spoken to Suzanne in the early evening, he announced that he would be arriving late in the day tomorrow.

Naturally, Suzanne had immediately become more alarmed at this when Tim first told her. After only two and half days there was no need to panic yet. Granted, it was getting near that time – another day without hearing anything? She had tried not to think about this preferring Jodie's more positive outlook. "David knows what he is about," she kept saying. Fortunately, her attitude had infected the children. Michael had forgotten about the two days and both of them had ceased asking questions.

Tim quickly told her it had more to with stopping Christine or their mother coming. He just did not think it would do any good at this time.

Roz Maidment decided it was time for her to get more upfront, though mostly on her husband's coercing. She stayed on after work in order to spend the evening at the Dower-house with Jodie and Suzanne. It was very much a lengthy coffee after supper before she drove home to Patterdale.

Fly was starting to show signs of disquiet. He spent the entire night sleeping by the front door.

CHAPTER THIRTY-NINE

A LONG LINE OF MARINE PIRATES.

Late that evening, after Roz had left and Jodie had gone to her room, Suzanne checked on her two children before going downstairs and switching on their video recorder. She decided it was time to have a look at the film Jack Twentyman had given her.

She kept the volume low in order not to disturb anyone else in the house. The film, an old black and white western classic titled *High Noon,* was not exactly her scene. But she did grasp the overriding message especially from the theme song, *'Do not forsake me oh my darling.'*

Despite being dull eyed with her distress Suzanne's attitude when she awoke in the morning had completely changed. Immediately after breakfast she gathered Jodie, Emma and Michael together making sure Fly was present. She wanted him to pick up on the mood. Without hesitation, she told her children that their father was delayed because he and David where lost in the underground river and they must be given time to find their way out. Unfortunately, they were not able to contact them. "No telephone, no letter – we just have to wait until they find their way above ground." And then she added, "It might take a few days." She knew something like this had to be said, especially before Monday morning when Emma returned to school. With all the media attention something was bound to reach her ears.

It worked. Michael wanted them to climb up a mountain so he could hear his father calling. 'Why not,' thought Suzanne. 'Better than sitting at home moping.' And so that was what they did. After tending to duties at the animal rescue centre, she took the children up White Crag on a beautiful early summer's day. Jodie was needed at the riding school and could not come with them

When they reached the summit, with admittedly Michael having to have the odd lift on the way by an exhausted mother, they were treated to a view of Lastwater in all its royal blue resplendent glory. Michael and Emma shouted for their daddy and listened to the far away echoes. Before leaving little Michael asked, "Do you think daddy heard us?" His mother assured him he would have done because he had called so loudly. The little boy looked really pleased with himself.

Earlier that day, Dalmar awoke David from his snug ensconced position in the submersible. "Come on. Saturday morning. You are supposed to be at rugby practice by ten o'clock." The strange words echoed around them in their subterranean world of water, rock and – nothing else really.

David audibly cursed wondering what and where in his part subconscious mind. When he finally came round, groaning but secretly pleased that he might just have spent his last night on the rocks, "Yer daft wassus," he muttered.

"Pardon? Didn't quite catch that," Dalmar gave him a good morning grin.

After two whole days without a shave beard growth was showing on both men. David's, from a distance, being fair, was not all that noticeable and in the dull light of their present world hardly worth a mention. Dalmar – quite the reverse: already showing a short full beard. It suited him from a masculine point of view, but as neither man had thought to bring a mirror of any description, David could get away with accusing him of looking like the very worst of a long line of marine pirates.

Breakfast was not very appetising, dry cereal and a glass of water.

As soon as possible they tidied up and put everything back in its place in the submersible before setting off again on their journey. Every day, up until now, in terms of subterranean scenery, they had come across something unique and dramati. Both men wondered what they might see today. It must be said that most of the time it was just more of the same; a slow-moving black river of varying width from thirty odd feet down to fifteen. When narrow, their progress dramatically increased due to the faster current. Both men enjoyed these periods because it was less boring provided, that is, it did not go on too long, and was difficult to find a suitable place to dock Charlie when they needed a rest.

Late in the morning, sometime before noon, both men got a shock. Dalmar thought they must be approaching the open sea and his spirits soared. David could just not understand what was happening.

There was light showing around the next bend in the river. There was no mistaking it. Dalmar who was using his head torch at the time, immediately switched it off. As they rounded the bend both men kept completely silent. No expletives – no questions – just mouth open expectation.

As a dimly lit cave came into view flickering like the light from a thousand candles, Dalmar felt acute disappointment. It was not daylight.

Now David spoke. "What the ma of da is this aall about man?" The Geordie dialect went acute with the surprise.

Coming up close to the first of the many small lighted objects twinkling before them on the bank of the river and above their heads, it became known, at once, that some of them were moving – very slowly – like snails. For that matter, they were about the same size as the average fully grown slug and looked just as disgusting, especially with their transparent luminous bellies all oozing a slimy substance as they progressed on their seemingly pointless travels.

"Some sort of glow worm?" asked a confused Dalmar.

"Who knows," commented David giving the nearest one a poke with his forefinger. The result was dramatic. The thing extinguished its light and curled up in a ball at once. "Thing is. What do they live off down here?"

"Quite," said Dalmar, offering nothing further, as though summing up his opinion of this form of life by having anything to say about them.

"Well, there is nothing on the rocks – must be in the water – I don't know. Doesn't make sense."

"There has to be hundreds of them too. They must have a food source."

Suddenly David put down his paddle and peered over the side. Almost straight away he put his right hand in the water and pulled up a small bleached white object. "A fragment of bone, if I'm not mistaken man." He handed it over to his companion and went back to gaze into the river nearest him. Soon he pulled out a handful of them – not the same shape by any means but lots of bits of what appeared to be bone – animal bone.

"Okay but where do they come from – whose body, originally, I mean."

"The sixty-four-thousand-dollar question." David scratched at his blond locks. "Look – if our friends here have nibbled at these bits," he cast a hand over the water, "Where do they come from, or – what?"

They had no time to think further on this problem. David spotted it first. The tell-tale signs of a line running across the river surface about thirty yards ahead, clearly showing up in the collective light from the glowing slug like creatures, told him they were approaching a weir or waterfall. He could make out the slight brake of disturbed water caused by its transparency at the top of the fall. "Get your oar in!" he shouted to Dalmar, who having seen the oddity himself readily obliged.

David virtually slammed back both sides of the canopy windows. They had no time to stop their craft and investigate. Whatever it was, they were going over.

As Charlie dipped on the very edge David shouted, "It's okay!" The reason was obvious – the drop was only about eighteen inches – like a man-made weir. The submersible sloshed down onto the new level as though nothing had happened, such was the cleverness in its buoyancy design. However, the panic was not over for after a little settling, Charlie started going backwards into the weir. Both men slid a window back and went to grab their paddles. Unfortunately, they got each other's crossed and David ended up with his head in Dalmar's lap.

"Shit!" he yelled before desperately getting into the upright position so that he could use his paddle. Dalmar had already started back paddling but it needed both of them do so, one each side, in order to keep the submersible straight. By the time they were in unison they were practically under the natural weir and the water started to splash down on the rear of the craft. By paddling hard, they were able to start moving forward again before water entered the cockpit. Both men used all their strength to get away and clear of the reverse current until they were safe to rest.

"Sorry mate," said David recovering his composure. "It would have been far more practical to have kept the canopy closed and started the engine. Mind you we have managed to conserve battery power – you never know, might be vital for our survival later." This sobering thought prevented Dalmar from making a bantering comment. Instead he kept it just as a thought, 'and for my next trick.' But he could not resist a smile which did not go unnoticed by his companion. David chuckled, grinning himself.

Now they could study their partly changed environment. There were still plenty of the glowing slugs and they had no need to use their torches, however, the nature of the river itself had changed. It appeared to be a milky white going deep into its depth. This very depth had dramatically increased in that they could no longer see the bottom. As their eyes became accustomed, they realised they were looking at a giant bed of small bones encrusted with the white slugs. This then was their food. The remnants of sea creatures no doubt brought about by the equinox bore, where fish and crustaceans had become trapped in the underground river. This basin was the trap in which water circled into the depths of it under the weir.

David explained this to Dalmar. However, he was not entirely a layman on the subject. "You know I'm thinking that maybe the life-form that keeps these glowing things alive has not come from the lake – but the other way around – from the sea – in which case...

"Oh, very good," said David. "But don't get excited. You see those bones might look as though they have come from small sea creatures – but they probably didn't – and, if so, they are originally from larger fish or mammals, which have been broken up having travelled a long way and over some considerable time."

Dalmar gaped at him. Once again, he felt disappointment.

It was time for David to execute his photography. While he was shooting Dalmar pondered, "All right, but this is the first time we have some possible evidence of something other than saltwater coming from an ocean. So, it must be good news – yes?"

"Aye," came David's reply muffled into the viewfinder of his camera. "That's the way I'm thinking as well. Once we are clear of this lot, I'll take a salinity reading. And I think I'll have another go at getting our compass to work. It would be nice to know where we are heading man." Not for the first time he very much regretted not bringing along a standby liquid compass, the type that divers wear on their wrist instead of steadfastly trusting the instrument in the submersible. After all they might have had to abandon Charlie and continue on foot. David did just not envisage the direction would have been that important. This was a tidal bore he was investigating and, therefore, the route must be to the sea. Also, it was highly likely that any compass underground in these conditions would be subject to too much interference in the earth's magnetic field, unlike conditions under the sea.

Dalmar thought it odd that the approach to the weir had been silent. He related this thought to his companion. "You would have thought falling water on that scale would make a considerable noise?" he said.

"I thought so too," David agreed. "But when you look at it the whole mass just keeps moving as one. There is no pressure in the actual fall – so no noise."

"Remarkable," commented Dalmar.

As soon as they left the basin of bones and glow-slugs, things returned to normal and on coming across a small harbour, they tied up Charlie in the usual manner with pitons hammered into the rock face. David set about carrying out a salinity test while Dalmar prepared lunch, more packet soup and biscuits followed by the proverbial hot tea made with powdered milk, which both men disliked. They made up for it by adding extra sugar.

The test showed that the salinity had, in fact, declined from earlier readings. Dalmar expressed puzzlement and hidden disappointment in his, "Oh," when he heard the result.

David explained. "Actually, it should lessen because we are in a river with water provided by rainfall over the Cumbrian mountains and maybe elsewhere en-route. The salinity should only increase at the time of the equinox bores."

An hour later, there was a complete change to the river course and surrounding rock formation layout. It seemed to come across them out of a gloomy area of low roof line with a misty quality to the surrounding air. It was still breathable but there was definite moisture evident. David's head torch shone through a diffused light area. The reason for this became intelligent very soon. The sound of turbulence could be heard dead ahead. Immediately, David signalled to Dalmar that they needed to tie up urgently. A single piton was used for the purpose. They clambered onto the narrow bank on the right-hand side of the river and carefully made their way forward. Both of them had their lamps switched on.

After a short distance, sometimes on all fours, they

could see the cause of the rough water noise. It was not that loud but the sight ahead of them was frightening. It reminded David of the vortex he had seen off Shimdorie Island last autumn, except that it was not spinning, but appeared to be going backwards and forwards in a segment of the river about thirty feet wide. It was not just this that captured the geologist's attention. Large slabs of rock face rose off each side of the river course and, if studied, it was fairly obvious that the rock on the far side was different in texture to that on their side. David knew what he was looking at. But he did not know where it was.

"This is a major fault line somewhere in the United Kingdom," he announced.

Dalmar knew that a geological fault line occurred were two tectonic plates rubbed up against each other, shifting about over millions of years. There were lots of fault lines in the U.K., especially in the north and west. If it was a major one, however, there were only a few so his next comment, quite naturally, was, "Which one?"

"Haven't a clue," was the reply. "If the compass was working, I could tell you, but as it isn't... However, I can tell you that we are either entering Wales or halfway up Scotland."

"Right," said Dalmar. "Now, I don't want to sound negative – but how do we get to the other side of that maelstrom. Swing?"

David gave him a despairing look. "Can't you see over there – on the other side? There is a quieter channel."

Dalmar followed the pointing hand. "Ah," he said. "Just as a matter of interest though, how do you know we are at a fault line?"

David pointed out the two different rock cliffs and then he gave his thoughts about the rough water. "What's going on there is this. Between the two sides, one is higher or lower than the other and there is a gap between them which has eroded over eons. Water is rushing in on our side, falling and after hitting the bottom bouncing up the other.

That hole will be getting larger and deeper over thousands of years until there is a move in the fault altering everything. Needless to say, the last thing we need is a jolt right now."

"Quite," said Dalmar nonchalantly. David grimaced. Sometimes this man's coolness got to him.

They made their way back to Charlie and after retrieving the piton set off with some strong paddling to get to the far side of the river, so that they could navigate their way through the small side stream with the canopy closed up – just in case.

This turned out to be a great deal easier than they had expected. Although the current wanted to drag them into the maelstrom, if that is what it may be called, for on closer viewing it looked to be a vigorous but untroubled affair: a great sweeping low wave going in, with the surface showing as a strong deep transparent greeny-blue, instead of the usual black or dark brown and the same going out the other side in a long lazy curve. Once they were over to the safe side, in the narrow channel, only some four feet in width – enough for Charlie thankfully – they could let the current's own momentum take them through to the other side.

Then they received a nasty shock. The current ordeal on the fault line was far from over for dead ahead was another similar situation with an ugly looking area of troubled water in a wider basin, this time, with no safe channel for passage on either side.

They were heading fast towards it. There was no time to try and reach the banks and secure a hold. They were going in.

David was glad of their decision to come through the last obstacle with the canopy closed because there would have been little time to doing anything about closing it now. He shouted back to Dalmar, "Hang on!" knowing full well that if the drop in the middle was too great, they had had it. It might be all over. He made an instant decision not to press the start button for the engine. If they came back out the other side, there should be quite enough power in the water surge itself.

As they went over the edge with hearts in mouths, they had no time even to be terrified. The submersible dipped at almost seventy-five degrees causing David to put his feet hard against the forward bulkhead and Dalmar to push his up against the unfortunate geologist's back. Stuff stored in the back came flying forward, fortunately, through careful planning, nothing breakable.

There was a tiny moment of time when Charlie, without hitting the bottom, levelled out and the very next second the occupants found themselves, it seemed, flying through the air with water rushing by on all sides. This time David got his unintended revenge and cannoned back into Dalmar who was squashed up against all sorts of equipment at the back. With a slosh and sudden settling, the craft came to a near standstill. They were out and over, bruised; feeling silly, but safe.

Dalmar was the first to speak. "Should have done that on the first one – would have been halfway home by now."

"Ha bloody ha!" said David while trying to extricate himself from his entanglement with the man behind him.

CHAPTER FORTY

AND SUDDENLY RELEASED.

By Sunday evening there was not a single media person, who did not actually live in the vicinity, left in Cumbria.

A colossal depression had settled over all the staff at Bray Castle. It was time now to understand, or, perhaps, to realise that Dalmar Hunter was a popular and respected leader. This was not just about the distress caused by the loss of a colleague. It had a great deal to do with the teamwork provided by his marriage. They would have been equally depressed if something were to happen to Suzanne. It was just the fact that they worked. The trouble was that one without the other, the man without the woman, Dalmar without Suzanne, or vice versa – in the circumstances, how do you resolve the future management of Bray Castle? – but – that was not for now.

Nothing had been heard from the two men since they set out four and a half days ago. The greater percentage of those knowledgeable people from the geological world, not just in the U.K., but, also, internationally, reckoned they should have surfaced by now. Privately, the majority of these experts had already given up hope and, certainly, if there was no news within the next forty-eight hours all of them would.

The press were either thoroughly negative or the opposite – some giving out goodbyes and even short biographies, while others blatantly claiming there was still hope according to such as astrologers; the clergy or just celebrity well-wishers. However, there was one particularly distressing individual: a medium who claimed that he had already been in contact with the two departed beings.

Jodie Fresher sort solace in the arms of her lover. At least she had him, although Nick seemed just as sad as she was. The two of them were taking an after-dinner stroll down by the lakeside. Jodie did not want to look at the water, but this was hard to do. Whether you went up or down, east or west, there was always a view of Lastwater. And on each occasion, she cried inside for her beloved lost brother.

For the last two days it had hardly stopped raining. The Lake District was living up to its name. It was raining now, although, under the trees it hardly bothered the young couple. The dull light fitted their mood.

The lights had gone out in Suzanne's eyes, and she continually nursed a physical ache in the pit of stomach. Jodie was off duty now and this meant Suzanne could busy herself as much as possible with her children. She was paying them far more consideration than she normally would.

Emily could not be fooled any more. She had picked up on everyone else's ambience, although her mother insisted that her father was only lost in a world without communication and would be bound to contact them soon. Michael though, seemed to accept it all, unless he was shielding his brain from something unbearable. It was hard to tell. Anyhow, he was the only partially cheerful soul about – currently enjoying the extra attention. The little boy did, however, spend a lot of time being concerned about their dog. Fly was definitely not his usual self. Both Suzanne and Jodie worried about the extra strain on his heart. They tried not to show their distress in front of him.

Tim Westward, as promised, had arrived yesterday evening, but Suzanne and the children had hardly seen him. He had spent the larger part of Sunday helping out with a diving team from the National Geographic Society. The purpose of the four-man team's visit was to establish that the mouth of the underground river by Shimdorie Island existed, and that there was no sign of the submersible.

While it was accepted that it was hardly likely that there would be, the Society had deemed it wise to check. The result was absolute confirmation of David Fresher's location and that the entrance and first fifty yards or so of the river itself was completely clear of any foreign matter.

After the dive, Tim went with the team to the castle canteen for some refreshment. His job had been not to participate with the descent but to assist with the surface team in any way he could. They used him mainly as the communications radio link with the divers. Jack Twentyman joined them before they departed on their long journey back to Cheshire. All of them, when pressed, were not hopeful of the outcome as things stood now. This was a cold professional opinion, nevertheless, sincere.

When Tim and Suzanne finally sat down for a late supper, he tried to comfort his sister. The trouble was, his hopeful suggestion that the whole thing was just taking longer than expected rang hollow. He did not believe himself. Tim's knowledge of underground rivers was not extensive, but he did know enough to reason that time was running out. He was not going to tell his sister that. Not yet.

The next morning after Jodie had taken Emily to school and Michael to playgroup, a red eyed Suzanne told her brother that she must carry on and the best way to do that was to go and help Bea with the animals. There was plenty to do, especially with this season's new-born lambs out in the pasture; checking that things were in order and then there was specialist feed to be ordered. Tim left her to it. He persuaded Roz to let him take one of the ponies out on his own.

Jack found Suzanne in the office later in the morning. He had never seen her looking so wan. She had made the effort to look presentable because of the public showcase they were constantly under – now even more than usual. But her usual healthy complexion looked blotched and pasty. Her eyes – well, they were dull and almost life-less. As a result, Jack put off what he was going to ask her, instead vowing his unstinted support – no matter what.

Two more whole days went agonisingly by, sometimes far too fast, sometimes jarringly slow as though punishing them for being optimistic in the first place.

Jack finally summoned up the courage on Wednesday 29th June before one o'clock, approaching one week exactly since David Fresher and Dalmar Hunter had disappeared into the waters of Lastwater, to ask Suzanne a question. His superiors at The National Trust had been pressing him. Bray Castle flew a flag. While it was a Trust flag, it was still a flag and should not be flying high at this time. Either the flag should be taken down or flown at half-mast. The decision would be Suzanne's.

When Jack asked her, at first, she was shocked. It was not something she had even considered. With tears in her eyes she asked him, "A flag at half-mast – surely that means someone has died?"

"Not strictly. It can signify a death, but, also, mourning or distress. It is the last of those three which is important just now."

Suzanne immediately discounted the option of taking the flag down. She was thinking of her children as well. They would be less likely to query a flag at half-mast than one missing altogether. Jack made the suggestion that perhaps it should be flown in the traditional naval situation; that being, one flag width from the top thus making it less obvious. Suzanne agreed. He did not go on to tell her that the gap left at the top of the mast used to indicate the space for an invisible flag of death.

And so, at three o'clock the flag above the main tower at Bray Castle was lowered fully; raised right to the top and then lowered to one flag's width from the top.

Shortly after that Suzanne had an unexpected visitor. She was working with Bea in the bird sanctuary area when one of the students helping out in the canteen shyly approached her. "Mrs Hunter there is a lady to see you. Says her name is Mrs Tewk." Suzanne almost smiled. The name sounded comical.

"Ask her to come through. Don't want to go out to reception looking like this." She looked perfectly alright, but felt unwashed after all the cleaning out tasks they had been engaged in. There were only a few birds in residence, a poorly sparrow recovering from a broken wing, probably as the result of a collision with a telephone wire; three overweight pigeons and a glorious cock pheasant that had been treated for poisoning from an unknown source.

When she was shown through, Suzanne found herself confronted by a well built, albeit, attractive red-haired women with a polite smile. "My name is Andrea Tewk," she announced offering her hand. "Before I was married last year your husband may have mentioned me – Adred Dread?" Her glorious pale blue eyes explored Suzanne's face for recognition.

She got it almost at once. "Oh – yes. How do you do? Your family used to live here?" And then, as an after-thought, she added, "I'm Suzanne Hunter."

Andrea nodded before saying, "Well – here abouts – yes. But I haven't come about that. I thought – well Henry, my husband suggested I call."

Suzanne encouraged her. "Yes," she said.

"You see I am calling in my capacity as a medium." Her voice was clear and although Suzanne knew she had been well educated, the clear diction surprised her. "Not many folk know that about me – but it is something I cannot hide, especially at times like this."

Suzanne suddenly realised where this was going and felt a pulse of panic. The blood rushed into her cheeks and she felt unsteady on her feet, putting an arm out for support on the nearest cage upright. Sensing the distress, she might be causing, Andrea placed her hand on the other woman's arm and looked earnestly into her eyes. "I thought you would like to know that I have not heard from him."

Suzanne looked blankly at her, now rapidly going pale. Bea hearing all this came to her side – very suspicious of

Andrea's intentions.

Sensing the confusion, Andrea, with her hand still firmly in place on Suzanne's right arm went on to say almost inaudibly, "Don't you see ... he must be alive."

The relief flooded into her brain as Suzanne heard those words, realising what this woman meant, and, at the same time becoming aware that Andrea was a perfectly sane individual who had come to see her out of sheer compassion. Bea's shoulders, also, quickly relaxed.

Although Suzanne was not entirely convinced about the spiritual world, there was no doubt that this encounter did make her feel a little better. Her brother noticed it when they met at teatime. She told him why. He made no comment but gave her an encouraging smile. "Whatever you may think about that – it is good news," he said.

Tim could not know this, but the event had all but eradicated a dreadful feeling Suzanne had developed, especially in her dreams, that her husband and David had, in fact, perished almost as soon as they had submerged and entered the underground river.

Late on the following day two very despondent, tired, hungry and, it must be said, bad tempered men could be found somewhere under the British Isles.

For the last four days they had progressed through similar and, therefore, tedious underground scenery travelling, approximately, twenty-five miles per day. So – if they were in Wales, they must by now be at, or, very near to the sea. David had expected that they would be headed south towards, perhaps, Milford Haven, but the geological formations they had passed through in recent days would suggest either the Cambrian mountain area of mid Wales, or the Grampian range of mountains in Scotland. This information did not help Dalmar's general mood, because of the distress that was bound to be upsetting his wife and no doubt by now – others. He was desperate to try and make contact to alleviate sorrow for his children and, at times, could not suppress the feeling that David had not been entirely honest in his optimism for an early end to the exploration. However, this was not true; David was even more surprised, and, more alarmed at their predicament. He simply did not expect an underground river in, what is not exactly a large country, to be of this length. In fact, he was dumfounded and considering his companion's obvious terse mood, he decided to tell him so having, up to now, opted for caution rather than cause undue worry.

Dalmar cooled down at once after the declaration. Neither of them knew it, but the event marked a turning point in their association for this trip, which was the very reason why David had, without knowing why, asked Dalmar along in the first place. He was the kind of guy you would like to have around in a crisis. Anyway, our man hardly had much to complain about, he had had plenty of opportunity to pull out, and he had made it clear that if he had not had this chance to exonerate himself honourably by taking part in the expedition, he would have resigned as curator of Bray Castle after the deaths of Pat and Trevor last year.

Over a breakfast of stale digestive biscuits and a mug of tea obtained from one tea bag they took stock of the last of their provisions. They had another packet of biscuits, a bar of Kendal mint cake covered in dark chocolate, two packets of raisins and six tea bags. That would have to do. At least there was plenty of water. Both men cut out of their depressive bad humour and made silent vows to get on and get out.

Unfortunately, it would not be that day. It passed the same as those immediately before. Dalmar began to hallucinate with a fixation, again, that they were going round in circles. He had to punch himself hard in the chest at one point in order to drive home the point that to be going round in circles was impossible. They were following the course of a river – downstream.

He did raise one point with the Geordie. "What do you reckon to our battery power?"

"I have completely given up trying to calculate that. Tried and tried until my brain just tires of it. We seem to have the same strength on our light beam. What do you reckon?"

Dalmar had no hesitation in replying with a suggestion. "Might be an idea to dim it ourselves." As David was the one with his head lamp on at the time, Dalmar followed up by mentioning that it might be worthwhile trying his power reduction control. The result clearly showed them that they could get by on half power, which would go a long way to conserving the main charge on their accumulators. David was quite convinced that they must have exhausted at least one bank by now.

That evening, in order to try and improve moral, Dalmar decided to ignore the cold and take a plunge in the dark river and give himself a quick all over wash. They had one towel between them and a bar of soap. It was put to good use with David following Dalmar's example. The exertion in the chilling water did them both a great deal of good, not to mention improving their body odour. Their cries and shrieks echoed like a flock of squawking parrots in the confined, low ceilinged cavern they were occupying at the time.

While they were at it, they washed some socks and under garments. How they would ever get them dry was another matter. For the time being they left them isolated in a plastic bag. There outer clothes; the heavy stuff designed to keep them warm would just have to stay as they were – lank!

Dalmar now had a growth of black beard and even David sported some wispy strands of reddish/blond bristle. Certainly, they both looked the part of senior cave dwellers. While they were still supplied with essential toiletries, the one item they both missed was a mirror. It amazed Dalmar how something like that had been taken so much for granted in his normal life. He kept trying to get a decent reflection in the water, but it was always just too indiscernible and, therefore, utterly frustrating.

It was David's turn to sleep in the submersible, but neither man got a good night. Both of them were, by now, utterly fed up with their damp, chilling and claustrophobic environment. It would help if there was some variety but after eleven days of just river, rock and more rock in dim lighting, it was bound to affect their moral. And, add to that, in the morning, the discovery that they were about to open their last packet of raisins – well – the general atmosphere declined into the negative.

And then something happened which caused a rapid change in David's demeanour. Initially it went unnoticed by his colleague. The reason was a subtle but definite widening of the river course with a resultant slackening in the current.

It was a full half an hour before Dalmar made a comment. "Current seems a bit sluggish today. I'm having to work harder." By his tone it almost sounded like a complaint.

"Canny lad. Could be good news. Have you noticed the extra width in the river?"

"I guess so." Dalmar could see what was coming but he was not terribly convinced yet.

"Better stand-by in case we need to get the canopy windows closed." And then as an afterthought. "If it gets any wider, we'll have to don our wet suits."

However, this optimism was short lived, for the river, quite suddenly got narrower, rougher, and, it looked as though they were in for a change of scenery.

Not even David with his extensive knowledge could have been prepared for quite such a change. It started with a roof line expansion in height and scale that seemed almost transparent with a kaleidoscope of colour, and as both men simultaneously switched their head lamps to full power, partly out of concern, but mostly out of sheer curiosity to see more clearly, only to have to shield their eyes with their hands immediately due to the strength of colour – moving colour – constantly flashing with alternating bands, and geometric shapes: reds, blues, greens and white, although the white was made up of tones as though emanating from different types of electric light bulbs.

"What is it?" shouted Dalmar. He was excited and terrified at the same time.

"Quartz," replied David in a quieter, almost hushed tone.

"Quartz?"

"Yea – quartz – but like you have never seen it before." Then he added emphatically. "Or like no one has ever seen it before – or knew anything like it existed – anything. Man – it is just awesome!"

And it was. The rock walls lining each side of the extensive cavern were now joining in, almost down to where they met the riverbank. It was like having The Northern Lights with additional colours thrown in right on top and all around them. Their powerful torch beams had caused the quartz formations to explode with this kaleidoscope of light. Beautiful iridescent colours that, it seemed, had been trapped for millions of years, now suddenly released. The quartz was formed into many different crystallised shapes; some extending in pillar formations, some two feet in length, others huddled in honeycombs of all sorts of dimensions. The effect only added to the general beauty causing refraction and reflection into each other.

All at once matters progressed further. A single bright flash exploded from the cavern roof about twenty feet away from them. It shot down in a straight line: a brilliant white light that died as suddenly as it was born with a pop and a fizzle in the dark river. And then there was another one there – and another over there.

"What the hell?" shouted Dalmar.

"Static – I think," yelled David. "God, I hope one of them doesn't hit us."

"Now – that would be interesting," said his teammate in a considerably quieter tone.

David just raised his eyelids up in exasperation, before scrabbling to locate and get his camera set up, fearing the effect might subside by losing energy. He had only taken a few photographs before they found themselves passing into another phase of the show – a new cavern with predominantly red light. Thankfully, the static electricity phenomenon vanished at the same time. This was followed by another cave with mostly flashing tones of green and, finally, they entered a vast grotto of clear quartz which, basically, amplified their head light beams and bounced them back at them, although, not before diffusing the light all over the surface and side of the cave.

By the time they had passed through into a much quieter and fairly wide-streamed system of smaller caves with the expected rock formation of ancient volcanic masses, they were both exhausted, not from physical exertion, but entirely due to the strain caused to their eyes from all the colour and sparkle they had just experienced. It was a strange feeling and they both commented on it. David had to give both eyes a vigorous rub with balled fists to alleviate the discomfort.

CHAPTER FORTY-ONE

IT WAS AN EXTRAORDINARY MOMENT.

At seven-thirty that evening there was a knock on the door of the Dower-house at Bray Castle. It was a knock from a person who desisted in using the bell for fear of disturbing small children.

Jodie Fresher opened the door. "Hi," she said looking at a stockily built, slightly balding young man standing there with one hand, supposedly holding up the other, cradled in front of him. He smelt of perspiration but not overpoweringly so.

"Mrs Hunter?" The accent was local.

"No – not me," Jodie looked at the man. He had a serious but friendly face. "She's a bit tied up at the mo'. Who shall I say is calling?"

"Torry – um" … He looked unsure before saying, "I'm a member of her husband's mountain rescue team."

"Oh." Jodie was taken aback at this. She had been quite prepared to shield Suzanne from any unnecessary distress, but this was different, and, maybe, important. "Just a minute, I'll see if she's free."

"Ta."

Suzanne, not looking at her best came to the door. She was one very, very sad soul and looked it.

The two shook hands in silence before Torry said to her. "Just wanted you to know that myself and other members of our rescue team held your husband in great regard. Not just' a good team leader, he was. He were … sorry – is a very brave man. We know you see. Seen it with our own eyes." He paused briefly while Suzanne gaped at him. "We just wanted you to know that we are thinking about you – and hoping – you knows?"

Finally, Suzanne said something. "Thank you Torry. Won't you come in?" Then she smiled for him. "Dalmar has often talked about you guys. Come on – come and have a drink."

Such was the warmth of greeting, Torry, who had not planned to stay, went in and said hello to Emma and Michael before they went to bed. He did not stay long, just enough time to have a small beer and to pass on well-intentioned messages from other members of the team. As he left Suzanne asked where he had parked his car.

"No – walked," was the reply.

"Oh – would you like a lift back?" immediately asked Jodie over Suzanne's shoulder.

"No – be fine ta – nice evenin'. See you good folk." And with that he strode away down the lane away from the castle.

When he was out of earshot, Jodie asked if he lived at Grasmere, which was about three miles distant.

"Don't think so," said Suzanne almost in awe. "Sure he lives at Ambleside." This meant Torry had a five mile walk home – making a ten-mile round trip.

"Perhaps he's calling on someone else on the way," said Suzanne in a hopeful manner.

"Likely – yes," added Jodie.

The two women had another chilling evening in front of them: a night of despair with nothing to look forward to – nothing at all – for it was beginning to feel as though there was no hope. Somehow, they had to keep going for lots of reasons. Not just the children. There were their jobs, so much additional responsibility without Dalmar even though Jack Twentyman came by every day and often spent several hours here. Mike Parsons and his intended had sent a message through Roz and Frank wanting to know if he could be of any use. The word *use* had struck Suzanne. Most people offered help but wanting to be of use was somehow different – genuine. And who knows? – could be that in the weeks ahead a teacher might well be of *use* in all

418

sorts of capacities.

In the morning, David and Dalmar were starting to get seriously hungry and as with most people suffering from the lack of sustaining food, they were both short tempered. David still held forth that journey's end could not be far. Dalmar was not convinced after yesterday's disappointment, although, considering the lack of nourishment, he certainly hoped so, because with starvation came lethargy.

Sometime towards the middle of the morning their minds became otherwise occupied. Seriously so.

It started as a distant noise. Dalmar actually got excited. He thought it might be the sound of heavy surf braking on a shingle shore. But it became obvious that it was a far too constant noise. A water noise – yes – and big – very big. After every turn on a bend in the river it became louder.

David had been ominously quiet for quite a while since they had at first become aware of the sound. Finally – he said it. "Waterfall. A big one." And that was all.

He did not have to tell his colleague how serious this could be. Dalmar knew that if the fall was too high, they could be trapped... There was a limit to how high Charlie could tumble.

The river was definitely quite a bit wider. There had been good reason to suppose they were, in fact, nearing journey's end until now. The sound of the distant fall had got to the stage where there could be no doubt that there was a fall of considerable status ahead of them. The speed of the current in the river was increasing. David half turned in his seat and pointed towards the right-hand bank. It was time to take precautions.

They took it in turns, while one held the submersible still, a task not without difficulty, the other changed into his wet suit complete with hood, placing the head torch over the waterproof material above the face mask. Even the compressed air cylinders had to be placed over their shoulders. Fins, belt with knife – everything they needed in case of accident and the loss of Charlie had to be taken into account.

In the rear compartment, wearing the air cylinder made matters extremely cramped for Dalmar. He had to put up with it though. Neither man used the paddles for propulsion. They held them at the ready in case it should suddenly become necessary to back paddle and get into one bank or the other. They just let Charlie drift forward. It did not matter how slow their progress. Caution was essential.

The roof of the long, long cavern seemed to be ultra-smooth. The sight caught by their head torches was a never ending grey and brown blend of hard rock passing along relentlessly above their heads. The river, itself, seemed almost evil in its silky black appearance. What did it herald ahead of them?

It was Dalmar who spoke first. Although the sound of the fall had not got appreciably louder, it did seem more urgent to him. "Don't you think we ought to tie up and do a reccy on foot?"

There was a long pause before David, with a visible shrugging of shoulders, replied, "I reckon."

The submersible was left anchored to a large slab of rock by two pitons hammered into a crevice. They took off their air cylinders, face masks and other encumbrances and left them in the boat. With just their head torches in place and extra foot-ware over the waterproof material on their feet, they started to make their way forward along the narrow, often very slippery, right hand bank of the river. It was very confined and Dalmar, leading the way, was aware of a claustrophobic atmosphere of such magnitude that it eclipsed all such feelings he had experienced during the whole of the expedition so far.

They must have painstakingly made their way forward for well over half an hour covering perhaps a quarter of a mile before it became clear that due to the deafening sound of falling water they were almost on top of the fall. Neither man could hear the other speak unless it was shouted mouth to ear.

Quite suddenly, Dalmar's head lamp highlighted the edge. The river came to an abrupt halt, virtually in a straight line across the cavern; beyond was only blackness.

What was utterly alarming was the realisation that the dry bank of rock they were edging their way along came to an end as well. The river joined right through to the wall leading up to the roof of the cave – about eight feet above them.

David's face looked very pale. There was no answer there. He seemed, without warning, to have given up.

Not so Dalmar. His mind was working something out in quite a different direction to his companion's. Catching hold of David's left arm, he shouted into his ear close to. "I need to get a look over the edge of the fall! See how far down it goes!"

David gave him a listless look with his pale blue eyes. He understood but feared the result desperately.

Literally inching his way along now, Dalmar lay flat on his stomach until the water started to push its way all around him. Fortunately, it was shallow, so he was able to keep prone without having to put his face underwater for too long. This was going to test the water tightness of the headlamp, but he had to have vision otherwise the whole exercise would be pointless. There were a few coughs and splutters mostly caused by the strong current swirling the cold water up his nose. With the wet suit just leaving his mouth, nose and eyes exposed, discomfort was kept to a minimum.

At last his lamp began to show something beyond the chasm – mainly spume but that was good news for it meant the fall was not too high. As his body finally reached the overhang the scene below him came partially into view. The fall fell straight down for approximately fifty feet. Dalmar knew this was too high to risk going over on-board Charlie – but there was another way. It all depended whether a man could climb down the side immediately below him. Climbing by hand and foot holds was out – the rock surface was very smooth. Might as well be a wall of ice under the falling water. Dalmar turned over and studied the roofline immediately above him minutely. Then he turned back and started to make his way towards the waiting David who was sitting on the bank looking at him with an expression of, *don't tell me written all over his face*. Due to increased confidence Dalmar made the short return trip in a crouched standing position – very carefully.

It was now nearly one o'clock. When he came up to his colleague, Dalmar yelled, "Not good but not impossible." To David's amazement his quite exuberant teammate divulged a plan of action. When the height of the fall had been communicated to him, together with the geographical lay out right across the river, privately, David could consider only one option. They should leave the submersible and set off with just their wet suits and air tanks taking their chances by plunging over the fall, hoping to escape drowning before continuing on foot.

Dalmar had other ideas and after painstakingly making sure the plan had soaked into the Geordie's brain, they set off back to Charlie. The return trek took half the time, mainly because they knew how having learnt on the way the best method of progress without slipping into the river, which constantly moved in the opposite direction absolutely adjacent to them.

Charlie was still held fast by the two pitons. The craft looked quite small against the wide width of the underground river with its low cave ceiling and narrow banks each side. It was a strange sight, like a toy tangerine coloured boat in a large pond at night.

While David held on to the submersible, Dalmar loosened the two pitons with sideways clouts from his rock hammer. They would need these. It had been estimated that it would be safe to let Charlie drift as slowly as possible for about ten minutes, then, they must gradually, hand over hand, ease the vessel forward until they were within twenty-five yards of the edge of the waterfall. By the time they had accomplished this another hour had gone by.

Before starting on the next task, the most difficult as far as Dalmar was concerned, David insisted they broke out the remaining bar of chocolate covered mint cake. They were going to need as much energy as possible. The effect on their taste buds and, as a consequence, their moral was dramatic. Suddenly, because of the assuredness showed by Dalmar with his plan, David's depression eased. Maybe they *could* make it with Charlie intact.

Because the task involved suspending the submersible on a rope held by one man, it was essential to remove the eight batteries first. There would be no possibility of anyone holding the combined weight of the craft and accumulators. Using the spanner supplied in the small maintenance kit on board, the two men disconnected the two banks of batteries and placed them, securely, on the narrow riverbank.

As soon as they had completed the task, Dalmar, with a rock hammer and three pitons set in his belt, made the hazardous journey back to the fall edge. Once there, immediately, he rose to his full height and locating a slight fissure in the rock hammered home the first piton. David, meanwhile, had come up behind him with his upper body covered in rope. He was standing precariously with his feet covered in the flowing water; the quite considerable extra weight of the rope not helping matters. First, he passed up a short length of rope which he extricated from around his right shoulder. Dalmar tied one end through the eye of the piton with a round turn and two half hitches.

Next, he positioned another piton halfway up the wall so that when he placed a foot on it, he would be able to reach the first one. This done, he tied himself on to the rope giving him a hanging position where he could touch the roof with both hands. Now he set about putting another piton above his head. As well as being essential for the current operation this piton would also serve as the point where they could lower themselves down to the base of the fall on the extreme right-hand side. Although very turbulent it should be possible to make it to the nearest safe bank some ten feet away.

Having secured the piton with a great deal of care, David passed up the end of another length of short rope, which, again, Dalmar tied through the eye and bowlined himself to it. There was no way he could test the piton's hold in advance, so he simply slackened off the first rope and dangled there with his full weight. David held his breath. It was an extraordinary moment. The tall man suspended – hoping.

Placing the hammer back in his belt as securely as possible, Dalmar now had to reach out to place the last of the pitons into the rock ceiling. This one had a section of screw thread at the upper end of its travel. First, Dalmar felt around with his arm extended at full stretch until he found a likely fissure in the rock. Taking the last piton out of his belt he put the end, with much grunting, into the crack. His right hand caught hold of the hammer and extracted it from the other side of his belt. For five long extremely strenuous minutes Dalmar hammered away. Any sound was completely deadened by the overall thunder of the waterfall. Once he had done this he put the hammer back into its cover on his belt, and took a steel spike out of a sheath also secured onto his belt. He placed one end of it through the eye of the piton and grabbed hold of both ends with each hand, then with all his strength he screwed clockwise into the rock another half an inch or so. That would have to do. This was the piton that would hold Charlie while they lowered it down. It would be in a position far enough out from the right-hand extremity of the fall to give sufficient clearance. When he had finished securing this piton, Dalmar needed to rest while hanging suspended from the cave roofline. The enormous noise from the fall did not take away or add to the abject trepidation of their situation. Whenever the beam from his head light, now turned fully on, penetrated the blackness encircling him, he received glimpses of an awesome setting especially when he chanced a look downwards. The plume from rising spray could not occlude the dramatic drop into an abyss of nothing ahead of him; with a solid curtain of falling tons of water immediately adjacent. In all he was only some eight to ten feet above the lip of the waterfall itself.

David now had to throw out and up, the end of the remaining rope. With one hand, Dalmar caught it at the first cast and looped it through the piton eye pulling out some slack before tossing the end back to David. They now had a line with which they could pull the submersible up to the fall and using the other end, hopefully, quickly drag it clear of the turbulence once it had reached the lower basin.

Dalmar re-tightened the short first rope as much as possible, bearing in mind he was now a further two feet out over the river, and then he untied it on the main piton. He tossed that back to David. He missed. It did not matter. It had served its purpose and disappeared over the edge of the fall.

Dalmar let himself go, swinging into the bank, but not before his legs caught in the full drag of the mass of water about to plunge over the edge. Fortunately, he did not go with it. With David's help he was held.

The next task was to ascertain just how much rope would be needed to lower Charlie down. They carried on with this straight away even though recent exertions had exhausted Dalmar, and the constant thunderous sound of the fall itself had left his brain numb.

While David held tight to the end of the rope trailing from the main piton's eye, Dalmar took the other end, after some considerable de-ravelling from around David's body, he took it right to the edge and then he let it fall. David pulled it back and as it rose through the eye, Dalmar yelled when he saw the end bouncing around in the turbulence at the base. Keeping hold of the rope to mark the point, Dalmar extracted his knife from its sheaf and cut through it at this point, being careful not to let go of either end, otherwise the whole operation would almost certainly end in failure. Once through the rope, which took a while, testifying to its strength, he tied the end left dangling from the piton to a karabiner attached to his belt. He checked the success of his round turn and half hitches before proceeding with a series of sharp pulls.

Dalmar now simply had to tie the rope end hanging over the edge to the piton immediately above him. Then, without faltering, he turned to give David the thumbs up and started his descent.

The plan was for Dalmar to make his way down by abseiling through the falling cascade so that once in a stable position away from the immediate waterfall, he could mastermind getting Charlie down without damage or loss. It would take some considerable strength but should be possible providing he did not fall over during the operation.

David retraced his steps back far enough so that he could stand on dry land. Before doing anything else he gradually bailed out the main rope, as it lengthened through the piton, while Dalmar made his way down. The full force of the waterfall, even though on the very periphery, hit Dalmar as he made his initial progress. Instead of being able to place a boot clad foot against a solid rock cliff when he abseiled after his first swing, he found his legs whipped away from him by the truly massive force of the falling water. While hanging onto his shoulder lock position with a very wet rope, he had to force his knees, literally, through the fierce current so as to allow a foot to penetrate before finding solid rock. It was going to be a slow progress. Dalmar got an eyeful of water. He had forgotten to replace his face mask after the rock climbing where it would have been a handicap. Too bad, he would just have to get on without it. He could feel some of the wet stuff seeping under the suit's skin around his face. It was very cold, but, if anything, seemed quite refreshing due to all the nervous energy he was expending.

After a while David began to wonder if something was

wrong, he seemed to be paying out the rope so slowly, but he could do nothing about it. He must not let go at his end or move back to the edge of the fall to investigate. He still had no idea what lay beyond. This rankled him, as the geologist here. However, he realised he must be patient.

In about ten minutes, Dalmar finally got down to where the water hit the rocks at the base of the fall. Huge great boulders, smooth as polished stone, formed the surface. With, it felt like, tons of water hitting him constantly on his head; trying to scrabble over these rocks while still grimly hanging onto the rope was extremely difficult, and he picked up many a bruise on his chins as he slipped and stumbled. With relief, he finally managed to brake clear and within a very short space of time, the water basin gave way to a sound rock bank where it started to take on the form of a river once again.

He let go of his abseil rope to let it fall back against the fall ready for David's descent. He was secretly pleased with his efforts so far, and, also, for planning that additional rope length to allow an easier passage over the base rocks. It may well have been easier, in some ways, to have done without it once having made the descent, but he felt he needed that extra security in case he fell into the tumbling maelstrom. Otherwise he would have had to rely totally on David's rope going up to the main piton, and from there down to the karabina fixed to a rope around his waist. Apart from the fact that this might have caused David to lose his balance with the sudden weight exerted, the poor man would have wondered what was happening.

It did not occur to him until this moment that throughout all the deluge on his head, the lamp had kept working without a flicker.

CHAPTER FORTY-TWO

"TELL YOU WHAT – LET'S CALL IT A DAY."

At long last, David, with considerable relief, received Dalmar's signal. Three distinct pulls on the rope. He had sufficient play to make his way back to the submersible and, once there, he withdrew his knife and cut the rope before securing it onto the eye in the bow. The line went all the way up to the piton above the fall, and from there down to the waiting Dalmar in the basin below. David then tied the remaining piece of rope adjacent to the other on Charlie and, also, to the karabiner on his belt. It looked to be long enough for its purpose. This was the rope with which David would haul Charlie out of the maelstrom. However, to be sure, he intended to keep alongside the underwater craft all the way up to the fall as best he could. Once he was happy with his knots and ready in himself, he grasped hold of the main rope and gave it a hefty tug, bearing in mind that a lot of it was submerged. He did this three times, very nearly going with it on the last attempt. He slipped and had to scrabble wildly to prevent himself from falling into the river.

Dalmar received the signal and started hauling away at once causing David to move quickly to keep up with Charlie's advance. This became increasingly difficult when the bank ran out and he had to go on his hands and knees through the water.

For Dalmar this part of the task was full of anxiety, although easy in terms of exertion. The anxious part was waiting for Charlie's bow to appear on the lip of the waterfall. He knew that it would happen over to the left side, but he could not be sure as to exactly where. The craft might have drifted, in which case, it would be important not to let it dip over the edge, and he must pull with all his might to get the submersible to hang from the piton. Now that Charlie was at the mercy of the powerful force of the mass of water, he knew there were so many things that could go wrong. The powerful current could spin the boat about without Dalmar's knowledge causing a collision with the bank. David, who would be trying to prevent this, could easily loose his balance and then, disaster of all disasters, the piton might not take the weight and Charlie would plunge into the maelstrom at the bottom of the fall to be almost certainly lost, or damaged beyond repair. All this passed through Dalmar's mind until, suddenly, there it was, the bright orange tip of the bow standing out against the smooth black edge of the fall. Dalmar instantly pulled hard on the rope. The underside of Charlie came up facing him. He held fast without loosening his grip. The craft swung free of the water suspended from the piton – just like that. But now Dalmar felt the full weight of it. He knew he must hold on during the length of time it would take David to abseil down through the fall while keeping his rope connected to Charlie free. He was dimly aware that the leverage effect caused by the rope hanging acutely against the embedded piton in the age-old rock took much of the overall weight of the craft; he would not have been able to hold on otherwise. It was time to just bear the exertion for as long as necessary. His shoulders and upper arms were pumped up to full capacity and his face bore evidence of that, however, he never once closed his eyes.

Meanwhile, David, having briefly taken in the scene below him, mostly in wonder, grabbed hold of the rope ready for his descent and swung out on his first abseil loop. Unlike Dalmar he kept going straight down without hanging pauses. This was not just because of the urgency to relieve Dalmar of the strain, but simply because he was wearing gloves and was able to avoid any rope burn on the palm of his hands. Matters were not quite so straight forward when he arrived at the bottom. The large rounded boulders caught him by surprise. It was a good job Charlie's support rope was tied to the karabiner on his belt. It would have been lost otherwise, not once, but twice, as he slipped and fell heavily picking up sizable bruising in the same manner that Dalmar had done. The Geordie ignored the pain and he was soon standing alongside his friend. He wrapped his rope twice around both wrists, individually, so that the rope was locked against his glove gauntlet's sleeves. Then he gave Dalmar a ready look.

That man had an expression on his face, at this moment, of envy looking at the gauntlets worn by his colleague. "Alright for some!" he shouted against the strain he was undergoing holding Charlie aloft. David managed a grin. Dalmar was unaware how much the confident tone in his voice reassured his companion at this time.

Now it was time to lower away. Dalmar, standing legs astride, with the rope heading upwards taught and straight looped around his left shoulder and held fast with both hands, gradually began to release the strain. For a fraction of a minute nothing happened and then Charlie dipped. Dalmar reinforced his pull to steady the descent. Once on the move he was able to control that descent as the boat bumped up against the sides of the fall, but due to the piton being placed a little in advance of the fall's edge, the craft did not enter the deluge, although it was getting a thorough soaking.

As Charlie's stern neared the spume and thrashing water at the base of the fall, David stood ready, keeping his rope taught to the craft without slack. The plan was that as soon as the submersible was down, David would start hauling away while Dalmar would let go his end and assist his companion as much as possible. No one knew just how powerful the force dragging Charlie down into the maelstrom might be. It could be considerable and would need both men's maximum effort to haul the craft clear.

Well – it certainly needed that. After Dalmar had disentangled the rope from around various parts of his body and thrown it clear, he went immediately to David's aid who was fighting a losing battle slipping closer and closer to the bank of the river. Dalmar grabbed at the rope and pulled as hard as he could. This stopped David's momentum going forward, but with regard to progressing backwards, nothing happened. It seemed like stale mate. One force equalling the other.

Dalmar realised that they must both pull in unison. "One – two – three!" he shouted. It needed two attempts at this before they got it right and then slowly – very slowly they realised they were moving away from the water's edge. They were winning, or they thought they were until David slipped and fell backwards right down on his buttocks. Dalmar just grimaced and held on for all he was worth, however, he was unable to prevent a creeping back towards the water. By the time David had recovered and regained his balance, both men were at the end of their physical capabilities. It required one last sustained effort that seemed to go on interminably with Dalmar bellowing out the numbers over and over again.

Suddenly, Charlie was free. The craft came bouncing towards them across the sudden calm waters of the basin finally clear of the giant cascade reflecting white water in their head torches' light. Both men tumbled backwards. They lay there on their backs breathing heavily. The immediate job was done.

After a while David scrambled to his feet. He wanted to examine the submersible. One look into the interior of the cockpit gave him considerable relief. It was dry. Of prime concern to him had been the safety of the camera and the films he had already shot, even though they were sealed in watertight bags. It did not occur to him that this showed a considerable improvement in his attitude, against the despair he had felt when they first became aware of the large waterfall that barred their way. Then, he could not have cared less about the photographs. Dalmar noticed this with satisfaction. He grinned to himself while looking up towards the cave's ceiling.

Because David's hands were in better shape than Dalmar's, he volunteered to climb back up through the waterfall, using the rope still attached to the piton on the left side of the fall. Surprisingly, he found it less difficult than he thought it was going to be, although, this might have had something to do with his radically improved motivation. Once right at the top having spent most of the ascent under a continuous thundering fall of ice-cold water, he turned and shouted something down to his colleague. Dalmar did not hear a word of it. What he said was, "That was fantastic!"

It took him a full forty minutes to, one at a time, convey and lower four accumulators down to Dalmar's waiting elevated and outstretched hands. David had to precariously man-handle each battery in turn from their safe place on the right bank of the river near where Charlie had been tied up. Carrying a single battery to the lip of the waterfall had to be done very slowly and deliberately while maintaining his balance, and to his great credit he achieved it. Once at the top of the fall, it was necessary to tie a parcel style side and over knotting on the accumulator at the end of the rope before lowering away. Unfortunately, there was no handle of any description, so this was the only secure way to do it. Even then, Dalmar had to make a frantic grab at the last one where it had worked loose on one side through the constant deluge of heavy water hitting it. Fortunately, these batteries were completely waterproof.

After this, David descended rapidly himself. When he started to come down, Dalmar was at first puzzled, wondering why he had not finished the job and set about obtaining the last four batteries. Then he realised that David must have checked the S.G. reading and decided that the first bank of accumulators, being nearly exhausted of power, might just as well be jettisoned and left behind.

Both men elected to get on their way, primarily to get clear of the fall's noise so that they could hold a conversation without shouting at each other. David asked Dalmar to sit in the front of the craft. There was no propulsion or steerage required for they would only require the paddles for momentum. Dalmar did not question the request and took up his knew station without a murmur.

Once they had left the sound of the waterfall way behind them where it could only be discerned as a distant background hiss, Dalmar made for the nearest bank. He did not care what might be around the next bend. He had an urgent need to get out of his wetsuit and relieve himself, although he had fully appreciated the value of the suit during their recent ordeal.

When this was accomplished and David had joined Dalmar by changing back into his outdoor winter clothes, he brewed tea. The horror was they only had two more tea bags left after this. Also, there were a miserable six digestive biscuits and that was that.

"Three tonight and three tomorrow morning. Then hope for the best," suggested Dalmar. David looked at him. "Presumably that means one and a half biscuits each tonight?" Dalmar gave a small nod.

This made David cross. However, after a salinity test in the river, he cheered up considerably. "Canny! The sea water element has increased by ten percent," he announced. "And it's definitely fresh sea water." He could tell this from the chemical composition reading. It was unlike anything they had come across so far.

Dalmar raised his eyebrows. "Perhaps we should make that two whole biscuits each tonight!" And then he added, "Gosh." David spluttered in mirth and they both dissolved into maniacal laughter.

Jodie Fresher, had looked better. Having returned from her stint out on the lower fells in the rain with two young pony trekking students, she was covered in a kind of sandy solution of mud and wetness. It was even liberally plastered into the blonde curls on her head, although most of that had probably been due to the rubbing down of the ponies on their return to the stables at Bray. She was glad that tomorrow, it would be Roz's turn, even if the weather did become more clement. Still hurting every waking hour with full on despair about her missing brother, her usual lovely brown eyes and soft complexion were far from their best. She was just in time to receive yet another telephone call from her mother in Newcastle and to catch up on news about her sisters who were, understandably, utterly distraught. Unless there was an announcement on the news broadcasts, her mother, really, had only one place where she might keep in touch with up to date news of her son and that was Bray Castle.

So, this time, she came up with a proposal. She asked her daughter if it would be possible for her and her husband to come and stay at the Dower-house for a couple of days. Suzanne had suggested this, but just then they had not wanted to intrude. However, as time had gone on, David's mother had realised that her daughter might well be more in need of comfort than her son, not to mention her own distress. In fact, joint consolation was what was required.

Suzanne was hardly off the phone during the early part of the evening. It seemed all her closest relatives and friends had decided to try and contact her including a distressing call from Dalmar's elder sister, Judy, in South Africa. This was mainly because of an announcement over the radio and television networks that Cumbrian police had called off their search for the two missing men. It might seem surprising that any kind of search had been taking place at all. This was just not so. Along the northwest coast of England, the coast guard had kept up a constant lookout for a bright orange submersible during daylight hours, and the police made frequent sorties into the quieter areas of the river Derwent's course just in case they popped up there.

Suzanne was relieved to find out that no action would be taken with regard to her husband's replacement at Bray Castle for several weeks. Dalmar had no life insurance policy in place so there was no problem there and, even if there were, more time would have to pass before a *missing*

presumed dead official notice would be issued. Anyway –
the distressed woman still hoped – all the time – shredding
doubts in her mind especially at night when there was
absolutely nothing to distract her – just the empty space in
her bed.

The prime concern now effecting nearest and dearest
was the fact that it was known what the explorer's
compliment of rations were, more or less. It did not take
much to realise that the men, by now, would be without food
and suffering from the beginnings of starvation. It was
assumed they had water. All this, that is, if they were still
alive. Nobody close to David and Dalmar wished to think
about the later including members of staff at Bray. This
positive attitude was constantly passed on to some tourists
who, quite frankly, might well not have visited the castle and
its grounds but for morbid curiosity.

Emily kept herself busy throughout the day helping out
with animals, but Michael was, by now, starting to show
distress at the prolonged absence of his father without a
satisfactory explanation from his mother. Fly ... he grumbled
at the rain, because it prevented him from taking up his
station on the front lawn. Instead, he lay in the Dower-house
porch with his head laid out between extended front legs
and viewed any visitor with great big sad eyes.

At twenty to eight that evening, Dalmar was looking for
a suitable place to berth Charlie with their one remaining
piton and a few feet of rope. Earlier, they had decided to
push on in the hope they were near journey's end, however,
enough was enough. Both men were tired, not just from
constant paddling, but, more especially, the strenuous
efforts used on the waterfall. Also, the dreary scenery was
getting to them, especially Dalmar. It was always the same:
nothing but the usual geology of dark rock and black water.
Better to get some sleep, even though it would, almost
certainly, be fitful with hunger discomfort.

This was going to have wait though, for, out of nowhere,

the river course tunnel ceiling shot up in height and they entered what seemed, to be an enormous cave. Their head torches showed that there were no stalactites or stalagmites. All the rock was very smooth in texture. Parking Charlie, as best they could, David reached into the far-right hand corner behind him to locate one of the two powerful black Mag-lite hand torches.

He switched it on and arched the beam around into the farthest reaches of the many side-caverns, at first, there seemed to be nothing unusual. Suddenly, something large and stark white showed itself above a shelf like structure in the rock formations fairly high up in one of the corners of a distant cave. When Dalmar, after an exclamation of surprise, asked David to go back with the beam, he finally held the torch still over what looked like a large bleached bone sticking up towards the cave's ceiling. "Jesus!" said David. "If that's what I think it is."

"Go on," asked his curious travel partner.

"A bone. And not just any old bone – must have belonged to a large sea creature – got to be." He switched the big torch off. "Can we get across to the other bank? Should be able to climb up for a look-see."

"Don't forget, we have no climbing equipment left." Quite apart from that Dalmar was in no mood to do any more difficult mountaineering today.

"Don't think we will need it. Looked fairly easy man. Come on, start paddling."

To get across the river as near to the shelf were the strange object was hidden took only a few moments. Dalmar secured the piton and tied up. David switched on the big torch again to get another look. The bone or whatever it might be was hidden from view. Presumably it would be somewhere above them. As David had thought it would be, the climb was gradual, however, it was extremely slippery, not due to moisture, but due to the smooth slate-like surface of the rock, which was exactly what it was in unbroken form.

Dalmar found the light from the Mag-lite almost too bright for his sensitive eyes, after over a week trapped underground with only very low wattage lamp light to illuminate their way. They had not used the submersible's main light once since the initial descent at Lastwater lake. Every time David swung the beam of the powerful torch, even just a little, in his direction his eyes stung, and he had to shield them with his hand. David kept apologising.

As they ascended, with difficulty sliding about on the smooth slate incline, they soon realised that there were many high shelves throughout the upper reaches of the cave network, no doubt with their own basins beyond.

As David reached the lower edge of the steep shelf in which, he hoped, lay the odd bone-like structure, he was relieved to see there were several fissures in which they could get hand and footholds for the climb to the top. However, it was time to lay the big torch down in a safe place where it would not roll backwards. He would need both hands free from now on and would have to rely solely on his head light for illumination.

Before he even reached the top of the shelf wall, a huge tapering object started to show itself beyond, visible due to its paleness even without a full beam from one of their torches.

"Good grief!" The loud exclamation, which echoed rudely under the giant cave's ceiling came from Dalmar. He had climbed up another shelf adjacent to the one David was ascending and found himself higher, and, therefore, able to look down directly into the depths of the hollow on the other side. It was full of large broken bones from the skeletons of some enormous creatures. At least it looked to be so. What else would something of that look and texture be? The basin itself must be fifty to sixty feet in length and the same again wide. Most of the bones were submerged in a dark pool like an underground raised lake. David looked up towards his colleague with a questioning look. "If those are bones," Dalmar suddenly reduced the strength of his voice, there was absolutely no need to shout and the echoes were very confusing to the recipient's ear, "then – they belong to some mighty animal or fish?"

Quickly making the last few manoeuvres to the top of his route, David looked over the edge. After a short while he let go a piercing whistle which reverberated everywhere. It was meant to have been a low whistle of wonder through his teeth. He looked back at Dalmar who was peering down into his own basin. "Anything in there?" he asked.

"More of the same, except the one on the top looks to be a whole skeleton."

"Has to be a sea creature," said David almost in a matter of fact manner.

"Well, I may not be an expert, but I can tell this chap here is – was – definitely not a whale." He based this on the fact that what he was looking at had a reptilian appearance. The head was far too small to belong to a whale.

David suddenly got interested. He climbed down quickly and came up behind Dalmar on his miniature cliff to join him looking over the edge. He let out another whistle. "That's a big un."

"Big what?" asked Dalmar.

David shook his head. Referring generally, all around him, for there were lots of these basins isolated high up in the cave complex he said, "Some of these bones will be very old. I mean could be millions of years. I am willing to bet that the equinoxal bore does not always get this high, but, when it does, it would certainly account for the smoothness of the bones – except this one. I mean I'm no archaeologist, but I reckon it's more recent." He turned to look at Dalmar before saying. "What do you think?"

"I don't know the first thing about ancient life, however, the fact that it is whole might well back up your theory."

"Yea." David suddenly made a fist and thumped the soft side against the rock. "Darn it! Forgotten the camera."

"Tell you what. Let's call it a day. We've got a feast in store and I need some sleep. Tomorrow morning you can come back and take your photographs."

Carefully, they made their way back to Charlie. On the way, David mentioned that the Norwegians reckoned that they might soon find evidence of a giant sea creature that lived one hundred and fifty million years ago." Dalmar encouraged him to go on. "They are excavating on a remote archipelago looking for fossils. It has long been thought that a giant predator known as a Pliosaur, anything up to fifty feet long existed. That bone sticking up back there could be part of one of its paddles for all I know."

"Just a minute – if you reckon this," he pointed downwards in a jabbing motion with an outstretched finger, "belongs to a creature that died in more recent times – how have they survived for – how long did you say?"

"One hundred and..." David did not get to finish.

"Yes well – when it comes to modern times, something that big would have been seen by a ship or what-have-you."

David made no comment.

"Do you reckon they got trapped in here? Maybe got swept in with the bore." Dalmar probed.

"Could be," said David, "or they came here to die. Who knows? I'm willing to bet though that all those small bones we saw – a few days ago – remember – are connected."

"Also – makes your bore a trifle long in the tooth," Dalmar commented through the side of his mouth. Not for the first time, David gave him an exasperated look.

After their meagre meal, strangely, David entered into a political discussion. What had brought it on was a mystery. Considering their plight, sorting the world's problems could wait. Being from the North-East of England his own politics were, quite naturally, left of centre. While discussing the plus factors of a decently run democratic state, he abruptly asked Dalmar where his political preferences lay. He replied that he usually voted right of centre, but sometimes veered towards the centre ground. David went further and asked him if he supported capitalism, with as he put it, "No frills."

Dalmar's reply put an end to the conversation.

"Capitalism works – if it works for you." David looked up at his colleague and gave a profound nod, apparently satisfied.

Two very tired men went to sleep. Both were hungry. Both were uncomfortable, nevertheless, they slept soundly.

CHAPTER FORTY-THREE

SUNDAY, 3rd JULY.

Sunday morning at Bray Castle dawned with the same overcast sky and intermittent rain that had existed over the last few days. Jack Twentyman was having a day off, leaving Brian Cussen in charge. The astronomer was not busy at night due to the lack of visibility. His students had been enjoying the national park's more usual pursuits so ensuring a normal night's sleep routine for him. However, life at Bray was far from pleasant due to the current situation. It was not the extra responsibility that bothered him; it was the dreadful atmosphere about the place. This kind of extreme grief and anxiety was not something, nor ever would be, that he could deal with. Even when he lost his wife after a forty-year marriage, he ran away from the grief separating himself from family and friends for quite a while. Right now, he went out of his way to avoid any member of the Hunter family and Jodie Fresher. This morning though, it was inescapable. He felt he would not be carrying out his duties properly unless he went across to the Dower-house to enquire about the well-being of its occupants.

Making his way from the back entrance by the kitchens, he thought wryly that maybe he should have put on a raincoat: it was falling quite hard now, not like the light rain that had been evident throughout the last week. He threw back his head to loosen up his greying locks in a futile effort at protection from the elements. 'One good thing,' he thought, it did look as though it might not last. There was some light in the sky over to the East. He noticed that the lake water had lost some of its dowdy diluted gunmetal grey where sprinkles of white light broke up the flat calm in places. There was a distinct breeze in the air as well.

He found them all dressed, finishing off breakfast. With Bea away until Monday, Suzanne had a busy day ahead of her on animal sanctuary duty and Jodie would be looking after Emma and Michael until her parents arrived sometime during the afternoon, then Suzanne would take over.

Answering Brian's knock on the door, Suzanne greeted him with one of her wan smiles. "Morning Brian. Do you need me?" She was dressed ready for work in her green N.T. light jacket and trousers. Fly stuck his head between her legs, grunted, tossed his nose in the air and retreated. It was not dislike of Brian that caused this. It was the weather.

The astronomer gave Suzanne a brief smile in return. "No. Other way around. Do *you* need me?"

Suzanne shot him a thankful glance with bowed head. She did not like anyone noticing her blood-shot eyes, especially this early in the day. "Sweet of you Brian – but no – I will be on duty directly in the rescue centre, so you need not worry. Just do whatever it is you would normally do standing in for Dalmar," and then she added, almost reluctantly, "or Jack."

His duty done, Brian; it has to be said, with some relief, went back to the castle noticing that Edna had arrived. Or, at least her car was in evidence as the driver made their way to the lower car park. On the way he waved to Rosalind Maidment in her five-year-old Volvo estate, wheels crunching on the gravel, as she drove by on her way to the stables. Through the windscreen, she gave him a cheery, if subdued smile, in return.

Both David and Dalmar awoke almost at the same time. The trouble being, it was ridiculously early – about five-thirty. Hardly enough time to have secured sufficient sleep after the rigours of the day before. All the nights without a decent bed had not got them used to either; the hardness when lying on the rock bank, or, the cramped conditions when taking their turn in Charlie's cockpit. Far from it. Both men longed for a mattress. Hunger was the main problem – particularly the lack of certain vitamins which were not provided by biscuits and water. Although they did not realise it consciously, the absence of daylight played a major factor. It was not just psychological. Anyhow, there was only one way to alleviate all the problems and that was to carry on.

After the last of the solid rations, David set out to get his photography accomplished up on the shelf rims. He wanted to obtain as much photographic reference of the mysterious bones belonging to supposed marine creatures as practical. Although this was not his subject, the geographical society had amongst its members eminent archaeologists specialising in animal life who would be very interested.

While David was about this, Dalmar got things ready at the submersible. Early or not, he was anxious for them to get on their way, especially with the water around them, apparently, getting ever saltier. He was almost ship-shape when a cry caused him to spin around and look up the deep grey ascending terraces of rock formations towards David. He was in time to see him rolling over, at first sideways, before falling head over heels and coming to a thudding stop on a large flat shelf of slate. His camera, which had kept pace with him, clattering on its own in headlong descent, kept going right over this shelf. David let out an agonising groan while lying on his left side. He had his back to Dalmar, so his face was hidden from view. The camera finally came to a halt, carrying strap flapping, about twenty yards from the river.

Dalmar ignored it and went straight up towards his prone colleague. At first, he moved as fast as possible on the dangerous slope, but, realising that if *he* fell and injured himself, their situation could become crucial, he slowed to be sure of each firm footstep. As he got nearer to David the groans became louder. Although this was a good thing in that he, possibly, did not have a head injury, it was still not very encouraging.

"What have you done?" asked Dalmar as he came up alongside the injured man. He went around to the other side of him so that he could see his face which was contorted in pain. It soon became obvious, however, that this was partly an expression of extreme annoyance as well.

He was supporting a limp right lower arm with his left hand. "Think ... I may have broken something," he eventually muttered finishing in a wide mouthed grimace.

There was no way of knowing whether this was the case right now; anyhow, he had certainly damaged it in some way. Dalmar got him into a sitting position. "We had better get a sling sorted. Have you any other injuries?"

"Five hundred brusies!" The exclamation reverberated against the cave roof and echoed about going up and down river.

"Stay here," ordered Dalmar. He had to get to Charlie and the first aid box.

"How's – camera?" Asked David amid winces, as he found other bruise orientated pain while shifting position to allow his injured arm to lie across his lap.

"Will find out. Hasn't gone in the river you will be pleased to know." David did not reply. The fall might have wrecked it. Neither did he tell Dalmar that he had slipped before taking any photographs. While placing himself in a situation that he could bring both hands to bear on the camera; his feet, he thought, securely niched in footholds near the top of the clif, a small fragment of slate had cracked and given way. At first, using one hand to grab the basin rim, he thought he would be alright, but another slice of slate gave under his other foot and down he went dropping the camera as he fell.

One look at the camera told a distressing story. The lens in its holder was hanging loose. That meant the film would have been ruined. He placed the whole thing in the submersible and locating the first aid box extracted the large square of muslin, which was obviously intended to be used as a sling for a broken wrist, arm or shoulder. Alternatively, Dalmar reckoned it could be cut up for bandages.

Getting the sling fixed up went well. Dalmar tied a secure knot behind David's shoulder allowing a generous wide loop for his arm to rest inside. After he had fixed it, he broke the news about the camera.

"Let's just check the shutter mechanism. I've got another film. You never know," David said hopefully."

Dalmar thought to himself, 'It'll be me who has to come back and try to get a shot or two.'

Very carefully, with Dalmar supporting his good side, David made it back to Charlie where he was transported, with much complaining and 'ouches' to the back seat in the cockpit.

The camera, unfortunately, was completely wrecked in all departments. This depressed David, "Bloody shame," he said. Considering the knowledge that might have been apparent from photographs of the large skeleton, in particular, there was no doubt that he was right in this assumption.

"If you think I am going back up there with a sketch pad and pencil, which, fortunately, I believe, we do not possess, then you have another think coming." Dalmar said this without a trace of a smile on his face. "Anyhow my drawing capabilities are pathetic."

David shrugged his good shoulder, and then wished he had not done so as pain travelled to his injured arm anyway. He grimaced before saying, "Just have to rely on our verbal observations. Hope you have a good memory." This was not a question.

"Why – do you think we are still a long way from surfacing? Going under the bloody Atlantic Ocean, I reckon.

Next stop Belle Isle, Nova Scotia." There was a small parting of lips, just visible under the black beard growth, suggesting some amusement.

David managed a grin. "I'm a little more hopeful than that." Then he went serious trying to adjust his seated position to give the maximum comfort. "Mind you – need to be."

Dalmar clambered into the pilot's position. Progress would be a lot slower now. He would have to do all the paddling: two or three strokes on one side before moving the paddle over to the other and repeating the operation and so on. This would be far more difficult to execute than in a canoe due to the extra overall width of their craft. To make things easier he opened up the entire canopy to give him more freedom of movement. Once on the move, however, he managed to find a satisfactory rhythm.

And then, as though to tell him he was wasting his time, the current in the river suddenly increased. They had left the big cave far behind. Dalmar brought the paddle in board urgently so that he could have a hand free to operate the rudder control and keep them in the middle of the river course. His head torch beam kept playing off the water as Charlie started to roll more. It became obvious that this was not caused by rapids or white water ahead. Not only was there no noise indicating this, but the river, if anything, had widened.

David spoke over Dalmar's shoulder. "Might be an idea to test the engine. Could be – we may need it soon."

Dalmar did not require a second invitation. The engine had not been used for ten days, since their descent into Lastwater and the first, and only, so far, completely filled tunnel of water. They had only used the accumulators to charge up the head torches over the night-time and, it was hoped, there would be plenty of power left. But it was with some trepidation that Dalmar pressed the red button which activated the power supply to the engine. Nothing happened. He waited for approximately ten seconds. Then he pressed it again – more definitely this time. This time it came to life with a subdued rumble. David let go a loud sigh of relief. He appeared to have been correct with his calculations. His sigh was followed by a low whistling sound expelled through clenched teeth.

Dalmar opened up the side fins to facilitate his steering and give him braking power by turning the planes vertical if it became necessary. Then he pulled the right and left acrylic side panels into place ready to receive the overhead canopy if required in a hurry.

It was as well he had done so. Matters happened so fast that even David was caught unawares. The roof line of the underground river course began to descend on them. Dalmar immediately turned around and grabbed the two handles of the canopy pulling it over them. He had time to secure the right hand catch and David helped him with the other using his good arm. Then, urgently, Dalmar closed down the side screens, securing them to ensure water tightness. Almost desperately, he started to use the engine to fill the ballast tanks so that they could submerge before the canopy top crashed against the hard rock ceiling.

As Dalmar switched on the powerful front lights both men instinctively turned off their head torches. There had been no time to get into their wet suits and prepare their compressed air equipment. Dalmar could not care less and David had been secretly dreading the operation because of the pain he would suffer, due to his, almost certainly, broken arm.

The lights became almost superfluous in seconds. At first, Dalmar could not believe it was happening. David felt a thrill beyond belief. The blackness in the water ahead became dark grey and then a kind of filtering lightening took place, until they suddenly found themselves suspended in deep water – with – there was no doubt about it – daylight somewhere above them! Both men blinked as the light, even though they were well submerged, stung their eyes. Instinctively, they cast their eyes down. Below them was only water until something flat, thin and lazy swam under the submersible. A flat fish! The same realisation confirmed itself to both men at once. They were at sea. Which sea, they did not know for certain, but if David was right, in that they had just completed an underground traverse of Wales – then this would presumably be the Irish Sea.

"Quick Dalmar, in that compartment!" David extended a hand over his colleagues left shoulder, "the shades."

"The wha – what?"

"Sorry – I mean dark glasses."

Dalmar released a flapped drawer and took out two small sealed packages. He let go of the controls, broke the seal on one and passed it back, then he broke the seal on the other, and, blessedly, placed the pair over his ears. Even with them on, he still blinked about him.

Nothing can describe the thrilling euphoria that each man felt deep inside them – initially – in silence. And then they both started to babble at once. "Wonder where we are."

"Shall I surface?"

"Hope there is cloud cover. Can't cope with strong sunlight yet."

"Christ – we made it – I think. Haven't we?"

"Yes – we have – we must have."

"I'm going to surface." And as they did so – very slowly – both men remained utterly silent waiting for that canopy to breakout into the open air and proper – marvellous – daytime light.

Charlie broke surface at half past seven, British Summer Time. Water cascaded down over all sides of the canopy until the occupants realised they were bobbing about in a not exactly calm sea. On the other hand, it was not that choppy either – it was just that Charlie was not really built for the open ocean in this part of the world.

Dalmar released the catches on the canopy and commenced, with caution, to pull it open leaving the side screens in situation. They were greeted with more blinding light, even with their dark glasses firmly in place. There was also a sudden fairly strong wind. Well – it was strong to them after days without feeling that element whatsoever. But it was not the strength of the wind that grabbed their immediate attention – it was the sound of it. Suddenly their ears were filled with extraneous noise, something they had not heard, apart from the waterfalls, since leaving Lastwater. And then there was the change in temperature, even taking into account being out at sea, it was considerably warmer than they had been used to for some time. There was something else. Something more important than all of that. The smell of fresh air. The feel of free air. After days without it and, most of the time, not knowing if they would ever experience it again. That feeling cannot be described in any language. It is just felt.

David was the first to notice that the onboard compass had sprung to life. So, when they could focus their eyes on land lying about a quarter of a mile away, he realised that it was to the south. Not what he expected at all. 'They must be in an inlet,' he considered.

The land, however, did suggest Wales. Short stretches of sandy beaches rising up through woodland to low fertile fields showing mid-season green growth and those were definitely mountains in the distance, though more to the West. They should be to the North-East. Although the sky was overcast, to David and Dalmar it was incredibly beautiful. Even the colours in what would normally be a dull light appeared bright and uplifting, whether looking around them at the water or the coast not far away.

Dalmar turned Charlie shoreward at a careful engine speed, otherwise they would get drenched as the bow bucked against the spray. Obviously, he kept the side panels in place.

Catching them by surprise, a pair of dolphins swiftly arrived, out of nowhere, cresting and leaping in beautiful arches clear of the water. They came quite close giving the watching men a good view before going away toward the open sea.

In the distance, away to the north of them, were what looked like two fishing vessels. They could even hear a chugging of motors fluctuating in resonance as the breeze influenced the travel of their sound.

Once further into shore both men started to look for somewhere to beach the craft. There were plenty of areas with soft looking sand, but it was what lay before them that bothered Dalmar: too many reef-like low rocky structures protruding from the shallow water.

On rounding a promontory their prayers were answered: a long jetty sufficiently within reach of the current tide situation.

"O T E L," said David. "See – there is a sign partially visible up there on that building. Could be a hotel. If so, we will be in time for breakfast."

Dalmar suddenly felt ravenously hungry. All he could think about was bacon and eggs. It was so powerful that saliva built up inside his mouth. It seemed an absolute age before they got within hailing distance of the jetty – not that there was a sole about to shout to.

They tied Charlie up alongside the small pier and Dalmar switched off the engine. He could not resist giving the craft a pat on the edge of the carbon-fibre bulkhead next to him before clambering out. He was desperate to give himself a good stretch to relieve his cramped muscles, but, instead, held out an arm so that David could extricate himself safely.

Once disembarked, David held onto the jetty rail with his good hand and looked down into the submersible wondering whether they should locate the photographic films used earlier in the expedition.

Meanwhile, Dalmar was casting his gaze down the jetty landwards to ascertain how they could make their way up to the hotel. While studying what he thought were steps leading up through a wooded area; predominantly pine trees by the look of them, he noticed a man making his way down from the building. He had just come through an attractive terraced area set before a large sun lounge type construction. "Someone is coming," he said to David.

It did not take the man long to reach the end of the jetty. He must have been in a considerable hurry and, even from that distance, looked annoyed.

CHAPTER FORTY-FOUR

A FLASH OF TRANSLUCENT BRIGHT GOLD

The man, probably middle-aged, with a glorious mop of red hair, a rather unhealthy-looking ruddy complexion, using a raised voice, said, "Are you guests at the hotel?"

David, quickly very interested, caught the dialect. To him, it sounded like the unmistakable accent, with the finest English language clarity in the United Kingdom – that of the area around the City of Inverness on the east coast of Scotland.

Dalmar did not reply to the irate gentleman straight away. Instead, he walked towards him to avoid having to shout. David let him go on so as not to intimidate the fellow.

The hotel owner immediately grew concerned. The man walking towards him with a lazy kind of languid stride was not something you saw everyday around here. The black beard growth; sunglasses on a cloudy day: his filthy looking unkempt clothes – totally out of season – more suitable for a cold winter's day out there on the estuary.

Also, his accomplice did not look any more encouraging apart from the obvious incapacity due to the sling-ed arm. 'And what a strange looking boat.' For a daft moment he considered the possibility of some kind of modern pirate, but, much more likely - men who dwelt on the wrong side of the track. If Dalmar had not spoken to him right then, he would have turned and run.

"Our apologies for the intrusion," he said, and, instantly, the man was calmed by the measured deep sincere and cultured voice. "My name is Dalmar Hunter and the gentleman with me is David Fresher. We have arrived here along an underground river from Lastwater in Cumbria. Have you heard anything about us on the news?"

The man's face, as the realisation dawned as to who his unexpected visitors were transformed from a worried scowl to a look of sheer amazement. His mouth opened so wide, Dalmar thought it impossible. "Ye –es, yes. My god – they had given up on you. It said on the television." His hands went into a mutual ringing together as something began to implode in his mind ... *Publicity!*

Dalmar came right up to him. "Would it be possible for us to purchase a breakfast from your establishment? We have not eaten for a few days. And the use of a bath would be gratefully accepted. Oh, and my friend needs to get to a hospital." Pausing he added rather selfishly. "In that order."

"By all means," said the suddenly amiable fellow now grinning all over his face. "Anything – do come on up."

By this time David had drawn up to them with his good arm outstretched. He said "Hello," while shaking hands with the proprietor, before asking if, as a priority, they could use a telephone. Sensing the man's anticipation in the sheen of joy in his eyes, he quickly added. "If you wouldn't mind – perhaps we could leave off informing the press until I have spoken to The Royal Geographical Society. They will do that for us."

The man who still had not given his name became even more impressed and shook Dalmar's hand enthusiastically. "Yes – of – of course. Completely understand."

Joining them, David could not wait any longer. "Where are we?" he casually asked. Dalmar looked at him wondering why *he* had not asked that and then realised that breakfast was far more important.

The man went quizzical, scratching his right cheek quite vigorously, before replying. "Why – that is the Moray Firth out there. And about fifteen miles in that direction is Inverness." Even allowing for their extraordinary travels, it puzzled him that they seemed to have no idea of their whereabouts.

Now it was Dalmar's turn to look astounded. David had already worked it out from the gentleman's dialect. He pointedly looked at his bewildered companion for quite a long time. "Inverness is connected to a certain large inland waterway by a river – that waterway is Lochness." David waited for the realisation to enter his colleague's brain. He did not have to wait long, but, infuriatingly, it was acknowledged by a simple nod.

"Breakfast then," said Dalmar looking expectantly at the man who had now developed a thoroughly curious look ... "Mr?"

"Macdonald," replied he at once. "James Macdonald." Becoming anxious again he waved a calming hand at them, "Take your time. I will go on ahead and organise things." As he turned to go, he said something that cheered Dalmar enormously, "Porridge, smokie, bacon and egg, followed by toast and marmalade made with malt whisky suit you?"

Oh – would it just," replied Dalmar and David gave out his widest smile.

After a long tiring climb, for David Fresher with his by now badly aching arm, James Macdonald took the two men with a fussy, concerned rotund lady in attendance, obviously his wife, through to the front hall where a telephone was waiting for them to use.

David picked up the handset and then beckoned Dalmar over. "You first," he said, "and if Jodie is there, I'll have a word after you."

Dalmar gave a grateful nod. He dialled the number at Bray Castle.

Edna, on duty, at the entrance reception took all incoming calls at the weekend when she was on duty. She was close by when the telephone tringed loudly in the large hallway.

A few moments later a jubilant Edna running faster than she had run for years, skirts billowing about all over the place was rushing towards the Dower-house. She had not bothered to try and put the call through. She almost knocked Suzanne over as she came out of the front door on her way to visit the rescue centre. "Oh, praise be!" she yelled out loud to anyone within earshot. Fly came bounding out. He sensed a rapid change in the atmosphere. Edna grabbed Suzanne by the hand and started to almost drag her. She pointed at the castle entrance. "The tele – phone," she was out of breath - "Your husband!"

Jolted by Edna's radiant joy, Suzanne's face burst into life – her eyes suddenly took on their marvellous brilliance almost at once. She had difficulty understanding what was actually happening and was absolutely tongue-tied. But she did know it was good news – the best news!

Attracted by the shouting, Jodie Fresher appeared in the doorway. "What is it Edna?" Jodie yelled after her.

Edna slowed letting Suzanne run on towards the castle's main entrance. She shouted back over her shoulder. "They're alive!" Despite being breathless an enormous smile was covering her face caught in a rare moment of sunlight. Blessedly, the rain had stopped for this special moment.

Jodie let go a huge, "Yippeee!" And the leaden atmosphere of days past vanished as her joyous shout seemed to invade every part of Bray Castle's ground's, most especially into the interior of the Dower-house where two young children, not yet knowing why, felt a blood rush of sheer excitement envelope them.

Wrapped up in two of the hotel's white towelling gowns, David and Dalmar devoured a breakfast in the dining room. David's progress through the meal was only marginally slower than his companion's, despite being handicapped with the use of only one arm and the wrong one at that. Both men had taken a bath while their clothing and been, literally, confiscated by Mrs Macdonald to be laundered. Dalmar rated it the finest meal of his life. He had gone for porridge followed by bacon and egg, while David elected to have the smoked haddock instead. They were sensible and asked for reserved amounts. A big meal after days without could have made them feel very uncomfortable afterwards. Before they had had a chance to take off their clothes, Mrs

Macdonald had insisted on inspecting David's arm. This resulted in a replacement clean and fuller sling being applied, which did give David a little relief. She then dragged him off to another room ignoring the Geordie's protests and with much tut tutting helped him disrobe.

The hotel guests had already breakfasted by the time the two men had entered the dining room, however, many a curious, gaping visage appeared at the window. After only eleven days their beards were not too full and David's, certainly was definitely not so. Now without the dark glasses, washed and scrubbed, the two men had been transformed into pleasant looking beings again.

As they both sat back enjoying the toast, marmalade and strong percolated coffee, James informed them that a private ambulance would be calling to take them to the Raigmore hospital, at Inverness, in about one hour. He reckoned their clothes should be dry by then.

"You can expect a visit from the press sometime after we leave." David told him. "The Geographical Society has arranged it, so they won't ask you questions you don't know the answers to – or they shouldn't. Hope that is okay?"

James almost sputtered that it was just fine. He was delighted.

"Would appreciate it if we could beg one further kindness," David asked.

"By all means ..." James opened his hands wide by way of acquiescing.

"Please don't tell the media where we have gone. A press conference is being arranged, so hopefully they won't ask – but – you never know." A sudden thought flashed into his mind. "It would be okay to let them photograph Charlie – that is our craft tied up alongside your jetty, but please don't let them touch it. We will arrange suitable transport to have it taken away by road – O.K?"

"Of course," James further obliged; the publicity strength was getting better and better. David had good reason to make the last request; while he was nervous about the media getting too near Charlie, he also knew he had to give the manufacturers maximum coverage.

After the breakfast and before they left, James and his wife flatly refused any form of payment. Dalmar extended an invitation that if ever they were in the vicinity of Lastwater to give them a call.

They caught up on the news from the hotel's newspapers in their lounge, saying hello to some of the guests who were enthralled at meeting them.

David had not complained once about discomfort during the morning, but once in the ambulance and on their way, he let go a long moan. Dalmar gave him a sympathetic look. "Soon have you fixed up in a cast, David."

"Ah – now," David seized on the chance to talk to Dalmar, while their conversation could not be overheard, provided they kept their voices low from the driver, "there are a couple of points arising out of the knowledge of where we finished up. One is that the massive tidal wave that hit the north-east coast of Britain caused by a huge undersea silt landslip – approx – 6000 years B.C., just after the last ice age, must have caused an unscheduled massive bore all the way to Lastwater. Not for now I guess, but we should be able to find evidence of that." Dalmar looking slightly fuzzed at this and merely nodded. And then David came up with what he had been itching to talk about ever since their arrival, "What do you reckon? The proximity to Lochness?"

"Presumably, you are referring to the large skeleton in the cave – and the other bones?" Dalmar encouraged him.

"Too darn right. Nessie of course. What do think? Damn shame we didn't get a photograph – not even one!"

Dalmar pondered the matter without making a comment.

"Too much of a coincidence – yes?" asked an impatient bubbling David.

After a further pause, Dalmar said, "Possiibly."

David Fresher tried to hit him, but he chose, involuntarily, his injured arm. The attempt achieved no more than a raised wrist by a couple of inches before he cried out in pain.

"Careful now," said his companion hunching his shoulders and pushing both elbows into his body to enjoy the comfort of the clean fabric around him. "You mentioned that the, apparently, whole skeleton could relate to a recent demise?"

David, cheered by the fact that his accomplice was, at least, continuing with the same subject replied, "Well – recent centuries perhaps."

Dalmar rubbed the beard on his chin looking thoughtful. "Thing is – I can't see the Loch Ness monster swimming down the river to Inverness without being spotted before it reached the Moray Firth and open sea."

David looked slightly stunned. 'Why had he not thought of that,' he reprimanded himself. The oversight had been caused by the excitement at a possible solution to the legend of Nessie. He did not make a comment straight away, then he came up with a face-saving idea. "Yea... reckon there must be an underground river from Loch Ness which joins the one we have just arrived on. While we still have Charlie – fancy taking a look?"

Dalmar looked at the roof of the ambulance and closed his eyes. While David was grinning hugely, his confidant answered him.   "And then, perhaps, we could return to Lastwater the way we came. In fact, if we hang around until September ... we could hitch a ride on the autumnal bore."

This finished up with both men, even David despite his discomfort, cackling at each other in uncontrollable hysterics. Relief ... of course.

Roz Maidment, on Stargazer, led her two young girl pupils on the Irish cob and the gypsy cob, along the short segment of road before they reached the small parking area below White Crag. They had wound their way up on a series of traverse pathways from the woodland beyond Bray Castle. Roz intended to stop at the viewpoint where the pupils could dismount and let the ponies graze for a while. Usually, she went on further, but it had not stopped raining since they left the stables at ten-thirty this morning. All of them were very wet. When the weather was like this Roz wore blue jeans: somehow, they felt better wet than the heavier material of jodhpurs.

Once on the plateau below the crag summit, she could not resist taking off her riding helmet and letting her long blonde hair cascade down. She shook her head to let it disentangle naturally. "Would you like to dismount for a while?" she invited her charges. They did so and started chatting to each other a little way off. Roz let them have their privacy. She turned Stargazer's head to look out over Lastwater.

The lake, in the rain curtained scene, had gone its usual gun metal hue. One of the United Kingdom's much photographed landscapes looked depressing from north to south. Bray Castle was just a half hidden grey buttressed edifice of no particular attraction, in fact, quite the reverse. Roz tried to cheer herself up thinking about the work due to start at the top end of the meadow at Bray – the jumping course for the equestrian centre. And then there was the rowing club regatta to look forward to – the first since the tragedy – bringing much needed colour and activity of the right sort to the often - lonely waterway.

As Roz looked on, she was not aware of any other presence apart from the body movement of the horse under her. It was at times like this that melancholia could come upon her. Before long a single tear started to fall from her right eye. It came to a stop halfway down her fair skinned cheek. *'I have never loved so much in the rain.'*

As if, in answer, a flash of translucent brilliant gold broke free from the cloud bank over the eastern fells way above the other side of the lake, followed by the most amazing transformation, as strong bright light gradually spread across the centre of Lastwater, causing a vibrant blue colouring to spread over the waters. The sunlight hit the western bank of the lake immediately below Bray Castle – coming up and over – changing the buttresses to a much more appealing pale grey; in fact, almost white.

Roz blinked in the startling bright light. "Look at that!" exclaimed one of the girls away to the left of Stargazer. "Quick Jill. Get your camera."

Roz took no notice. Her attention had been grabbed by the sight of small figures on the castle roof, two of whom were tiny. They had to be children, but what had really caught her eye, helped by the sudden sunlight, was that they were definitely agitated as though jumping up and down and – yes – waving – arms above their heads. The other two, grown-ups, possibly young women were waving as well: waving with their hands held right up in a side to side motion. Then Roz noticed something else. The Flag! The flag on the tower was flying high and full – right at the very top of the mast.

Roz did not wave back straight away; first she raised her head and looked towards the break in the clouds squinting against the brightness of the light. Then she cast her eyes back towards the joyous looking figures on the castle roof. Holding onto the rains of Stargazer with her left hand, she raised her right arm high above her head and arced it from left to right several times. The woman with long golden hair on a horse with a golden mane, standing out on the crag above the western shore of Lastwater could be seen by the jubilant few below, and they responded by waving back even more vigorously than before.

Jill noticed what was happening. She took a picture. Her and her friend obviously knew about the missing explorers. They could not have failed to do so, and they had been very aware of the sombre atmosphere at the castle. All that appeared to have vanished. She went to whisper something to the other girl.

When she turned back, Roz was once again looking towards the sun. The tear lying against her cheek had dried, and the smile she wore seemed to be apart from the

present happening as though intended for someone else.
"Thank you darling," she said.

THE END

Acknowledgements.

My grateful thanks to Lisa for her advice on equestrian matters and to Shelagh for giving an early draught of the novel a read through.

A special thank you to Maxine for her understanding.